B

FAR FROM HEAVEN

FAR FROM HEAVEN

GREG MATTHEWS

WALKER AND COMPANY
NEW YORK

All the characters and events portrayed in this work are fictitious.

First published in the United States of America in 1997 by Walker Publishing Company, Inc.

Published simultaneously in Canada by Thomas Allen & Son Canada, Limited, Markham, Ontario

Library of Congress Cataloging-in-Publication Data
Matthews, Greg.
Far from heaven/Greg Matthews.
p. cm.
ISBN 0-8027-3303-4 (hardcover)
I. Title.
PR9619.3.M317F37 1997
823—dc21 97-9608
CIP

Printed in the United States of America
2 4 6 8 10 9 7 5 3 1

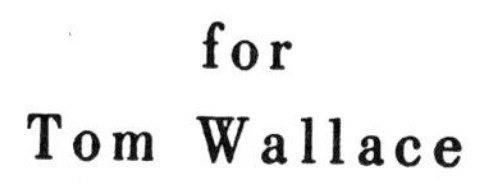

for
Tom Wallace

FAR FROM HEAVEN

1

HIS DOOR, AS he approached it each morning, caused a sense of despair he had to fight for at least fifteen minutes before commencing work. His name was spelled correctly but had never been painted onto the door, as was usually the case with writers at Empire. On either side of his own door, and stretching away to the farthest ends of the Writers' Building (called by its occupants, with heavy irony, the Writers' Block), were the names of other men, some of whom had worked at the studio for less time than himself, all of them neatly painted, with a crispness suggesting permanence of place.

It was not that he wished to be assured of a position at Empire Productions forever—surely greater things lay in store—but the absence of a painted name indicated a deliberate attempt on the part of studio management to disparage his role. He supposed it was because he wrote the Westerns.

KEITH MOODY, announced the strip of paper thumbtacked to his door, and beneath it was another, stating his current project: SIX-GUN JUSTICE. It made him sigh. It made him cringe inwardly and close his eyes for just a few seconds. His hand, as it turned the doorknob, did so with a weariness that should have come at the day's end, not its beginning.

Once inside, things were easier; he could not think why, since the walls were covered by movie posters for each of the productions he had authored, and a great many more created by his predecessors. These garishly colored reminders should logically have depressed him even more than the paper strip outside, but here his name was hidden away among the tiny print at the bottom of each sheet—"Screenplay by Keith Moody"—along with the composer of the musical score. It was better that way, he decided, since every one of his scripts was an embarrassment. But he should still have merited a painted nameplate on the door.

His two years and five months at Empire had resulted in fifteen screenplays so far, all of them produced, and all of them moneymakers for the studio's cowboy star, Smokey Hayes: *Border Law; Deadwood Stage; Hellfire in Abilene; Sunset Trail; Cripple Creek Showdown*; the posters aimed pistols at him, shrieking of success.

Moody hung his jacket behind the door and sat before his typewriter. The room measured eight feet by twelve; a small bathroom lay behind a door to his left. The posters were his only distraction, and he avoided looking at them as he fought the usual discouragement that preceded his first striking of the keys. *Six-Gun Justice*, he reminded himself, was only halfway complete.

He had left Smokey the previous day tied to a chair in a cabin where at any moment the outlaw boss was scheduled to return, which was bad news for Smokey, since he would instantly be recognized for what he was—a railroad detective. It was a tight situation to be in, and Moody was unsure how best to extricate Smokey. A means of escape should already have been worked out in his original treatment for the project, but Moody had submitted less than the usual detailed outline, and had been surprised when the go-ahead was given despite his proposal's sketchiness.

So now he was in a tight corner, along with Smokey. Outlaw boss. Recognition. Confrontation. Bluff? "I never saw you before in my life, pardner, now tell your friends here to untie these ropes." It was a ploy unlikely to work, since Red, the leader of the claim-jumpers, had been bested before by Smokey and could not possibly mistake him for anyone else, no matter how many denials there might be. Smokey would have to remain tied, and endure quite a bit of physical punishment when his identity was made clear to the rest of the gang. Escape would have to be postponed until later. Smokey always looked good with bruises, and had on several occasions requested more violence from Moody. "Don't go making it too darn easy for me," he'd say. "Have them bad hombres put me through the wringer some 'fore I gun 'em down. Kinda makes it better that way, watchin' them varmints fall, when you know they done what they done to me, you follow? They have to deserve it, see what I mean?"

Moody's hands lay in his lap like sleeping cats. The typewriter squatted before him, a miniature temple of darkness, its interior awaiting the arrival of a sacrifice. And Moody knew what that sacrifice would be. The smacking keys would mangle every original thought, every line a convincing character might utter, every plot Moody might conjure up that resembled reality, however glancingly. There was no place at Empire Productions for such stuff, at least not within the department Moody worked for. He was a two-hundred-and-fifty-dollar-a-week man, scarcely a Faustian bargain. Marvin Margolis owned his soul, at least that part of his soul concerned with artistic honesty, with integrity, with concern for the higher things Moody knew himself capable of.

He had done it to himself, and there lay the true thorn, the one that pricked deepest; all blame for his misery lay with himself. He carried it with him to the Writers' Block each day and carried it home again. He carried it to the bank every week. The hands that carried it had to be persuaded each morning to lift themselves and begin work, that they might continue to carry Moody's burden. Moody was not any kind of tragic figure, even in the private theater of his thoughts. He was, he concluded several times a day, the worst kind of hack. An ordinary hack could do no better than his masters required, but hacks of the worst kind were smarter than that, knew themselves able to create work of much grander vision, but did not; they accepted the devil's wage and churned out what was demanded of them.

Moody was unaware that a story he considered his best had brought him to the attention of the studio. "The Samaritan" had been its title, and it concerned a man who had one day seen an incredibly ugly child in a store, accompanied by its equally ugly mother. So forlorn a picture did these two present that the narrator promptly decided he must save them from the life their physical appearance restricted them to. The woman wore no wedding band, and Moody's narrator followed mother and boy home before concocting a plan of conquest. He insinuated himself into their lives the following day, and within the space of several weeks persuaded the woman to marry him. He adopted the ugly boy also, and fully expected contentment to arise from his philanthropy.

Instead, his new family turned on him, demanding all manner of things he could not supply. They did not appreciate his generosity at all and hounded him to provide everything the world had denied them. The narrator was not a wealthy man, although he considered himself rich in spirit for having done for the woman and boy what he had, and he quickly came to see that his act of charity, freely chosen, was in fact the worst mistake of his life. When finally his wife and son began jeering at him for his inability to give them what they wanted, the Samaritan killed them both in a fit of rage directed not so much at his detractors as at himself, for his foolishness in having assumed that good intent would result in some kind of expansion of the soul.

Moody had been proud of that story for its unrelenting bleakness, and only succeeded in having it published in an obscure literary quarterly after having it rejected by every other magazine in America carrying short fiction. Eight months passed before he saw his creation in print, and he was not paid for its inclusion in the third (and last) edition of *Scribe*. The story did serve to bring him regular employment, however, when it was noticed by a script developer at Empire Productions. This man was under imminent threat of dismissal from the studio for having failed to provide sufficient material suitable for production. When word of his dismissal finally came, his last act before walking through the studio gates forever was to submit a glowing report on an obscure writer named Keith Moody. "This fellow, with his rootin' tootin' cowboy yarns, has what Empire needs," he had written, in the only act of vengeance he could think of, and forged the name of his successor. His bogus memo passed through the usual channels without drawing suspicion; Moody was summoned to Hollywood by mistake, and assigned a room in the Writers' Block.

Western Writer was his official designation, but Moody had not become aware of this until too late. He was by that time in debt to his aunt in Kansas City for the cost of rail fare to California, and so had begun his first screenplay for her sake, hoping that the silly misuse of his talent could soon be straightened out and his abilities redirected toward more worthwhile outlets. After six months he realized it was not to be, and his unhappiness had increased in direct proportion to the amount of time spent concocting nonsense for Smokey Hayes. Of course, two hundred and fifty dollars a week was more than he could ever have dreamed of making back home.

His hands lifted slowly and reached for the keys.

SMOKEY
You're makin' a big mistake, friend.
OUTLAW #3
I reckon you're the one made the mistake.
SMOKEY
I guess we'll be seein' about that.

Moody read what he had written, muttered, "Christ on a stick . . . ," and began typing. Salvation would not come today, nor was it likely to come on any other day.

Marvin Margolis did not believe it necessary to provide his writers with telephones that they might be tempted to use during working hours in pursuit of matters unrelated to the work he paid them for, so the summons, when it came, was a hasty knock at the door. "What!" Moody yelled, but the door had already been opened. He saw briefly the head of a gofer who blurted, "Chief wants ya right now!" before he disappeared without bothering to close the door again.

The Chief was Quentin Yapp, head of B-feature production. Moody had spoken to him very few times, and was uneasy at the prospect of holding a conversation with someone he considered boorish and without intelligence, but there was no way he could think of to avoid the meeting. If nothing else, it would provide a break from the trash he was creating.

Yapp's secretary sent him directly through, a disturbing contrast to his previous visits, when he had been obliged to wait for at least twenty minutes.

"Moody, what the fuck is this all about!"

Yapp was swiveling his chair briskly from side to side, as if attempting to bore a hole through the carpet, his knuckles on the armrests white with the effort of gripping slippery leather.

"Pardon me?"

"He wants to see you! What the fuck's it mean, Moody, huh?"

"Who wants to see me?"

"Who the hell you think! *Him!* What did you do to make him want to see you without he tells me first what it's all about, huh, Moody?"

"Mr. Margolis?"

"Who else you think wants to see you around here! Tell me first, Moody, and maybe I can help you out. You go in there not prepared, and he'll slice you six ways from Sunday. You tell me right now what it's all about, and maybe I can be in your corner."

"I don't know what it's all about."

"The fuck you don't! You tell me now so I don't have shit coming down on my head. Shit I don't need right now on top of the shit I already got, so speak!"

"To Margolis I'll speak," said Moody, adopting Yapp's manner.

Yapp stood up, then sat down again behind his desk. "Listen," he said, "if it's about the schedule, we're on top of it. The new one, *Six-Gun Whatsit* . . . ?"

"Justice."

"You tell him you're just pages away from completion, you got that? Pages away from completion, and it'll be ready pronto, hear me? That's what you tell him if he asks, which he won't, because that's what I'm here to be asked, so he wants you for some other shit, so what is it, huh? Listen, just tell me so I can get prepared, okay? That too much to ask?"

"I can't tell you what I don't know, Mr. Yapp."

"Mr. Yapp—shit! Quentin, for chrissakes! We're a goddamn family here, aren't we? Aren't we a family here, telling each other the shit we need to know?"

"Quentin, I really don't know—"

"Get outta here, Moody, and don't put my name on any kinda shit you've got yourself into, you hear me? You shit on my name and I'll shit on you from way up high, so help me!"

Walking back past Yapp's secretary, Moody looked to see if she had been upset by the words that must have penetrated the door, but she was filing her nails and did not look up. If he had been an actor she would have, or a producer, or any kind of studio executive, even one as ordinary in appearance as himself, but a writer earned no favorable glances.

He was on his way to the front office before it occurred to him that he could think of no reason at all why Marvin Margolis might have sent for him. He had never met the man, had seen him only once or twice from a distance, and would have preferred that matters remain as they had been until now. What possible cause could there be for a summons to the inner sanctum of the one man every individual at Empire was truly afraid of? Had the sloppy construction of Moody's latest proposal caught up with him? Surely it was Yapp's job to discipline him for that. It must be some other transgression, or maybe it was all a mistake, an order given to round up the wrong man. Moody had no illusions he would be told he was overdue for a raise, or given some worthwhile project to work on as a reward for having endured so long under Yapp's foul mouth and absolute lack of taste. It was a mistake, that was all, and when it had been cleared up he would return to his room with the paper strip on the door and resume work on rescuing Smokey Hayes.

Moody experienced the first pangs of terror when Margolis's secretary smiled at him as he gave his name. "He's expecting you," she said. "Go right in." Moody's heart plummeted. It was no mistake after all, but some kind of sentencing for Kafkaesque crimes beyond his present understanding. He approached and pushed weakly against bronze doors leading to the place he had heard tales of but never before seen.

The room that opened before him was long and broad, and Moody's eyes were drawn immediately to the desk at its far end, and the figure seated behind it that beckoned once to him before lowering its head to something on the expanse of teak before it. Moody began to walk across carpeting so plush he felt his soles sink into its creamy thickness, like spongy grass on some alien planet that sucked strength from him as he trod upon it, his confidence diminishing with every step. The figure behind the desk raised its head again.

"Faster," Moody was told, and he lost more esteem in his rush to present himself at the nearest edge of the desk. A hand indicated the two ornate chairs there, and Moody perched himself nervously upon one of them. The man behind the desk was young yet balding, his face belonging to some other pate less depleted.

"Seen this?" asked Marvin Margolis, suddenly lifting the thing before him and presenting it with a rustling flourish. Moody recognized the red oblong with its four familiar capitalized letters in white. "*LIFE*," he whispered, then added, in case Margolis should consider him a fool, "*LIFE* magazine."

Margolis nodded slowly. "*LIFE* magazine," he confirmed, "and what else, Moody? See anything else?"

"It's . . . someone in uniform. An airman, I think—"

"An airman. Right again. See the airman's face, Moody?"

"Yes . . ."

"Know him?"

"No, no I don't."

"Moody, do you keep in touch with your family at all?"

"Well—"

"This is your cousin, I'm told. Is it your cousin, Moody?"

"I . . . well, it might be. . . . Which cousin?"

"You're asking me? Am I in a position to know? Is it your cousin, or isn't it?"

Moody leaned closer. Margolis's hand grasping the edge of the magazine occupied him more than the picture; the fingers were short and powerful, the nails beautifully manicured, yet Moody could swear they had been filed to a distinct point.

"It's . . . Russell," he said, and true recognition came only as the name passed his lips. "Russell Keys," he read aloud, noticing the print alongside the photograph.

"Definitely your cousin?" inquired Margolis, lowering the magazine.

"It's him," confirmed Moody, attempting to sound sure of himself. How had Russ managed to have his picture presented to the nation on the cover of *LIFE* magazine? No less likely candidate for fame could have been dredged from a list of everyone Moody had ever met. He hadn't even been aware that Russ had joined the armed forces.

"Makes you proud, doesn't it," said Margolis. It was not a question.

"Yes," said Moody, whose chief emotion at that moment was bafflement.

"This is someone we can all be proud of, wouldn't you say?"

"I would, yes . . . most definitely say that."

"How long since you saw this hero?"

"Well . . . it must be . . . seven years at least."

"Seven years," mused Margolis, staring at his perfectly white ceiling. "That's a long time, Moody. Get along okay?"

"Sir?"

"You and him, you get along okay seven years back? Did you like each other, Moody, is what I need to know."

"Yes," lied Moody.

"So he'd listen to you if you had a suggestion to make."

"I believe he would, yes."

Moody could not think of a single suggestion made to Russell Keys that had not been met with a faint sneer and a slow-motion lowering of the eyelids to denote a complete disinterest in the suggestion and its source. Russ had been that way with his foster parents, with the police, with anyone who ever spoke more than a few words to him. Russell Keys had looked at Moody on the half-dozen times they met as boys with the level gaze of a snake too lazy to strike, a rattler with a rat inside it, mildly annoyed at having its digestion interrupted, not sufficiently angry to lunge and bite. Moody had not liked him, and had even, he admitted to himself now, looking at the upside-down picture on Margolis's desk, been somewhat afraid of his lanky cousin with the straight corn-silk hair and lazy manner of moving and talking and those snake eyes that observed without malice or friendliness or anything but cool regard.

Moody, a youth of considerable anxiety the last time they

met, had been envious of his cousin's slow-moving ways and apparent contempt for any of the societal or familial niceties. It was a persona he had attempted to recapture in front of a mirror many times before convincing himself that Russ was probably a dunce of some kind, and unworthy of imitation. Before leaving Kansas for California, Moody had once or twice heard news concerning Russ, but could recall nothing other than the fact that the snake-eyed boy had somehow become a flyer, a crop duster who swooped low over the fields in a buzzing biplane to scatter bug poisons.

"You know what he did," said Margolis; again, it was not a question.

"I . . . don't, as a matter of fact. We haven't spoken for some time."

"Your cousin's an ace, Moody, in fact he's a triple ace. That means he shot down fifteen enemy planes. You didn't know he did that?"

"As I said, we haven't . . . corresponded."

"But family should always correspond, Moody, even as far away as America is from China."

"China?"

"Where he shot them down, those fifteen Japs. Moody, you aren't aware he's a Flying Tiger? You didn't know this about your own cousin, the triple-ace hero?"

Moody knew who the Flying Tigers were. Republic Pictures recently had made an execrable movie about them starring John Wayne, and Moody had taken a girl to see it in the hope of winning his way into her bed by indulging her passion for the Duke. The evening had been a disappointment on all fronts.

"Over there fighting the little yellow-bellies before the rest of us even thought about the need to do just that," Margolis reminded him. "Way out in front of us all, those Tigers, defending the Chinese against the sons of Nippon raping their country the way they'd like to rape ours. You're 4-F, is that correct, Moody?"

"My feet," Moody said, shuffling his Florsheims unconsciously, "and my eyes." He raised and lowered a fraction of an inch the tortoiseshell frames resting heavily on the bridge of his nose. It hurt Moody to refer to his weaknesses. Every week since the atrocity at Pearl Harbor he had seen the newsreels exhorting men to join up, and had finally ventured into a naval recruiting office, fully expecting, and receiving, dismissal from any further consideration as a member of the fighting forces. Those feet and those eyes had plagued him since childhood and provided the original impetus to reject the world of actuality for the world of fiction. Russell Keys had arches that flexed like bent bows and eyes that could read automobile number plates three blocks distant. If I can see as far as a sheet of paper in an Underwood, Moody had told himself, I can be better than anyone ever expected I would.

"Soldiers of fortune," Margolis continued, "over there hitting the Japs where it hurts even before they did what they did to us at Pearl. Those were men of vision, Moody, knowing what they had to do to stop evil from spreading across Asia."

Moody suspected that the reward of five hundred dollars per downed Japanese plane had prompted most pilots to join the American Volunteer Group under General Chiang Kai-shek's banner, but he said nothing; Marvin Margolis clearly was feeling patriotic. Moody suddenly found himself envious of his cousin's fame and felt a fool for knowing nothing of his triple-ace status and the picture on *LIFE*'s cover until he entered Margolis's office. Russell, a killer of men? He could not conceive of it, even if the fifteen men killed had been Japs. It made his own work even more wretched by comparison, and he avoided the eyes of his employer.

"Quite a story there, wouldn't you say, Moody?"

"Yes."

"And who better to bring it to the screen than Empire, am I right?"

Moody looked up. Margolis was smiling at him. Now he saw the motive behind his summons. "It's been quite a while—"

"Among family, time is immaterial. This is your cousin. This is someone who, God willing, and family ties being what they are, will listen to you where he hasn't listened to Metro and Warner's and all the other vultures circling to pick up options on his story, a story that needs to be told now that the nation is at war, wouldn't you agree, Moody? Here's an inspiration to us all, but the hero in question is so modest he won't sign with anyone, and frankly, Moody, we've had our own representative trying to get your cousin's name on a contract, but he won't, not with us or anyone, and the military brass won't let us bother him anymore. But you're family, and if he says he wants to see you, they'll let him, I'm sure. Would he want to see you, Moody, do you think?"

"I . . . really couldn't say."

"Couldn't say?"

Margolis invested the words with incredulity. Moody felt his stomach lurch; he had disappointed the man behind Empire Productions, and no reasonable excuse presented itself.

"Do you believe in fate, Keith?"

"Fate? I believe in . . . free will."

"It's an important question, the difference between those religions, Keith, but humble men such as ourselves won't solve anything today by arguing over it. I'll just say this: a matter of an hour or so ago, I happened to hear an amazing fact, a small piece of information that wouldn't ordinarily have reached my ears if not for—and here you'll have to bear with me, Keith—if not for *the hand of fate.* I heard, as if the information had been whispered in my ear by friendly angels, that the man whose story all Hollywood wants to tell has a cousin right here at Empire Productions, a fellow who just happens to be one of our finest screenwriters. Can this be just coincidence and nothing more, Keith, or has that fateful hand I happen to believe in scooped yourself and your cousin and Empire Productions up and rolled us all against each other like dice? Can you tell me the answer to this amazing development, Keith?"

"I'd say it depends on how you choose to look at it—"

"And I say it's a fool that flies in the face of fate, and my enemies and friends alike will tell you, Keith, that I'm no fool. Do you see the direction we're taking, Keith? Can you see for yourself how it is that fate has seen fit to bring your cousin to us, the studio best equipped to portray him on the screen? I'll make it plain, Keith, the assignment's yours. Need a break from Westerns? Consider it done. A war movie, Keith, during a time of *actual war*. We're talking about an example to the American people, not just some forgettable adventure flick. This is real!"

Moody was panicked into replying, "Yes, sir."

"Good. Here's where your free will theory comes into play, Keith, if you wish to see it that way. You can choose to go on down to the Wilshire Hotel and ask to see your hero cousin, or you can choose not to. A perfect test of faith, I'd say. Would you say it's a test of faith?"

"Certainly," said Moody, who saw it as no such thing. Margolis, for all that he controlled a movie studio and was presumably worth millions, was every bit as much a fool and ignoramus as Quentin Yapp. The intellect of these men and others at Empire had, of course, no bearing upon the very real predicament Moody found himself confronting. It was not so much a question of talking with or not talking with Russ as it was of keeping his job or losing it, regardless of fate, whose hand, Moody acknowledged, would have thick fingers narrowing to manicured nails that came to a point.

"Pick up the contract as you leave. Bring it back signed, Keith. The terms are generous, be sure to assure your cousin, cash on the barrelhead. Take a pen, Keith, and report back to me personally when it's done."

The young-old face nodded at him, then was lowered again

to the magazine, and Moody saw that his interview was over. He stood and took several steps backward before turning to leave. He was angry with himself, as he made his way across the carpet, for having acquiesced, without the least resistance, in a plan without honor. If Russell Keys had not been his cousin, there would be no part for Moody to play in bringing Empire a contract bearing the signature of the hero. He was an errand boy, nothing more, a messenger fortuitously privileged by mere association, sent on winged feet from the Olympian office of Margolis to fetch back a piece of the Flying Tiger's soul.

The secretary handed him two envelopes, one thin and one fat, as he passed her desk, and Moody walked out into the searing sunlight of a California morning.

PASSING SOUNDSTAGE FOUR, he was grabbed by the elbow and spun around.

"Hold it right there, pardner." The man attached to his arm smiled. "You just saw the Big Chief himself, ain't that right?"

"Yes, how did you know?"

Smokey grinned his trademark grin and tipped his Stetson with the trademark fingertip. "On account of I'm the one set 'em on your trail, pard."

"Excuse me?"

"Yep, I'm sure the one. 'Member that time you said to me about that ol' cousin of yours back home? 'Member that?"

"No."

"Russell Keys from Russell, Kansas—you said that one time, and I remembered the name because of an uncle that died in that town. Whooping cough. Ever hear of a body dyin' of that? That's what happened, they say. Never met the man myself, too little when it happened, but it happened in Russell, Kansas. Say, you must be prouda that cousin I bet. Seen him in the magazines? Son of a gun killed fifteen Japs."

"I know. Who did you tell?"

"Told that little gal calls herself Margolee's secertary. She's a cute one."

"I see."

"Fifteen Japs. Hell, I never got that many badmen in a single picture. Got to be some kinda sharpshooter to scratch that many little yeller fellers."

"I have to be going, Smokey."

"Sure, sure. Margolee give you the job like I figured he would?"

"Well, yes, he did."

"No need to thank me, pardner."

Moody's elbow was squeezed and shaken with genuine affection. Smokey Hayes credited Moody with putting him onto a winning streak at the box office with his cornucopia of scripts, each one exactly what Yapp and Smokey required to perpetuate the public's notion of the Old West.

"That new one, you finished it yet? Got to finish that'n for me 'fore you go writin' 'bout that flyboy cousin of yours, hear?"

"Of course, yes—"

Moody had often wondered if Smokey saw him as some kind of substitute progeny, the cowboy star being childless, so far as Moody was aware. He had several times been obliged to share an evening of food and drunkenness with Smokey to humor the man's apparent affection for him, and he assumed it had been on their latest foray into the nightspots of Los Angeles that he had talked, however fleetingly, of his cousin, who had indeed been born in the town after which he was named. It was pure chance that had caused the name to stick in Smokey's less-than-alert mind, and now Moody was caught up in the web he had himself spun so carelessly that night. The evening, he now recalled, had ended at a fashionably discreet brothel much frequented by Smokey, who thrust Moody into the arms of a platinum blonde with the exhortation, "Let fly with Mandy, son, she knows how to do it all." Moody had made the attempt for Smokey's sake but failed embarrassingly and spent his time with Mandy explaining to her the philosophical subtleties behind his only published story, "The Samaritan." Mandy had not been impressed by it. Any man, she said, who chose to marry an ugly woman out of sympathy for her ugliness deserved what he got.

"You make darn sure you put in plenty of action now," said Smokey.

"I always do."

"And laughs, just a couple or three, you know? Hell, sure you do."

"I'll remember."

Smokey punched him good-naturedly on the shoulder and grinned even more widely. "Son of a gun," he said. "Must run in your family, pard."

"I suppose so. I have to go somewhere now, Smokey."

Moody could understand Smokey's gratitude for the run of successes that had flowed like hot tar from Moody's typewriter to the soundstages and back lots of the studio. Smokey was a true presence there, squinting at the cameras to convey the meanness he reserved for bad *hombres*, grinning the big grin he bestowed upon children and clever animals (one or the other of which tended to be instrumental in rescuing him from mine shafts and cabins filled with hissing dynamite), and presenting his most famous expression of all three—the one that earned him more fan mail than any other, in Smokey's opinion—his bashful look, the one he allowed to sneak up on him when confronted by the schoolmarm or the rancher's daughter. It drew audiences into the theaters nationwide every week. Moody happened to know that Smokey's real name was Mortimer Pence, and that he was from Rhode Island.

"Git along then, li'l dogie."

Released, Moody hurried away and lost himself among a passing caravan of Bedouins.

2

THE DESK CLERK made it known to Moody even as he crossed the lobby of the Wilshire that he considered him an unsuitable presence among the massive potted ferns and expensively attired guests. It was Moody's walk while passing through the fixtures and aromas and stares of the wealthy and important that revealed his intimidation. He gave way several times in just a few yards to individuals more powerful than himself, granting them passage across his own inferior path, and by the time the desk was reached, the clerk behind it was filled with mild contempt for the young bespectacled man whose clothing bore out everything suggested by his gait.

"May I help you, sir?"

"Russell Keys," said Moody, then added, "He's here, isn't he?"

"Mr. Keys has left instructions not to be disturbed by anyone."

Moody thought the desk clerk sounded just like a desk clerk in a movie. He even looked like a movie desk clerk.

"Could you just call him and let him know his cousin's here, please?"

"His cousin?"

As he watched the desk clerk's left eyebrow lifting minutely, the way a suspicious and haughty desk clerk's eyebrow would in a movie, Moody realized he was facing a part-time or would-be actor. It was a depressing discovery.

"Yes, his cousin, his actual cousin. Tell him it's Keith."

"I'll try," said the clerk, lifting the house phone and dialing. Moody watched the performance and found it convincing. Someone should hire the desk clerk to play a desk clerk.

"A gentleman referring to himself as a cousin of Mr. Keys wants to see him."

A soft buzzing of words was returned through the phone, and the desk clerk said to Moody, "You'll have to wait while they ask if he wants to see you."

"He has someone up there with him?"

"Of course," scolded the desk clerk. "Mr. Keys is a triple ace."

"I know."

The clerk attended to a beautiful woman who demanded the Wilshire's finest suite. Moody glanced at her once, wondering if she was a movie star, but her profile was not identifiable. Moody knew it wasn't always easy to spot a star off the set. They could disguise themselves, cloak their splendor with anonymity if they chose to, but he was fairly sure the woman beside him was no one special. She returned his second glance with a look that penetrated Moody as if his flesh were mist.

Minutes after the woman had been escorted away by a flotilla of baggage-bearing bellboys, the desk clerk's phone rang. He picked it up, listened, then asked Moody, "What was the bad thing you did at Aunt Mildred's birthday party?"

"Bad thing?"

"That's what he wants to know."

Moody felt his face begin to flush. It was typical of Russell to pull such a prank as this, solely in order to humiliate him.

"I . . . peed in a flowerpot. I was only five."

The clerk made little effort to hide the smirk beneath his pencil-line mustache.

"He says he peed in a flowerpot when he was five. Yes." He covered the mouthpiece and asked Moody, "Are you very, very sorry for what you did?"

"Tell him to stop the nonsense. It's Keith, and I have to see him."

"Your guest is not amused, I'm afraid, Mr. Keys."

He hung up the phone. "Two twenty-nine," he said.

"Thank you."

The elevator rose silently. Moody, already upset by the incident at the front desk, did not look forward to his reunion with Russell. The doors slid open with a rumbling hiss, and he stepped out into a windowless corridor brilliantly lit by sconce lamps. Two twenty-nine was not far away. He knocked and waited. There were voices beyond the door, and loud swing music. A uniformed man not much older than himself suddenly flung open the door and shouted, "What!" into Moody's face.

"I . . . want to see Russell Keys."

"Hey! Hey, it's the cousin!" the young man called over his shoulder.

"Bring him in!" called a woman, and a jerked thumb allowed Moody inside.

The suite, a warren of lavish rooms, appeared populated by midnight revelers, since all the curtains were closed, including the blackouts set up in case of a Japanese bombing raid on California. There were sixty to eighty people that Moody could see immediately, and the traffic to and fro through several doorways suggested plenty more in the adjacent rooms. The shouting and laughter and outright screaming was not enough to drown out the phonograph; Moody now was able to recognize the song: "This Is the Army, Mr. Jones." It was a party, a noonday party, a glass or bottle in every hand, the air blued by cigarette smoke, made jagged by noise.

"He's in back," said the young man, "this way. Want a drink?"

"No, thank you."

His guide steered Moody through the shifting crowd, at least half of which was young and female and dressed, or undressed, for seduction. Moody was shocked. How could this bunch of screaming good-timers have anything to do with dour, sullen Russell? Most of the men present were in uniform, but where was their military discipline?

"In here. Ask him if he needs anything."

Moody was nudged through a doorway and heard it close behind him, muffling instantly the sounds of revelry. A lanky figure sat in an armchair by a window left open to allow sunshine inside the room. His hair was considerably shorter, and he appeared much slimmer than Moody recalled, but it was Russell. A half-empty Coke bottle swung from his long fingers. His jacket was off, and his tie was loosened, the knot hanging over his breastbone. The Coke bottle was lifted a few inches in lazy salute.

"Hey, cuz."

"Hey, Russell."

Moody came closer. His cousin appeared much more than five months older than Moody, his face unshaven, dark crescents beneath his eyes. His expression was benign, without joy or resentment at Moody's intrusion.

"Quite a party you've got going out there."

"It ain't my party."

Russell lifted the Coke and drained it, his Adam's apple bobbing. When it was empty he set the bottle carefully down beside his shoes. "Sit yourself," he said.

Moody chose a matching armchair, arranged by the management to facilitate intimate conversation by the window. Russell's eyes roamed the ceiling for a while before settling on him. "So, you live in this town?"

"For a couple of years now. Mildred never wrote you about me before she died?"

"She might have. I moved around a lot. When'd she die?"

"Last year. It was cancer."

Russell merely nodded.

"China," said Moody. "That must be a fascinating place."

"Smells like an open crapper. Those chinks live like dogs, most of 'em."

"But having the chance to see another culture that way, from the inside—"

"Couldn't wait to leave, you want the truth. You want China, go see it for yourself. I had enough."

"I suppose . . . seeing it the way you did, being at war, I mean, would make it less enjoyable."

Russell shook his head a little and smiled, lifting only the corners of his mouth.

"Keith, you don't know a goddamn thing."

"I'll listen if you want to educate me."

"Forget it. What kinda work you do nowadays, cuz?"

"Hollywood."

"Hollywood what?"

"Screenwriter. I write movies."

"You're shittin' me."

"No."

"Movie writer?"

"Uh-uh."

"Jesus H. Christ. What movies? Any ones I might've seen?"

"Well, actually I specialize, just for the time being."

"Specialize in what, cartoons or something?"

"Westerns."

"Westerns. No shit. Gary Cooper, maybe?"

"I mainly write for Smokey Hayes."

"Smokey Hayes! That dumbfuck? Jesus, cuz. Excuse me, but Jesus. You write those movies? You're the one?"

"Yes, I am."

"Now you sound sore at me."

"I'm not sore."

"The hell you ain't. I don't blame you, though. Those Smokey Hayes movies, we saw a bunch over there in Kunming. How about that, huh? The stuff you wrote here went all the way over there. We had movies in the mess sometimes, you know."

"You didn't notice my name on the screen credits?"

"Hey, who reads that stuff? It's a Smokey Hayes flick, so you don't read a goddamn thing except what it's called."

"Thanks."

"See, I knew you're sore. Look, I just want to know one thing; how come every movie starts out the same way, you know, with Smokey sitting there by his campfire with the coffeepot and all, and then he hears these gunshots coming from way off and he jumps on his horse, that prissy-looking palomino, whatsisname?"

"Jake."

"Right, jumps on old Jake who happens to be all saddled and ready with his ass pointed toward old Smokey so's he can jump straight over it into the goddamn saddle and start riding in around two seconds flat."

"That's how Smokey wants it."

"And when he gets to where the shooting's at, there's this buckboard tearing along with the horses going hell-for-leather and this pretty girl who's lost control of the reins, and a bad outfit riding down hard on her, shooting but never hitting her, but Smokey hauls out his forty-five and starts knocking them off from so far away he couldn't do it without a Winchester at least, and they all get scared and ride away, so then Smokey rides alongside the buckboard and yanks the girl off the seat just before the linchpin busts and the whole shebang goes over a goddamn cliff, only the horses got loose just in time so the kids don't see something that's gonna make 'em cry."

"That's only happened a few times with me. Smokey had other writers before."

"That's all I've got to say on the subject."

"Good."

"I didn't mean to make you sore at me."

"I'm not. How does it feel to be a hero?"

"Just between you and me, it feels like they're talking about someone else. This is just the dumbest setup. That bunch out there, they don't know me and I don't know them, and I don't wanna know 'em. Bunch of assholes and whores. The whores have got the tits and the assholes have got the uniforms." He gestured toward his jacket, dumped in a pile on the bed. "Guess that makes me an asshole too."

"It takes all kinds."

"You know what this one general told me? He said they should give me a medal, but they can't do it on account of I shot down most of my Japs before this war even got started."

"I thought they gave medals for individual acts of bravery, not just how many enemies you killed. I don't mean that the wrong way."

"I know you don't. I wouldn't know what you get a medal for. I don't even want one, or any of the rest of this bullshit." He pointed to the door, behind which music throbbed and voices mingled in uproar. "They're all here for the beer, that's all, the beer and the cooze."

"Tell me about China."

"Why should I? What's there to tell? I flew lucky and killed a bunch of Japs that shouldn't be there, so they got what they asked for, invading someone else's country like that. Fuck 'em. *Fuck 'em!*" he yelled at the door. Moody was unsure if his cousin referred to the Japanese or the party revelers outside.

"Russ—"

"What!"

"I feel that I'm here under, I don't know, false pretenses maybe."

"Say what?"

"I'm told that the studios have all been hounding you for the rights to your story."

"Yeah, they have. There's even a couple hanging around out there still, sucking up the sauce and waiting for me to do the same so they can talk me around. It won't happen, cuz—you know why?"

"Why?"

"Because I don't give a shit if they make a movie about me or not, in fact I'd prefer it if they didn't, so they're wasting their time. They're just a different bunch of assholes is all. I wouldn't take their money if they paid me."

Moody squirmed in his chair.

"Russ, that's why I'm here too."

"Well, I'll be goshdarned, like old Smokey'd say."

"The studio sent me. It wasn't my idea. Someone told them you were my cousin. It all happened just this morning, but I want you to know it wasn't through any intention of mine. This is an accident, so to speak. Frankly, Russ, I didn't even know about you being a Flying Tiger ace. I couldn't believe it when I saw you on the cover of *LIFE*."

"Ain't it a hoot? Couldn't believe it myself. I was maybe just a leetle bit drunk when they took that picture. I don't like having my picture taken."

"I know. I remember Mildred having to tell you over and over to smile."

"So, they sent you down here to make me sign on with your bunch. Sign on the dotted line, as they say."

"I feel like apologizing for it."

"No need. Hey, would you be the one that writes it?"

"It's been broadly hinted at. I think it's the carrot that brought me down here. The stick is knowing that if I don't bring back a contract I'm stuck writing for good old Smokey Hayes."

"Oh, brother, I can't let that happen to family. Sure, you can do a movie about me, what the hell. Who they gonna put in it as me, John Wayne? Errol Flynn? Hey, you know who I'd like? Jimmy Stewart, he's about as tall as me."

"They're all under contract to other studios. I don't know who they'd use, but you can bet they're already thinking about it."

"A movie about me. Who would've ever guessed, huh?"

"Funny world," Moody agreed, now grateful; his cousin had responded to honesty, a straightforward approach, with just a hint of family obligation thrown in. Russell's mood seemed to have been altered by the sudden and casual nature of the deal. He was smiling now, nodding his head in a distracted way, looking at the carpet, possibly picturing his movie-self diving through the clouds over China, sending streams of bullets into the invaders from the Land of the Rising Sun. It was probably an intoxicating notion, Moody reasoned, now that Russell had turned around and agreed to let it happen. As for himself, landing the deal had been almost too easy.

They spoke briefly then about the life they had known in Kansas. Russell was disinclined to talk about his foster parents, and Moody wondered, not for the first time, if his cousin resented the fact that he had not been brought east to Kansas City when his parents died but had been fostered out right there in Russell, Kansas. Moody's own parents, dead now from an automobile accident at a railroad crossing in 1934, had never explained to him why they had not offered to take in the orphaned boy, and Aunt Mildred, when he went to live with her, could offer no explanation either, other than to suggest that Russell was "difficult" and "hard to manage sometimes, not like you."

Moody wanted to ask his cousin's opinion on the matter, but having already achieved more than he'd hoped to in a professional capacity, he felt Russell might become irritated by questions relating to the distant past, when he had been a nobody, about as likely to appear on the cover of *LIFE* magazine as the family cat.

"Need a drink, cuz?"

"I wouldn't mind. I didn't want one before."

"Nervous, yeah, I felt the same. It's dumb, us feeling that way."

"Yes, it is."

"Go get us something, will you? I hate to look at that bunch out there."

As he went to the door, Moody was reminded of those times Russell had ordered him around when they were children. Moody had obliged him then because he was afraid of him, and wondered why it was that he obeyed today without hesitation. He was not afraid of Russell anymore, had lost that childish sense of intimidation, and it was not that the request to fetch liquor was unreasonable, given Russell's stated opinion of his short-term companions outside. Moody doubted his own manhood when he sprang up to do his cousin's bidding, and he told himself, unable to think of any other reason, that he did so out of gratitude for the contract Russell soon would sign. The drinks would probably facilitate that act in any case, so Moody comforted himself by pretending he was merely being an attentive agent for Empire.

A redhead screeched boozily into Moody's ear as he wormed his way through to the suite's built-in bar, "You send that long drink of Kansas water out here, or I'm gonna come in there and give him what he deserves. You tell him that for me, okay, sugar?"

She was expensively beautiful, like a tropical fish in an aquarium. It was unfair that such an exotic creature as this should be throwing herself at Russell, who was no better looking than Moody.

He returned to his cousin's room with a bottle and closed the door.

"A hot number outside wants you to know just how hot she is."

"One of the assholes can cool her off, or you can if you want."

"It isn't me she's interested in."

"Any cock'll do, as the rooster said at sunrise."

"I got Scotch."

"Fine by me."

They drank. Moody found himself drawing the contract from his jacket long before he had intended doing so. He tried to make the act appear casual by tossing the folded sheets onto a small table, but Russell's eyes followed.

"That the thing I have to sign so's Smokey gets off your back?"

"That's it. A thousand in cash right now, on signature of the contract."

"You brung it with you, the money?"

"I'm surprised they didn't make me sign a receipt for it before they handed it over, just to make sure I didn't run away and buy an island in the south seas."

Moody's laughter was unconvincing. He thought Russell looked at him with pity.

"Shoot, gimme a pen right now so's we can concentrate on the liquor."

Russell signed it without reading a word.

"You should be aware of what it is, Russ," said Moody, shocked by such carelessness. He drew an envelope and slip of paper from his jacket.

"I trust you, so why bother."

"Well, here's the cash, and if you wouldn't mind signing again, just here, so they know I really gave it to you."

"They don't trust you farther'n they can throw you, those movie people, do they?"

"No, I guess not. It's just business, nothing out of the ordinary."

"Something they'd most likely do a coupla times a week, huh."

"Maybe not that often."

The receipt was signed, the envelope left where it was on the table. Moody felt guilty, he was unsure why. Being Marvin Margolis's envoy was disquieting work.

The whiskey quickly began to affect Russell's speech. Moody watched his cousin become someone else within the space of five minutes and concluded he was one of those unfortunates who could not take alcohol without inviting disastrous results. There was little conversation between them as Russell poured and drank repeatedly. Moody sipped and observed, and eventually was caught observing.

"What the hell're you lookin' at?"

"I'm just drinking my drink, cousin."

"Don't call me cousin. I don't like that word."

"What would you prefer?"

"I'd prefer to be fishing."

"I remember that place Uncle Frank took us to, that place where he said there'd be plenty of bass, but we didn't catch a single one."

"Fuck Uncle Frank."

"What's wrong, Russ?"

"Uncle Frank, yeah he took me fishing, but he wouldn't take me when the old man and old lady died. The goddamn house burns down, I get left on my own without a goddamn thing, but what's he do? He says to have me fostered out, the son of a bitch."

"Frank knew he was a sick man, that's why. He was dead himself within a year. Mildred told me later they wanted to take you in, but it wouldn't have been fair to let you lose another father, and my folks couldn't do it either, not with things the way they were back then, with Dad losing his job."

"But he got another one, right?"

"Later, after you were taken in by . . . what was their name?"

"The Deavers."

"And my folks were killed too, later on, after the Deavers and you moved away. Mildred would've taken you in then, along with me, but you were gone. Frank left her a pretty nice insurance policy."

"Ain't that swell."

"No need to sound that way about it. You had all the bad breaks back then, but now it seems like you're getting the good ones."

"Is that what it seems like? That what you think?"

Russell was ugly drunk now, his face twisted, body slipping farther down into the chair. Outside the door a woman screamed, then the scream became laughter.

"Russ, if my coming here has upset you in any way—"

"I said not to call me that."

"You said not to call you cousin."

"I know what I said!"

"Maybe you'd like me to leave."

"Maybe I would. You've got your piece of paper. That's what you came here for, wasn't it, just the paper, like all the rest."

"If you want to, you can tear it up, I don't care."

"Bullshit you don't. Go on, get outta here. Go write a movie, but you know what? It'll never be about me, you know why? Because there's not a man alive knows a goddamn thing about me that's worth knowing. Go ahead and write what you want, only get out now, because I'm sick to death of looking at your face."

Moody picked up his jacket and went to the door. "I'm sorry," he said, "I don't know what for, exactly."

"Add it to everything else you don't know."

Moody walked through the party as fast as he could, his face burning.

"KEITH, THIS PROJECT has the earmarks of a classic. It's not usually my nature to make predictions even before pre-production gets under way—listen to me, we don't even have a treatment yet!—but I strongly suspect, call it instinct if you will, that this one will be big. Big! Do you share that feeling, that hunch, at all, Keith?"

"Yes, I do," lied Moody.

He had felt terrible since leaving Russell's room, but it would have been unwise to speak of this to Marvin Margolis, who had been astonished to receive word, mere hours after despatching Moody to the Wilshire, of his success. Margolis ordered in a late lunch for them both and insisted on hearing every detail of the visit.

"What kind of man are we talking about, a slow-to-anger-but-you-better-not-get-him-mad kind of guy? Is that what he is? We've got someone perfect for that character. What about background, Keith? We don't want to just put him in his plane and send him up to kill Japs. Have you seen this? That's how a fighting plane should look."

The issue of *LIFE* was again thrust at Moody, opened at the article about Russell Keys. His cousin stood before a Curtiss P-40 Warhawk with its air-intake cowling painted to resemble a wide-open mouth filled with sharp teeth. Pieces of the fuselage had been torn away by enemy bullets.

"So is he interesting? is what we need to know. You already know, growing up with him like you did, but now you need to share your special knowledge with me, Keith, and the production team, when we get one assembled. You've taken us by surprise, I don't mind saying it out loud, but we'll catch up with you, Keith, just give us time, so is he interesting, this cousin of yours? What kind of interesting, Keith? because this is crucial, this pinning down of the essential character, I think you'll agree, so tell me now."

"He's an unusual personality type, Mr. Margolis."

"Unusual. Unusual how? Not in some strange and peculiar way, I hope you're not telling me that, Keith. He's likable, am I right? The quiet type, but there's depth behind those eyes. You fellers from Kansas, you look way off into the distance, don't you? looking for something that isn't there, because in Kansas there isn't anything to look at, so you have this look, which is good, we can use that, it fits right in with the farm boy image."

"Russell was never on a farm, Mr. Margolis. He was a townie."

"That can't be right, Keith. I looked up Russell on the map, and it's a tiny place in the middle of nowhere. We need that faraway look in his eyes. What else about him?"

"He lived with foster parents."

"Adopted—!"

"Fostered. His parents were killed when their house caught on fire."

"It's perfect! Cast into the world at a tender age . . . How old was he, Keith, when this terrible event unfolded?"

"Thirteen or so."

"Perfect! A kid, all alone, but then along come some people to stop him being an orphan. These were good people, or cruel?"

"I really don't know. The family moved down to Oklahoma,

I believe, and the rest of us more or less lost sight of Russell after that, although he did write once or twice to Aunt Mildred in Kansas City. She's the woman who took me in when my own parents died."

"Was he always looking up at the clouds, Keith, you know, imagining himself a brave pilot, anything like that?"

"No, when I knew him he was more interested in marbles and so forth."

"But it was there anyway, buried inside him, this yearning for the wild blue yonder. This is wonderful material, wonderful. Any death among the stepfolks?"

"Foster folk," corrected Moody, but when Margolis's eyes narrowed he hurried on. "No, not so far as I know, but as I said, we pretty much lost track of Russell until he showed up right here on *LIFE*."

"How about China? Any romance there, some slant-eyed young thing full of Eastern promise, someone whose family got bombed out by the Japs? How about she has a little brother who was injured, and that's how they meet, when Russell picks him up and carries him to shelter during a bombing raid. She's grateful to him for that, but shy, like these Chinese girls are, so he doesn't see how she's falling in love with him, not at first, but then later on he does. Go on, Keith."

"He said it smelled."

"What did?"

"China."

"Well, what can we expect from a society that doesn't have toilets? Let's put more emphasis on the good side here, Keith, and not criticize the Chinese for what they unfortunately don't have. The courageous Chinese character, that's what we need to stress, their resistance to aggression from the Japs, bravery in the face of superior odds, that kind of thing. We have some marvelous character actors who can bring this off perfectly. Her family objects at first, him being a foreigner, but then they see what our boy from Kansas represents—in the grand scheme of things, that is. You know what I'm talking about, don't you, Keith? It's the thing that's more crucial to the production than anything else, the real meat and crux of the matter. Be candid with me, Keith—what does your cousin represent to you, and is it the same thing he represents to the rest of us, from the average American citizen right down to your Chinese peasant in his rice field? Is it the same, Keith?"

"For me, it's—" Moody grasped for something large yet formless. "—the principle of the thing."

"That's it exactly! We're seeing this eye to eye. I said my instinct was good on this, didn't I. He's there to protect the innocent, because by God they deserve protection, don't they?"

"There's also the matter of the bonuses."

"Bonuses?"

"The five hundred dollars a pilot got from the Chinese government for every Jap plane he brought down. It's something we can't really ignore."

"Of course not, and that was going to be my next point on the agenda. He gives the money to the girl, so she can get her little brother the hospital treatment he needs. What's he got, a broken leg? Better make it a flesh wound, something they can put lots of bandages around, but not the face, we need to see this kid's eyes light up whenever Russ stops by and sits at his bedside to cheer the little guy up, and incidentally, Keith, I think that's where he should first become aware of Lin-Ming's love, when he glances up and sees her on the other side of the hospital bed, staring at him with the unmistakable look of love, which is an international language, as we all know. The kid sees it too, and says something cute, but Lin-Ming's too embarrassed to translate it for Russ."

"Is Lin-Ming an actual Chinese name?"

"It'll be something like that, something close to it. You don't like the sound of Lin-Ming, Keith?"

"It has a very pleasant ring to it."

"Damn right. Instinct. Say, did he leave a girl behind in the States when he went over there? That could be an interesting angle, him being torn between two women, East and West, the eternal struggle. He isn't married, is he?"

"No, not that I'm aware of."

"Good. The lone wolf of the China skies, that's the angle we need. Make that lone tiger. God, I love the way these planes look. We'll have to get a few dozen from the War Department or someone. Like avenging angels tearing across the sky, blasting evil out of existence. It was evil what the Japs did at Pearl, Keith, pure evil. A day of infamy. They'll pay, and big, very big, thanks to men like Russ. Is he going back to China or what?"

"I really don't know."

"It doesn't matter. He's *been* there and seen and done the things he did. This is an important picture for the studio, you know that, don't you, Keith, what with a war on, the situation being what it is internationally and people out there needing reassurance that decency and American courage will prevail against that kind of disgusting evil. You'll have a new office. Yapp'll scream when he hears you're off the new Smokey picture, but we'll substitute someone. This is a big step up for you, Keith. You did a magnificent job, getting a contract out of Russ when no one else could, magnificent job, and he didn't raise any kind of fuss over the money at all?"

"He just signed the contract without even reading it."

"That's trust, sheer outright trust. That guy trusts you, Keith, because you share the same blood, and we won't betray that trust, that's why you're the one who'll work on the script, making sure of its authenticity, its inner truth. Who else could write so knowingly about your own cousin, am I right? This is something only you can do for Empire Productions, Keith, and for Russ, and even more importantly, for the American people out there who need to know, who need absolute assurance that there are heroes waiting in the wings, heroes *with* wings who'll protect them and serve the cause we all know is the most important in the world right now. This is your job, Keith, and you've earned it, this sacred flame. I have a meeting."

MOODY'S NEW OFFICE, when he approached it the following morning, bore his name on the door in fresh paint, and beneath it the title *China Skies*. He had stayed awake much of the night trying to conjure up the perfect title, and eventually settled on *Out of the Sun*, this being the place from which successful aerial sorties were launched against an opposing force in order to blind them until too late; it also suggested the origins of the Japanese war machine currently grinding across China and the countries of Southeast Asia. Margolis apparently had already arrived at the correct title, and Moody accepted it with only a little regret.

Inside he found that the research people had covered his walls with pictures of Chinese peasantry and American warplanes, the P-40 predominant among them. All the pictures from *LIFE*, including the cover, were also there. Moody looked at Russell Keys and felt only resentment and puzzlement rather than inspiration. His cousin had told him nothing of events in China, offered no unique perspective on the battle there, given him nothing but a signature enabling Empire Productions to concoct a scenario of its own choosing, a hastily assembled notion of war as witnessed from a great distance, shot through a soft-focus lens with a distinctly rosy tint. Moody knew there would be no severed limbs on the screen when they were done with *China Skies*, no mangled American airmen, no Japanese pilot who would not be blown out of the air by the final reel.

It was shaping up to be nonsense of the lowest order, if Margolis's suggestions of the day before were to be the blueprint for production, as they often were. If Margolis purchased a book for filming, he tended to treat it with a measure of consideration for its actual content. But when there was no book, and little time or opportunity to develop a treatment cognizant of basic truths behind the project, anything could happen, since Margolis tended to embrace these opportunities and impose his own creative impulses onto the production. For all the reality that would emerge from his new assignment, Moody was already aware, *China Skies* might just as well star Smokey Hayes and announce itself to the public as hokum, pure and simple.

A typewriter of distinctly newer vintage than he was used to sat waiting for him, and Moody felt a faint professional pride in its appearance, as he had when he saw the nameplate outside his door. He was moving up. Margolis seemed to like him, and so he should, considering the near-impossible feat Moody had performed in eliciting from Russell Keys a contract with definite advantages, creatively and monetarily, for Empire. Russell should have read it before he signed, but he had not, and so would pay the usual price Hollywood demanded—a complete rewrite of actuality. Moody refused to feel guilty; his cousin had treated him abominably, as he had when they were children. He would deserve whatever Empire chose to say about him, however they decided to depict him. Of course, the picture would be so flattering it was unlikely Russell would object seriously to its structure. In any case, it was now out of his hands and in the hands of Moody, who was in turn held firmly in the larger hands of Marvin Margolis.

Moody sat and began working on the standard twenty-page treatment, bearing in mind every inspired twist Margolis had delivered himself of the previous day. Margolis would be the final arbiter before production began and would expect to see much of his own original contributions featured in Moody's outline. Lin-Ming was there, as was her injured little brother, the impish but loyal Hung-Lo. Moody removed that name with a nervous titter and replaced it with something less suggestive;

Chin-Li would be much better. Chin would use a crutch for most of the time while recovering from his Jap-inflicted wound, an Oriental Tiny Tim. Margolis would love that.

Russell's life before he arrived in China as part of the American Volunteer Group was more challenging; Margolis had said nothing about that, offered no insights, so Moody went ahead and included the known facts: the death by burning of Russ's parents, his adoption by the Deavers (no mention of the aunts and uncles who might have taken him in but hadn't; it was irrelevant, dramatically speaking), and his growing fascination with flying. Moody created an old-time barnstormer–turned–crop duster to act as Russ's mentor in all things aerial. His name would be Dusty Fields, and he would take the boy up and make of him an airplane addict, teaching him the rudiments of those risky, ground-hugging maneuvers that were the staple of his profession. Russ would master the techniques (and use them later in China, somehow, Moody was not quite sure in what capacity, possibly some outrageously low attack on a Japanese airfield that would yield devastating results), but Dusty Fields would die on a routine crop-dusting job because a mechanic had failed to fix something amiss with his engine. And that mechanic would wind up in China also, providing natural enmity between himself and Russ; in fact the mechanic would vie with Russ for the affections of Lin-Ming, but would be absolved of all bad behavior by sacrificing himself somehow for the rest of the Tigers and Russ in particular in the final reel, some act of heroism involving many explosions and the deaths of a great number of Japs. It was perfect.

He was halfway through the second, expanded draft, when his door opened.

"Mr. Moody, I believe. Hi, Baxter Nolan. Bax."

The studio's newest leading man strode in with a practiced smile and offered his hand. Moody was on his feet by then, mouth hanging slightly open. The handshake was firm and hearty, Moody's responsive grip too inadequate, too late. The handsome face so close to his own exuded a faint aroma of breath mint and aftershave lotion.

Nolan glanced around the walls. "Already up and running, I see."

"Yes, yes . . . Mr. Margolis is very excited about this one, raring to go."

"I guess he's told you."

"Told me?"

"You're looking at your cousin, cousin."

"They're casting you as Russell?"

"Thought I'd drop by and get the family seal of approval." He looked more closely at the *LIFE* cover portrait. "Guess there's not too much in common there. They tell me he's one lean and lanky fellow."

"He's around six-three, long in the face, as you can see."

"Well, we can't get everything right, can we, Keith? Mind if I call you Keith? Call me Bax. This is one helluva big step for us both, wouldn't you say?"

"Yes, it's very—timely."

"The perfect word for it. A story that's happening right now as we speak, and you and I are basically the ones responsible for bringing it alive. Okay, the director's an important choice too. I heard they're giving it to Blackwell, and he'll do a damned good job. Did you see *Fall of the Dice*? Mississippi gambler, steamboat race. He steered me through that one, so we both know how the other thinks and works. Great team, and now you're on board too, Keith. Did you say you saw it?"

"I didn't actually get a chance to. They've been keeping me kind of busy."

"Smokey Hayes says you're a writing machine, swears you're the greatest thing to happen to his career since Jake learned to count with his hooves. Roy Schutt's got his sights set on making this the best war movie since *All Quiet on the Western Front*."

Roy Schutt was in charge of the studio's most prestigious projects, and the mention of his name made clear to Moody the irreversible turn his career had taken. If Schutt was the one shepherding *China Skies* through its various metamorphoses from idea to finished product, then little could go wrong, and Moody's own status within Empire would be enhanced by association with the great man. Baxter Nolan would not have taken the time to visit Moody if not for Schutt's official involvement at the highest level. Moody's star had risen in just twenty-four hours.

"Well, that movie had more of an antiwar message. I think Mr. Margolis wants this one to be very . . . patriotic, very rousing."

"Exactly, and there's very little distinction between the two notions if you examine them closely, just a sadder ending on the antiwar picture. Don't forget, Keith, that was told from the German point of view, so naturally it had to be about death and defeat, ultimately. This project isn't saddled with history, so we can be as patriotic as we like."

For a brief moment Moody thought Nolan had said "idiotic" instead of patriotic.

"Yes, that's certainly true . . . Baxter."

"Bax. Truth is, Keith, I came over to see if you had anything prepared yet, just to give me a few clues in advance for my character development. You can't start too soon, shaping the character, it's the clue to your success on the screen."

"You're welcome to look at what I've done so far." Moody picked up his original draft. "This should give you a rough idea."

"Thanks, Keith, I really appreciate this."

Baxter sat in Moody's chair and read quickly, then said, "Keith, I don't see any mention here of Russell's girlfriend back home. Roy was very clear about the two-woman setup, said he got it straight from MM himself."

"Well, that's just the first draft. I'm working on the second."

"Put the girl in, Keith, a decent American girl who's prepared to wait for the man she loves, even if he's on the far side of the world. Listen, just a hint from me to you, write it with Sandy Ryder in mind. Roy says MM is very much concerned with advancing her as fast as we can."

This news did not surprise Moody, who had heard through the commissary grapevine that Baxter and Sandy had been seen together recently in Hollywood's places to be seen. "Thanks for the tip, Bax."

"No charge, Keith. We all need to give each other that extra helping hand now and then, or we'd get in more trouble than we deserve. Any chance the second draft'll be ready for Roy today?"

"I'll work on it till it's done."

"That's what MM likes to hear—team spirit and sacrifice. See you around, Keith, and make sure there's a scene for Sandy to get misty-eyed about what her man's going through over there in China when she gets a letter from him. That'd go down real big."

"Okay."

Baxter winked and was gone. Moody stared for some time at the door and reviewed the actor's performance and his own. He could not decide who had been the bigger phony. Baxter was more intelligent than Smokey Hayes, but his quickness of mind was not as appealing as the cowboy star's absolute conviction, the total involvement that enabled him to believe himself an ex-cowhand who had drifted to Hollywood and been discovered. Baxter's friendliness was of a different order, a surefooted weaselly approach that made Moody's skin crawl as he recalled the visit; and yet the man was not unlikable. The worst of Moody's criticism he reserved for himself. He had been almost as unctuous and ready to please as a star-smitten fan, but Baxter probably accepted that kind of behavior as routine and would not dismiss him as some kind of servile toady.

Staring at the draft in his hand, Moody could not deceive himself about its worth, and for several minutes he was overtaken by a phenomenon he had experienced at irregular intervals since his arrival in California. He called these visitations the Jiminys, after Pinocchio's conscience-laden insect pal, and they served to remind Moody not so much of the difference between good and bad moral acts as the difference between what he was engaged in doing on his typewriter, and what he would have preferred to be doing on his typewriter. He was a hack, no doubt about it, and the distance between *China Skies* and "The Samaritan" seemed wider than the Grand Canyon. The Jiminys soon had him feeling fit to weep, but Moody resisted such self-pity, knowing it for the futile exercise it was. He should be glad he had been lifted out of B features at last, and see the current assignment as a means to better things. The world was a practical place, and Moody would have to be a practical man while living in it.

He went back to work, and by noon had received a message via gofer from Roy Schutt, informing Moody he was as of today a five-hundred-dollar-a-week man. He could almost hear Jiminy tut-tutting in his ear, but drove him away by the simple expedient of giving a little whistle.

IN THE COMMISSARY for a late lunch, Moody was approached by a girl he had seen several times before around the studio. She was unremarkable when viewed from a distance, but closer observation revealed a startling set of deep green eyes, quite the most attractive Moody could recall ever seeing. She sat at his table without waiting for an invitation, smiled, and said, "Hello, are you Keith Moody?"

"Yes."

"Myra," she said, extending her hand in a brusquely mannish gesture. He took it and pumped her fingers several times.

Her smile was every bit as appealing as her eyes, and he approved of the dark sweep of hair over her shoulders.

"Bax told me you're someone I should meet."

"Oh, he did?"

"He said you were the right kind of person for the job."

"What job is that?"

"Are you moonlighting as a night watchman? You're a screenwriter. That job."

"Oh, well . . . that was nice of him."

"Most people think Bax is nice."

"Yes. Are you . . . under contract?"

"An actress, you mean? I'm not pretty enough, but I'm too proud to play frumps, so the answer is no, I'm not under contract, and I'm not in the wardrobe department or makeup either."

"Then—?"

"Research. I'm part of the *China Skies* team."

"It's all happening very quickly."

"You bet. Today's story, made today. Margolis is jumping up and down over what you did."

"You're researching the project?"

"I need to know what kind of farmhouse your cousin and you grew up in. One of those tall, boxy clapboard things with a big front porch?"

"We weren't raised together, and neither of us ever lived on a farm."

"But you're both from Kansas."

"Would it surprise you very much to learn that I've never shucked corn, I don't carry a straw in my mouth, and I've never seen a tornado in my life?"

"Oh, gosh, looks like I've offended you. Oodles of apologies."

"I was born in Olathe, which is just outside Kansas City, and Russell was born about halfway across the state in Russell. Yes, he was named after the town. His parents were proud the family had been there for three generations."

"But no farms."

"Around Russell, yes. Russ's father was a John Deere salesman, but they lived in town, not out on the windswept prairie, surrounded by empty space and howling savages."

"You haven't forgiven me."

"I'm sorry. I get a little peeved when someone who's never been there assumes Kansans are all a bunch of hicks, that's all."

"I hate to say this after what you just told me, but Bax says he's seen the outline in draft, and Russell's a farm boy. Explanation, please."

"MM gets what MM wants."

"So I should just go ahead and pull some pictures of typical midwestern farmhouses."

"By all means."

"Does it get you mad, what they want you to do?"

"I've already been diagnosed as clinically insane, so I'm indifferent."

She laughed. Moody liked the way her two front teeth were separated by a slight gap. He reviewed the conversation so far and found that he had been unfriendly.

"Can I buy you lunch?"

"Nope. I already ate, then I saw you over here and thought I'd get my ten cents' worth of info. Can you tell me what type of plane this Dusty Fields character will fly?"

"I know nothing whatever about airplanes."

"That's okay, I can always look it up. That's my job, looking things up."

Her smile seemed not to go away. Attracted to her, he looked for signs that she might reciprocate. It was difficult to tell; she might very well be the kind of girl who was bouncy and vivacious with everyone, regardless of how she felt about them.

"His parents died in a house fire," said Moody. "It'll be a farmhouse in the script."

"That should wrench a few tears out of the customers."

"My own parents died in an auto accident. I believe it wrenched a few tears out of me at the time."

"Oops, did it again, didn't I? You wouldn't believe how I can get my big feet crammed in my mouth so often, or maybe you would. I think I owe you dinner."

No female had ever before suggested buying dinner for Moody. He was unable to respond for a moment, then heard himself say, "All right."

"I like to eat early, so how about we meet by the front gate at six?"

"Fine."

She stood, lifted her fingers in his direction, then began threading her way through the tables of costumed extras and the din of cutlery and conversation. When she was gone, Moody had to think fiercely to remember her name. Mary, that was it.

She had a roadster that seemed far too expensive to belong to a researcher, and she drove it at speeds Moody found alarming, given the blacked-out street lighting, to a place she called "my favorite watering hole. I call it that because there's an aquarium behind the bar. That's about the only water there, unless you go out back and wash dishes."

The tables were candlelit, the service discreet. Aware of the murmuring couples around them, Moody found himself wondering how many other men his companion had brought there. They ordered from the menu and drank a wicked martini apiece. "One of these before the meal, and one after," said Moody's host. "Any more, and you pay a steep price next day."

"I really appreciate this, Mary. I've been working pretty hard lately, and a night out is just what I need."

"Keith, I hate to bring this up, but my name is Myra."

"Oh, excuse me. I don't know how I did that."

"Mary, Myra, what the hell, it's my winning ways that count, isn't that right, Keith, or is it Kenneth?"

"Touché."

"God, that sounded sophisticated, Ken. I never met a man before who actually inserted 'touché' into the chitchat."

"Can we accept that the score is now even and proceed like nice people?"

"I believe we can. Tell me about what happened when your parents died."

"I went and lived with my aunt Mildred. She didn't have any kids of her own. Her husband was dead, and she had a house to herself."

"How come she didn't take in Russell too?"

"I don't know. All three families were reasonably close until the fire. Russ had more or less disappeared by the time Mildred took me in, gone to Oklahoma with the people who fostered him."

"And the next thing you heard, he's a national hero."

"It was quite a shock."

"Is he heroic? In the flesh, I mean."

Moody took a sip from his martini. The olive bobbed like a sea-green buoy.

"What difference does it make, how he is? The movie won't be about him."

"You sound very disillusioned. How can you go ahead and do it, feeling that way, or is that a silly question?"

"I'll be getting five hundred silly reasons a week."

"Sounds absolutely daffy. I'd go berserk for three if they offered."

"And he looks nothing like Baxter Nolan, of course."

"Bax is certainly good-looking."

Moody resented such a claim, even if it was true. It was a childish way to feel, and he fought it by agreeing with Myra, then analyzing Baxter's appeal to women.

"I think it's his profile that gets them, the perfectly regular spacing, the classic proportioning of the features, and that thick, wavy hair. Let's not forget the shoulders."

"Keith, you're not queer for Baxter, are you?"

"Good God, no!"

"I'd just hate to think I was buying dinner for someone who wouldn't want to take me home later."

Moody, unaccustomed to risqué talk from women, found himself blushing. He could not decide if Myra was easy or simply outrageous. Either way, he wanted her very much by then, and he took heart from her line of talk.

"I'll . . . be happy to take you home."

"Actually, Keith, I'll be taking you, since the car's mine."

"Well, yes—"

She laughed, and he blushed even more, hating himself for being unable to control it. He hadn't met anyone quite like her before, and he was relieved when their food arrived to distract them.

SHE DROVE FASTER than before to her apartment in Alhambra. They drank Tia Maria and eventually fell into bed, where Moody acquitted himself through strenuous application to the task. Myra made no comment on any of it but remained friendly and alert despite the liquor in her.

"All right, Keith, here it is, the question you've been dreading—how did you get into movies?"

He was drunk and relaxed enough to be honest. "It was the woman with the cart," he said.

"What woman?"

"Back in Kansas City. It was a Fourth of July fireworks display in Shawnee Mission Park, and she had her kid with her. A young woman, but very ugly, and her kid was too. I don't mean plain, or merely unattractive; she was downright ugly, and after the fireworks were done I watched her take her kid home. He was sitting in one of those little red wagons you see kids with, and his mother tied a rope to the handle and wrapped the other end around her waist and started hauling him away to God knows where, they certainly didn't belong in Shawnee Mission. She was like some pioneer woman hauling her possessions across the plains, swinging her arms, concentrating on getting to wherever she was going. She'd dragged her ugly kid to the park to see the fireworks, and now she was dragging him home again. Sacrifice, that's the word for what she was doing. I was embarrassed to look at her, but impressed too. She was an admirable woman in her way, and I wondered at the time what would happen if I went up to her and started talking. I didn't do it, though, I just wrote something more or less based on the woman, and for reasons I've never understood, the story got me a job out here. What I've just said probably sounds ridiculous."

"No, it doesn't."

Myra laid her head on his chest in a sympathetic manner and listened to his heart. Moody felt he could hear his own heartbeat better through her head, strange though that struck him. It had all been emptiness and waste since "The Samaritan"; maybe if he had simply written about the woman as he had described the encounter to Myra it would have been a better story, less dramatic, less phony. He might have been a legitimate writer by now if only he had remained faithful to the initial moment of inspiration. And now it was too late. He wished himself alone so he might wallow completely in the sense of worthlessness overtaking him, but Myra had him pinned to her bed with hair and light perfume and affection. He was trapped.

Myra shifted and raised herself to turn on the bedside lamp. She reached for a pack of Chesterfields and shook out two. Moody seldom smoked, but took one and accepted the flash and heat of her lighter. Settling back, he noticed a framed picture of Baxter Nolan beside the lamp.

"I didn't realize you were a fan," he said.

"Oh, I'm not, but it's a nice picture. I guess I keep it there for sentiment's sake. I'm his sister."

4

HE WORRIED ABOUT it all the next morning. She had slept with him within hours of their meeting for the first time; what kind of girl did that? Was he simply being prudish and old-fashioned; was he acting like a rube from Kansas? And the fact that she was Baxter Nolan's sister but had chosen not to admit it until Moody saw the picture struck him as devious in some way, he was unsure why. He had left Myra's apartment shortly after, claiming it had been a longer than usual day. She had not made any kind of fuss, had watched him dress with a look of bemusement on her face. It was all a considerable distraction.

His treatment for *China Skies* had been left with Roy Schutt's secretary the previous afternoon, and word came shortly after Moody's lunch break that Schutt wished to see him. Moody, confident that his efforts would be found acceptable, entered Schutt's office with what he hoped was the look of a man in charge of his life.

Empire's head of production was an angular man, tall, his head bristling with salt-and-pepper hair, his narrow chest emphasized by an expensive and ornate silk waistcoat. Moody suspected this was worn solely for effect, to convince others, and perhaps Schutt as well, that he was more than just an office and telephone type of man, was in fact an artist himself.

"Take a seat, Keith. Coffee?"

"No, thank you."

"How do you feel about the transition from Westerns to something a little more serious? Are you comfortable with the nature of the project?"

"Very comfortable, Mr. Schutt."

"Roy, since we'll be working together on this. . . I've read your treatment, and it's clear you've taken everything Margolis wants into consideration. Just between you and me, I don't know if that's necessarily a good thing at this stage. MM has some very fixed ideas sometimes, but he can usually be persuaded to let go of them with a little cajolery and professional expertise."

"You don't like what I wrote."

"Not so fast. You wrote what the boss wanted, but I think we can come up with something better. I'm not talking about major changes, but for example, this fellow who teaches Keys how to fly, does he really need to be called Dusty Fields? There never was such a guy, was there?"

"I don't know who taught Russ how to fly, frankly."

"It's not the character I object to so much as the name, just a little too close to Smokey Hayes for comfort, wouldn't you say? And how about this business of the other Flying Tigers all calling him 'Kansas.' Did they do that?"

"I have no idea. Knowing Russell, I doubt it, but it seemed like something that Margolis might like."

"We need to think in terms of leaving behind your previous work and concentrating on achieving something of a higher caliber. Don't take that personally, Keith. I know your options for creativity were limited over in Yapp's department, but you're with me now, and I know we can come up with the changes that'll make *China Skies* a great movie."

"I'll work with you on your terms, Roy. There are some changes I'd like to make myself, but as you said, Mr. Margolis more or less demanded certain things. I left a few out of the original draft, then Baxter Nolan came along and read what I'd done and recommended putting them back."

"Nolan? What the hell's it got to do with him? He's an actor, not a writer. He hasn't even been firmed up yet as the lead."

"He said you definitely wanted a two-woman situation, one Chinese and one American, with Sandy Ryder in the American role."

"The little shit, I told him no such thing. Well, don't worry about it. I'll take this up with Terry Blackwell—you know he's penciled in to direct?—and together we can work on Margolis. That's not your concern right now, Keith. You leave it to Terry and myself, and if Baxter Nolan comes around again, wanting to read stuff that isn't ready to be read, you tell him to go soak himself."

"His sister's working on research for the project."

"Is she? Oh, yeah, I think I know the one. We tested her once for a bit part, but she didn't come across with the lens. Cute kid anyway. So you've got a cousin who's a hero. How do you feel about that?"

"Fine. He's helping me get out of B movies, so I'm grateful."

"MM says you're the one who got the actual contract, is that right?"

"Walked right in and had him sign."

"I can tell you the other studios are pissed at you, Keith. They've all been trying for days to pin him down with a pen, and then you walk right in and it's done. Great work. You know, we need this picture to go over big, and I don't just mean small big, I mean big big. Empire's had a few flops in the last year or so, and Margolis is getting a royal bug up his ass about it. That's why this picture has to work. You've given us a tremendous head start, Keith, not just with the contract, but the way you hammered out the treatment in record time. You always work that fast?"

"Yapp wants as many Western scripts per year as he can get Smokey to play in. They don't take long."

"I'll bet. Okay now, you probably know what you need to do this afternoon."

"No, I don't."

"You didn't see this?"

Schutt tossed Moody a copy of the *Los Angeles Times*. The headline read: SINGAPORE SURRENDERS. "Halfway down," said Schutt, and Moody saw ACE TO FLY COAST TO COAST. He hurried through the piece; Russell was scheduled to fly from Los Angeles to Washington, D.C., in America's newest fighter, the P-47 Thunderbolt. He would refuel in Salt Lake City and pass over Denver at approximately 11:00 P.M. mountain time. The citizens of Denver would be asked to leave their lights burning in tribute to Russell as he passed overhead, and he would drop three flares of red, white, and blue in acknowledgment of the city's patriotism before flying on to Hays, Kansas, for his second refueling. He would proceed to St. Louis, then on to Columbus, and reach Washington one day after his departure. The Thunderbolt would cruise at well below its maximum speed to avoid giving the Axis powers any clue to its performance, and Russell would take his time at each of the stopovers. The War Department made it plain that this was not some kind of attempt to break the cross-country speed record. While in Washington, Russell would address a war bonds rally and attend a gala reception at the White House. He was scheduled to leave Los Angeles at 4:00 P.M.

"He didn't mention any of this to me."

"Maybe it got dreamed up yesterday. The government needs men like your cousin to be splashed with a lot of publicity. When the Japs are getting away with crap like this"—he indicated the newspaper—"Washington probably figures it can't do too much to make the military look good. Margolis has already got us the use of some planes for the production. Anything that'll put an American hero in front of the people, the government brass makes it happen in a jiffy."

"It's a production in itself, all this fuss."

"No real difference. It's all showbiz, Keith. Take the rest of the afternoon off, and be sure you're down at the airport for this big sendoff. See if you can't get some more biographical details out of your cousin. I've got to have something concrete to hit Margolis with if I want him to drop some of this other stuff, okay?"

"I'll do what I can."

"Don't just do what you can, Keith—get us what we need."

HE WAS LATE, arriving at 3:47 without any excuse for his tardiness other than a personal reluctance to look into the face of his famous cousin again, so soon after having been invited to leave Russell's suite at the Wilshire. That had been nothing less than humiliating, but Moody had shrugged it off as typical. Being ordered back into the shadow of the hero was something he had no wish for, and so he had hesitated and found other things to occupy himself with when he should already have been halfway to the airport. It was a childish reaction to an unwelcome assignment, he could see that clearly, and it moved him through the afternoon not one bit faster. He entered a bar and drank and thought of Myra Nolan, squeezed duty from his thoughts for as long as he could, then was roused from this unsatisfying reverie by a glance at the wall clock. He had to do what he didn't want to do, or else be obliged to lie to Roy Schutt.

The airport lounge was overrun by newsreel and radio crews jostling for a final word, one last glimpse of the man already on his way through the doors and onto the tarmac. Moody saw the fair hair of his cousin for just a moment before the entire entourage began spilling out in pursuit of the man representing America that day.

He attempted to follow but was prevented from leaving the terminal building by police. The knot of adulation twining about Russell moved across the flatness outside toward a plane that Moody, never an aviation enthusiast even as a child, could see was something special. It sat like a fat toy, silvered by the afternoon sun, a massive four-bladed propeller at its blunt nose, a Perspex bubble glinting on top of the stubby fuselage. There was a general massing by the ladder at its side, then Moody saw the pilot in his bulky flying suit and leather helmet climb up and into the machine, and the small crowd that had accompanied Russell to the Thunderbolt began moving back.

Moody watched through the terminal windows as the propeller began to spin and blur, and felt the glass beneath his fingertips vibrate as the engine was throttled up. The plane turned slowly and taxied to its takeoff position, turning again to face the runway's length. It began to roll, picking up speed quickly, then seemed to be catapulted into the sky. Cameras tracked Russell's plane as it dwindled to a speck in the northeast, and then the event was done, all sense of its passage gone.

Moody turned from the window and walked slowly to the parking lot. He felt a burning in the pit of his stomach from the unaccustomed drinking. He had not done what Schutt had told him to, and now he would have to make something up.

"HE SAID HE didn't want to be famous, but it was okay with him if that's the way things worked out, so long as it was the people of America who wanted it that way, not just himself."

Moody delivered this lie in a conference room adjacent to Marvin Margolis's office at 7:30 that evening. Also present were Roy Schutt and Terence Blackwell, who had that afternoon officially been named as the director of *China Skies*. The unusual lateness of the meeting was occasioned by the haste with which Empire was obliged to bring the project to the forefront of the studio schedule.

"These were his actual words?" Margolis asked.

"To the best of my remembrance. Frankly, Russell isn't the most articulate fellow you're likely to meet."

"But what you just said is the true essence of what he said?"

"Yes."

"To you personally, in a private moment before he took off."

"That's correct."

Moody looked across the table at Roy Schutt, who wore an expression so blank it could only have meant he believed nothing of what Moody claimed. Blackwell, a small man whose habit it was to wear a fedora, indoors or out, was staring at the polished wood before him. Moody wanted to confess his untruth to them, but Margolis appeared pleased by his message from the hero.

"We can use this. This is good. The reluctant warrior, how does that sound, Roy?"

"It sounds fine."

"He doesn't want the fame, being a naturally modest individual, but if that's how the people want it, that's how he'll play it. Selfless, shouldering the public burden thrust upon him by fate." Margolis turned to Moody. "Fate," he said again, and Moody disappointed himself by smiling and nodding.

"Terry? Your feeling on this."

Blackwell raised his head. "A nice touch to finish off with, but we'll have to be careful not to make it sound corny."

"It won't, because a message as heartfelt as this goes beyond sentiment, gentlemen. It can't be misinterpreted as mush because it's real, it's a genuine emotion. Russell Keys is no fake, isn't that right, Keith?"

"No fake," Keith parroted, and had to endure the blank stare of Schutt for several seconds.

"Besides," added Margolis, "in Keith's hands the dialogue will ring true. This is his own cousin we're talking about, a boyhood companion, someone he knows inside and out. You worry too much about the wrong things sometimes, Terry. Now, where do we do the exteriors?"

"Up around Barstow would be best. It's close, and the landscape is rough, pretty much like the area around the Flying Tiger air base over in China."

"What's the name again?"

"Kunming."

"Kunming, I like the sound of that. It's very Oriental sounding, which we need plenty of in this picture, atmosphere, the Far East, a different world our Kansas boy finds himself in, but deep down, those people over there are really no different from us, those Chinese, not so very different at all, with their hopes for peace and liberty. That's an angle to bear in mind, Keith, the fact that East and West are united in a common bond."

"But not the Japanese," said Keith.

"Of course not the Japanese! They aren't from the East anywhere near as much as the Chinese. The Chinese are farther east than the Japs. The Chinese are a separate race entirely, and they're our friends. There is no connection between them and the Japs at all, and I want you to make that perfectly clear in the script, just like there's a world of difference between us and the Germans. Roy, the planes, tell me about the planes."

"The aerial camera crew will be given the use of two old training biplanes with open gun cockpits in back of the pilot. Getting good aerial footage shouldn't be any problem. Soundstage four is the one that's free for Kunming streets and all the interiors. We'll do back-projection for the Kansas segments, those that require wide open spaces, anyway. We've already got the Keys farmhouse on the back lot."

"The one used in *Free as the Wind*?"

"That's it, but we're remodeling the porch and moving the trees."

"Do they have trees in Kansas, Keith?"

"They do around farmhouses, Mr. Margolis."

"Good. Now about this business with the women. Sandy Ryder is someone we need to bring along fast. This is perfect for her, and without a girl at home to keep him on the straight and narrow path, morally speaking, the temptation for Keys to do something foolish with the Chinese girl is very strong. They're our allies, and a very brave race of people, and this is a nice girl, this Lin-Ming, but that's no reason for suggesting she does anything but love him from afar, and he treats her with respect, the way an American would in those circumstances, so the girl back home stays in the script, for the good of the hero and the good of the film. I won't have it said that Empire Productions promotes the notion that interbreeding is a good thing. Roy, you had some objection to—what was it?"

"Dusty Fields, the crop duster guy who teaches Keys how to fly."

"What about him? I think Keith has done well in introducing this character. Okay, he's made up, but someone had to teach the kid how to use an airplane, and they have lots of crop dusters out there in Kansas for the crops, don't they, Keith?"

"Yes, they do."

"So there it is," announced Margolis.

"It's just the name," said Blackwell, exchanging a look with Schutt. "We need to call him something else. It's too corny."

"You've got corn on the brain tonight, Terry. Corny message, corny name. Corn, corn, corn. Maybe you're thinking about Kansas too much. Plenty of corn in Kansas, am I right, Keith?"

"Plenty of corn," Keith admitted, slumping deeper into his chair. He didn't dare look across at Blackwell and Schutt.

"I like Dusty Fields," declared Margolis. "Anything else?"

No one spoke.

"Keith, Quentin Yapp tells me you're the fastest writer we have, but with quality also. How soon can you give us a script?"

"Well, I'd say—"

"It has to be soon, very soon, Keith. Time waits for no man. This picture has to be playing across the nation before December seventh rolls around, kind of a symbolic thing, gentlemen, less than a year after what the Japs did to us, here's this picture showing how we fought back, even if it's set before the actual Pearl Harbor incident. It's what it says about those little yellow sons of bitches that makes it count. Are we all in agreement on that very crucial point? You didn't answer my question, Keith."

"A month?" Keith suggested.

"Three weeks. You know the material inside out, so there shouldn't be any difficulty or delay. How much are we paying our young man from Kansas here, Roy?"

"He's just been made a five-hundred-a-week man."

"Make it seven, but hold back the extra two hundred until we see if Keith can give us what we need inside of three weeks. Sound fair to you, Keith? Incentive, that's the name of the game. I reward talent that deserves rewarding, but the talent has to be proved to my satisfaction. That's the basis for success in any business."

Marvin Margolis stood and left the room. The men remaining were quiet for almost half a minute, then Schutt said, "Moody, did you go to the airport like I told you?"

"Yes, I did."

"Your cousin really said that?"

"More or less."

"A friend of mine over at Movietone said he didn't see Keys have two seconds to himself, he just made a god-awful speech and climbed in his plane and took off. Sure you're not bullshitting me?"

"Absolutely."

"There's plenty of bullshit in Kansas, isn't there, Keith?"

"Not around my part of it."

Blackwell said, "You two aren't helping anyone, if I can just squeeze my opinion in around here."

Schutt ignored him. "Moody, this picture's being made ass backward to save time, sets being built before there's even a first draft script, let alone a shooting script. Everyone's taking a tremendous risk on Margolis's say-so, and he says so because, for reasons unclear to me, he believes in you. That means if this house of cards collapses before it even gets built, you're the one who'll carry the can. That's the shitcan I'm referring to, Keith old chum."

"I'm aware of my responsibilities," said Moody, in what he hoped was a hard voice. Blackwell caught his eye and shook his head a fraction of an inch, but Moody was disinclined to back down from Schutt, not if Marvin Margolis had expressed faith in him.

"Roy, you're worried, and who wouldn't be, but it wasn't me who started this ball—this *oddball*, I might say—rolling. Smokey Hayes just happened to recall my cousin's name from some conversation I had with him sometime, and when Russ became famous Smokey took that information to Margolis. I didn't ask him to do it. In fact there's no one more surprised than me by what's happened."

"You two need to cool off and cooperate," offered Blackwell.

"Words of wisdom," said Schutt, rising from the table. "Go ahead and write your script, Keith, and be sure to include every aspect of the story Margolis wants, but show me you're a real writer by making those aspects believable, all right? You do that and I'll buy you a drink."

"A mai-tai," said Blackwell, "for the Oriental angle."

"Mai-tais it is. Do we have an agreement, Keith?"

"Certainly."

Schutt headed for the door. When it closed behind him, it was Blackwell's turn to rise. "Don't worry about any of this," he told Moody. "This is more routine than you might think. It's just the accelerated timing that's got Roy upset. Everything around here's a compromise. Nobody gets what he really wants, not in this town. Everybody bends a little, or even a lot. Check your ideals at the gate—that should be carved in stone someplace. Over the gate, maybe." He smiled.

"Thanks," said Moody. "It's all more nerve-racking than B features ever was."

"You climb up the stairs a little way, it's farther to fall. See you around, Moody." Blackwell turned for the door.

"Is Baxter Nolan getting the part?" asked Moody.

Blackwell paused. "So far as I know," he said. "Any objections?"

"No, not at all, I was just wondering."

Left alone in the conference room, Moody wished he had a cigarette on him.

"KEITH, WHAT A charming surprise."

Moody was unsure if this was simply Myra's manner, whatever the circumstances, or if he was subtly being mocked. The light beside the doorway was not turned on for fear of attracting Jap bombers, and Myra's features were shadowed.

"May I come in?"

"You surely may." She stepped aside to allow him through. "To what do I owe the whatsit?"

"I just wanted to drop by and see how everything was with you."

"How sweet. Have you eaten?"

"No, I had a late conference with Margolis and the *China Skies* team."

"Moving among the powerful nowadays."

"I wouldn't say that, exactly."

"I have chicken to offer, or chicken."

"I'll take the chicken."

"Sharpen the ax, Henry!" she yelled over her shoulder.

Moody laughed, a little nervously. Was Myra drunk? He followed her through to the kitchen and watched her carelessly prepare a meal. There were no glasses of liquor standing around that he could see. "How's the research going?" he asked.

"I'll have to look into that," she said.

He laughed louder this time, but was no more set at ease by her manner than before. Anyone who kidded as much as Myra, he reasoned, had to be hiding a painful inner torment of some kind. He liked her even more in that tragic light. Maybe she required rescuing. "I saw my cousin off at the airport this afternoon."

"Really? How was it?"

"Kind of impersonal. There were too many people around. I couldn't even speak to him. He must be somewhere over Utah by now."

"Miss him?"

"No. What do you mean?"

"Blood being thicker than water, I just thought you might have been sad to see him go winging off into the blue that way."

"No. We were never close. I should have brought wine," he said.

"There's a liquor store about a mile and a half down Valley Boulevard. Here," she said, tossing him her car keys. "Better make it white, to go with the clucker."

"I drove my own car here."

"Your car's boring, Keith, if you don't mind my saying so. In California you need a convertible so you can feel that Pacific breeze in your hair, and that old Santa Ana wind. Go on and take mine. This'll be ready by the time you get back."

Driving slowly through the darkened streets, the night wind curling about his ears, Moody asked himself if he was being a fool. She had made no move toward him, nor suggested by way of a look or posture that she wanted him to approach her for a kiss, at the very least. It was as if nothing whatever had occurred the night before. Although he had never done it himself, Moody knew that lovers could separate after just one night, having satisfied their bodies with each other, but he had never heard of a woman being the one to finish it. It was entirely possible that Myra was simply being nice to him, with her offer of a meal, and was not at all interested in pursuing what was begun twenty-four hours earlier. He supposed he had been a terrible lover. He wished he was driving his own car, so he might continue on home and forget ever having met Myra, but it was too late for such easy cowardice. He would get the wine and enjoy the meal and make believe, as Myra clearly wished to, that they were nothing more than acquaintances.

Stepping back into the roadster with his purchase, two bottles of expensive chardonnay, Moody felt the sole of his shoe crush something on the car floor. Feeling around in the darkness, his finger was pricked by something sharp. He swore, and retrieved from beneath the front of the seat the tip of what was unmistakably a hypodermic syringe. He felt for the plunger but failed to locate it, if one was there. Why should such a thing be in Myra's car? Was she a dope fiend? It was too absurd a scenario to contemplate for more than a moment or two. He dropped the bent needle into his pocket and drove back to Myra's.

"Do you have any antiseptic?" he asked, placing the bottles on her kitchen counter.

"What for?"

"I pricked myself with a needle."

"I've told you before, Keith, if you must make those doilies, use a thimble, for heaven's sake."

This time he did not laugh. "It was on the floor of your car."

"My car? I don't sew, nor do I knit, or crochet or weave."

"It's a medical needle, a hypo."

He set it on the counter. Myra glanced at it, then said, "In the bathroom cabinet, if you think you might get an infection. Are you bleeding?"

"No, but you can never be too careful."

He felt less than manly as he doused his fingertip, the needle scarcely having broken the skin. The incident, trivial in itself, was upsetting when viewed as part of an evening that was not working out as Moody had planned. He contemplated his image in the mirror and found himself as unprepossessing as on the thousand previous occasions. He would eat the meal and leave as soon as he possibly could. Seeking out Myra had been a colossal error of judgment. With luck and a healthy appetite he could be gone inside an hour.

The chicken was indifferently cooked, but Moody ate quickly.

"Good as Aunt Mildred's?" asked Myra.

"Better," he said, nodding for emphasis.

"You fibber. I can't cook worth a damn. You'll probably get indigestion."

"No, really, it's perfectly all right. It's fine."

"At least we have wine. Not a bad selection, Keith. Do you know about wines?"

"No, I just asked the guy running the place."

"Ambrosia, ambrosia," Myra intoned huskily, "da bubbles get up ya nosia."

"You're very funny."

"I know, everyone tells me that. I could be the next Fanny Brice, they tell me, but I tell them right back, who the hell wants to be Fanny Brice? Marlene Dietrich, now that's someone worth being."

Moody was unsure how best to proceed with this girl who, it was beginning to dawn on him, was sharper and more interesting than himself, and very probably more intelligent. It was a difficult moment. He set down a chicken bone and stared at his plate.

"Keith," she said, "you look like a lottery winner who lost his ticket."

"Do I? I guess I do. I think I'll go home now, before I drink any more."

"Well, I suppose that's very sensible of you, but wouldn't you prefer to stay and rumple my tumple like we did yesterday? It's the least I can offer you after a meal like this, Keith."

He watched her face for the beginnings of laughter. She winked at him, and Moody became exasperated. "Myra, I haven't the least notion of why I'm here."

"Oh, you do too know. Don't be a mealymouth."

"I'm serious," he insisted, attempting to convince himself it was so. "I just don't know . . . don't think I know . . . I don't know."

Myra placed her elbows on the table, her chin in her hands. "You didn't do well in high school debating, did you, Keith?"

When he didn't answer, she said, "That's all right, Keith, most men can't handle a girl who's a joker. They want a poke, not a joke. I guess I'd feel the same if I went to some dishy man's place and found all he wanted to do were my tax returns. Tell you what, I'll just go take a cold shower, and you can leave without saying another word about anything at all. I can't make it easier than that, now can I?"

She stood immediately and left the table. Moody presently heard the shower running. He stood, then sat down, stood and sat down again, made angry by his own indecision. He supposed there might exist, among the littered plates and smell of badly cooked chicken, the possibility that he was in love with this unlikeliest of choices.

He was still at the table when Myra returned in a bathrobe, her hair piled in a towel. "I'm giving you every chance, Keith. I don't ever look worse than this."

"Stop it," he said. "I'm not going."

She sat opposite him. They looked at each other.

IN THE MORNING Myra asked if Keith would appreciate a little normalcy and subservience, by which she meant an offer of breakfast. Moody said yes, he would. Myra promised him toast done to blackness and coffee to match—"The taste, that is, not the color." Moody assured her this would be fine. He heard her go to the front door, open and close it, and then nothing at all for a short while. Myra returned slowly to the bed, a newspaper in her hand. "Keith, look at this." She handed it to him.

TIGER ACE'S PLANE CRASHES
BODY NOT FOUND

"AS LONG AS there's the possibility that he's alive," declared Marvin Margolis, "the project remains on track and on schedule. Nothing gets canceled until and unless they find him in a nonliving condition."

He paced behind his teak desk like an animal of nondescript genus in a zoo, its head scraped bald by futile rubbings against the bars of its cage. Moody could not shake free the notion that a furred arm might at any moment stretch across the desk and rake open his cheek with vicious claws.

"This is fate at work here, Keith, just like I told you, and I can't believe fate went and set up this wonderful deal we have going, just to knock it down a day or two later. Fate doesn't work like that. I'll tell you what I honestly believe, Keith, and I wouldn't talk this way with just anyone, but you're involved here more than myself even, being that he's your cousin." Margolis paused and leaned across the desk. Moody drew back despite himself. "It's all to give the picture a triumphant ending. That's what I truly believe. He's out there somewhere between Utah and Kansas, alive and unharmed, but far away from anyplace he could phone and say so, that's what I think, and it'll make a tremendous ending for the picture, the finding of the hero after everyone worries so much about him being killed. It's fate, Keith, working for and on behalf of Empire Productions."

The newspapers and radio had given what little information there was. Russell had departed from Salt Lake City on schedule and begun his crossing of the Rocky Mountains as darkness approached. He did not drop his red, white, and blue flares over Denver, although many people in that city swore they had heard a plane pass overhead at approximately the appointed time. The Thunderbolt fell from the skies later in the night near Leoti, in Wichita County, western Kansas. Russell was not on board. The plane had not burned, since its fuel tanks were completely emptied. Despite this, there were mysterious burn marks on the fuselage and wings, the paint having risen in blisters. A thorough search of the area had begun at first light, and Russell was yet to be found. It was known that he had been equipped with a parachute, and the generally accepted theory was that he had been forced to abandon the Thunderbolt in midair while its autopilot system was engaged, causing the plane to follow its prearranged flight path until the fuel tanks were emptied.

Somewhere along a line between Salt Lake City and Leoti—a line that crossed Denver as planned—the airman was on the ground, presumably safe. There had been reports of thunderstorms along the Great Divide throughout the night. In an ironic twist made much of by city editors and broadcasters alike, it was postulated that the Thunderbolt had been struck by its namesake, causing a temporary dysfunction of the engine, at which time Russell had bailed out. The engine, it was assumed, then began working again, and the plane proceeded according to the dictates of its autopilot. A lightning strike, or a series of them, would account for the blistered paint. The story had for the time being supplanted all war news on front pages and hourly bulletins across America.

"Do you share this faith of mine, Keith?"

"Naturally I hope he's alive, Mr. Margolis."

"But the picture, Keith, do you believe fate is working for the picture? is what I'm asking. It can't be anything else. We've gone out on a limb, and if your cousin met with a terrible end it means the same thing for us, for the project, because you can't end a picture that way, Keith, and have your audience go home happy and inspired."

"The picture could end with Russell taking off and flying into the distance."

"No, it couldn't, and I'll tell you why, because everyone in this entire nation will know how it really ended, even if the picture ends while he's still in the air, and that would be box-office death. That's how I know, deep inside my heart, Keith, that your cousin is alive, because that's exactly the right ending for *China Skies*. It's custom-made for our particular needs, and that's why my gut tells me that's what they'll find sometime today, a slightly battered but still grinning hero, maybe with a broken arm, or possibly a broken leg he had to drag for miles through the unfriendly wilderness. It's still pretty cold up in those mountains this time of year, but he'll be found. I want you to keep on with the script and ignore all this drama, Keith. We can't afford to wait for outcomes, especially since we know what the outcome will be."

Leaving Margolis's office, Moody saw Schutt and Blackwell approaching.

"Keith, do you have any information that hasn't reached the rest of us yet?"

"I don't, Roy. I wish I did."

"Damnedest thing," said Blackwell, shaking his head.

"What's the word in there?" asked Schutt, indicating Margolis's door.

"He says we continue on. He's convinced Russell's going to be found safe and well, giving us exactly the ending we need for the picture."

"He said that?" Blackwell asked.

Schutt was already moving away, in the direction Moody had just come from. "If you hear anything, Keith, pass it along."

"I will."

He watched them enter Margolis's office.

Moody returned to his new room in the Writers' Block, ready to begin working on the script. The night spent with Myra had filled him with a confidence he could see no actual cause for, unless it was true—as he had allowed himself to suspect—that he was in love with a woman who was in love with him. Such things happened all the time in the movies, so why not to him? He could not help feeling a little guilty over his happiness, given the news about Russell, but it was likely that Margolis, for all the wrong reasons, was right about the outcome; Russell would be found limping along some rutted back road in Colorado and would be made an even bigger fuss of when he was returned to civilization.

Smokey Hayes was leaning against Moody's door, drunk. Moody was not pleased by his presence; Smokey represented in one awful package everything Moody wished to forget concerning his time to date at Empire.

"Howdy, pard."

"Hello, Smokey. Can I help you?"

"Got all the help I need right here."

A hip flask was drawn from Smokey's jeans with the split-second draw he employed for his .45 on the screen. "Want a leetle taste?"

"No, thanks."

Smokey followed him inside and sprawled himself in Moody's chair. He took a long swallow from the flask and said, "I got me a big problem, pard."

"What might that be?"

"That new picture you were workin' on, *Six-Gun Justice*? They went and canceled it."

"Really? No one told me. I'm sorry, Smokey."

"Hell, they never even told *me* till I heard it from someone else and went and asked 'em outright in the main office if it's true, which it is, pard. And you know what else them skunks has got planned? They don't aim to renew my contract, how 'bout them horse-apples."

"Not renew?"

"It's that asshole Gene Autry over at Republic. Everyone wants a goddamn singin' cowboy nowadays. I ask you, what the hell kind of a sissy'd want to be a singin' cowboy? It's crazy!"

Moody was aware that Autry's last two movies, *Sierra Sue* and *The Singing Hills*, had done phenomenally well, their profits eclipsing easily the two Smokey Hayes pictures released at around the same time, even though both *Mustang Bride* and *Borderlands* had made a profit. Moody felt responsible in a way for Smokey's plight, even if the decision to end Empire's longstanding association with the cowboy star probably had been made by Margolis alone.

"I don't know what to say, Smokey—"

"Shoot, it ain't your fault. It's that fairy cow-pie Gene Autry! He's gone and messed up the whole notion of what it is to be a Westerner. You ever see one of that shithead's movies? I did last night. Good God almighty, what a chunk of butt-breeze! He talks the bad guys outta killin' him by singin' 'em a goddamn song! What the hell kinda reality's that!"

Moody found it no less absurd than the idea that an actor from Rhode Island could call himself Smokey Hayes and convince not only his fans but himself that he was indeed a genuine cowboy who just happened to have drifted from the rangelands onto the screen. "It's a terrible thing, Smokey. I'm really sorry about this."

"I don't know, I just don't know, pard. There's this war they got now, and it seems like all the real men are gonna be in war movies, not Westerns. The goddamn Japs are the bad guys now, and where does that leave a feller like me, huh? Leaves me swingin' in the prairie wind, that's where. A singin' cowboy! It ain't right! It's the wrongest thing I ever heard of, but that son of a bitch Margolee, he's gonna climb on the old bandwagon and do what Republic done with that faggoty Gene Autry—he's gonna get hisself a singin' cowboy!"

"Are you sure, Smokey? I haven't heard anything about that."

"Sure I'm sure. I got friends here who tell me what the big man don't want me to know. Ever hear of a radio fairy calls hisself Jesse Wilder?"

"I believe I've heard the name."

"He's the one. They're gonna make him a big star, pronto. You seen him atall? Stands 'bout up to my titties and don't hardly shave yet, looks like. I ain't so sure he's got a cock and balls in his pants, he's such a sissy-lookin' piece of cow-pie. Silk shirts with fringes all over, and silver on his belt and boots. Big-deal radio singer, and now he's gonna be in the movies. It ain't right, nosiree."

"It's a terrible thing to happen," agreed Moody.

"Hell, I oughtn't to be makin' you suffer this way. You just got yourself a promotion on accounta what I told Margolee's little secertary gal, I heard."

"That's right, I did, but I feel bad about it now, Smokey, in light of what you've told me."

He watched the actor empty his flask. "Yessir," said Smokey, "it's a peculiar world sometimes. I can't figure it all out, drunk or sober. You started that flyboy movie yet?"

"I was just about to. Of course, what happened last night puts the project in jeopardy to a certain extent."

"How do you mean?"

"You haven't heard? Russell's plane crashed in Kansas."

"You're shittin' me. No, I never heard."

Moody explained the situation, and Smokey shook his head. "Here's me tellin' you 'bout my troubles, and all the time you got troubles of your own. I'm sorry as hell to hear this, I really am. You figure he come down easy someplace with that parachute?"

"I'm hoping so."

Smokey levered himself up from the chair. "I won't occupy you more'n I have already, pard. Looky here, you tell me when they find that boy, okay?"

"I will, Smokey, and . . . you know what I'm going to do? I'm going to recommend to Margolis that he makes Roy Schutt cast you as a crop duster pilot in my new picture. That's the guy who teaches my cousin how to fly, a very important role. You wouldn't mind crashing and dying, would you, Smokey?"

"Wouldn't bother me one bit. You serious? You'll try and get me into this flyboy picture?"

"Can you change your accent just a little, make it more Oklahoman? That's where Dusty Fields is from."

"Dusty Fields. I like that name. Pardner, I love you like a brother. You swing this deal for me and I'm your pal for life, I mean it, and even if you don't swing it I'm your pal, 'cause it's the thought that counts."

He went to the door, tipped his Stetson, and was gone. Moody wondered if he hadn't promised more to Smokey than he could deliver. The thought of asking Margolis to include an ex-star on such an important project made him wince, but he had committed himself to make the attempt now, and would not back out.

He turned to his typewriter. He saw a twisted, blackened plane. He saw a hypodermic syringe. He saw no part of himself in the smooth whiteness of the page before him, no single thing representing Keith Moody, who once had thought he was a writer but now knew he was not. The blank page was his motto and his epitaph, an expanse of perfect nothingness. He was expected to cover it with lies, and he would do what was expected of him. Every smacking key would erase another tiny portion of the world's elemental truths. The ink would blacken everything worthwhile, the ribbon strangle virtue in its cradle. He was the monster of artifice and emptiness, or rather, a small part of that leviathan, a fingernail perhaps. He raised his hands, a weary conductor summoning the squeaks and rattling of orchestrated disbelief. It was a dirty job, but someone had to do it.

WHEN SHE ANSWERED the door, Myra saw a man different from the one who had awakened beside her that morning. Moody drifted past her and fell into an armchair, his eyes unfocused. His tie was loose, his hat worn carelessly. He seemed unwilling to look at her.

"Can I have one of your cigarettes, please?"

She lit one for him and placed it between his lips.

"Have you heard anything more about Russell? I've been listening to the radio. Everyone has been, all day."

"There's nothing new. They're searching the mountains."

Even his voice was listless. She sat beside him, but Moody inched away.

"Is it something else? Something that has nothing to do with your cousin?"

"Yes, oh, yes . . . and no."

"Oh boy, a riddle."

"I'm sorry . . ."

"Don't be sorry, be hungry. We're eating out."

"I couldn't. Do you have any of that wine left?"

"In the kitchen," she said, unwilling to fetch liquor as well as light cigarettes for him. Her resistance to his mood seemed to stir him somewhat, and his expression became more alert. "I shouldn't drink. What would that prove?"

"Umm, let me see. . . . No, I give up."

"It's just awful, really awful."

"They'll find him."

"No, the crap I'm working on, and I helped shape it. My own cousin, and I'm turning him into a figure that has nothing to do with . . . anything."

"Uh-oh, sounds like you're coming down with a bad case of tinselitis."

"I'm serious."

"I know, I can tell. There's only one cure, you know—sew leather elbow patches on your jacket and find a tenured position at some college or other. Take up smoking a pipe as well, just to make sure you've done the job right."

"Myra . . ."

"Yes?"

"I made a promise I can't possibly keep."

"Not to me you didn't."

"To Smokey."

"Smokey Hayes? The cardboard cowboy? What'd you promise him, riding lessons?"

"Please don't joke. I promised I'd try and get him a part in the picture."

"As a Texas pilot who lassoes Japs outta the goldurn sky. He'd be wonderful in the role."

"I'm serious!"

"You said so, and I believe you, but honestly, Keith, how could you promise that idiot anything? He can't act at all, unless you call that phony Texas accent of his acting. If the picture's going to be as bad as you think, why louse it up even more by putting Smokey Hayes into it? You know his name's really Mortimer Pence, don't you?"

"It's a harmless deception he practices on himself."

"Margolis wouldn't let it happen, anyway. They let his contract expire today."

"How did you know?"

She placed fingers over her eyes. "I am Myreena. I know all, see all. One dollar gets your fortune told."

"I feel guilty about it, that's all."

"Don't you have something bigger to fret about?"

"I know, I . . . I don't know what's wrong with me."

"Would food help?"

"No."

"Would satisfaction of any other physical appetite do the trick?"

He stood. "I think I'll go on home. I don't know why I came here. I'm sorry to intrude. I'm just not myself tonight. It's . . . everything."

"Nice of you to drop by, Keith."

He thought she slammed the door rather too loudly behind him.

IN HIS APARTMENT, Moody stared at the wall. He knew this was what writers were required to do when struck by any kind of creative crisis. He discovered wrinkles in the lightly flowered paper he had been unaware of, but did not find salvation or sustenance, and so fetched from hiding a bottle of whisky. He did not often drink, and loathed whisky, which he compared unfavorably to floor polish, but it was a writer's drink, and a man's drink too. He wondered, as he poured a stiff shot, if he was either. He had spent the day concocting the opening scenes of *China Skies*, then gone across town to Myra's, only to make a fool of himself. Moody felt a familiar inadequacy creeping over him, and fought back with a mouthful of whiskey.

How could Margolis and Schutt and Blackwell possibly consider the story of Russell Keys, as planned, to be anything but shit of the worst kind? It was a stupendous act of self-deception on their part, unless, of course, they too were staring at a wall and swigging liquor to bring on forgetfulness and encourage acceptance of what was inevitable. There should have existed a way in which Moody could wriggle free of the trap he had stepped inside, but he knew there was not.

PINNED TO HIS office door, as he approached it next morning, was a note. Moody stripped the paper clumsily from its thumbtack and took it inside. He was badly hungover, barely able to read the scribbled message: SEE MM NOW! He deciphered the instruction on his third attempt and aimed himself at the door, his head pounding to a new, more urgent beat.

Margolis's secretary pointed to the bronze doors behind her, indicating that Moody need not waste time asking permission to enter. Marvin Margolis was waiting, a single sheet of paper before him on his massive desktop, and beside the paper an opened envelope. "This is addressed to you, Keith."

"Me—?" Moody was barely halfway across the room.

"Read it and explain, if you please."

Moody stretched his arm to pick up the letter and envelope. It bore his name and the address of Empire Productions, but Moody did not understand why this should be.

"Read it," Margolis repeated.

"Who opened it?"

"This is wartime, Keith, and extraordinary measures apply. All mail in and out of the studio is vetted for information that might conceivably assist the enemies of the nation. You haven't read it yet. Aloud, please, so I can be sure you've understood."

" 'This is to let you know your cousin the hero is a . . . a shitbag. I know the reason why and will tell every newspaper and radio station and also magazines why there should never be any movie about this . . . shitbag cousin who is not what you think, and the movie studio either. So be outside the studio gate at noon on the fifteenth or I will do what I said, I mean it. Yours truly, One Who Knows.' "

"A fairly threatening tone, wouldn't you say, Keith?"

"I suppose so, but what does it mean?"

"Empire Productions is hoping you can provide the answer to that question."

"I don't know, Mr. Margolis. It's blackmail, isn't it?"

"The blackest of blackmail, Keith. This is the work of a crank or deranged person."

"But why is it addressed to me?"

"Obviously word has passed beyond the studio that you, and you alone, are to pen the movie this deranged individual wants to see strangled in its infancy. Can you imagine why this might be, Keith?"

"No."

"Empire Productions doesn't take kindly to blackmail, especially the kind based on nothing but the threat of bad publicity. It isn't possible, is it, Keith, that this crazed person might have actual proof of some misdeed committed by your cousin, is it? Your cousin is a true product of the heartland, is he not, virtuous in his own simple fashion? I've got that right, haven't I, Keith?"

"I can't say, Mr. Margolis."

"At noon I want you at the studio gates. You'll be watched from cover. When this blackmailing filth approaches you, he'll be nabbed by studio security. They'll be in disguise, of course, so as not to scare him away. Confrontation with authority, that'll put the fear of God into this fellow. This is extremely upsetting to me, Keith, I hope you're aware."

"Yes, sir, I'm sure it is." Moody felt he was being accused of something.

"Noon is some considerable time away, Keith. Get back to work."

"Yes, sir."

FOR ALMOST THREE hours Moody struggled to bring Russell Keys to life, or the Hollywood approximation of that state, and eventually became so engrossed in the task, despite his still-pounding head, that he was obliged to leave his office and run toward the studio gate at just a few minutes before the time appointed for the rendezvous. The guard on duty studied Moody with dispassion as he leaned against the wall several yards from the entry and exit booth, catching his depleted breath.

By Moody's watch it was three minutes past noon before his heart began pumping normally. His head hurt still, and he was desperately hungry, having left his apartment without benefit of breakfast. The blackmailer was nowhere to be seen. A man in the uniform of a city cleaner was sweeping the gutter nearby, and Moody was impressed by his thoroughness in removing every speck of dirt from the curb in front of the studio gates before realizing he was staring at someone who was not a street cleaner at all but one of the disguised security staff promised by Margolis. Back and forth went the broom, grooming concrete and asphalt. Moody cast about for other signs of inauthenticity and noticed a gardener ostensibly weeding the flower beds several yards inside the gates. This figure's trowel performed work of a limited and repetitive nature while his eyes strayed toward Moody every few seconds. The trap was set.

At 12:20 the sweeper finally appeared satisfied with his handiwork and set aside his broom to light a cigarette. The gardener, observing this, did likewise. Moody was inclined to join them, but he had left his smokes back on his desk. He was considering asking one of his escorts for a cigarette when he saw the car.

It was a gray Ford coupe, and it rolled quietly to a stop a

short distance down the boulevard, its motor still running, the brake lights glowing faintly in the noonday brightness. An arm extended from the driver's window and waved, jerking at the wrist like a landed fish. Moody understood that the hand signal was intended for himself.

The gardener was chatting with the studio guard in his glassed booth, and the sweeper was watching them both, drawing calmly on his cigarette, his back turned to Moody. The hand beckoned again, impatiently, and Moody began moving crabwise in the direction of the Ford, hoping that before he reached it the sweeper and gardener would become aware and spring into action, apprehending the culprit before he had the chance to engage gears and drive away. Moody maintained his hope for the entire twenty-three seconds required to move from his position against the studio wall to the curb, and beyond the curb to the double-parked Ford.

He could see a hatted profile inside. The beckoning hand had been withdrawn once Moody began his awkward progress toward the vehicle, and now the driver turned to face him, a cigarette dancing on his lower lip.

"You gonna get in, or what?"

"Are you waiting for me?" Moody asked, playing for time in what he imagined was a convincing tone.

"Nah, for Betty fucking Grable. Get in here."

Moody did as he was told, certain the sweeper and gardener already were aiming themselves at the idling Ford. He closed the door behind himself slowly, to allow them a few precious seconds more for their act of arrest, and could not understand why the driver was able to move away from the curb and enter the flow of traffic without flooring the accelerator, with barely a backward glance in his rearview mirror.

"Them putzes, what a joke. I went past three times and they never even saw it's the same car. Who you got watching out for you, the Marx Brothers?"

"I don't know what you mean."

"The hell you don't. You're Smith, right?"

"No, Moody."

"Just checking. Coulda been some other skinny guy with glasses, see what I mean? Coulda been another Marx Brother."

"Who are you? This is just ridiculous. You can't make threats against a major studio and expect it to do what you want when there's nothing to use against it. I'm sorry, but you're wasting your time. That's what I'm here to tell you. You could be arrested for doing something like this."

Moody turned his head; no sweeper or gardener was running along the sidewalk in pursuit. Margolis would be furious. Several sheets of paper were placed in his lap.

"Take a look at that," he was told.

The papers, wrinkled from overfolding, were covered in graceful symbols arranged in vertical rows. "What's this?"

"Chinese, stupid. What it is, it's a police report. What it says, your cousin, he did something he shouldn't oughta done, but he was drunk, see."

"No, I don't see. What is he supposed to have done? This means nothing—"

"What he did, he killed someone. A dwarf, that's what. Ever heard of someone that killed a goddamn dwarf? That's some kinda lowlife that'd do a thing like that."

"Excuse me, but this is ridiculous—"

"You already said so, but you're wrong, bub. It gets worse. This dwarf, it was a woman. Keys bashed her brains in. Stone dead, that's how he left her, and just walked away in front of witnesses. It's all there." A hand indicated the indecipherable sheets in Moody's lap.

"I don't believe you—"

Even as he said this, Moody knew it was a lie; he *did* believe what the stranger with the hat pulled low over his forehead was telling him. It was not inconceivable to any great extent that

Russell, mean and slow-moving Russell, could have committed the grotesque act described. Moody was briefly ashamed at this instant acceptance of his cousin's guilt, but not one iota of doubt arose to cloud his horror and belief.

Something heavy was dumped on top of the sheets of Chinese characters.

"That's what he used. Not what you'd expect, huh, except maybe in China. Them chinks, they don't live like us. Anything can happen over there. Doesn't mean a damn, most of it. This evidence, it cost maybe a dollar-fifty. A Chinaman cop, he doesn't care. A buck-fifty, that's a fortune where he lives."

The object was long and blue-green, bulbous at one end, like a stone gourd.

Moody had to study it for a moment before understanding its form and nature.

"Jade cock," said the driver. "Heavy, ain't it. I calculate fifteen pounds maybe. Real solid. Grabbed the knob end and hit her with the balls. Straight to the head. Caved it in like an egg. Brains everywhere. Why he did it, I can't say. I've seen things happen in a whorehouse wouldn't happen anyplace else, but in a China whorehouse any goddamn thing can happen if a feller's got a mind to do it. It ain't the same as here."

"Whorehouse?" Moody set the phallus beside his thigh on the seat.

"She was a whore, this China dwarf. What she did to make him mad I don't know, but that's the weapon right there, and the police report like I said. That's something you wouldn't want reporters and such to get hold of, I bet, with the movie and all you want to make about Keys."

"There isn't going to be a movie. He's probably dead, don't you read the newspapers?"

"Sure I do. Wouldn't be nothing so easy as a parachute bailout that killed old Russ. He's alive and kicking. Got a way about him makes death go around. You couldn't kill

Russ Keys with a machine gun. I want fifty thousand dollars."

"I have no authority whatsoever, and how did you get my name anyway?"

"Put the cock and the papers on the backseat. Do it right now!"

Moody set them behind him. The car was slowing to a halt.

"Get out. You tell them what I told you. The cock and the papers for fifty grand."

"It simply isn't going to work. Empire Productions has no traffic with blackmail."

The Ford stopped. The driver turned to Moody. The cigarette was plucked from its perch on his bottom lip, and the driver breathed cheap tobacco into Moody's face.

"Traffic is what cars are. You're a stupid idiot that don't even know how to talk right. You go ahead and say what I said, they'll come around. Now get out, and don't try to read the license plate, or I'll plug you and get some other stupid idiot to run my errands."

A pistol was pointed at Moody, who kept his eyes on it as he backed out of the Ford. The barrel never wavered for a moment.

"Turn around and count to a hundred."

Moody turned from the street and studied his reflection in a storefront window. It was a clock repair shop, and a sign inside declared, on behalf of Big Ben Clocks, VICTORY WON'T WAIT FOR A NATION THAT'S LATE. Whitewash ads on the plate-glass window of the grocery store next to it announced to pedestrians that there was a sale on all canned goods.

"I'll be in touch real soon, Moody."

The car, its reflection in the window dim as a half-remembered dream, slid away from the curb. Moody did not turn around to watch it depart. Campbell's soup was just a nickel; he seriously considered going inside and buying some.

ROY SCHUTT WAS summoned to Margolis's office to witness what Moody had to say. When Moody was done, a steady silence filled the air, riding the air conditioner's hum.

"What kind of man are we dealing with, Keith?" Margolis asked. "Is he of the criminal class, do you think, or someone of higher intelligence?"

"He didn't strike me as being particularly intelligent, Mr. Margolis. Cunning, maybe. He wasn't well spoken. He looked like a taxi driver."

"Keith," said Schutt, "this isn't some kind of prank you've dreamed up, is it?"

"If it's a prank, it's none of my doing. I'd prefer not to hear any more suggestions like that, if you don't mind, Roy."

"No need to take it personally. It was a question that had to be asked."

"And I've answered it. He wants fifty thousand. I'm simply a messenger."

"Of course you are, Keith." Margolis smiled. "No one doubts you're nothing more than an unfortunate pawn in this filthy business. You're sure the papers were genuinely Chinese?"

"Mr. Margolis, I can't be sure of anything. They *looked* authentic, but they might just as well have been pages from a cookbook, for all I know. The . . . the phallus certainly *looked* Oriental in appearance, like something you might see in a museum. It was . . . yes, I'd have to say it was beautifully carved, a work of art in fact."

Margolis shook his head. "I have to disagree. Nothing serving so vile a need as the object you described could possibly be called art. Art is something I happen to know just a little bit about, Keith, and I can assure you that all true art, from the time of the ancients down to the present day, is uplifting in nature, concerned essentially with the human spirit and its need for hope and greatness and the finer emotions that exist inside us all. All, that is, but the kind of scum who resort to disgusting practices with the . . . the kind of thing that was shown to you."

"Assuming this individual has a genuine Chinese artifact," said Schutt, "can we assume so easily that his story is nothing but bluff?"

"You're suggesting, Roy, that Keith's cousin is a pervert and a murderer?"

"I wouldn't know about that, Mr. Margolis, but we have to make a decision based on either acceptance or rejection of the fellow's threat. Let's say for the moment it isn't true. What happens if he approaches the newspapers? The documents may be bogus, but if they accuse Keys of murder, and the translation confirms it, then Empire faces a massive problem. I don't need to remind you of the time and capital already invested in this production. Interiors for the Kunming sets are being prepared on stage four, and the external sets are under construction on the back lot. Several fighting planes have been made available for our use by the War Department. To shut the project down because of the mere possibility of this story being true will create a scandal in any case."

Margolis tipped his swivel chair back several inches and studied the ceiling. "Unless we give the blackmailer what he wants, and receive in return the supposed evidence. Then our problem would presumably be solved."

"Only if you feel we can trust him not to come back for more. The things Keith was shown may only be a part of what the blackmailer has to back up his story."

"I'm waiting to hear a plan that works, gentlemen. The good name and financial integrity of Empire Productions are at stake in this matter. Do I hear any suggestion that makes better sense than my own?"

Schutt was breathing heavily through his nose, an indication, Moody assumed, of frustration or anger. Margolis appeared unruffled. Moody was himself more upset at Schutt's implication that he was involved in the plot than he was by the thought of the studio being faced with calamity.

"It's just . . . I hate to cave in to something like this!" Schutt finally said.

"Of course you do, Roy. Any man of honor would share your view, but in the real world, compromise is sometimes necessary. I have to concern myself with the larger canvas. Our hands will be soiled, yes, but Empire will carry on with the picture, and no one outside this room need be any the wiser."

"Except the blackmailer," said Moody.

"Who'll cease to bother us once he has his money, I'm sure. Gentlemen, thank you for your time. Keith, you'll report to me the instant this despicable fiend makes contact with you again."

"Yes, sir."

Moody and Schutt exited together. In the corridor, Schutt said, "If I ever find out this is something you cooked up with your cousin . . . Was the thousand bucks not enough for him? All he had to do was follow the great American tradition of demanding a raise, Keith, and with a bit of persistence on his part, Empire would have dug a little deeper into the kitty."

"Excuse me, Roy, but I don't have to listen to this . . . bull!"

Moody strode away from Schutt, realizing too late that he had made his departure in the wrong direction and was heading back along the corridor toward Margolis's secretary. Reversing himself with what he hoped was a confident about-face, he marched past Schutt and out of the building.

MYRA APPROACHED HIM in the commissary as Moody fell upon a delayed lunch.

"Burning the noonday oil again, Keith?"

"I got caught up in something."

"Typewriter all hot and sweaty from overwork?"

"Certainly."

She sat opposite him, her arms filled with large sheets of drawing paper. Moody saw an upside-down farmhouse, presumably the mythic abode of the mythic Russell.

"Want me to go away? I'm just passing through from Research to Production. Have you seen the Chinese set on stage four? It's really coming along."

"Not yet."

Myra took a fingertip of whipped cream from Moody's caramel dessert and popped it into her mouth. Moody watched her do this a second time before asking if she'd like to order some caramel for herself.

"I just want some of yours, Keith."

Moody placed the bowl before her. "As much as you want," he said.

"We're angry with each other, aren't we."

"I wouldn't know. I have a lot on my mind right now."

"I heard on the radio they're calling your cousin's disappearance the biggest mystery in aviation since Amelia Earhart."

"Russell went down over the Rocky Mountains, not the Pacific, so if they keep searching they'll find him. One way or another."

"You mean alive or dead."

"Yes. I have to go back to work now."

"Bax was asking me how the script's coming along, strictly off the record."

"It's fine. Bax'll love it. He'll play a handsome, selfless individual whose chief characteristic is a burning need to right the wrongs of the world, especially those wrongs perpetrated by Japs. It'll be Bax's greatest role to date, possibly the most endearing in his career. Quintessential hero, see."

"Jeepers, lay off the sarcasm just a tad, please. I'm only asking."

"And now you've been told. If Bax wants further information

I suggest he go to Roy Schutt. Roy's a big Bax fan, in fact he's almost as big a Bax fan as he is a Moody fan."

"Uh-oh. Did you and Schutt have words?"

"An exchange of views, that's all."

"About Bax?"

"Something quite different. Nothing whatever to do with Bax, strange as this may seem to Bax."

"Ouch. Any other family members you'd like to bash while you're about it? I must've done something awful to get you into this state."

Moody rose and set his chromed chair under the table. "I apologize. None of this has anything to do with you or Bax."

"None of what?"

"Nothing."

"None of nothing? Is that something Einstein might understand?"

"Please, I have to get back to work."

"The door's always open, Keith, if you'll overlook the obvious Freudianism."

"Yes, good-bye."

Myra watched him weave clumsily between tables on his way out.

THE LOVE SCENE between Lin-Ming and Russell was presenting problems, chief among them the obvious language barrier. Moody decided to turn the scene's weakness to his advantage by utilizing the lovers' inability to communicate; they would simply sit and hold hands and gaze at each other for a short while, maybe fifteen seconds of screen time, then Russell would take out a cigarette and Lin-Ming would light it for him. She would blow out the match, and the pouting of her lips to perform this task would be sensual in the extreme, if shot with flair and sensitivity.

Terry Blackwell would probably like it. Moody had heard that such visual scenes were often preferred over dialogue by directors who wanted to let the world know they could achieve artistic greatness without the aid of a screenwriter. Of course, Moody had written the scene and described the atmosphere required. In the end, it was the actors who would most likely win praise for their talent in bringing the tender moment to life, despite the best hopes of Blackwell and himself.

"It was ever thus in Hollywood," Moody told the wall behind his typewriter.

A knock at his door made him jump.

"Come in!"

He had seen Sandy Ryder several times around the studio lots, once as a harem girl in an Arabian Nights fantasy and several times in less revealing attire, playing the kind of role that had become her forte—the girl next door. She was pretty without being glamorous, although the effect required at least as much time in the makeup department as had the role of harem girl.

"Hi there!" she said, her cheeks creased by the dimples that were becoming her trademark. Moody could see, even at this early stage, that by the time she was thirty-five Sandy's dimples would have become so indented she'd resemble a rodent with a mouthful of forage.

"Hello, Miss Ryder. What can I do for you?"

"Sandy. It's Keith, isn't it? I've been told to stay away and not bother you, Keith, but I just had to sneak in and ask if you're shaping things up for me. MM said I had the part, so I just had to come say hi to the guy who's writing it. What's her name, the hero's gal back home?"

"Kathy."

Sandy frowned thoughtfully. "I guess I could get used to that. Katherine?"

"Kathy. We don't want her to sound too sophisticated. She's a small-town girl."

"Shoot, just like little old me." Sandy dimpled.

"Exactly."

Moody knew Sandy Ryder was playing a role for his benefit—the eager and intense starlet-in-waiting anxious to nail down the role that will determine her future. It was so obvious a blend of concerned sincerity and blatant grasping for inside information that Moody almost felt sorry for her. He was mildly perplexed that Sandy and Bax supposedly were an item around town. She appeared so much less fascinating than a man of Bax's classic good looks deserved, in a Hollywood sense. Moody wondered, studying her dimples, if the match was a studio invention, a story to feed the endless shoals of movie fans yearning for their preferred food, the rumor of love.

"Any chance of a leetle peek at the story so far?" Her dimples deepened alarmingly.

"I'm afraid I can't do that, Sandy. Roy Schutt won't allow any sneak previews."

"Not even for me?" Her eyebrows arched to vaudevillian heights.

"I'm sorry."

The eyebrows fell, the dimples were erased. Sandy clearly was not pleased.

"Well, you tell Mr. Schutt when you see him I think he's an old poop."

"I'll be sure and pass the message along."

She gave him a stiff smile and departed. Moody stared at the door. Sandy Ryder, like Baxter Nolan, was concerned solely with her career. She had not asked if he had news of his vanished cousin, nor expressed commiseration with Moody over his presumed agony as the search went on. Moody supposed he should despise Sandy for her self-centeredness and shallow conceit, but found he could not. He was himself busily writing a story about Russell that bore no resemblance even to the former reality—Russell prior to his disappearance—and was even farther removed from the Russell more recently revealed—the murderer of a dwarf prostitute in faraway China.

Moody's five hundred a week, and the promise of a two-hundred-dollar-per-week bonus if he finished the work quickly enough, were what concerned him, not whether Russell was stranded on a mountaintop, nursing a broken back. Moody accepted the blackmailer's accusation and felt a mild sense of guilt over it, but he wanted Russell found, alive and well, for the publicity it would create, and the rising tide of Empire's fortunes (and Moody's own) that would follow a successful production and release of *China Skies*. Russell the killer of Japs was a hero; Russell the killer of a Chinese, albeit at the lower end of the social spectrum, was a business liability rather than a study in moral degeneration.

"And there's a war on, too," Moody told the wall.

THE WORK HE took home with him grew by several pages per hour until nearly midnight, when his doorbell rang. Moody sprang up from his chair at the kitchen table, sure it must be Myra. Making his way toward the door, he was unsure if pleasure or annoyance was predominant in his thoughts. He turned out the hall light before opening the door, as per blackout regulations.

"Swell place, bub."

The blackmailer stood outside, leaning one shoulder against the doorjamb.

"How did you find me?" Moody kept his voice under control.

"Followed you from the studio. Gonna ask me in, bub?"

Moody stepped aside.

"Call me Tony," said his guest, easing past him and into the living room, trailing the aroma of freshly chewed Juicy Fruit in his wake. He wore the same clothing, a loose-fitting leather jacket and wide-brimmed hat that remained on his head, pulled down low, Moody reasoned, to keep his nondescript face in shadow. Tony stood directly beneath the overhead light sconce, when it was turned on, as if to prove Moody right, jaws pumping noisily.

"So, you told 'em about it like I said?"

"Yes."

"They gonna do what I want?"

"No actual decision was made while I was in the room."

"Is that right? That ain't so good from where I stand. I want what I want, and I want it pronto. You better shake 'em up for me, bub. I'm a busy man, and fifty grand, that's peanuts for a big movie studio, so don't tell me different. I want it tomorrow night, you tell 'em. Nothing bigger than fifties, and it all better be old money, no sequential numbers, nothing like that, or it's no deal."

"I'll tell them. For what it's worth, I think they intend to cooperate with you. That's the impression I have."

"So they believe me about Keys, huh?"

"Well, not necessarily, but they want to avoid trouble."

Tony shook his head; Moody caught a glimpse of the wry look on his face beneath the hat brim. "Jesus Christ, you tell someone their golden boy ain't what they think, and you show 'em the proof, but still they don't wanna believe. So what's your opinion? You're his cousin."

"Nobody wants to believe a thing like this, not when it concerns a family member. You haven't convinced me, I have to say."

"Makes no difference, I guess. The fifty grand, that's all I want, not to make you guys tell me you don't think I'm a liar. They didn't find him yet, did they."

"No—at least, I don't think so."

Tony inclined his hat toward the mantel radio. "Just gone midnight, and you weren't even tuned in to the news on the hour.

Maybe you figure the morning edition's plenty soon enough to find out what's happening."

"I'm busy. I wasn't aware of the time."

"Sure you were. I'm a busy man myself, like I said." He took a small sheet of notepad paper from his pants. "This is the instructions you're gonna need. I wrote it all out clear."

Moody accepted the sheet without looking at it. "Who are you? If everything you've said is true, how do you know about it? Do you know Russell personally? The more facts I can deliver, the more convincing you become, and the more likely they are to do what you want without any delay."

"Think I'm stupid? I tell you all that, you figure out who I am and set the cops on me. No, thanks. And if they believed it, I mean if it got to where they really believed he did what he did, you think they'd wanna make a picture about the guy? You better hope they keep on wanting me to go away, just to keep the boat from rocking, that's what you better hope, or there ain't gonna be any picture for you to write, is there?"

"Possibly not."

"Definitely not. You think about it awhile, and you're gonna see I'm right. This way, the payoff way without no more details, that's the way that's best."

"I'm sure you're right."

Tony snickered. "That how you talk to 'em at the studio? Yessir, nosir, I'm sure you're right, sir? You a paid yes-man, Moody? I heard they got 'em in all the high places."

"Excuse me, are you passing judgment? I would've thought a blackmailer couldn't afford the luxury of criticizing others."

Tony slapped him hard and fast across the cheek, and Moody's head snapped sideways. He touched his face in some surprise, more shocked than hurt. Tony was already moving toward the door.

"See you tomorrow night." He paused, his hand on the doorknob. "By the way, just to put you in the picture all the way, you mess me around at all, you have cops or someone else waiting for me when there's only supposed to be me and you and a bagful of cash, I'm gonna come find you again, wherever you're at, hiding or running, and I'll kill you stone dead. Nothing personal."

Alone again, the sound of the door latch loud in the room, Moody found he was shaking.

MARVIN MARGOLIS STUDIED the note for some moments before looking up again.

"Comments, Keith?"

"He's perfectly serious, Mr. Margolis."

"No doubt in your mind at all? No hint of bluff, no sweating upper lip to give him away? A large amount of studio money depends on your realistic assessment of the situation before us. Think about it."

"He's confident, sir, very sure of himself."

"The kind of confidence born of knowledge, Keith? Is he blackmailing us with the actual truth, do you think?"

"Not truth as you and I might understand it. He simply understands that the studio can't afford to allow the least hint of this . . . abominable story to escape."

"You still have faith in your cousin, I take it."

"Absolute, unshakable faith in him, Mr. Margolis. He's my own cousin, after all, and I think I'm in a position to know. Russell could never have done what this 'Tony' says he did."

"Good. I accept your opinion, Keith, because it coincides in every detail with my own. My instincts are seldom wrong when I detect a story or incident I feel will make a fine picture. This entire sordid diversion from our work leaves a taste in the mouth foul to contemplate. I want it taken care of, tonight, as per the instructions."

"Yes, sir," said Keith, imagining a snicker from Tony.

"Sometime this afternoon you'll be summoned back here to my office and given the money. You'll guard that money with your life, I don't need to tell you. I want this filthy business taken care of smoothly and professionally. The mere fact of it taking place while the subject of the blackmail is lost and alone even as we speak is an inversion of the norms our society is founded upon."

The studio head's face was reddening as he continued. "This kind of thing belongs in Nazi Germany, not in America. Maybe the Japs are experts at blackmail too, I wouldn't be surprised, and it burns my gut to have to pay out good American money to the likes of this blackmailing filth, and why? Because all we're trying to do here is produce a good clean movie about a good clean Kansas boy who defied the odds and brought to a justifiably fiery death the enemies of this nation and all of mankind!"

Moody nodded in appreciation of the sentiments. Margolis pointed to the door.

"Go back to your typewriter and continue working on the script this animal wants to prevent us bringing into the light of day! Write the words that will cause him to feel shame if he should happen to join decent citizens in a darkened theater to witness the kind of heroism given to very few, *very few*, to perform on behalf of us all, and when he hears the lines you're about to write, I want him to squirm with shame, because he'll know those lines are intended for him and him alone! Write the lines that will defeat this criminal, this degenerate! Make them immortal lines, Keith, worthy of Empire Productions and America!"

Moody began backing away, bobbing his head in agreement, and fled the room in a welter of patriotic fervor and personal shame, pursued by the lingering resonance of Margolis's words and the distant, knowing snicker of Tony.

Halfway back to his office, Moody saw Myra approaching from the alley separating soundstages six and seven. She waved to catch his eye, and Moody was obliged to stop and wait for her. Myra even broke into a trot to complete the last few yards separating them, eager to be by his side, Moody thought.

"They need you over on six!" said Myra, confusing Moody for a second or two.

"Who does?"

"It's Smokey Hayes. He's drunk and creating a disturbance, and he keeps asking for you. He's holding up production on the Jesse Wilder set. They don't want to send security to throw him out, so they asked me to get you. I've been phoning all over the place."

As they hurried toward stage six, Myra said, "I called Margolis's secretary last of all, and she said you'd just left. You're spending a lot of time over there with the big guy."

"It's *China Skies*. He wants to keep his fingers on the pulse of it, that's all. It's his pet project."

"That makes you his pet writer, I bet."

"I don't want to have an argument, Myra, I've got too much on my mind."

"Who's arguing? There are writers who'd give their teeth to be over in Margolis's office half as often as you."

"Let them keep their teeth. Myra . . . I haven't been pleasant company lately, and I want you to know it isn't because of anything between you and me."

"There's nothing between you and me?"

They skirted a cavalry troop exiting stage seven.

"No, that's not what I meant. It's . . . difficult to explain for the moment."

"Why don't you drop by my hacienda sometime after working hours, and I'll ply you with strong drink until we both know what you're talking about."

"Yes, certainly. I'll do it, thank you."

"God, Keith, it sounds like I just sold you an insurance policy or something."

"Please . . . please, don't ask me about anything!"

"These will be my last words until you notify me by telegram that we can talk again."

"I'm sorry, it's just that I have a lot to concentrate on."

Myra began humming loudly, and maintained it until they entered the massive concrete barn with SIX painted above its door.

The director, identifiable by his bandanna and beret and agitated manner, saw them approach the Western saloon set where soundmen, the camera crew, and a bevy of costumed actors all stood in awkward limbo, illuminated by arc lamps, surrounded by the interior darkness of soundstage six. Jesse Wilder, smoothly handsome and fifteen years younger than Smokey, stood with his guitar and an amused smile, the spangles on his shirt glinting brightly.

"Are you Moody?" the director asked.

"Yes."

"Take care of *that*, would you, and I'll let you write my next picture."

The director's extended forefinger aimed itself at Smokey Hayes, seated at one of the saloon tables, his Stetson awry, boots splayed belligerently, a shot glass and whiskey bottle occupying his hands. Smokey waved as he recognized Moody.

"Actually, I don't write Westerns anymore."

"I don't give a damn if you wrote the fucking Bible, just get that shitty drunk off my set! Excuse me," he added, for Myra's benefit.

"Shit, I don't care," Myra assured him.

Moody went directly to Smokey's table and sat down.

"Hey, pardner! You're never the one wrote this piece of cowflop they're shootin' here, are you?"

"What's it called, Smokey?"

"*Tumbleweed Turkeys*, thass what it's called. Big chunka cowflop, got that fairy boy in it, Jesse Wilder."

"Not one of mine, Smokey, I guarantee it."

"Thass him over there." Smokey gestured with his glass, slopping drink onto the table. "The one next to the gal in the purple dress, or maybe he's the one wearin' the dress, hard to say with that faggoty boy."

Jesse Wilder strummed a fast and dangerous chord, making the crew laugh. Smokey's expression of contempt turned to anger, and he attempted to rise from the table. "Faggot! Singin' cowboy—!" His left boot slipped from under him, and Smokey fell back in his chair. Jesse Wilder strummed something in a comical vein.

Moody placed his hand on Smokey's denim sleeve. "What say you and me get out of here and find a real bar to drink in, pardner."

"Real bar, thass what we need, where they got real men drinkin', yes sirree."

"Let's do that right now, Smokey."

"You get me that role like you said, huh, Moody boy?"

"Role?"

"In your China pisher. Gonna be a crop dusser pilot, you said. You get that role for me yet?"

"I'm talking to Mr. Margolis about it every day, Smokey. He's giving it his serious consideration. It's a big jump for you, going from cowboy roles to pilot roles."

"No it ain't! Ride a horse, ride a goddamn plane! Whassa difference!"

"Probably not much at all. Why don't we talk about it in my office?"

"In a real bar, you said!"

"What's a bar but somewhere you can get a drink? You bring that bottle along, and my office becomes a bar, see?"

Smokey began laughing deep in his chest. "Office bar," he said. "Okay—"

Moody assisted Smokey to his feet and, aided by Myra on Smokey's other side, steered him away from the set toward an exit door. Jesse Wilder strummed a march, and the director blew Moody a kiss in passing.

Myra helped bring Smokey to Moody's office and place him on a chair. Smokey had staggered and sworn all the way from stage six without losing his grip on the bottle and glass. Propped up in a corner, he poured himself a drink and demanded two more glasses for his friends.

"I don't think I have any," said Moody.

"What the hell," Myra said, "we're all real men here, ain't we?"

She took the bottle from Smokey's hand and drank, then handed it to Moody, who took a lengthy sip and returned the bottle to its owner.

Myra wiped her mouth with exaggerated satisfaction and declared Smokey's whiskey the "best panther piss I ever tasted, bar none."

Smokey slapped his knee and told Myra she was his "kinda gal all reet, yessir, and a real honey to look at too, you betcha by golly . . . Hey, you two oughta get hitched! Thataway my two bess friends are together when I need 'em, perty good idee, huh?"

"Perty good all reet," agreed Myra, "but we got ourselfs a maverick as don't wanna get hisself branded, Smokey. Old Moody here, he's agin the cabin in the pines and the young'uns underfoot, see what I mean?"

"The hell you say! Moody, what'n tarnation's the matter with you, boy? This here's a fine filly and no mistake, stands out all over, and you don't wanna tie the knot? What'n hell you waitin' for, you dang fool!"

"Well—" began Moody.

"Tell'm, Smokey!" Myra encouraged. "Consarned galloot don't never listen to his heart, I reckon."

"This is all very amusing—"

"Hear that, Smokey? The man I love just ain't interested, looks like."

"Guess we better hog-tie the son of a gun till he comes to his goddamn senses," said Smokey, rising from the chair. "Where's my lasso at? Anyone seen my lasso—?"

He tripped over his own boots and collapsed heavily at Moody's feet, the bottle still firmly held in his hand. Ragged breathing erupted from his open mouth.

"Goldurn it," said Myra, "there goes my secret weapon."

"All right, that's enough. It's bad enough his contract's not being renewed. You don't need to mock him on top of that."

"Let's put him on the sofa. You didn't have a sofa in your other office, did you? That's proof you're on your way up the ladder, Keith."

Smokey was established in comfort, strangulated snores gusting from his nose. Myra looked down at him with genuine pity. "Poor old fake cowboy."

"Poor old fake everyone," said Moody.

"Including us? I thought we were real."

"I didn't mean you."

"That means you included yourself. What's fake about you, Keith?"

"Nothing. I should get back to my work. And I'm expecting to hear from Margolis."

"My, but he's taken a shine to you. Well, see you around, cowpoke."

"Thank you for helping me with Smokey."

"Anytime. Did Dimples come see you yesterday? Bax told me she did."

"Dimples? Oh, Sandy Ryder. Yes, she did."

"Pushy little thing, isn't she?"

"I suppose so."

"Does it strike you that she and Bax are an odd couple?"

"They're both actors. What's so odd about it?"

"Nothing, I guess. 'Bye now."

" 'Bye."

Moody waited until her footsteps receded before seating himself at the typewriter again.

THE TWO MANILA envelopes that passed across Margolis's desk and into Moody's hands were fat and heavy. Margolis watched Moody feel their weight before he placed them inside his jacket.

"The contents are your responsibility now, Keith. I don't need to tell you that things must go exactly as per arrangement. I want this matter ended, once and for all, tonight. Understood?"

"Yes. Mr. Margolis?"

"What is it, Keith? Your instructions are crystal clear, I think."

"Yes, sir, they are. It's about Smokey Hayes."

"Hayes? What about him? I've been informed he made a public disgrace of himself over on six this morning, is that correct?"

"Well, he was just a little drunk, yes, but it was taken care of, Mr. Margolis."

"So I was told. You saved the studio money by getting him out of there as fast as you did. That's good work, Keith, and don't think I'm not watching you closely. Empire knows who its loyal friends are in times of crisis."

"Thank you. The thing is, I was wondering if Smokey couldn't be given a role in *China Skies*."

"What kind of role would that be? There are no drunks in *China Skies*."

"Well, I thought maybe the barnstormer-turned-crop-duster-pilot who teaches Russell how to fly."

"Dusty Fields is an American hero on a minor scale, Keith,

just as your cousin is an American hero on a major scale. Dusty Fields is a courageous pilot engaged in dangerous work. They fly very low to spray those fields of corn, Keith, and I admire any man who can do dangerous work day in and day out. I won't give the role to a drunk. Frankly, Smokey has been a disappointment to us. His last four pictures have shown evidence of sharply diminished returns at the box office. America is tiring of Smokey Hayes. Naturally I don't disparage your part in this, Keith. I'm sure your screenplays for those last four films were perfectly adequate. No, it's simply that Smokey must be laid to rest, professionally speaking. He can't begin a new life as an actor portraying other types, it's too late. Smokey is no more. If another studio wants to offer him a contract, that's entirely their business, of course."

"I just thought he should be offered another chance, Mr. Margolis. His pictures made a lot of money a few years ago."

"Ancient history, Keith. I don't need to tell you that stardom is a hard-won condition, and easily lost. There is an elite in Hollywood, as you know, and their names and faces are part of our world. We see them gracing theater marquees, smiling at us from magazines, and most important of all, towering above us on a million silver screens, veritable gods of today, Keith, as I'm sure you understand. They are unique, and Smokey Hayes was never really placed among them. Smokey was a contender on the narrow pathway to immortality, but he has stumbled and fallen along the wayside."

"With just a little help, sir, I'm sure he could get back on that path."

Margolis shook his head, a pitying smile on his lips, eyelids lowering briefly, the picture of a man patiently explaining the obvious to a child.

"Once fallen, forever down. The kings of old, Keith, would place their favorites at the head of the banquet table, where they could reach the salt, which was a very precious commodity in those days, I'm told, and it was a privilege, Keith, to be seated above the salt, where you could reach for and take as much as you wanted. But the tables were long, and many others were seated there, below the salt, according to their lower rank, and they were obliged to chew their meat without benefit of such precious stuff. Smokey must take his place alongside these lesser folk."

"Yes, sir."

"I know your motive is pure, Keith. You feel sympathy for an old associate, and I approve of that, but kindness must never stand in the way of true reality, and so I have to say no, once more and for the last time—no."

"I understand."

"Please see that the latest pages from *China Skies* are delivered to Roy Schutt before you leave today. And Keith? About your task tonight, let me say that your cooperation in regard to this distasteful business is duly noted. That's all."

"Yes, Mr. Margolis."

"You'll need time to reach your rendezvous. Take the rest of the afternoon off."

THE MAP PROVIDED by Tony was well drawn, the directions explicit. By sundown Moody was waiting at a roadside picnic area some eighty miles from Los Angeles, just a few miles south of Victorville on the road to Barstow. The country surrounding the site was barren, low hills sparsely dotted with desert brush, without visual appeal except to the south, where the San Gabriel and San Bernardino Mountains interrupted the horizon with their blueness in the evening haze.

Moody parked his car and got out to stretch his legs. There were no other cars in the dusty parking lot, and the picnickers, if there had ever been any at such a forsaken spot, had departed long before. Moody wandered over to the sun-blasted wooden tables and benches and inspected the forty-gallon drum converted for use as a trash bin. There were several Coke bottles inside, and some crushed paper wrappings smelling of old food. Moody wondered if desert scavengers ever plundered the bin.

He sat and looked around in the deepening twilight, breathing air so dry it seemed to shrivel his nasal passages. There was a small toilet block of blistered corrugated iron at the edge of the picnic area, and Moody's nostrils told him, despite their dryness, that he was seated downwind. He got up and strolled in aimless circles, waiting for Tony to appear. There was no birdsong around him, no sounds of insect life, not the least thing to attract his ears. He looked to the west as colors of startling vividness bled across the few wisps of cloud lingering there, and found himself becoming hypnotized as their permutations of hue—purple to red to gold—began to fade, rendering them invisible at last against a darkening sky.

The footsteps, when they came to him, were faint at first, and when he turned, Moody was surprised at the distance still separating him from Tony, identifiable by his hat. Moody guessed the sound was amplified by stillness, and the lack of competing sound elsewhere. Tony did not wave or speak as he approached. Moody wondered where his car was parked. He stood and waited. Tony carried a valise. His shoes and the lower legs of his pants were covered with alkali dust.

"Like my little spot? Good scenery, huh?"

"Inspiring."

"Maybe to the artistic type like yourself. Me, I like bright lights, you know. I like it where there's bars and cars and broads, that's what I like. You got my money?"

"Enough to buy you at least one bar, a couple of dozen Cadillacs, and as many women as you could possibly cram into all of them."

"That's funny, yeah, that's a funny thing to say to me, which is why you hear me laughing."

"I don't write comedy, I'm sorry."

"Don't waste my time. Where is it?"

"First I have to see the things you showed me before."

"First you got to take off your jacket so I can see you don't have no gun."

"Oh, please, can we stop pretending this is a detective movie? I'm here to give you what you want in exchange for what the studio wants, as per instructions."

"Nice speech, now get it off and give me a twirl like those fashion dames do."

Moody removed his jacket and turned slowly in a circle, his arms outstretched.

"Satisfied?"

"Perfectly satisfied, only where's the cash?"

"May I see inside your valise?"

Tony unzipped it and presented the interior to Moody. "Trusting guy," he said.

"It's too dark to see inside."

"Jesus, Moody, you're hard to please." He moved closer, removing the jade phallus and several sheets of paper. "Here, get your nose right up against it."

Moody took the papers and studied them, tilting them toward the remaining light. Beautiful ideograms ran like stylized rain down the sheets in his hand. It was difficult to reconcile their fascinating appearance with the message of criminality they conveyed.

"Okay? Happy now?"

"Yes."

"So gimme my money."

"Very well." Moody reached for the inner pockets of his jacket.

"Whoa there, nice and slow so's I know it ain't a gun."

The fat envelopes were drawn slowly out and handed over. Tony opened them both, then took a small flashlight from his pants and aimed its beam at the bills fanned out fatly in his other hand.

"All fifties," Moody said, "and nonsequential, the way you wanted."

"I said nothing *bigger* than fifties, not *all* fifties. Now I gotta break 'em down in a half million stores and gas stations."

"I'm sorry, I must have misunderstood."

"Hold the goddamn flashlight."

Moody obliged, and Tony began counting. He counted badly, and became bored halfway through. "Looks like it's all there," he said, stuffing it back into the envelopes. "You got an honest face, Moody."

Tony placed the envelopes inside his jacket.

"Just out of curiosity," said Moody, "where's your car?"

"Over there." Tony gestured behind himself.

"I don't see it."

"The green coupe, dopey."

"That's my car."

"Right, and I'm gonna use it to drive to where my car's at, which is quite a ways. See, Moody, I got here two hours ago from over the other side of them hills, on foot, so's I could see if you set something up that I didn't like, another guy hiding out in the brush maybe with a gun, or maybe he'd take a peek at my license plate and track me down. I wouldn't have liked a deal like that, but you did the right thing. Just you and the money, so here's your cock and the rest of it. Keep the bag, that's how generous I feel. The flashlight I keep."

They exchanged items. Moody said, "Am I supposed to walk all the way back to Los Angeles?"

"You could, or you could hitch a ride, but that won't be till morning, after someone comes along and lets you out of the crapper over there."

"Are you joking? I can't spend all night in there. The doors on those things lock on the inside anyway. This is ridiculous.

Look, take the car and tell me where I can find it again. By the time I've walked there you'll be miles away in your own car. Be reasonable."

Tony rummaged inside his pants and produced a padlock and short length of chain. He dangled these in front of Moody. "I figure this'll keep you inside where I want you. Those doors have got handles on the outside. I just put the chain through the his and hers handles and lock it up tight and you're there till someone comes along with a crowbar, boy. I came out here before and got this all planned out."

"I'm not going in there. You can't make me."

"Come on, Moody, it won't be so bad. Worst thing can happen is you get cold. They say the desert's cold at night. Hey, you got a blanket or traveling rug in the car? You can take that in there with you. I got no grudge against you, but it has to be done the way I planned."

"I don't have a blanket, and I like my way better."

Tony reached into his other pocket and withdrew a small automatic pistol.

"Okay, this'll hurt you even if it don't kill you, so get in the john right now."

Moody turned and began walking toward the toilet block.

"This is good," Tony said. "When people have to get shot, that's bad. There's this war now, and there's thousands of guys gonna get shot. You don't wanna be like them, I bet."

They stopped before the doors. It was dark enough now that Tony had to illuminate them with his flashlight. "Go ahead," he told Moody.

The door with the outline of a trousered man stenciled on it would not open.

"Try the women's," Tony suggested.

That door opened, and Moody stepped inside. He knew it would be the smell rather than the cold that would keep him awake. The flashlight beam raked briefly across a metal drum

beneath a holed plank. "All modern conveniences," said Tony. "Stay right there."

The door closed behind Moody, the metal latch falling into place. He turned and watched the door's outline dance uncertainly as Tony set about untangling his chain. Metal links rattled as they were passed through the outside handle, then the light moved sideways toward the men's door. Moody heard that door open. Why had it not opened before?

He heard a gunshot. The detonation was so loud, so unexpected, he jumped backward and stumbled against the toilet seat. Something heavy fell against the door outside and slid to the ground. The flashlight had gone out, or was aimed elsewhere. Then it returned, accompanied by the sound of chain links being drawn back through the handle.

"All right, Mr. Moody, you can come out now, it's all over." It was not Tony's voice.

Moody stayed where he was, confused, suspicious. The door was pulled open against a resisting weight. A light shone into his face. "Let's go, Mr. Moody."

He stepped warily outside. The light was lowered to reveal Tony's body slumped against the door. His hat had fallen off.

"Is he dead?"

"He'd better be. Where'd he put the money?"

"Inside his jacket . . . Were you behind the other door?"

"Since about six hours ago. Didn't have a single motorist need to use the place. They shouldn't spend state tax money on a place like this. Get the money, and take his wallet too. No sense in leaving anything the police can use to identify him. Mr. Moody, are you hearing me?"

"Yes—"

"The money and his wallet. Get his gun too."

Moody extracted them from Tony's jacket and pants. The flashlight, aimed at Tony to assist in their removal, revealed a startling amount of blood across the front of his plaid shirt.

Tony's eyes were open. Moody offered the wallet and envelopes to his rescuer, who told him to put them in the valise along with everything else. While Moody attended to this, Tony was bundled into the women's toilet, and the padlock and chain were utilized according to the dead man's plan.

"Why are you doing that?" Moody asked.

"Buying time, a day or two if we're lucky. Let's go."

They walked quickly to Moody's car. The man with the valise got into the backseat. "Don't look at me, Mr. Moody," he said, when Moody sent an inquiring glance into the gloom. "Get in and drive to Victorville."

Moody started the engine and steered north.

"Is that where your car is?"

"Correct."

"Is this something you planned with Mr. Margolis?"

"Never heard of him. Don't ask questions, Mr. Moody, just drive."

"I don't quite know what to say—"

"Then don't bother. No more talk."

The man in the backseat lit a cigarette, and Moody glanced in the rearview mirror to catch a possible glimpse of his features, but the smoker kept his head down. He used a lighter, not matches, and despite the lengthy flame, his hat brim obscured everything but a long jawline.

The drive to Victorville was shorter than expected. The town, too far from the coast to be affected by blackout regulations, was well lit. Moody was told to pull into a parking lot beside a tavern. Swing music poured from a jukebox inside. His passenger pushed past him and exited through the right-hand door, keeping his face turned away from Moody as he did so. Over his shoulder he said, "Go home now, and forget any of this ever happened."

"I doubt that I can."

"Mr. Moody, you damn well better try."

"I'll take that valise, if you don't mind. I'm responsible for the money and the evidence. I signed a receipt for the money."

"It's all taken care of."

"I only have your say-so for that."

His passenger sat back inside the car, sideways, his legs outside the vehicle, his back still turned to Moody. "Listen carefully. None of this happened. You spent the evening at home. You went nowhere. Tomorrow you'll go back to work, which is a happy place, Mr. Moody, without problems or difficulties of any kind. Your bosses are happy and you are happy. Everyone is happy, because there's no reason for unhappiness. You won't discuss any of this with them, and they won't discuss any of it with you, because there's nothing to discuss. Write a nice picture, Mr. Moody."

He got out and slammed the door but did not move away from the car.

"Mr. Moody, why are you not driving away?"

"I don't think I have to do what you say."

The man turned, and a large-caliber revolver was aimed at Moody's face through the open window. All he could see of the gunman was his chest and arm and gun.

"Get moving."

Moody engaged the gears and steered back onto the highway, this time heading south. When he had gone two blocks he suddenly wrenched the wheel sideways and turned off the main road. Two minutes later he was back at the tavern, approaching the parking lot by way of an alley, and in time to see a late-model Buick leaving the lot, just as he had done. Every other vehicle that he could see was either a farm truck or else so antiquated it simply did not jibe with the crisp manners of his recent passenger.

Moody decided to follow the Buick, well aware, as he motored across the lot and onto the highway again, that what he had embarked upon was totally uncharacteristic of him. It had a giddying effect, this hasty veering in the direction of danger, and Moody, concocter of too many cheap adventures, was able to recognize the emotion his writing was intended to promote in audiences everywhere—he was in the grip, unsubtle and unyielding, of wild excitement. The Buick was already at the edge of town, its taillights moving into the darkness beyond the last streetlight. Moody turned his own lights off and pressed the accelerator.

The drive back to Los Angeles was without incident. Traffic was light; not a single vehicle passed Moody as he tailed the Buick at a distance of less than a quarter mile, hidden, lightless. When the darkened outlying districts of the city were entered, the Buick's driver turned off his lights. Moody was confident enough, in the increased traffic flow, to ease his car closer.

He had felt a powerful urge to urinate for the past twenty miles, and hoped the man he was following lived on the north side of the city. By the time the Buick came finally to a stop in front of a stucco apartment building in Monterey Park, Moody was in considerable distress, moaning and squirming behind the wheel.

The man got out of his car. Moody, parked along the opposite curb, did too. Clenching what felt like his entire abdomen, Moody entered the courtyard, passing beneath a sign—ORINOCO APARTMENTS. Staying in the shadows as the movies had taught him to do, he was able to watch the man with the valise climb an outside staircase to the first floor and pass along a lengthy balcony to the last door. He paused to insert a key, then went inside.

Unable to proceed without relief, Moody sought cover behind a trash bin collection wall and voided his bladder for sixty-seven seconds, according to his slow count, while listening to Jack Benny on a radio program wafting from behind the blackout curtains in the nearest open window.

His fly rebuttoned, he proceeded up the stairs and along the balcony. The number on the last door was eleven. Moody turned and retraced his steps to the front of the building, and consulted the mailboxes there. Number eleven was occupied by E. Mauser.

Moody went back to his car, very pleased with himself. He had no idea what to do with his knowledge, but was glad he had it anyway.

Driving home, filled with a satisfaction so novel he wanted to sit in contemplation of it, Moody was suddenly overtaken by a wish to see Myra, and not just to visit but to make robust love. He knew it would be different from any previous intimacy, because Moody was himself different, transformed from within. All he had to do was present himself on Myra's doorstep, and she would see the difference and be his completely, offering herself in new ways, eager to sate the more powerful man Moody felt he had become. He was hungry, but food could wait.

Approaching her door, Moody heard voices inside Myra's apartment, voices raised in argument. Myra's words were indistinct, but the man she was arguing with shouted loudly enough for Moody to catch the phrase "Since when did you ever understand! When!"

He didn't bother with the formality of ringing the bell; instead he turned the door handle and walked straight in. The argument was being held in the kitchen, and when Moody came around the corner he was prepared for a fight, a notion that prior to this evening would have frightened him but now seemed the perfect way to end this unusual day; he would defend his girl against a ruffian.

The man was shouting again, his back to Moody, and Myra appeared to be protecting herself from his words by turning from him to face the sink. "All I need is your support, just for a little while!" the man yelled at Myra's hunched shoulders. "Is it too much to ask? Is it?"

Moody tapped him on the shoulder, and when the shouting

man turned in surprise, Moody threw a punch at his jaw. It was a weak punch, despite Moody's best intentions, and the man—Moody saw too late that it was Baxter Nolan—reeled back several steps in surprise rather than from the blow's impact. Baxter staggered against Myra, who turned, and all three became quite still, watching each other like alley cats caught in a ritual standoff.

"Bax—I'm sorry, I didn't know it was you—"

"What the hell is this, Moody! Damn, I ought to punch your lights out, you idiot!"

"I'm sorry—I heard the shouting and thought Myra was in trouble—"

"You're the one in trouble, Moody! I've got a screen test tomorrow, and if there's any swelling in my face I'm telling Roy Schutt and Terry Blackwell who's responsible!"

"Shut up! Shut up, damn you!"

Both men looked at Myra. Moody had never seen her in such distress. Her face was twisted in what he saw as helpless rage of some kind. She clearly was not pleased to see him, or to have been rescued so unconvincingly from her own brother.

"Get out!" Myra said.

Moody and Baxter looked at each other. Which one was supposed to leave, or did she mean both?

"Bax," she said, more calmly now, "just leave."

Baxter shrugged. To Moody he said, "There won't be any swelling. You hit like a girl. And next time, knock, for Christ's sake."

He took his hat from the kitchen table and brushed past Moody, who waited until he heard the front door slam before approaching Myra where she stood at the sink, both arms wrapped around herself, fingers gripping her shoulders so tightly her knuckles had whitened.

"Looks like I blew my rescue scene," said Moody.

She smiled at him, making an effort to reassure him. The

result was more like a rictus, stiff and artificial. "Were you rescuing me, Keith?"

"That was my intention. Are you all right?"

"Yes, perfectly. I need a drink, how about you?"

"A double, I think."

He followed her to the living room and across to the tiny bamboo bar. Moody watched her pour two stiff rum and Cokes. She kept her back to him deliberately, it seemed, in order to calm down and collect herself before handing him a glass. He waited for her to speak.

"I went back to your office this afternoon to see if Smokey had peed his pants or anything, and you weren't there. I went back a couple more times. Smokey left, eventually, but you didn't come back. Where were you?"

It was a query, but it sounded too much like an accusation. Moody was instantly defensive. He could tell her nothing of what had happened.

"I had an errand to run for Margolis."

"Is that what you are now, his errand boy?"

"No, and I don't think you need to be quite so sarcastic."

"Of course I shouldn't be, not to a man who just got off his white horse."

Moody drank deeply. "I'll just finish this and go, if you like."

"How would I know what I like? Who asks *me*?"

He had never seen her this way. All the humor was gone from her. Moody felt inadequate, unable to understand or give comfort. He had driven over in anticipation of sweeping Myra away to some plateau of self-glorification where she would worship him, and had even gone so far as to hit someone like a Hollywood tough guy, pursuing this fantasy of rescue and passionate reward.

Now Myra was glaring at him, radiating irritation beyond anything he could grasp, and Moody's dream of greatness, of virility and mystery and conquest, was melting away like the ice cubes in his drink. He was not any kind of man at all. He had been told to go inside a women's toilet to spend the night, and had done so without any real protest. Why had he not wrestled with Tony for possession of the gun? He had himself been rescued from harm's way by a mysterious stranger, and assumed that man's mantle on the drive south. He was ridiculous, a thing of straw, wholly unworthy of Myra, probably unable to help with whatever it was that had caused the fight between Baxter and herself. Moody took another swallow of his drink, its sweetness turning to bile in his mouth.

"It was a family argument," offered Myra.

"Oh."

"Nothing new. Bax is a typical actor, cranky when he wants to be, and that's pretty often. There's only me to listen to him. Some family."

"Why doesn't he bother Sandy Ryder with his problems?"

"She's one of them. Oops, let my claws show, didn't I."

This sounded more like the Myra that Moody was familiar with.

"I came around here to make amends," he said.

"How, by socking my sibling? Not that he didn't deserve it, the jerk. Amends for what?"

"For not appreciating you."

"Aww, shucks, Keith, you don't have to get romantic and gushy on me. A girl gets all embarrassed when her feller says he actually appreciates her. A girl's not ready for that kind of sugar talk."

"All right, all right. I take it back. Thanks for the drink."

"Not rushing away, are you, Galahad?"

Moody threw his glass against the wall. It shattered into a surprising number of pieces. He hadn't planned on doing it. Ice cubes went slithering across the sofa cushions and fell onto the carpet. Moody was appalled. He had no idea what to do next.

"Bejesus and bejabbers," said Myra. "So that's how you give up drinking."

Moody began to laugh. He couldn't stop himself, and his laughter sounded so foolish it deserved more laughter, so he and Myra laughed at it, both of them winding up breathless.

Myra, when she was able to, said, "We'll sweep up the glass in the morning."

8

THE EARLY NEWS broadcast offered nothing new regarding the search for Russell Keys. The army had sent men from Fort Riley in Kansas to assist in a massive sweep back along the path Russell's plane was calculated to have followed before falling from the sky. Thousands of men were covering a theoretical line hundreds of miles long. It had been three days now since the Thunderbolt was found, and not a single trace of the missing pilot had been located. There were still snow flurries in the Rockies, and the general feeling was that if Russell had bailed out over the mountains, rather than the plains of eastern Colorado or western Kansas, then little hope could be held out for his survival. "The nation awaits with bated breath further news of the hero," concluded the radio announcer, in hushed and reverent tones.

"Not to be flip or anything," said Myra, lighting her first cigarette of the day, "but what the hell is baited breath? Is it something you use to lure flies into your mouth?"

"It's spelled b-a-t-e, not b-a-i-t."

"Thank you, my literary friend."

Moody laughed despite himself. It was probably wrong to make light of Russell's death—Moody had no serious doubts about his cousin's demise—but his mood was effervescent that morning, and the death of a man like Russell was not something Moody intended to allow into his thoughts.

He had caused Myra to cry out with pleasure the night before, something he had never experienced with his few sexual partners, and he was elated. It had not been any kind of fake performance, of that he was certain, and he assumed that the gratification they both had achieved was a direct result of being in love. He was ready to admit it now; he loved Myra Nolan and hoped, with some confidence, that she loved him also, in equal measure. This, after all, was supposed to be the fullest expression of human existence, according to ancient wisdom and Hollywood movies alike. Such disparate sources arriving at the same conclusion gave the theory a veracity that Moody, reclining in bed, replete as a well-fed otter, could not fault.

"I wonder how Bax's face is this morning?"

"Knowing Bax, he probably held an ice pack on it all night long."

"Or had Sandy hold it for him," Moody suggested.

"Can we please not profane the air with that person's name?"

"Sorry. None of my business, but what exactly do you have against her? Is it some kind of sisterly jealousy, you know, not considering her good enough for Bax?"

"Maybe she did something to Bax that I don't like. Maybe I have definite reasons for not liking her."

"Such as?"

"Nothing I'd care to discuss right now. And while we're in an analytical mood, you don't seem at all broken up about the fact that your cuz from Kansas is most likely dead and buried under the snow a thousand miles from here. Care to explain?"

"Nope."

"Tit for tat."

"Are you talking dirty to me, Myra?"

"I could be persuaded to."

Moody set about accomplishing this.

MOODY HALF EXPECTED, despite what E. Mauser had told him to the contrary, that Margolis would summon him to his office for an accounting of the previous evening's events, but no word or summons came throughout the morning, and by midafternoon, still hard at work on the script for *China Skies*, Moody accepted that the business of Tony the blackmailer had been settled to the evident satisfaction of Empire Productions.

Moody sometimes paused at his typewriter to ask himself the question a thinking, intelligent individual must ask, granted the circumstances: Did it matter, in a moral sense, that Tony had been shot to death as a result of his criminal activities? Moody had to admit he did not care that the man who had intended locking him into a toilet overnight was dead. It was a revelation of sorts, this cavalier attitude toward so grotesque a denouement as he had witnessed at the picnic area. Moody had always assumed that murder committed before his eyes, if he should ever witness so unlikely an event, would have a profoundly disturbing effect upon him, but that had not been the case, and this puzzled and worried him somewhat.

Tony had met with justice of the roughest kind, and should not be mourned simply because he was no longer among the living. The wages of sin, Moody reminded himself, were held to be self-evident, at least in the world of Hollywood scenarios. Tony had brought shame and ignominious death upon himself by his actions, and should not be the object of remorse, at least not on Moody's part. Moody, after all, had not pulled the trigger; E. Mauser had done that.

What manner of man was E. Mauser, and how had Margolis (or could it have been Schutt?) known whom to contact for the services of a hired killer? Moody wanted to know the answers, simply for the knowing. The logistics of such an arrangement intrigued him. He was preparing, at top speed, the cinematic

biography of a man for whose secret life another man had been killed. It was fantastically complex, from an ethical point of view, and quite beyond the purview of his own assignment—to present a respectable image of his cousin to the world.

THAT AFTERNOON TERRY Blackwell paid Moody a visit to inform him that Baxter Nolan had been given final approval to play Russell Keys, following a screen test that morning and a script reading that afternoon, using several pages of what Moody had already written. Tipping his fedora to the back of his head, Blackwell said, "You and Bax have a falling-out lately?"

"Why do you ask?"

"He wanted to keep the camera on his left side, when I happen to know for a fact that his right side is his official good side. Thought I saw a little swelling there under the makeup, nothing to jeopardize the test, though."

"Why does that point to a falling-out?"

"Well, he had a few unkind words to say about the pages of script I handed him. Said it was lame stuff and needed a rewrite. Just for the record, I disagree with him, and there isn't time for rewrites in any case. It was unnecessary criticism, and that's where my falling-out theory comes into play. You don't have to tell me anything."

"I hit him. Last night."

Blackwell whistled. "Any particular reason?"

"He was shouting at his sister."

"Oh, whatsername—Mary, isn't it?"

"Myra. I didn't like what I saw and heard, so I socked him."

Moody felt he did not have to admit that he hadn't known it was Baxter Nolan he hit until the blow was delivered. A fist to the face of a third-tier star was good gossip to have passed around the studio, as Blackwell assuredly would. Moody might just earn himself a reputation as a hardnose if things went well.

"Bax can be a handful all right," Blackwell said, placing a cigarette in his mouth. "He was all smiles and please and thank you when he got signed up a couple of years back, but after he had a few successes under his belt, directed by yours truly, he got cocky. I've seen it before. You take someone off the street and make them into something big, they go gaga for a while. Sometimes they straighten out. Bax had that accident to cope with, of course."

"What accident?"

"Oh, he cracked up his car last year, broke a leg and some ribs and put his back out, but he seems okay now. Physically, that is. His temper's gotten worse. My advice is to stay away from him. You're both essential to the production, and any bad blood between you is only going to bring grief down on my head."

"I'll keep out of his way, so long as he stays away from Myra."

"You and her an item, Moody?"

"You might say so."

Blackwell pulled his hat down. "Say, have you seen Smokey Hayes lately?"

"Not since yesterday."

"He'd better watch out, or he'll be banned from the studio, the way he's been carrying on. Seems you're his special pal."

"Kind of. He can't get over his contract not being renewed."

"Smokey's yesterday's hero. Well, see you around, Moody."

Moody had to wonder, later in the day, if Blackwell had already circulated the story of his tangle with Baxter Nolan. Nothing else would explain the appearance in his office doorway, at several minutes to five, of his old boss Quentin Yapp, head of B-feature production.

Yapp's feral snout seemed to quiver with inquiry. He had entered without knocking, as if Moody still worked beneath him and was not deserving of politeness.

"So, Moody, they gave you a bigger box to scribble in, huh?"

"Yes, they did."

"And a plum project, this cousin guy of yours, the war hero. What's the deal, he jumped outta his plane or what? That Thunderbolt, that's an expensive ship, not even in full production yet, and he lets it go down. He never heard of gliding, that cousin? Makes the plane look bad, it falls outta the sky like a rock on accounta the pilot bails out."

"Were you there?"

"What there? How could I be there? Dumb question."

"I think we can assume he had no choice but to bail out."

"Yeah, well, nobody's ever gonna know, are they?"

"Russell will tell us what happened when he's found."

"Found!" Yapp snorted noisily, an act Moody knew was as close as Yapp could come to laughter. "Found where? How? They already looked. He's up a tree somewhere, owl food."

"Owls eat mice, Yapp."

"Mice, men, what difference."

Yapp had produced a witticism, but he was too stupid to be aware of it.

"What's to smile about, Moody, huh? Your cousin's dead, and you smile. You know something I don't? Hey, when they call off the search it makes him officially dead is what I heard, which they'll do anytime now. You think he'd still be missing if he's alive? There's more than bears in those mountains. Somebody woulda seen him by now if he's walking around. And you know what else, Moody? When that happens, when they call off the search, you can call off your flyboy movie, because they don't make movies about dead guys that bailed outta their plane and forgot to pull the rip cord on their parachute, or whatever he did or didn't do. He's a dead guy, that's all. If he got shot down by Japs, that's different."

"Yapp, you have the most obnoxious personality of anyone I ever met."

"I call it like I see it, and I don't go picking fights with movie stars either. That's a good way to get your ass canned outta here."

"This is touching. You're concerned for my welfare."

"Help is what I'm giving. Good advice. You think you're somebody now, but you're on thin ice, Moody, only you don't even know it. You and Smokey Hayes. That bum, he's been around my neck ever since yesterday, moaning and groaning. Shit, the studio didn't give him plenty of cash while he was big? The hell they didn't. Now he wonders what he's gonna do with his life. I told him, buy yourself an automated laundry. That's a business that brings in cash steady. There never was a time in history when clothes didn't get dirty, and now we can clean them with a machine. You think the dumb bastard's gonna go buy himself an automated laundry and sit back and count the profits? Like hell he is! Wants another role, a different role, something without a big hat. Says you're gonna get him that role in your flyboy movie. That right, Moody?"

"I've made the suggestion to Mr. Margolis."

Yapp snorted. "Yeah, and what'd he say, Margolis, huh? Said go take a hike, right? You think I don't know what goes on around here? Think I don't have ears? The big guys, Margolis, those Jew financiers back in New York, you think they can keep any secrets I don't hear about? The hell they do, Moody. You watch your ass is what I'm saying, and don't think I don't know what I'm talking about."

"I'll bear it all in mind."

"Sure you will. You're saying to yourself right now, what the fuck's Yapp shooting his mouth off about something he doesn't know about, but I do, Moody, I do."

"Fine."

"Fine yourself. You take care of your health, only don't go out in the desert for it. People think the desert air, it's good for them on accounta it's dry and clean, but deserts, they're dangerous places, Moody, you know? A guy could get killed in the desert. I heard of guys that died right next to the road, that's how it is out there."

Moody, until then amused by Yapp's performance, became alert.

"What guys?"

"Just guys that thought they were smarter than they were, and what's it get them but getting dead in the desert, that's what. I gotta go, only think about it, okay?"

Yapp almost ran from the room. Moody was mildly alarmed. Had Yapp's talk of death in the desert been a reference to the shooting of Tony? What could Quentin Yapp possibly know of that? Guys dying right next to the road, that had been what he said. Tony had died that way.

THE OFFICE OF a private detective, Moody had learned from the movies, is seedy and unglamorous to the point where its lack of aesthetic charm becomes appealing. He was not aware that a private detective might work out of an office located in his own home, but that was the setup he encountered when his first visit with Horace Wheat took place on the fourth morning after Russell's disappearance.

The address was near his own, and Horace Wheat was amenable to a meeting very early in the morning if that was what a potential customer required. Moody learned that the effort of leaving his home for an early appointment at the office was, for Horace Wheat, minimal. In fact, he greeted a slightly bewildered Moody at the front door while still wearing a dressing gown.

"Had you fooled, I guess" were Wheat's first words after beckoning Moody through the screen door and into the kitchen, where a bowl of cornflakes indicated the detective had not completed his breakfast.

Wheat was six feet three and at least sixty years old. Moody wondered, as he sat on a chair, where the office could possibly be, since the house was itself tiny, a stucco box on a street of tired palms.

"Garage," said Wheat, apparently able to read thoughts. "Had it converted. Keep my car at the curb. No hailstorms or snow, damn-all rain, so why fill up a garage with my automobile? Color's fading on it, though. Too much sun. Did you have breakfast yet, Mr. Moody?"

"I did, yes."

"We can go out to the office in a minute. Got to get my vittles first thing, or I get to feeling weak later on in the day. Outfit's not what you expected, is it?"

"Frankly, no. Are you a licensed private detective, Mr. Wheat?"

"Couldn't advertise if I wasn't. Came out here to retire. Did police work in Michigan. Now, there's a cold place. California's different. Didn't like being retired, though. You can sit around and eat oranges just so long, is what I found out. Then my wife died, and I thought, go back into police work, why not?"

"You've been successful, I take it."

"Moderate. Haven't been doing it too long. I see doubt in your eyes, Mr. Moody, and I want to assure you of one thing—I'm honest, smart, and diligent."

"Three things."

"For the price of one, and damn cheap it is. What's your difficulty, Mr. Moody?"

"Difficulty?"

"Nobody wants to hire a detective unless there's a difficulty in their life they can't resolve."

Moody looked around the room. The place had a threadbare appearance but was neat and clean. He suspected the few items of decoration reflected the taste of Wheat's late wife.

"I want to know everything there is to know about a certain man."

"What man, and why?"

"Why? Do you really need to know?"

"You might be fixing to rob him if I give you all the details about his daily itinerary. I have a broader obligation to society that overrides my obligation to paying clientele. Professional ethics, Mr. Moody."

"I'm glad to hear that. Ethics are in short supply, I sometimes think."

"We think alike. What's his name, and what's your beef?"

"His name is Mauser, E. Mauser, and he lives in number eleven, Orinoco Apartments, Monterey Park. You're not writing this down?"

"Got a good memory for dry facts. Go on."

"The reason I want to know all about him is . . . he wants to marry my sister, and I just don't trust him. It's hard to explain. An instinctive thing, I guess you'd call it."

Wheat spooned cereal into his mouth. "What kind of work's he in?"

"He told Celia, that's my sister, that he owns several automated laundries."

"But you don't believe that."

"It might be true, but the thing is, I happen to know he carries a gun. Why would the owner of a laundry need to do that?"

"Protection, if he collects the money out of the machines himself."

"I don't find that a convincing argument, Mr. Wheat."

"Sounded kind of feeble to me too. Might be the answer, though. Some people think the ordinary answer's never the right one, but they're wrong about that plenty of times. People see too many movies, in my opinion, and get all kinds of crazy ideas. What line of work are you in, Mr. Moody?"

"Oh . . . insurance."

"Which company?"

"I don't want my firm to be involved with this in any way. If you're worried about my solvency, I'll give you a cash advance now, to get you started."

"Twenty a day and all reasonable expenses incurred in the course of my investigation. Sound acceptable?"

Moody placed forty dollars on the table next to a saltshaker in the shape of a blue parrot; the pepper was in a red parrot.

"Look at that," said Wheat. "We've gone and concluded our business and didn't even get out to the garage. You might think me a trifle on the informal side, Mr. Moody, but don't be fooled by appearances. I did good work as a police detective, and I'm constitutionally reluctant to change anything about myself."

"I'm sure that's true." Moody stood.

"And we'll find out if this Mauser is the right kind of fellow for your Suzie."

"Celia."

"Correct."

"Do you carry a gun, Mr. Wheat?"

"Seldom. Got one, my police weapon. Shot a rat with it the other day."

"He . . . wouldn't surrender?"

"Not that kind of rat—a rodent with a tail. He kept coming in and eating whatever's in my pantry. Too smart to trap with cheese, so I shot him."

Moody began moving toward the door. Wheat stood and followed, dabbing at his lips with a checkered napkin.

"I'll be in touch tomorrow night," Moody said.

"Fine, fine, ought to be enough time. Come on by in the evening, after you're all done with your insurance claims and such."

"I will. Thank you."

Driving to the studio, Moody chided himself for having wasted forty dollars.

LUNCHING IN THE commissary, he was joined by Baxter Nolan and Sandy Ryder. They came steering toward him through the sounds of clashing cutlery and the swirling colors of a band of Gypsy minstrels, bearing their lightly laden trays before them like heraldic shields, and sat opposite Moody without invitation, their only excuse a pair of dazzling smiles.

"All right, Mr. Keith Moody," Bax declared, eyes narrowed with comical intent, "I'm here to offer the hand of friendship and apology. Whaddaya say?"

"Certainly," said Moody.

"Oh, that's so gentlemanly." Sandy beamed. "Bax told me about what happened, and I just have to say he deserved a darn good sock in the puss, giving his little sister grief like that, honest to God. He's a lug sometimes, but I have to put up with him, you know, because love is blind. But you don't have to, Keith, and you didn't!"

Bax threw his head back and laughed, displaying his many caps and crowns, and Sandy did the same. The occupants of the nearest table, hussars in splendid uniforms, turned to stare.

"Aggravation is a waste of time," Moody said.

"That's right," agreed Bax, "so the hatchet gets buried here and now."

"So long as it isn't in my skull," said Moody, and Sandy piped laughter for several yards around herself. The hussars raised eyebrows at one another and pulled wryly at their false mustaches.

"Seriously, Keith," Bax went on, "we're all three of us joined at the hip on this production, so friendship is the first order of the day."

"Fine by me."

"And we think the script is just wonderful so far," Sandy

contributed, "at least, the parts we've seen. I did my reading and screen test this morning."

"And passed with flying colors," assured Bax.

"So it's official, Keith. You write it, and we speak it."

"Very good," said Moody, unable to conjure up any other response. He looked at his ham on rye and wondered if eating the rest of it without further comment would be rude. Bax solved Moody's dilemma by attacking the soup on his tray, and Sandy took her cue from her lover.

For half a minute they ate in silence, then Bax said, "Did Myra explain anything that night? I feel badly about it, really. I get so wound up sometimes, and do things I shouldn't, and then I have to face the music afterward. She say anything at all?"

"No, except to say it was personal."

"That's what it is, but that's no excuse. Listen, Keith, when you see her next time, tell her I'm sorry, okay?"

"I think that might be your role, Bax."

Bax nodded. "That's true, I can't deny it's true. Isn't it, honey?" he said to Sandy.

"God, yes. She's your sister." To Moody she said, "Family, they stick together."

"So they should," offered Moody, and his table guests nodded their agreement.

"Script coming along okay, Keith?" asked Bax.

"Fine. Almost half done."

"That's incredible. You know, you've got a reputation at Empire for being the fastest writer on the lot, and that's no bull, I can see it now. How do you do it?"

"Take one grindstone," said Moody. "Apply one nose. Result—work done."

Bax and Sandy found that hilarious. One of the hussars leaned over and spoke to Moody. "Hey, feller, whatever your friends are on, we'll take some."

Sandy overheard and told the hussar to buzz off. All the

hussars began buzzing like bees and laughing between buzzes.

"Extras!" scolded Sandy, in a tone Moody imagined Marie Antoinette might have reserved for peasants.

They ate again in silence, then Sandy, reaching for her cigarettes, asked, "Any more news about your cousin, Keith?"

"Nothing. I'm afraid people are giving up hope."

"But not you," said Bax, offering Sandy a light from his gold Dunhill.

"Actually, I believe he's dead."

Bax and Sandy looked at Moody, then at each other.

"Keith, you can't mean that." Bax's voice was filled with earnest regret.

"I'm afraid I do. I'd be delighted to be proven wrong, of course."

Sandy exhaled smoke. "But the production, what would happen if he's dead?"

"I can't guess what Mr. Margolis might decide to do," Moody admitted.

"Not shut it down," Sandy said, looking at Bax for confirmation.

"Never," Bax stated. "It's gone too far. Have you seen the Kunming set, Keith? It's almost ready for shooting, they say. Roy Schutt told me they got it prepared in record time."

"So whatever happens, they'll go ahead." Sandy appeared to need more reassurance. Bax lit a cigarette for himself and squeezed Sandy's hand. Moody was startled to see that this stagy gesture brought actual relief to Sandy; the creases in her forehead were erased, and her dimples returned.

"I have to get back to work," Moody said, rising and pushing back his chair.

"Of course," said Sandy, as if granting him permission.

"I know you'll make every line memorable, Keith." Bax winked.

"Naturally," Moody said.

By day's end, he knew the script was more than half done, exceeding his own record for speed achieved during his efforts for Quentin Yapp and Smokey Hayes. He dropped the newest pages off with Roy Schutt's secretary and strolled over to the back lot. Passing through an English village being used in the new Elizabethan picture *Royal Pirate*, he came at last to what was unmistakably a piece of China, or what passed for such in Hollywood. Moody had to admit the streets of false-fronted buildings had an authentic look to them, although they were made of pine lumber and plaster and chicken wire. He stood for a while, smoking and wondering if Russell would have found the Californian Kunming redolent of the place he had known. This Kunming did not have a brothel, of course. Moody ground out his cigarette butt and went home.

HE APPROACHED THE home and office of Horace Wheat the following evening with little hope for his money's worth of information. Wheat welcomed him, this time appearing more professional in a jacket and slacks, and invited Moody into the converted garage. The walls were hidden by ancient filing cabinets, and the garage doors were blocked by a rolltop desk from the previous century. Moody took the ugly chair offered to him and waited for Wheat to select a file from one of the cabinets. When this was done, Wheat began packing a pipe.

"Did you find out anything?" Moody prompted.

"Interesting man, your sister's fiancé."

"Yes?"

"First off, the E. is for Edward, but he likes to be called Eddie. Eddie Mauser. He doesn't own any laundries, but he does own a dog kennel. Breeds French poodles. Went and took a look for myself, pretending like I was interested in buying one maybe. It's not the little yappy white ones, it's the bigger, black ones he breeds. Real intelligent dogs, he was telling me. Used as message carriers in the Napoleonic wars, something I never knew before."

"Anything else?"

Wheat applied a match to his pipe bowl and sucked noisily until the tobacco began glowing. Aromatic smoke wafted past Moody's nose.

"Well, I'd advise your sister not to marry the man, on account of he's already married to a lady lives with him in those Orinoco Apartments. The kennel's over in El Monte, looked after at night by a young feller who lives there full-time to watch over the dogs."

"Anything else?"

"No criminal record in this state. Might be one somewhere else. Want me to look into that?"

"No, I don't think so. So he's married."

"Checked it out at the registry office. Married nice and legal three years ago to a lady called Muriel, maiden name of Yapp, with two *p*'s."

"Yapp?"

"Nice name for a dog breeder's wife, don't you think? Too bad she's a Mauser now."

"This wife, does she have any brothers?"

"Didn't think to find that out. The point to consider here is, the man's setting himself up to be a bigamist if he goes through with marrying your sister. How long's she known him?"

"Oh, not long. Could you find out if his wife has a brother, or possibly a cousin called Quentin? Quentin Yapp?"

"Don't mind my asking, Mr. Moody, but what's that got to do with the matter to hand? Your sister's about to commit to a rascal."

"Yes, I'll tell her not to. How fast can you find out about Quentin?"

"Another day, I expect. I might have to buy a poodle to hang around and jaw about family matters like that with the Mausers. There's ways to do it, but they have to trust you and be relaxed. Fastest way to relax a businessman is to buy his wares. Ever felt the need of canine companionship, Mr. Moody?"

"No. I had a goldfish once."

"They don't count, in my opinion. A goldfish, it doesn't even know you're there, never mind giving you affection. I'd just as soon have a potted plant as a goldfish. A dog, now, that's different. Elsie and me, that's my wife who passed away, we had a number of dogs over the years. You can't beat a good dog when it comes to keeping you company. They were handsome dogs he had there."

"Mr. Wheat, go ahead and buy a dog, if you think that's what it'll take to find out about the wife's brother or cousin or whatever he turns out to be, but you have to keep the dog yourself. I live in an apartment."

"With your sister?"

"No, alone."

"Where's your sister live, with your folks?"

"No, alone, the same as me. She'd like to be married so she isn't alone anymore."

"Mr. Moody, no offense intended, but I don't think you're being entirely straight with me. You don't have an actual sister, do you?"

"Well, no."

"So what's this Eddie Mauser to you?"

"I'd prefer not to say." Moody took out his wallet. "That's another twenty dollars for tomorrow, and how much will a dog cost?"

"You can settle up with me tomorrow night. I'd really like to know a little more than you've told me so far. He has a gun, you said."

"So do lots of people. You have a gun yourself."

"I do, and I'm a law-abiding citizen. Is Eddie Mauser the same?"

"You said he doesn't have a criminal record."

"In this state."

Moody replaced his wallet. "I don't think he'll shoot you for asking a few questions, Mr. Wheat. Buy yourself the nicest dog he has. That should guarantee smiles all around."

"If you say so, Mr. Moody. Now, supposing it so happens the wife does have a brother or cousin called Quentin, will it make you happy or sad to find that out?"

"It'll make me . . . curious."

"That's what killed the cat, so they say."

"We were discussing dogs." Moody rose. "I'll come back at the same time tomorrow night, if that's all right."

"Fine by me."

Wheat escorted him to the door connecting the garage to the house, and went with him to the front door, talking along the way. "I like to keep a fairly complete record of my cases, Mr. Moody, so if you could see your way clear to explaining a few things to me tomorrow, I'd certainly be grateful. Mauser, that's a German name. This fellow isn't a Nazi spy, I hope."

"I really doubt it."

"Well, think about sharing your thoughts with me between now and then. The more a man knows, the better prepared he is for all kinds of things. That's what I've found out in this life."

"I'm sure you're right. Good night."

Moody walked along the front lawn's cracked paving to the curb and got into his car. He drove away knowing Wheat was standing in his front doorway still, watching him depart.

MOODY'S NEW OFFICE, like his old office, was not equipped with a phone, so the message that came before noon was delivered by a gofer.

"They want you over in Margolis's office."

Arriving from the Writers' Block, Moody found a scene dramatic enough to be worthy of the movies. Roy Schutt explained the situation while Terry Blackwell tried to calm Margolis's secretary, who was sobbing daintily into her handkerchief.

"Smokey Hayes is in there with MM." Schutt indicated the bronze doors to the inner office. "Terry and I were in there reviewing your script with MM when Smokey came in waving his gun around and demanding to be given a contract, any kind of contract, or he'd put a bullet in MM's skull."

"Good God—"

"You did an excellent job with Smokey the other day on stage six. Do it again now, Keith, and Empire will forever be grateful."

"Are the police coming, or studio security?"

"Don't be ridiculous. Not a breath of this can get out, or we'd be the laughingstock of Hollywood. The prestige of the studio is at stake, Keith, as well as MM's skin. Get in there and calm Smokey down."

"I'll do my best."

"Your best better be damn good," said Blackwell.

Moody approached the doors and knocked, then pushed the doors open several inches. A shot from within sent a bullet into the door.

"Smokey, it's me, Keith!"

"You can come on in, but them other skunks better keep their distance!"

"They will, Smokey! They've promised me!"

Moody entered the office, closing the doors behind him to muffle the sound of any more shots, should they occur. Margolis was seated at his desk, his expression stony. Smokey Hayes was over by the window, his favorite nickel-plated Colt .45 in his hand, his Stetson tipped to the back of his head, two days' growth of whiskers darkening his jaw. He smiled crookedly. "Hey, pardner."

"Hey, Smokey. What's the problem here, mind telling me?"

"Just a big ol' studio head that don't wanna do what's right by yours truly, that's the problem."

"What would you like Mr. Margolis to do for you, Smokey?"

"Gimme a contract is all, just an itty-bitty ol' contract so's I can keep my feet in boot leather and gas in my Cadillac. All them pictures I made for Empire and Margolee here, they don't seem to count for diddly-poo. That fair, you figure, Keith? You wrote 'em, and your reward happened just recent—you got to write the big-deal Flyin' Tiger movie, and I'm real happy for you about that, but see, I'm the one that starred in them selfsame movies, and the reward Margolee hands me is a kick to the backside. No more contract, he says. Says Joe Public don't wanna see me up on the screen no more, which is pure horse-apples, lemme tell you. I got my fans still, millions of 'em, and they sure as hell wanna see more Smokey Hayes pictures! Okay, so maybe I need to climb down outta the saddle and play some other roles." He addressed Margolis. "Moody here says he's gonna get me the part I want in his Tiger picture, some flyboy that teaches the hero to fly his first plane, a real good part, sounds like to me, only you don't wanna gimme it, do you, Margolee, huh?"

"The part is unsuitable for you, Smokey," said Margolis, his voice bearing only the faintest of tremors. "I'm sure there will be other roles."

"Not without I got a goddamn contract to act in 'em, there won't! Don't think you can bamboozle me with them slick promises!"

"No one's attempting to bamboozle you, Smokey," Margolis continued, "it's just that a career such as yours, based exclusively on Westerns, requires more than the usual effort to steer it in a different direction. If you want to be taken seriously as an actor, you must wait for a script that's . . . suitable, and we have none in development at this moment, that's all I'm trying to make you see."

"The hell you are! You can put me under a new contract while you look around for a suitable goddamn script, can't you?"

"Empire Productions will not be coerced into making any such decision. Put your gun away, Smokey, and we can discuss the possibilities like grown men, can't we, Keith?"

"Yes we can, Mr. Margolis. Putting the gun down is the first step, Smokey."

Smokey leveled his Colt at Margolis's head and cocked the hammer.

"I want to hear a good idea for a movie that's exactly right for me in the next thirty seconds, or there's gonna be one dead Margolee in here."

"For God's sake, man!"

"You heard me! Start thinkin'. You got twenty-nine seconds."

"Keith—" Margolis implored. Moody could see sweat sprouting from his head like resin from burning firewood.

"Smokey," said Moody, "it so happens I was working on a

scenario in my spare time just before the *China Skies* project came along, and it has the perfect role for you to play. It's so utterly different from anything you've done before, it's the ideal story to carry you away from Westerns forever!"

"Playin' the lead?" asked Smokey, suspicion narrowing his eyes.

"Of course! It's called *The Samaritan*, and it's about a man who one day sees an incredibly ugly woman in a store, along with her ugly little boy, and he feels so sorry for them both, because of their ugliness, that he decides there and then to change their lives, turn them into something much better, you see, and the way he does this is to pursue the woman and break down her defenses until she agrees to marry him, which eventually she does, and this is where the story really gets interesting, Smokey, because the man, the Samaritan, isn't just doing it to save the ugly woman and ugly boy, he's doing it to save himself, through an act of giving, you understand, an act most men would never consider, but this man does, in hopes of benefiting not only his new wife and son but himself, because he fully expects to be filled with a sense of righteousness and nobility when he does what he does, because it's such an unselfish act, basically, which is the payoff for him personally, but because life never works on a system of reward for acts of goodness, because life is fickle and cruel and capricious, the man doesn't get to experience the satisfaction he expected he would, and that's because the woman and boy don't behave the way he expects them to, mainly, being grateful because he took them under his wing, no, they aren't grateful at all, especially the woman, who thinks the man's an idiot for doing what he did, and she treats him like one, demanding this, demanding that, making him as unhappy as she can, because what the Samaritan never counted on was the fact that this woman who's ugly on the outside is also ugly on the inside, and her son's a rotten egg too, so you can see the position he finds himself in, Smokey, because after all this goodness and kindness that he invested in attempting to make three people happy, it turns out that he miscalculated so badly there's three very unhappy people instead, which depresses him terribly as you can imagine, and the thought of his failure begins to eat into the soul of the man, so much so that there comes a time when he feels the only way to salvage his act of kindness from absolute failure is to admit his total disillusionment and kill the woman and her son, who've both done the meanest things to him, so the audience will understand why he has to kill them, which he does—"

Moody ran out of breath.

Smokey stared at him. Margolis stared at him. Moody waited.

Smokey turned to Margolis. "What you think?"

"A truly radical solution," enthused Margolis, his face cracking open with a smile. "An absolutely brilliant premise. Extraordinarily daring. It flies in the face of every convention. Nothing like this has ever been attempted before!"

"Sounds kinda sad and miserable to me," said Smokey. "Hell, pardner, don't take it the wrong way, it's just I never expected somethin' like that. He *kills* 'em?"

"Well, yes, he has to, in order to restore . . . balance to his view of the world."

"Exactly, Keith!" Margolis beamed. "It's unorthodox, but it has its own . . . its own special kind of . . . its own actual brand of . . . Help me, Keith."

"Integrity?"

"Yes! The very word I was searching for! Integrity! This story, which is indeed grimly stark in the extreme, has integrity. It refuses to gild the lily. It says what it has to say, without apology, without compromise. It will represent a new direction for Empire, and you, Keith, and you, Smokey, will be carried along on this tide of . . . newness. The world will sit up and take notice of this picture, because there was never anything like it before in the history of motion pictures!"

"Mr. Margolis?"

"Yes, Keith?"

"I'd like to suggest we bring Eric von Stroheim back to Hollywood. I can't imagine a more qualified director to tackle a story like this. I know he lost a lot of money for other studios, but he has the merciless eye necessary for a project like *The Samaritan*, in my opinion—"

"Brilliant suggestion, Keith! Von Stroheim is a difficult man, but undeniably a genius! Where is he nowadays? Not in Europe, I hope, cut off from us by the Nazis."

"I'm sure he's in the States, sir. He could be found if you just give the order."

"And speaking of Nazis, Keith, is it possible that this woman and her son are Nazis? You said they're as ugly on the inside as on the outside, so it's not inconceivable that they're followers of Hitler, is it?"

"Well, I hadn't considered that—"

"We'll set the story in Hitler's Germany! Our hero meets and marries the woman just before war breaks out, and the boy is one of those little monsters in the Hitler Youth, always banging on drums and parading and spying on the neighbors to make sure they're good Nazis like himself and his mother, and the reason—are you listening carefully, Keith?—the reason the Samaritan kills them both is because he finds out that they intend to denounce him to the Nazis as a freethinker and Hitler hater which he revealed to them out of anger one night when they were badgering him to join the party, and after he kills them he's able to get away with the deed because there's an air raid and the building the bodies are in is bombed into oblivion! Then our hero escapes from Germany and makes his way across the English Channel to join the British in their fight against Hitler. . . . Wait! He doesn't actually have to kill them! He's tempted to, because he knows they're about to betray him, but before he can pull the trigger the bombs start falling, and *that's* what kills these monsters, proud British bombs!"

Smokey lowered his gun. "Mean to say I play a Kraut?"

"A *good* Kraut, Smokey, and there are such men, I'm sure. Not every apple in the barrel turns bad by association with badness. This is a challenge of the first order, a once-in-a-lifetime role, Smokey. Are you up to such a challenge?"

"Well, shucks, it ain't what I had in mind, exactly."

Moody said, "Smokey, try to imagine that you never played cowboys. Imagine, just for a moment, that you aren't from Texas. Picture yourself as a novice actor, coming from the East, talking like an easterner, like any regular citizen who has had nothing to do with horses and outlaws and guns, et cetera. Imagine that you were never Smokey Hayes. You have an ordinary name, not cowboyish at all, and the key to your new character is that name. Can you conjure up a name that might capture all of that in just a few commonplace syllables, do you think? It's the key to a whole new approach."

Margolis nodded. "I agree, Keith. A new name, not even a very glamorous name, nothing with adventure or romance in it, nothing dashing."

"A name for everyman," Moody continued. "A name you might once have imagined yourself called by, in a time long, long ago—"

"Mmmm—" Smokey began.

"Yes—?"

"Mmmmooort—"

"Say the name out loud. The name that is truly you. Say the name that will let you play the Samaritan like a new man, an actor out of nowhere . . . a natural actor, without artifice, not a shred of phoniness in his soul . . . What is the name of that man?"

"Mmmmmortimer—"

"Mortimer . . . I like that name," said Margolis.

"Mortimer who?" said Moody. "Complete the real name of that real man."

"Mortimer . . . Pence," admitted Smokey, his shoulders rising, squaring themselves. "I'm Mortimer Pence from Rhode Island."

"Absolutely the right name for the man to play this difficult and challenging role," said Margolis. "I congratulate you from the bottom of my heart—Mortimer."

"Mr. Margolis, I just remembered something."

"What did you remember, Keith?"

"The woman, when we first see her, should be hauling her son along in a wagon, one of those play wagons. That was my original inspiration for the story, a woman I saw at a Fourth of July fireworks display. She was hauling her son along in one of those little wagons . . ."

"Very well, Keith, but you must explain why the boy is in the wagon. Obviously he's too old to be moved around like that. An injury?" he suggested.

"A broken ankle . . . ," said Moody, his brow furrowing. "sustained during a rough physical workout at a Hitler Youth camp! They're always pole-vaulting and canoeing and hiking in those places!"

"Perfect, Keith. A brilliant suggestion, if I might say so."

"And the reason why he agrees to being towed along by his mother, which is something no boy would ordinarily submit to, is because she's taking him to see the biggest public rally ever held for the boy's hero, Adolf Hitler, one of those huge nighttime torchlight parades with the swastikas and the marching bands. There's plenty of newsreel footage to borrow for that scene."

"Yes, there is, and I believe we have the essence of the picture nailed down. Genius strikes swiftly, if it strikes at all. Well, Mortimer, are you with us on this perilous undertaking?"

"I . . . suppose so, Mr. Margolis."

Mortimer Pence's voice bore no trace of the open plains, no hint of saloons and trail dust and gun smoke. He sounded like the man he had been before reinventing himself for Hollywood. Moody imagined a psychoanalyst would feel much as he did, witnessing the rebirth of the original man, the emergence of reality from inside the buckskins and boots of a decade's pretense. Mortimer was calm, serene, as he laid down his gun. "I need to study up on Germany and the Nazis, Mr. Margolis, if I'm going to play this role."

"Excellent attitude, Mortimer. Every foot of newsreel we can find will be made available, plus private lectures by experts on the subject. Keith, this will be your next, and most important, project following the final draft of *China Skies*."

"Yes, Mr. Margolis."

"No other writer could do it justice. This story has come from a place deep within you, I can tell."

"Yes, sir, it has."

Moody felt lighthearted. Here was his one authentic story in the process of becoming a screenplay, the long-dormant larva at last granted an opportunity to emerge from darkness as a brilliant butterfly, Moody's masterpiece, rendered on celluloid by the master director von Stroheim. It would be a film of dazzling virtuosity, an instant classic, something the world, as Margolis had said, would sit up and take notice of. A wave of gratitude to Margolis swept through him. Thanks to the head of Empire Productions, a part of Moody that had been for too long denied would, like the resurrection of the identity of Mortimer Pence, come forth at last into its own rightful existence, its place in the sun.

"Mr. Margolis, I just want to say . . . thank you, for this opportunity."

Margolis waved his hand lightly, a great man dismissing homage from his underling. "It's always been my pleasure, Keith, as well as my profession, to bring out the best in creative individuals such as yourself, and Mortimer too, of course. I think today will go down in company history as the beginning of something damned important, and it was we three, like the musketeers of old, who caused this tremendous event to take place. Gentlemen, if I had champagne to hand, I'd propose a toast to us all."

"Yes, sir," said Moody.

"Amen," said Mortimer, with no trace of irony.

Margolis rose from his chair and gestured to the bronze doors at the far end of his office. "We'll discuss all of this further at the earliest available opportunity. Meanwhile, I have an over-burdened schedule I must try to catch up with."

"Yes, Mr. Margolis," said Mortimer, his face glowing with admiration.

Margolis escorted both men to his doors and turned the ornate handles with just the hint of a bow. Mortimer preceded Moody through the doors to the outer office and was instantly pounced upon by two burly men wearing white short-sleeved smocks.

"No!" yelped Mortimer, like a schoolboy dealing with bul-lies, as they wrestled him to the floor. Another figure, squat and bearded, stepped quickly forward and knelt by the downed man, a hypodermic syringe held upright with delicate intent in his hand. The needle was plunged directly into Mortimer's pulsing neck, and he screamed. Moody's hair stood on end at the sound. The man who had found himself moments before now resembled a helpless animal being prepared for slaughter.

"Just a minute," said Moody, "is this necessary?"

Mortimer attempted to scream again, but the drug already was coursing through him, and his breath was overwhelmed by it. He sagged against his captors, eyes upturned. Moody watched as Mortimer was carried away, the man with the syringe return-ing his equipment to a small black medical bag.

Roy Schutt was watching the departing group. Terry Black-well was watching Moody. "Called the cavalry fast as we could," he said.

"Dr. Weichek will look after things," Schutt assured him, "don't you worry."

"But you didn't need to—" Moody attempted to explain. "He was all right. He was *himself* again. . . ."

Schutt went past Moody on his way through the doors. Turning, Moody saw the face of Margolis peering from his office, assessing the receding level of danger. His eyes were bright with contempt for the man being carried away, and that contempt was directed at Moody as his head turned, then Schutt moved between them.

"MM, are you all right?"

"Of course, Roy."

Moody tried to follow Schutt through the doors, but Margolis barred his way.

"Mr. Margolis, are you thinking of another actor, maybe . . . ?"

"For what role? For what production?"

"For . . . *The Samaritan*, Mr. Margolis."

"Never heard of it. Get back to work."

The doors were slammed shut inches from his nose. Moody turned to Blackwell, who wore a look of burgeoning puzzlement on his face.

"Moody, what happened in there?"

Moody followed the path of the departed actor, his ears filled with a steady ringing that was, it seemed to the writer, merely a continuing echo, pitched at a higher tone, of the sound of those bronze doors closing. He began to run.

Outside, Moody saw Mortimer Pence placed in the rear of an ambulance by the men in white smocks. The other man, the needle plunger, stood watching.

"Where are you taking him?" Moody asked.

The bearded man turned. His head was no higher than Moody's chest. Without raising his eyes, he informed the top button on Moody's vest, "The patient will be well looked after."

"Yes, but where are you taking him? You didn't need to do what you did. He was perfectly calm—"

"Please, sir, you must allow professionals to make that decision."

The doors at the rear of the ambulance were closed. One of the men was inside with Mortimer; the other got behind the wheel. The short man opened the passenger side door.

"Dr. Weichek," said Moody, "you must let me visit him."

"How do you know my name?"

"If I don't see him soon, the moment he wakes up would be best. . . . You see, I helped him break free of . . . an actor's mania, I guess you'd call it, and now that he's himself again, it's absolutely essential that I be allowed to see him and help him . . . stay himself, so to speak."

Dr. Weichek shook his head. "I can promise you nothing. The patient has had a serious breakdown. You'll excuse me now."

He got into the ambulance and shut the door. The motor was running by then, and the vehicle began moving away. Moody, beginning to panic, saw discreet green lettering along the side: WEICHEK INSTITUTE.

For the rest of the day he found he could work for only a short while without pausing to review the events that had occurred in Margolis's office. It had been perhaps the most unreal ten minutes in his life, more frightening in its way than his encounter with Tony on the desert road outside Victorville. Only by reminding himself of his contractual obligations to Empire Productions was Moody able to complete several key scenes before preparing to leave for home.

It seemed to Moody he had entered a new and disturbingly alien world, where shifting screens and smoke and mirrors were being manipulated to ensnare him in some conspiracy he would never be allowed fully to understand. He was a mouse, a creature of no significance who had scurried by chance onto a boundless stage in the middle of act 2. All around him rushed shadowy, titanic figures bent on the demands of the plot, aware of Moody the mouse's presence, tolerating him, knowing they could, if it was required of them, simply deviate from their preordained moves by just a fraction and step on him. No more mouse. He wondered if Horace Wheat could shed any light from the wings.

"I BELIEVE I'LL call her Bess. She looks like a Bess, don't you think?"

Wheat could not seem to take his eyes from the dog. She was a handsome bitch, her coat black and curly, eyes shining with intelligence. He had prepared a blanket bed for her in the living room, and she seemed already to have accepted that it was hers. She looked at Wheat and Moody, her tail prepared at any moment to wag, if they should wish it.

"What did you find out about Quentin Yapp?"

"Muriel's brother, all right. What I did was, I asked the kid who works out there with the dogs—Herman's his name—if it was true what I heard, namely that Mrs. Mauser had a close relative called Yapp, and Herman said that she did have a brother who worked in the movie business. I kept him talking, making it all sound innocent enough, you know, asking Herman if he ever wanted autographed photos of movie stars from the fellow. Herman admitted that he'd kind of like a picture of Veronica Lake, only she isn't under contract to the Empire studio, which is where Mrs. Mauser's brother Quentin works. Does that satisfy you, Mr. Moody?"

"Yes. I suppose. Thank you, Mr. Wheat."

"You're looking a tad under the weather, I have to say. Is everything all right?"

"No. Nothing is right. I think there's a possibility that everything is wrong."

"Well now, that's certainly an intriguing statement. Care to explain?"

"Not really."

"Here, Bess."

The dog came willingly to Wheat and licked his proffered

hand. "Instant trust," said Wheat proudly. "She knows I mean her no harm and never will. A dog can always tell who its friends are. That's a faculty it's a shame more humans don't have, in my opinion. Folks'd recognize the ones who want to help them, and the ones who want to do them harm, just by looking, by smelling the air around them, whatever it is that a dog can do. That'd be right handy, wouldn't it, Mr. Moody?"

"Yes, it would. An enemy detector."

"That's right, and a friend detector too. You know, Mr. Moody, I kind of like you, despite the fact that you've been less than forthcoming with me concerning this Mauser and Yapp business. I suspect that you're a man in need of a friend, someone who'll help you work things out, am I right? Is that the kind of friend you need right now, Mr. Moody?"

"Call me Keith. I think they might try to kill me pretty soon."

"Kill you, Keith? Who'd want to do that?"

"I know too much, saw too much. It wasn't my fault, Mr. Wheat. I was drawn in all unsuspecting, like a bird into a turning propeller, and they're going to chop me up, Mr. Wheat."

"I answer to Horace when my friends drop by. You want a stiff shot of bourbon, Keith?"

"Please."

Wheat rose from his chair and moved around the dog, whose eyes followed him to the kitchen. Her ears pricked up at the sound of ice cubes hitting glass, then relaxed when her master reappeared with a bottle and tumblers on a tray. He poured generously and handed Moody his drink.

"Thank you."

"Maybe you should tell me all about it, son."

And Moody did.

ARRIVING HOME AGAIN just after ten o'clock, Moody had barely closed his front door when the phone rang. He picked up the receiver warily, expecting to hear a mysterious and threatening voice at the other end of the line.

"All work and no play makes Jack a dull boy."

"Myra?"

"No, darling, it's Bette Davis here. Is there another flame in your life, you dog?"

"Myra, I've been really busy—"

"Me too, cuddlebumps. You wouldn't believe how they're hustling us along from the front office—hurry hurry, rush rush. You'd think *China Skies* was going to rescue the studio from bankruptcy or something, the fuss they're making."

"The pressure has been building on me too, that's why I haven't called."

"I just wanted you to know that in the long days and lonely nights since our last encounter, I haven't forgotten about you, my only love."

"That's very sweet of you, Myra."

"Oh, gosh—is this Freddie Fanakapan I'm talking to? Freddie Fanakapan the millionaire playboy movie star?"

"No, this is Clark Gable speaking. I'm afraid Freddie's out of the country at the moment, following his conviction on a sordid morals charge. Few among his friends knew that Freddie was romantically involved with his spaniel. The poor beast has been pining ever since he flew the coop."

"Poor Freddie, poor spaniel. Love is so unkind. When are you coming to see me again?"

"I don't know. I'm so busy nowadays I just come straight home and fall into bed."

"That would account for the ten times I called this evening and got no answer. You were caught in the grip of uncontrollable slumber, right?"

"No, I was out, visiting a friend. I just this minute got home."

"Is she sick? Friends that get visited are often sick."

"It's a he, as a matter of fact, and he's quite well. He wanted me to see his new dog."

"Golly Moses, it wasn't a spaniel, was it?"

"Myra, I'm very tired."

"Okay, I can take a hint. You go on to beddie-byes, lover, and be sure you have your milk and dog biscuit, I mean cookie, before you turn the lights out."

"I'll call you tomorrow."

"You're never in the doghouse with me, Keith."

He laughed weakly. "Myra—"

"Hanging up now. So long, Spot."

"Good night, Lassie."

"Keith, that was so clever! You should be a writer."

She hung up. Moody wondered if he should keep her at a distance until he was sure no danger was heading his way from the office of Marvin Margolis.

10

RUSSELL KEYS WAS no longer front-page news. A story consisting entirely of nonresults could not be sustained indefinitely, and the war news swept back to prominence. The entire population of Japanese Americans was being rounded up and shipped away from the coast to camps in Colorado, and General MacArthur had been forced by the Japanese to leave the Philippines, promising that he would return.

Moody set aside the newspaper and faced his typewriter. Today's first assignment was the scene in which Sandy Ryder, as Russell's girlfriend, would read a letter, narrated in voiceover by Bax, assuring her that whatever happened, he would love her always. Sandy would read the letter and crumple it in her hands, then fall down onto her bed, weeping. He dispatched that nonsense within five minutes and moved on to the dogfight scene above the rolling hills of central China, in which the Jap ace Nakamoro would attempt to knock Russell's P-40 out of the sky once and for all, the contest between them having reached a personal level. Russell would send Nakamoro's Zero limping home, trailing a thin plume of smoke behind it, a humiliating reminder that American fighters would not be bested by anything or anyone from the land of Nippon.

Shortly before noon, Myra entered his office and locked the door behind her. She pulled the curtains, then began peeling

clothes from her body with comical haste. Moody watched, slightly dazed, as she reached her slip and bra. These were tossed in his direction. "Come on, Keith, for God's sake. I'm not here to change your ribbon."

Moody loosened his tie, then his belt, without removing either item. Myra completed the task and yanked down his slacks, having achieved total nudity herself, then applied her attention to the erection beginning to nudge the front of Moody's boxer shorts. Moody surrendered with grace and was pushed in the direction of the sofa Mortimer Pence had passed out on several days before, when he had still been Smokey Hayes.

Their coupling, vividly brief, was accomplished with a minimum of noise that might have attracted attention from outside. At no time was Moody able to step completely out of his pants, and when Myra was done with him, he fell onto the floor, his ankles entangled in silk and cotton.

"I'm trapped by my trousers," he said without sadness.

"At least they hide those awful argyle socks. Are you at all in love with me?"

"Yes, I am, I admit it."

"Good. There's a razor in my purse, and I would have cut your balls off if you'd said no."

"I like a woman who takes her love life seriously."

Myra began dressing. "This is supposed to be my lunch break. I'm starved. Think there'll be any tuna casserole left?"

"Why don't we find out together?"

"Why, you romantic fool, you."

His mood, made buoyant by contact with Myra, was unable to sustain its lightness. By the time he faced dessert, Moody's eyes were fixed on his tray, but he did not see the cherry cobbler there. He was with Myra, he told himself, and he had decided, hadn't he, that she should be kept away from him until all danger had passed.

"If you're not going to eat that," said Myra, "I am."

"Of course."

He pushed the plate toward her. She ignored it, watching him.

"Keith, either this is some kind of postcoital *tristesse*, or you're very much in need of a vitamin shot."

He looked up at her. "We shouldn't be seen together anymore. It isn't safe."

"Who's going to get upset? We're neither of us married. Or is that the problem? Not only not married to other people, but not married to each other. There's no morals clause that's enforceable in Hollywood. This is the new Sodom. No, make that the new Gomorrah. I think they were a bit behind the Gomorrahns in Sodom. That was a joke, Keith. Oh well, never mind. I'll just go ahead and eat your cherry dessert as if you heard a word I'm saying and could care less."

"Please—you shouldn't be anywhere near me. Things are happening to me."

"What things?'

"I can't discuss it."

"Awfully convenient. Have you been hitting the booze a bit too hard recently? Are the things that happen to you small and furry, and they only come out when the bottle does?"

"I simply can't explain it to you. You mustn't know."

"Oh, I see. You're beginning to worry me now."

"Good, that way you'll stay away."

"I'll do no such thing. Lunch break just wouldn't be the same without you to ravage behind locked doors."

"I'm absolutely serious."

"You're absolutely daffy. Fortunately I can overlook this, being fond of you."

"Myra, have you heard any kind of rumor around the studio that . . . someone was . . . is blackmailing Empire?"

"No, should I?"

"And has anyone seen Mort—Smokey Hayes recently?"

"I heard he'd been thrown off the lot and told not to show his face again. You should know why, after the way he behaved. Are you saying someone's blackmailing us over Smokey's rotten behavior?"

Moody laughed. "I wish someone was. I could forget about that."

"Then what?"

"Nothing."

"I'm thinking of shoving this dessert in your puss."

"I'm trying to do what's right for you, please believe me."

"And this means I have to buzz off, does it?"

"For the time being, yes, regrettably."

She studied his face. "All right, I'm going to buy the Brooklyn Bridge. I'm going to accept what you say, even though you haven't said anything that makes the least sense, and I'm going to keep away from you for a while. Not a long while, Keith, and I'll expect a full and complete account of your behavior before too much longer. Do we have a deal?"

"Thank you. I can't be worrying about you too."

"Are you really involved in something nasty?"

Moody said nothing.

THEY MET IN daylight this time, on a Saturday in Elysian Park, so Horace could walk his dog.

"Took me ten minutes to teach her to heel," he said proudly. "That's the smartest dog I ever had. I swear she can just about understand English."

Having learned that Bess had cost him sixty dollars, Moody was glad Horace took pleasure in her. They walked along the pathways, Bess sniffing the ground at every step, yet never pulling against her leash.

Horace handed a folded newspaper to Moody. "Page four," he said.

Moody read a short article concerning the discovery of a body locked inside a public toilet at a picnic site several miles south of Victorville. Local police had linked the corpse with a vehicle abandoned in a town parking lot. Documents in the vehicle identified the dead man as Clarence Anthony White, age thirty-one, of West Covina. The case was listed as a homicide. Readers were invited to contact the police with any relevant information. Moody handed the newspaper back after checking the date.

"This is yesterday's. I suppose you found out something about him?"

"Didn't have to," said Horace, producing another newspaper from his jacket.

"This one's today's. Page one."

MURDERED MAN
KNEW MISSING TIGER ACE

Moody stopped walking. Bess sniffed his shoes as he read. "Tony" White was an aeromechanic recently returned from China, where he had served as a member of the ground crew for the Flying Tigers. White had serviced the P-40 flown by Russell Keys. It was not known if the two men had been friends, but with one man missing and the other murdered, there was cause for inquiry into the possibility of some kind of conspiracy or plot, in the view of the reporter.

"This is going to make Marvin Margolis eat the rug," Moody concluded.

"If it's Margolis who's behind all this. Could be Quentin Yapp. It's Yapp's brother-in-law who pulled the trigger."

"Yapp's not an important enough man at Empire to be ordering guns for hire."

"Any idea why Tony would want to blackmail someone he worked alongside of?"

"He was blackmailing Empire, not Russell. I guess he

thought Russell was dead, so he could go ahead and try to make some easy cash. It's still a despicable thing to do, regardless."

"Killing a woman, that's kind of despicable too, wouldn't you say?"

"I'm not trying to excuse Russell's act. It's all a cesspit—what he did, what Tony did, what Margolis and Empire are doing . . . and what I'm doing."

"Trying to find out the facts? Nothing wrong with that."

"No, I mean writing this absurd screenplay. It has absolutely nothing to do with Russell. Even before I found out he was a murderer I knew it had nothing to do with him. It's just garbage for Mr. and Mrs. America, a story about a hero no real man could ever measure up to, but I'm supposed to portray him as a typical product of the U.S.A., and I'm doing just that, because they're paying me good money to. I'm a criminal too."

"Taking it a mite too far, aren't you, Keith? Exaggeration, that's your crime, as I see it. Doesn't compare to murder, not by a long shot."

"But I should be accusing Margolis, talking to the police about what I suspect."

Horace shook his head. "Think that'd get you anything but fired? You don't have a scrap of evidence that says he's got any part in this mess. All you've got is the fact that Yapp is related by marriage to the blackmailer's killer."

"The cops might lean on Yapp and get him to start talking about Margolis. Who else but Margolis has the motive to want to squash any bad news about my cousin the hero? The studio has a lot of money and prestige invested in this production. I'll bet it was Margolis who told Yapp to find someone capable of murder, so the story about Russell and the prostitute would never reach the public and put an end to *China Skies*."

"If that's true, then Yapp might keep his mouth shut for fear he'll get the same treatment Tony did. Anyone sucked into a shady deal like this, he watches his back all the time and keeps his lips locked. I'll say it again—you don't have proof of anything."

"Then what do I *do*?"

"You keep on writing your picture and collecting your paycheck. You didn't kill anyone. You think you know who did, but that and a nickel gets you coffee. Stay low, is my advice. I don't pretend to be any kind of moral authority, but you take a cold hard look at what's happened, and you'll see two interesting facts: Your cousin killed a woman, and now it seems pretty sure he met his own death under unpleasant circumstances up in the mountains. Tony tries to cash in on this, and winds up dead too. Both men deserved what they got, if you believe in a God that dishes out punishment."

"I'm an atheist."

"That doesn't matter if you know the difference between right and wrong."

"You're saying I should forget all of it, pretend it never happened?"

"You're not the pretending, forgetting kind. I'm saying you want to watch your own back for a while. Someday all this will blow over, and you'll still have your job and your health. What's done is done. I won't charge you for the philosophizing."

Moody patted Bess's curly head. "Dogs have it simple," he said.

"They do."

"All right, I'll take your advice. I have a girl. I don't want any of this to rub off on her. If lying low keeps me out of things, it keeps her out too."

"It's a practical decision. Doesn't mean you have to be happy about it."

"That's my problem."

"Exactly. You know, Keith, you and I see things the same, pretty much."

"I'll take that as a compliment, Horace."

"Best way to take it, I'd say. Let's just give Bess her head while we're here."

Horace unhooked the leash and his dog bounded away in pursuit of interesting scents.

"Horace, I want to visit Mortimer Pence. I want you to come with me. I want you to see what happened to a man who couldn't tell fact from fantasy for years, and then found out that fantasy can be less cruel."

"I'd be happy to see him," said Horace, watching his dog. "Look at her go!"

THE WEICHEK INSTITUTE was in Big Tujunga Canyon, where it clung, hugely white with a red-tiled roof, to the slope behind it, like a Tibetan lamasery. Moody parked his car and left the windows open a little for Bess; then he and Horace approached the entrance.

"Big place," said Horace.

Moody had already noticed that all the windows were barred, the bars having been painted the same bright white as the walls to disguise their purpose.

A sign in gold leaf on polished oak stood squarely in the vast entry hall, where a newcomer could not fail to see it and lose heart.

"Visiting by appointment only," Horace read aloud.

His voice carried to the front desk, where a woman in nurse's whites looked up from whatever work she was engaged in. She beckoned them forward. Moody's shoes made a tapping sound on the black-and-white-checkered tiles; Horace had dressed casually for their meeting and wore rubber soles.

"How may I help you, gentlemen?"

"We'd like to see a friend of ours, Mortimer Pence."

The woman, possessing all the attributes of a head nurse as prescribed by Central Casting—thick body, bunned hair, a well-scrubbed persona—consulted a ledger before her, then looked up, her features still wearing the same smile she had greeted them with.

"I'm afraid Mr. Pence is not allowed visitors today."

"What day *is* he allowed visitors?" Moody asked.

"That can only be determined by a qualified member of the staff."

"Could we talk with one, please?"

"I'm sorry, but no one is available at the present time."

"How about Dr. Weichek?"

"Dr. Weichek is in Chicago attending a conference."

"Then how are we able to see Mr. Pence?"

She handed Moody a pad and pencil. "Just jot down your names, addresses, and phone numbers, and I'll arrange for visitation at the earliest convenient time."

Moody was about to begin writing when Horace laid a hand firmly on his wrist. "Now then, son," he said, "you know you aren't supposed to write so much as a shopping list till that sprain heals completely. Just you let me attend to this."

To the woman he said, as he slid the pad away from Moody and began writing, "Tennis injury. My boy's got this idea he's a tennis-playing man, but his wrists are weak. Gets it from me."

"The therapeutic exercises have helped tremendously, though," Moody contributed. "I really think I can write our names, Dad."

"All taken care of," said Horace, handing the pad back to the woman, who studied it, still smiling.

"We'll certainly be in touch, Mr. Johnson."

"Thank you. Good day."

Moody and Horace began walking back across the hall to the glassed entrance doors. A young man with an athlete's build, his torso tightly encased in a white smock, was entering the hall from outside. He stepped aside to allow the visitors to depart, then continued on into the building. Moody and Horace walked to the car.

"That big fellow," Moody said, "he was one of the men who took Mortimer away."

"Think he recognized you?"

"When Mortimer was nabbed it was pretty hectic. I'm probably just another guy with glasses to him. Why didn't you want us to identify ourselves back there? This place has nothing to do with Yapp or Margolis. I don't understand."

"I'd call it a prudent move to keep ourselves faceless."

"Then how do we get notified when it's time to visit Mortimer? You left a phony address and phone number too."

"We'll find another way to visit your friend."

"By the way, I think calling me Jim Johnson junior is pushing the bounds of alliteration too far."

"Sorry, Junior. Look, maybe I'm being overcautious. We don't know anything for sure. Hey there, Bess girl!"

The dog was attempting to push her eager snout through the window space.

Horace teased the end of her nose while Moody unlocked the car.

Horace said, "I don't like the feeling I get from this place."

"It's just some kind of rest home," said Moody.

"Rest homes encourage their patrons to stroll around the grounds. See anyone out here? You don't need barred windows on a rest home."

"If it's a prison, where's the wall? Where's the locked gate? We drove up and walked right in. There's nothing sinister about it."

They got into the car.

"This friend of yours," said Horace, "is he connected to the China movie?"

"No, he's just an actor who had a nervous breakdown."

"Then maybe I'm wrong."

They drove away.

FOR MOST OF Saturday night Moody worked on the *China Skies* script, pausing only to drink coffee and visit the bathroom.

The air in his apartment became thick with cigarette smoke; he was fast becoming a two-pack-a-day man under the intense pressure Margolis seemed to require, and he hammered at his typewriter with a vengeance, smacking out scene after scene crafted according to the golden rules of Hollywood, which stated that in a story of this kind the hero must never suffer a moment's hesitation, and never exhibit anything other than moral probity of the rough-hewn type preferred by audiences nationwide.

His depiction of Russell was a clean-cut joke, but it didn't matter anymore. The subject of the script was doubtless owl food by now, as Yapp had suggested, and his erstwhile associate, the aeromechanic, was dead also, for having attempted to reveal the truth. Too much blood under the bridge, Moody told himself. None of it would ever be made public; Marvin Margolis would see to that, even if it meant ordering Yapp to set Eddie Mauser on Moody's trail to shut him up.

Moody elected to shut himself up. That way he would live, and be paid well for the living, for as long as he maintained silence. It was not a bad deal, not something he would be unable to live with as time passed. His position as screenwriter at Empire would be made secure not only by delivery of the kind of script Margolis wanted but by his ability to refrain from rocking the Empire boat. His reward for quiet cooperation would be a steadily rising income, and maybe one day the chance to write something worthwhile. Every now and then Hollywood produced, by fluke or accident, a movie of worth. The most he could hope for was the opportunity to see his name in the credits for just such a production. He was not greedy. He did not want the world at his feet, just a chance to show what he could really do. Moody felt he deserved that much.

His phone rang. Moody stubbed out his latest Chesterfield and picked up the receiver. He thought it might be Myra.

"Hello?"

There was no sound at the other end, then he detected breathing, hoarse breathing.

"Myra, is that you? Your heavy-breathing act is less than humorous."

His caller said nothing. Moody began to be a little irritated; he was being kept from important work by someone who had promised she would stay away from him for a while.

"Myra, I'm very busy. I told you I needed to be left alone for certain reasons, and you said you would. I can't afford this kind of distraction. Myra?"

The breathing stopped. "Thank you for that, at least," said Moody. "I can't think of anything witty to respond with; after all, this is my third obscene call this evening."

He waited for her to reply. Instead, he heard the whining of a dog.

BY DRIVING HARD he was able to reach Horace's house in eleven minutes. The ambulance he had called for before he set out had beaten him there and was parked by the curb, its red light spinning in violation of the blackout. Moody ran his wheels carelessly up onto the grass and raced into the house. Neighbors had gathered on their front lawns to witness the drama.

Horace lay on his back in the converted garage, Bess standing by his side. The telephone lay within his reach, the receiver yanked from its place on the desk. Two ambulance orderlies were checking for signs of life.

"You the one that called?" the first one asked.

"Yes. Is he all right?"

The second orderly, an older man, stood up. Moody heard his knees pop.

"Friend of yours?"

"Yes—please, is he all right?"

"No, sir, he isn't all right. He's dead, I'm sorry to say."

"Oh Jesus . . ."

"Heart attack, it looks like to me."

"They'll do a thorough examination," the younger man said.

"Full autopsy," assured his partner, "but I'm betting it's his heart. Seen it plenty of times. A man his age, it isn't uncommon. That his dog?"

"Yes—"

"Anyone else live here? Family?"

"No, he was on his own."

"Could I ask you to sign a few papers, just a formality, before we take him away? Ordinarily it'd be a family member."

"I'll sign. Where are you taking him?"

"Los Angeles County Morgue. Can we ask you to take care of things here, sir? There's the dog, for one thing."

"Yes, of course. When . . . when can I talk with a doctor about . . . what killed him?"

"Oh, late Monday maybe, if there isn't a backlog. Saturday night, that sometimes means a lot of work. It's the heart, though, I'd bet on it."

A stretcher was brought in from the ambulance. Moody fondled Bess's ears to stop her whining as Horace was loaded onto it and carried out. He had to shut her in the garage to prevent her following the stretcher through the house and out the front door to the curb and the ambulance's yawning doors. Moody watched as the red light was turned off. The ambulance drove away slowly, and the neighbors began drifting back indoors.

A woman older than Horace approached Moody. She wore a wrap around her shoulders despite the night air's mildness. "I'm Mrs. Gilroy," she said, "from across the street. He's gone, isn't he?"

"Yes," said Moody, "he's gone."

"Natural?" asked Mrs. Gilroy, her dentures producing the faintest whistle.

"They'll be doing an autopsy, they said." Moody wanted her to go away so he could think, and think some more, until he understood what had happened.

"Not suicide, then."

"Oh, no, not that. Definitely not."

"The reason I ask, gentlemen his age, after their wife dies, you see, they sometimes get lonely and morbid about things. He never struck me as that type, I have to say. I'm glad anyway it was natural. His wife, she was a lovely woman. She went eighteen months ago." Mrs. Gilroy pulled the wrap tighter around herself. "Well, reunited in the great beyond, as they say."

"Yes, I'm sure."

"Was it you here before?"

"Before? Oh, I've been here several times lately."

"Before it happened. Tonight, I mean."

"Tonight?"

"Only there was someone in there with him, earlier. I saw both their shadows just for a second, on the blinds. They were moving around, so I can't be sure. Was it you?"

"No," said Moody, "it wasn't me."

"Well, they're together again now," Mrs. Gilroy insisted.

"Excuse me."

Moody went inside and closed the front door. He released Bess from the garage and she went to the door, whining again. Moody went into the garage and stood for some time, attempting to reconcile the fallen phone and the departure of Horace Wheat on a blanketed stretcher.

Bess joined him, sniffing at the floor where Horace had lain dead. Moody hadn't the least idea what to do next.

He stared at the filing cabinets and, for lack of any sensible alternative, went to the nearest and pulled its sliding door out. The cabinet was empty. He went to the others and opened each in turn, only to find them filled with nothing but air. The last cabinet was not empty; a series of folders was arranged alphabetically in metal clips, some half dozen in all, representing, Moody supposed, the entire caseload of Horace Wheat, investigator.

He extracted them all, sat on a chair, and began reading. They were trivial cases, low-level spying on cheating spouses for the most part, and one request to ferret out the facts concerning a man who had invited a widow to invest her savings in a Bolivian silver mine. It was dismal reading, and only after he was done did it occur to Moody that one file was made outstanding by its absence—the file on himself.

Bess placed her jaw on his thigh and gazed at Moody's face. He patted her head, then found himself doing something he could not recall having done in years: Moody began to cry. He could not identify the exact source of his grief. It might have been the loss of an acquaintance who quickly had become a friend and confidant, or it might have been fear for his own safety, taking the shape of shadows the neighbor had seen on Horace's blinds. It might have been the eloquent sadness in the eyes of Horace Wheat's new dog. Whatever the reason, Moody succumbed for several minutes, until his shaking and stifled sobs drove Bess to renew her own whining.

Moody stood up, spilling the forlorn manila folders he had been reading from onto the floor.

"Enough," he said. "You're coming home with me."

HE DROVE WITHOUT direction for most of Sunday, unable to work on the script. Bess rode with him, her nose to the wind, as he followed one road to the next, and the next, winding his way through the hills and arroyos of outer Los Angeles. He wanted very badly to be with Myra, to tell her everything and share his burden, but Moody could not bring himself to turn the wheel in her direction. He had shared everything with Horace, and Horace was dead. Had he been frightened to death by his shadowy visitor? Maybe Mrs. Gilroy had been mistaken, and no one had been with him until the ambulance arrived. Maybe Horace had succumbed to an ordinary heart attack, and died simply because he was old.

"I don't know anything," Moody told the dog, then added, "and I don't want to."

There. He had said it aloud, even if his audience was dumb. It was admission of his own cowardice, Moody admitted, but he accepted that he preferred it this way.

Horace had died of natural causes, therefore Moody need fear nothing along similar lines for himself. He had not gone to the police with his suspicions over Quentin Yapp and the abrupt solution to Tony White's attempted blackmail, so he was not in disfavor at Empire. He had to shut up and keep writing and hope nothing bad would happen. Of course, once he had finished the script it was entirely possible that he might be rubbed out anyway, as a means of ensuring the truth would remain buried forever.

Moody stepped on the brakes, sending Bess sprawling onto the floor. The car slewed sideways off the asphalt and plowed dust from the shoulder before coming to a halt, blanketed by its own cloudy wake. Bess looked at him with reproach.

"Sorry," Moody told her.

He got out of the car and was joined by the dog. Together they walked a few yards to the nearest overlook along the road, giving a fine view of Pasadena and the city beyond. He could see the massive concrete barns of Empire Productions and other major studios to the southwest. Haze and distance gave them the appearance of sepulchres, row upon mighty row of Olympian burial vaults, the home of dead gods. He was aware, gazing at them, that a sacrifice would have to be made if he intended worshiping at the altar of those gods. The sacrifice would be himself, and he was willing to make it. What was done was done. It had not been pretty, but it had been justifiable, according to the laws of the jungle spread below him. A threat to the system had been thwarted, nipped in the bud before it could bloom into poisonous life and grow like a rampant vine, strangling the livelihoods of men like himself who had done no wrong. It was better this way. It was over and done with, and he had survived. No one would hurt him, because he had hurt no one, and intended never to do so. He was not a hero.

"I have my life to live," he said to Bess, who turned to him briefly, then looked away. They watched the city and Pacific horizon together. Somewhere beyond Moody's vision, men were sailing west to confront the Japanese with steel and blood. He would see none of that, but he might, if Empire looked on him with favor, be chosen to write a movie about the conflict taking place beyond the curve of the world. It was all he could do, after all.

BESS WENT WITH him to the studio on Monday morning. Moody arrived at his office clutching a sheaf of script pages in one hand and a leash in the other. He apportioned a corner of the floor for Bess, but she made it known she preferred the sofa, and Moody allowed it rather than waste time training her to accept the carpet. She had already begun to sleep at the end of his bed, on top of the covers, and he had been unable to deny her the closeness she seemed anxious to have from him.

He was, he calculated, somewhere between three-fifths and two-thirds of the way through the first draft of *China Skies* and was proud of himself. The scenes were all that was required, and he had produced them with record speed. He rolled fresh paper into his typewriter and took up where he had left off late on Saturday evening.

The scene was the humble dwelling of Lin-Ming. Russell had just brought home, in a motorcycle sidecar, Lin-Ming's little brother, Chin-Li. They had detoured en route from the hospital to Chin-Li's house, providing plenty of opportunity for narrow escapes at high speed along the way, the joke being that Russ, for all his prowess in the air, was a menace behind the handlebars of the machine he had only recently learned how to use. As he and Chin-Li pulled up in a cloud of dust and squawking chickens, Lin-Ming came outside to see what the commotion was all about. She and her brother exchanged a few words in Chinese, then Chin-Li said to Russell that he had been ordered to attend to the animals, all of which had been neglected while the boy was in the hospital. Exit Chin-Li.

RUSS

You're just about the best-looking lady this flyboy ever saw, Lin-Ming. I wouldn't say so ordinarily, but I know you don't understand a word of what

I'm saying, so what the heck. Every time I look at you I see someone I could get real fond of. That's what I'm trying to say, and it's not as easy as you might think, even if you can't understand me.

Moody knew the scene would be a success, because the audience would already have learned that Lin-Ming spoke English, having been taught by missionaries, only to keep this a secret from Russ out of traditional Chinese shyness. Russ was being set up for embarrassment of the nicest kind.

The knock at his door was perfunctory. Moody barely had time to look up before Quentin Yapp was in the room. Bess's head rose as Yapp entered, and she began to growl.

"Jesus Christ, Moody, what the hell's that?"

"It's a giraffe, what did you think?"

"Very funny. There's a studio policy against pets, Moody, or maybe you don't know that. No animals where there's only supposed to be humans, it says. Why'd you bring it, anyway, huh? That a Seeing Eye dog? You went blind, Moody?"

"What do you want, Yapp?"

"Yapp? Yapp you call me? Quentin, for chrissakes. Not Yapp, not between friends is what I'm saying."

"You can keep on calling me Moody."

"Okay, okay—Keith."

"No, I like Moody. It's less . . . how shall I put it . . . It's less like a floating turd."

"Turd? What's with the turd? You got a mental condition today, Moody—Keith?"

"My dog doesn't like you. Has she seen you before somewhere?"

"I don't like dogs, and dogs don't like me. Never have, never will. I live my life without dogs. No dogs, nohow. So listen, the script, it's okay? It's good? Or what? Speak to me, huh? They want to know."

"Who does?"

"Schutt, Blackwell, the usual. You got more pages? Gimme. I'll take 'em over, save you the trouble."

"Are you keeping an eye on me, Yapp?"

"What eye? They asked, I was heading this way, they said pick up those new pages. They like what you did so far, Moody. Don't fuck it up now, is my message."

"You tell them they'll get everything at the end of the day, when I'm ready to hand it over. You don't touch my work, Yapp, not ever. You can tell them I said so."

"Who wants to touch! I'm here to be nice! You're someone else today, is what I think."

"Get out."

"Jesus, what a way to act. Don't think I won't tell certain parties about this, Moody. You get cute, you mouth off, you get sorry, fast. Don't kid me you don't know what I'm saying. You wise up, Moody, and quit with the mouth."

Bess would not stop her low growling until Yapp left the room.

MONDAY EVENING AFTER leaving the studio, Moody drove to the Los Angeles County Morgue, stated his request for an interview with whichever doctor had performed the autopsy on Horace Wheat, and was told to wait.

He did so, reading an old *National Geographic* magazine containing pictures of African women with amazingly long necks encased in hoops of copper wire. He wondered what kept their vertebrae from separating under such abnormal stretching, but the article did not enlighten him.

"Mr. Moody?"

A middle-aged man wearing a stained smock was approaching him, lighting a cigarette. He carried a clipboard under his arm.

"Dr. Stern," he said.

"Hello."

"You're wanting to hear about a gentleman by the name of Wheat, is that right?"

"Yes."

Stern sat down, and Moody took his own seat again. Stern dragged deeply on his cigarette. "Cardiac arrest," he said, blasting exhaled smoke past Moody's ear.

"Just a plain heart attack?"

"Correct. Was Mr. Wheat on any kind of medication?"

"I don't know. Why?"

"Oh, there was a hypo mark on his arm. I thought it was a scratch at first, but there was a definite puncture, like he'd injected himself, then knocked the needle sideways accidentally."

"A needle? Why would he inject himself with anything?"

"Mr. Moody, surely you know that some people are dope addicts."

"Not this man. No!"

Stern held up the hand with the cigarette in a placatory gesture.

"Don't get upset. I know he wasn't an addict. After I noticed the puncture I ran some standard tests, and there was nothing in him, believe me."

"Then why was there a puncture mark?"

"I was hoping you could tell me. I assume no syringe was found at the scene."

"No, nothing like that. If there were no drugs inside him, why was there a needle mark? Why would he be injected with nothing?"

"I don't know. Maybe the puncture was older than it looked, and whatever it was that he used, it wasn't in his system anymore."

"Could there be drugs that you aren't equipped to test for?"

"Exotic drugs?"

"Yes. Curare and that kind of thing."

"I think I heard about something like that on *The Shadow*."

"Doctor, I'm serious. I want another autopsy, one that will look for drugs that aren't covered by your standard tests, something unusual and untraceable."

Stern checked his clipboard. "You're listed here as a friend of the deceased."

"Yes."

"Can I ask what profession you're in, Mr. Moody?"

"I'm a screenwriter for Empire Productions."

"Do you write thrillers?"

"I write . . . I *wrote* Westerns."

"I see. And you think we haven't done our job, is that right?"

"I think . . . I think that someone murdered Mr. Wheat. I didn't think so until you said you found a puncture mark that looked like something caused by violence. He struggled when they put the needle in, that's what I think."

"They?"

"Whoever killed him."

"Why would someone want to kill an old man, Mr. Moody?"

"Because . . . I don't know why, but they did!"

"Please don't raise your voice. Sir, do you know how many dead people we have coming through here in the course of an average twenty-four hours? A lot of people, and we have to attend to them all, determining what it was that caused them to die, and doing a pretty good job under conditions that sometimes are less than ideal, but we do our best, Mr. Moody, and that means reaching the conclusion we feel is correct."

"All I'm saying is, you should check for other drugs."

Stern dropped his cigarette onto the floor and ground it out with his shoe.

"Mr. Moody, I don't want to make light of your grief, but concocting bizarre murder plots against your friend won't bring him back."

"Excuse me, but I'm not concocting anything."

Stern stood up. "I think this is about as far as we can take this conversation, don't you?"

"Yes, I do," said Moody, standing also. "I want to speak to whoever is in charge here. I demand to speak to him now."

"With what object in mind, Mr. Moody?"

"With the object in mind of making an official request that further examination be made of the body of Horace Wheat."

"I could let you talk with my supervisor if you want, but there's very little point."

"Oh, and why is that?"

"We no longer have the cadaver."

"Pardon me?"

"Mr. Wheat's body has already been collected for burial."

"What! When—?"

Stern consulted his clipboard. "About an hour ago."

"But . . . who took him?"

"Resthaven Funeral Home, in Glendale. All signed for as per normal. You look a little surprised, Mr. Moody. Apparently you aren't the only one concerned for Mr. Wheat, and these other people are taking practical steps to cope with his death in a dignified manner, not making up stories about murder and plots . . . Mr. Moody!"

Moody was running down the corridor.

"Get some help, Mr. Moody!" was the advice shouted after him.

RESTHAVEN FUNERAL HOME was still open despite the failing light in the sky. Moody left Bess in the car and ran inside. The foyer, a set designer's dream in deep purple velvet, was empty. Moody saw a small silver bell on an ornate table and rang it frantically. Almost immediately a man came gliding out from behind a set of purple drapes, a professional smile tugging at his mouth.

"Do excuse me for being absent, sir. How may I help you?"

"Horace Wheat, he's here, isn't he?"

"Wheat, sir?"

"Horace Wheat. He's a dead man, and he was taken from the Los Angeles County Morgue just this evening, so he's still here, yes?"

"Ah, the late arrival. Yes, sir, Mr. Wheat is with us."

"I want to see him, please, before you put makeup on him and dress him up. I want to see his arm. And I want you to call the police and have them hold his body until another autopsy can be performed."

"Makeup, sir, for Mr. Wheat?"

"Hold the makeup! No makeup and no dressup for the coffin, and get the police here now!"

"Sir, we never apply cosmetic restoration unless instructed to do so by the bereaved. Sadly, to my knowledge, there is no family in this case."

"So you didn't do anything to him yet."

"We make it our practice not to prepare the deceased if there is to be no viewing by family members and friends in the Chapel of Repose. There would be no point, would there, sir?"

"No, no point at all, so can I see him, please? I'm his nephew."

"See him?"

"In the coffin. I don't care if he's been prepared or not, I just want to see him. And could I use your phone to call the police?"

"Police?"

"My uncle was murdered. Poisoned. It was a warning."

"Warning, sir?"

"To keep my mouth shut! But I won't! Where is he—?"

"Your uncle, sir?"

The mortician was clasping his hands tightly, struggling to maintain his smile in such close proximity to a madman.

"Where the fuck is he!"

"He . . . I regret to say, sir . . . he's in the Chamber of Immortal Flame, you see—"

"The what?"

"The . . . the oven, sir. Our instructions were to cremate the deceased immediately."

"Oh, God . . . You *burned* him?"

"Those were our instructions, sir."

Moody slumped onto a purple-cushioned chair. "Who gave the instructions?" he asked.

"The physician of the deceased, sir. We were told there was no family. . . ."

"His name?"

"The physician, sir? Weichek, I believe. Dr. Wendell Weichek."

ARRIVING HOME AND parking the car outside his apartment, Moody was aware that his mind was beginning to fog. Too much was happening. He could not keep attempting to fit together the jigsaw puzzle assembling itself in his head. The missing pieces were lurking at the periphery of his vision, dancing there, tantalizingly out of reach. He must ignore them. If he should ever grasp the emerging pattern fully, the completed picture would be unbearable—a gun aimed at his head; his car careening off a cliff and bursting into flame; a knife attack in a narrow alley. One moment he wanted to rush to the nearest police station and tell them everything; the next moment he wanted to hide under his bed and wait for a year or so to pass. Caught in a vortex allowing no escape, Moody felt himself spinning faster and faster, losing all notion of his place in the world, and he could think of no way to make it stop that would not break him apart.

Bess ran from the car and up the apartment stairs, then

began barking. Hurrying after her, afraid of what he might find waiting for him, Moody stopped several steps short of the top. Two men were standing by his door, one of them keeping an eye on Bess, the other watching Moody. If Bess had not already been mere feet away from them, Moody would have considered turning and making a run for it, but the fact that the dog was within striking distance of what he assumed were gunmen kept him rooted to the spot. *This dog is going to be the death of me*, he thought.

"Keith Moody?"

"No—"

"Police. Are you Keith Moody?"

"Not . . . necessarily. May I see your badges?"

The two men exchanged a look. Both wore long coats and broad hats; they might be cops, they might be mobsters. The taller one was dragging something from inside his coat. Moody expected to see the barrel of a pistol aimed at him, but it was a wallet containing a badge. The second cop was doing the same.

"Call the dog off, Moody," he said.

"Bess!"

She came to him, growling with discontent. Moody went to his door and unlocked it. Bess dashed through ahead of the men. Moody turned on the lights. The tall man had a mustache, the shorter man was clean shaven.

"Lieutenant Huttig, Sergeant Labiosa." Huttig was the tall one. "We need to ask you a few questions, Moody."

"This is in relation to what, exactly?"

"Your cousin the flyboy," said Labiosa.

"Have they found him?"

"If they found him, we'd be reporters come to visit," Huttig said, "not cops."

"I don't think I understand."

"The thing is, Moody," said Huttig, "there's stuff we don't understand either."

"So what we need," said Labiosa, "is for you to take a little drive with us."

"To the station?"

"No, not the station," said Huttig.

"Somewhere else," said his partner. "Now would be a good time for us."

"Is this a good time for you, Moody?"

"I suppose so. Can you be more specific about this?"

"When we get there we'll be specific as hell," Labiosa said.

"I'll just leave some food for my dog, if that's all right."

"Bring your dog along," said Huttig, smiling. "We like dogs, don't we, Vinnie?"

"We love dogs," Labiosa agreed, "especially faggoty poodle dogs."

Huttig said, "They're our favorite kind."

The drive to El Monte did not take long. Vinnie Labiosa turned off the road onto a long dirt driveway. At the end of the driveway was what appeared to be a farmhouse, but there were far too many dogs, their barking and howling awakening in Moody's ears the gradual scream of alarm bells. He knew now where they had brought him, and why Bess had been included. There was another police car parked haphazardly in the dirt yard, and a county coroner's ambulance, and the late-model Buick Moody had tailed from Victorville to the Orinoco Apartments in Monterey Park.

As the cruiser came to a stop by the front door, Huttig turned to Moody and asked, "Ever been here before?"

"No, never."

"Let's stretch our legs a little bit," Labiosa suggested.

The instant all three men stepped out of the car a barrage of renewed barking came from the nearby kennels. In the darkness all Moody could see of these was a series of tall wire fences. Bess was whining, staying close to his legs.

"Inside," said Huttig.

The farmhouse was small and not very clean. The smell of dogs was everywhere. There were two ambulance orderlies in the living room and a police officer in the kitchen.

In the bedroom, on the floor, were two dead people, a man and a woman. Both appeared to have been shot. They lay with their limbs sprawled at awkward angles, unreal in death as the dummies tossed off cliffs and buildings in front of turning movie cameras. The woman's eyes were open. Moody recognized the man: Eddie Mauser.

"Ever seen these folks before, Moody?"

"No."

"Hear those dogs outside?" Labiosa asked.

"Yes."

"Know what kind they all are?"

"No, how could I?"

"They're black poodles," Huttig said, "just like that one of yours."

"Really?"

"Yeah, really. Still say you were never here before?"

"Yes, I do."

Huttig called to the cop in the kitchen, "Get that Herman kid back in here."

The cop left. Labiosa farted. "No dinner," he said. "My guts are cramping."

Huttig said to Moody, "Sure you don't want to change your story?"

"No. What does this place have to do with my cousin?"

"We're here to find that out, aren't we?"

"Who killed these people?"

"Maybe you did, Moody."

"Don't be ridiculous, please."

"He's polite," said Labiosa. "Notice how he says please?"

"Some of the worst killers I ever came across were polite," Huttig said. "It don't mean a thing."

"Not a thing," echoed Labiosa, smirking at Moody.

The cop returned with a lanky teenage boy in faded jeans and a holed sweater. Herman's eyes took in Moody, then moved on to something of greater interest. He pointed at Bess. "That's one of ours!"

"We figured," Huttig said. "What about the guy?"

"I ain't seen him before."

"Take a good look at him, Herman. Isn't he the one that bought the dog?"

"No." Herman shook his head emphatically. Moody wondered if he was simpleminded. Herman was pointing at Bess again. "That's the dog Mr. Mauser sold just the other day. I know all of the dogs, every one. They all look the same, but they ain't, not if you look close."

"And this guy was never here?"

"I never seen him before."

"Okay, Herman, you can go back to your room."

"That's a real good dog," Herman said.

Huttig jerked his head at the cop, who led Herman away. Herman hadn't even looked at the two bodies. Moody assumed he had seen them already and was not interested in them. Might Herman in fact be the killer? Moody had heard of backward types who could kill and then sit down to eat a meal next to the corpse.

"Did he do it?" Moody asked.

"We wondered about that, didn't we, Vinnie?"

"For about five minutes. Then we figured Herman's so dumb he'd come right out and confess it. Herman has Sundays off to visit his grandma in Helendale. He gets back to work late today on account of car trouble. Around noon he walks in and sees this. His story checks out."

"Do I take it that I'm a suspect?"

"You might be," Labiosa said.

"Where'd you get the dog, if it wasn't from right here?"

"The dog belonged to a friend of mine."

"Belonged? That's past tense, Moody."

"My friend passed on recently."

"How recently?"

"Saturday."

"Saturday! That's pretty damn recent."

"He had a heart attack. He was old, at least sixty."

"What name?"

"Horace Wheat. He just bought the dog a few days before."

"That's a shame," said Huttig.

"I think I might cry," agreed Labiosa.

"You haven't explained why I'm here," Moody said.

"On account of your cousin the hero," Huttig told him.

"But . . . how?"

"Take a look at these people, Moody. Both of them shot, but you know what our forensics guys found? They were shot with two different guns. Mrs. Deadlady here, she was shot with a big gun, a forty-four, and Mr. Deadguy, he was shot with a littler gun, a thirty-eight. The guns were right here next to the bodies till our guys took them away for testing and checking the serial numbers. We got lucky then, didn't we, Vinnie?"

"Real lucky."

"See, Moody, both guns were legally registered, which is a rarity, guns being so easy to buy just about anyplace you go. Most people, they don't register their guns at all, do they, Vinnie?"

"Too lazy," said Labiosa, "or else they're criminals who don't want their guns traced."

"But these two guns were registered. The forty-four, that was registered to Mr. Deadguy here, name of Edward Mauser, but the thirty-eight, that wasn't registered to Mrs. Deadlady, was it, Vinnie?"

"Nope, not to her."

"The thirty-eight was registered to a Clarence Anthony White. That name ring a bell with you, Moody?"

"Umm . . . yes, I think so. I seem to recall something in the papers."

"Clarence Anthony White got shot with a forty-four, probably the same one Mauser's wife got shot with, we're checking on that right now, and dumped in a toilet up around Victorville."

"Ah, yes, I remember now. And he used to be an airplane mechanic with the Flying Tigers over in China, which means he probably knew Russell, my cousin."

"That's right."

Moody gave a little laugh, attempting to convey confusion, and saw immediately that it was a mistake. The detectives stared at him, their faces like stone.

"I say something funny, Moody?"

"No, it's just . . . I'm still confused."

"How come the gun that was owned by a friend of your cousin's turns up in a double domestic homicide of a couple of dog breeders that sold a dog to a friend of yours that also died just recent?"

Moody grappled with plausibility and actual knowledge, attempting to unite the two somehow. "Coincidence?" he said, looking from one detective to the other.

"Vinnie, you believe in coincidence?"

"Nope, not even in *Ripley's Believe It or Not*."

"Ripley's a goddamn liar, most probably," Huttig agreed.

"Made all those coincidences up just to fool people," Labiosa stated.

"But we don't let ourselves get fooled, do we."

"Nope, we're cops."

"But—" said Moody, "what brought you to me?"

"Charlene did," said Huttig.

"Excuse me?"

"My wife. Always reads the movie magazines. Loves to read that stuff, all that shit about movie stars. Me, I don't like movie stars. Vinnie neither."

"I hate 'em," said Vinnie. "The guys are all faggots, and the women are dykes."

"Except Gary Cooper. He's a real guy."

"Okay, I'll buy Cooper. The rest of 'em are scum."

"Anyway," Huttig continued, "my wife Charlene, she reads in some movie rag that they're gonna make a movie about your cousin the hero, and the fag they're gonna put in it is her favorite fag actor, called Baxter Nolan, and the writer of this movie they're gonna make is none other than the flyboy hero's own cousin."

"And you fellows don't believe in coincidence," Moody scoffed.

"Which is what brought us to your door tonight, Moody, just to ask a few questions on the off chance you might be able to shed some light, and what's the first thing we see but a black poodle, like all the poodles that live out here with these dead people. We smell poodles when we breathe the air out here, but we smell something else too."

"We smell a rat," said Labiosa.

"Because we still don't believe in coincidence," Huttig concluded.

"Then all I can do is ask that you take me back home," Moody said, hoping he sounded confident and just a little aggrieved, "because none of this has anything to do with me at all. Maybe Clarence Anthony White was Mrs. Mauser's lover, and Mr. Mauser found out about it and killed him and took his gun and brought it home with him to confront Mrs. Mauser with over her infidelity, and she grabbed the gun off him and shot him in revenge for killing her lover, but not before Mr. Mauser squeezed off a shot from his own gun, which you'll probably find is indeed the same one that was used on Mr. White. Classic love triangle. They make movies about this kind of tragedy, only we try to leave a few actors alive at the end or the audience goes away feeling sad, which doesn't sell tickets at the box office, gentlemen, so we tend not to make movies that resemble reality, which is what you have a sad case of here—cold hard reality, with a little bit of coincidence thrown in. Believe It or Not."

Huttig looked at Labiosa, and Labiosa looked back. Then they both began to applaud. Moody tried to remain dignified by saying nothing.

12

ON TUESDAY MOODY took an extended lunch break and motored out to Big Tujunga Canyon with Bess. He parked outside the Weichek Institute, went inside, and approached the desk in the entry hall. The same nurse from Central Casting was there, wearing the same professional smile.

"Hello, Mr. Johnson," she said. "I think your father left us with the wrong telephone number."

"Dad does that sometimes. Is Dr. Weichek here?"

"Yes, he is. One moment, please."

She worked the switchboard in front of her with expert precision.

"Dr. Weichek? Mr. Johnson has come back. Yes, Doctor." To Moody she said, "Just go up the stairs and turn left. The doctor will meet you."

"Thank you."

Moody's shoes made the same clicking sound as before when he passed across the entry hall tiles, and became louder as he climbed the staircase.

At the top landing he turned left and passed along a corridor flanked by many numbered doors, all of them closed. A large picture window at the corridor's far end allowed sunlight inside, and standing at its center, surrounded by a natural halo, stood a short figure Moody recognized from the day Mortimer Pence was sedated and taken away from Empire.

"Mr. Johnson, welcome, sir."

"Thank you."

Neither man extended his hand as Moody drew closer.

"This way, please," said Weichek, indicating that they should turn a corner and continue along another corridor.

"You wish to see Mr. Pence, is that correct?"

"I do."

"And you are—?"

"A friend."

"I see. And your father, Mr. Johnson senior, is not with you today?"

"Mr. Johnson senior is not with the living."

"Oh, I'm so sorry to hear that."

"Mr. Johnson senior was murdered last Saturday night."

"Good heavens! That's extraordinary. Why was he murdered, if I might ask?"

"He bought a dog from the wrong people."

"I don't think I'm following your train of thought, Mr. Johnson."

"Never mind. How's Mortimer?"

"Mr. Pence is not improving, I'm afraid. Are you quite well yourself, Mr. Johnson?"

"Perfectly fine, thanks."

"Good. In here, please. We can talk privately about your friend."

Weichek's office was paneled in fine woods that matched his broad desk. Artwork depicting such subjects as screaming faces and empty rooms with bleak landscapes beyond their windows hung on the walls.

"Some of our guests are of an artistic nature," explained Weichek. "Please sit down, Mr. Johnson. Have you known Mr. Pence long?"

"Several years."

"Really. Then you doubtless are aware that he once was known by another name."

"Smokey Hayes."

"You're in the picture-making business yourself, Mr. Johnson?"

"In a small way. I write them."

"Indeed. Were you by any chance the author of any of Mr. Pence's pictures?"

"Over a dozen, actually."

"Then your name, Mr. Johnson, must be Keith Moody."

"I think we both already knew that, Dr. Weichek."

"Are you and I engaged in some kind of adversarial relationship, Mr. Moody?"

"I think that's quite likely, don't you?"

Weichek stroked his short beard. "I'm not quite sure what to think. You come here under an alias, claim your father has been murdered, and then proceed to hint at something sinister that's beyond my present understanding. You're an unusual fellow, Mr. Moody. Perhaps you could benefit from a stay at our institute yourself. As I said, we have a number of creative individuals here, not least among them Mr. Pence."

"He wasn't my father."

"The allegedly murdered man?"

"The murdered man in fact was Horace Wheat."

"Not a relation."

"A friend, now deceased. Someone injected him with a rare drug."

"Unusual *modus operandi.*"

"It's untraceable, apart from the needle puncture, and even that can't be examined anymore because you had him cremated. If ever an act pointed to a guilty conscience, Doctor, that does. You don't deny that you ordered Horace's body taken away and burned?"

"I do not. Mr. Margolis, your employer, asked me to do so."

"Margolis?"

"As I understand it, Mr. Margolis heard of your loss and decided to assist you in the interment of your friend Mr. Wheat."

"Assist me? By sneaking him away so fast I didn't even get to see him? That isn't assistance, it's interference, and none of it was done on my behalf. It's disposal of evidence. And how would Marvin Margolis know about Horace Wheat's death anyway? I didn't tell him."

"No, but you did list Empire Productions as your employer on the sheet the ambulance men gave you to sign, did you not? No doubt they, or someone at the county morgue, contacted the studio."

"I don't accept that."

"I see. And why was Mr. Wheat murdered, in your opinion?"

"He knew too much."

"Regarding?"

"I was hoping you could tell me, Doctor."

Weichek steepled his fingertips and reclined his leather-upholstered chair several inches. "I must admit I don't know what to make of you, Mr. Moody. You don't appear to be insane, and yet the things you say are beyond reason, and are also, may I add, extremely insulting to me personally. Are you this way with other people, or have I alone been so honored?"

"I'm beyond politeness. I want to know why you killed Horace. He wasn't doing any harm. Did you kill the Mausers too?"

"The mouses? Surely a literary man would say mice."

"Eddie and Muriel Mauser. They breed poodles. Bred."

Weichek studied Moody's face for a long moment, then said, "Would you care to see Mr. Pence?"

"I would, yes."

"Come with me."

Weichek escorted Moody from his office and along several

more lengthy corridors, all painted white, all giving access to closed doors. Several men and women, all wearing white, passed them by with murmured greetings to the doctor, which he acknowledged with a discreet tilting of the head.

They stopped before 103, a door indistinguishable from any other except by number. Weichek produced a key and unlocked it, stepping aside to allow Moody to precede him into the room. Not wanting to be locked in, Moody insisted that Weichek go first. The doctor did so, with a smirk that let Moody know his suspicions were not only foolish but transparently so.

Mortimer Pence sat in a chair by the window. His room was small, furnished with nothing more than a bed and bedside table and the comfortable chair in which he sat, staring at the world outside.

Approaching him, Moody felt a sudden pang of disappointment; Mortimer's face was blank, without intelligence or emotion of any kind. He simply gazed at nothing, perhaps not seeing beyond the windowpane.

"What have you done to him?"

"Mr. Pence required electroshock treatment."

"He's a—a zombie!"

"Nonsense. There's always a period of adjustment following a course of treatment. In a week or so he'll be a different man."

"But . . . which man will he be? Smokey Hayes or Mortimer Pence?"

"That will be determined by the care and attention he receives while in our custody, Mr. Moody. Mr. Pence is an interesting illustration in separated personalities. Actors seldom are so completely swallowed by their stage or screen persona as was the case here. You may talk to him if you wish."

Moody squatted down beside the chair and took Mortimer's slack hand in his.

"Mortimer, it's me, Moody. Keith Moody? I've come to see how you are, Mortimer. Are they treating you okay?"

There was no response at all. Moody stood and looked through the glass. He could see dry foothills and the parking lot in front of the Institute.

"That's some view out there, isn't it, Mortimer? I could look at a view like that all day, just about. Is that what you do, when they aren't shooting volts through your poor goddamn head? They have to strap you down to do that, don't they, Mortimer?"

Weichek said, "Mr. Moody, really, this accomplishes nothing. Moderate your language and tone, or it may have a detrimental effect on the patient."

"What the hell could be more detrimental than what you've already done!"

"Mr. Moody, I must ask you to leave."

"In a minute," Moody said, lowering his voice and turning back to the window. "I want to talk with him some more—"

In the parking lot below, he saw a coupe convertible pull up some distance from his own car. The driver was a woman. The driver was Myra Nolan. She got out and began walking toward the entrance.

"Myra—"

"I beg your pardon, Mr. Moody?"

"What the hell have you got her coming here for! What's she got to do with all this, Weichek! You already killed Horace! Are you going to kill her too! Are you!"

"Mr. Moody, depart this instant!"

Mortimer's eyes slowly turned from the window. His mouth, until now slack, suddenly opened and began to emit a banshee wail that rose, strong and steady as an air raid warning, a siren song of madness.

Moody stared at him, aghast, then looked back out the window. Myra had disappeared inside the building below his line of sight. Moody ran toward the door, intent on intercepting Myra in the entry hall downstairs.

"Mr. Moody! Do not run! Come back here, Mr. Moody!"

But Moody was already out in the corridor, haring at full speed back the way he had come. Weichek stepped out of the room behind him and smacked a large red button mounted on the wall. Instantly the air became charged with sound, the bronchial barking of an alarm that seemed to penetrate every corridor Moody ran down, turning when he thought he should, then turning back when it became clear he had chosen the wrong direction, all the while pursued by the alarm's relentless hooting, until he could no longer decide which corridor represented the road to freedom; he could not even locate the stairs to reach Myra, and spun on his own axis in futile anguish.

Now there were footsteps clattering closer, then three men in white rounded a corner and saw him. "Okay, feller, just take it nice and easy and no one'll get hurt."

"Get away from me," Moody warned them.

"Just don't go making a fuss, and it'll be okay."

"I want to get out of here—I want to get back downstairs."

"And we're here to help you do that, so like I said, just relax."

"I'll be happy to cooperate, just don't touch me."

"Perfectly happy arrangement," said the spokesman for the three, all of whom continued inching closer.

Moody said, "Stay where you are! Just point the way and I'll leave, thank you—"

They rushed at him, snaring Moody's limbs with practiced ease, and lifted him from the floor, thrashing and squirming, shouting, "Let me go! I just want to leave here! Let go of me, you sons of bitches!"

"Ooh, listen to the nasty names. Naughty boys deserve a smack."

Moody received a quick slap across the face. His glasses flew off, and their loss caused him to panic as nothing else could. "I've lost my glasses—! Please—my glasses! I can't see a thing without them!"

"Can't you? Too bad, four-eyes."

Enraged, Moody began to kick with all his strength, his entire body writhing as it was carried along parallel to the floor. A shoe came off as he was transported down the stairs.

"My shoe!"

"Take it easy, Mac. You got another one still."

Seeing their struggling mass descend, the nurse at the reception desk turned off the alarm. Recognizing his surroundings as they carried him across the black-and-white tiles, Moody began screaming, "Myra! Myra, get out of here!"

He was carried, his movements weaker now, through the entrance and down the outside steps to his car, and dumped along the gap between hood and fender like a bagged deer. Inside the car Bess was barking ferociously. Someone shoved his glasses onto his nose, and another pair of hands crammed the toe of his shoe between his teeth. "Don't come back," he was told, and then the small entourage in white retreated from him.

Moody spat out his shoe and adjusted his glasses. He eased himself onto the ground and placed the shoe on his foot. Myra's car was twenty yards away. He considered waiting for her to leave the building but changed his mind when several of the muscular orderlies in white turned around and began walking back toward him.

Moody accepted defeat and locked himself in his car, then started the engine. They let him by as he turned in the direction of the exit. Bess licked his ear.

THE FACT THAT he could continue writing *China Skies* that afternoon, after his experience at the Weichek Institute, impressed Moody. He was impressed also by the way in which he had accused Dr. Weichek outright of murder. But maybe that had been reckless rather than brave, given the fact that someone was erasing the cast of a widening plot.

Maybe the scenario of a love triangle gone wrong that he had presented to Huttig and Labiosa was in fact the truth; it was not impossible. More than likely, Mauser and Tony White had been in cahoots on the blackmail plot, and Mauser had gotten greedy and knocked off his partner. In which case, Moody concluded, the only man he had to fear was the doctor, if the doctor had been the one who murdered Horace. If he had not, then Moody was still fair game for whoever was orchestrating the shadow play he found himself part of.

And was it mere coincidence that Quentin Yapp was the brother of Muriel Mauser? Yapp surely was implicated. Eddie Mauser clearly had brought home the gun he took from Tony, but where was the fifty thousand dollars? Had it been returned to Empire Productions and handed over to Marvin Margolis, or had the Mausers decided to keep it? Was Yapp the middleman between Margolis and the Mausers, or was he the murderer of Eddie, following Eddie's plugging of Muriel? A brother would do that for his murdered sister, wouldn't he? Even a weasel like Quentin Yapp could shoot his brother-in-law and leave the pistol in the hand of his dead sister.

Moody felt himself spinning again. Of all the deaths so far, he could feel remorse for only one: Horace Wheat had become involved in something too big and fast moving for the old detective to hunt down to its lair by wits alone. Moody truly felt responsible. And despite it all, he kept on writing.

"I amaze myself sometimes," he told Bess, sprawled comfortably on the office sofa. She did not respond.

"What about Myra?" he asked. Bess closed her eyes and let out a sigh. "She was there," Moody insisted, "in a place she had no reason to be. Why? And should I let on that I saw her there? Maybe Weichek'll tell her anyway . . . if Weichek even knows I know her. God, this is complicated, isn't it? And I'm talking to a dog. Work!"

He resumed typing. Then stopped. "She was visiting Mortimer! Like me! Someone told her what happened to him, and she went to see if he's okay . . . that makes sense. No, it doesn't. She always hated Smokey Hayes, always said he was an idiot. She wouldn't have visited him. So why was she there? To see Weichek? What's her connection to a guy like that? It still doesn't make sense. And now I'm talking to *myself*!"

More typing obliterated his misgivings, for the moment at least.

CAPTAIN

No squadron could ever make it through.

RUSS

That's right, sir, no squadron could, but a single plane, that's another thing entirely.

CAPTAIN

I guess it's yourself you're suggesting, Keys.

RUSS

I might be. It's the one chance we've got to turn the Japs around before they get their entire heavy armored division through that pass. One plane, one man, one bomb, that's all it'd take to bring that canyon wall down on top of them. The weather being what it is, they wouldn't be able to dig themselves out till next spring. It's worth a shot, sir.

CAPTAIN

I can't allow one of my best men to go up in conditions like this. The odds against a successful mission and a safe return are simply not good enough.

RUSS

Captain, you leave the mission to me, and we'll leave the safe return to the Guy Upstairs.

As he reread these lines, it occurred to Moody that Russ's

dialogue could have been spoken by Smokey Hayes. "I haven't gone anywhere," he said aloud, panic rising in his voice, then he reminded himself this script was just a stepping-stone to higher things. Greater projects lay in store if he could only make this a successful mission and please Margolis, the Guy Upstairs.

But Myra . . . What had she been doing at the Weichek Institute?

He got up and put on his jacket. "Stay here and don't pee on the floor," he told Bess. "I'm going over to the Research Block. I need answers."

He was partway to his destination, weaving through a bevy of bathing beauties having a smoke between takes of the new aqua-musical spectacular currently shooting on soundstage two, when he heard his name called. Turning, he saw Roy Schutt approaching, his expression unfavorable.

"Working hard, are you, Keith?" The sarcasm was unrestrained.

"Yes I am, Roy. If the truth be told, the kind of work I do, thinking things up, goes on all the time. I'm even hard at work when I'm on the pot, Roy, and you're very welcome to walk into my office and take the next twenty or so pages of script you'll find there, which will save me the trouble of finding you later. Good-bye, Roy."

Some of the girls in bathing costumes cheered, then shut up as Schutt turned to glare at them. Moody was by then on his way again.

Still a hundred yards from Research, Moody was hailed a second time. When he turned, it was to find Huttig and Labiosa bearing down on him.

"Where's the fire, Moody?"

"Good afternoon, detectives."

"Same to you, and where can we talk?"

"How about over there?"

They strolled toward the *Royal Pirate* set and sat down in the village square.

"What's this?" asked Labiosa.

"Elizabethan England," Moody told him.

"It looks dirty."

"It was. This is an example of authenticity. We do that with sets. It's the stories that avoid it."

"You sound like a man that don't like his work, Moody," said Huttig.

"Some minor carping." He felt almost buoyant after his successful telling-off of Schutt. "What can I do for you fellows?"

"How about you tell us why you were over at the Los Angeles County Stiffworks late yesterday, hollering and crying about how your friend Horace Wheat didn't have a heart attack like you told us he did, it was murder instead. How about that, Moody?"

"I was hysterical."

"Hysterical."

"Yes."

"Like what a woman gets."

"If you like. I was upset. I was talking nonsense, frankly."

"The same kind of nonsense you went and talked at the Resthaven Funeral Home later on?"

"Yes, probably. It's all been too much for me. My cousin vanishing, the stress of the project I'm working on, Horace passing away . . . I haven't been coping at all well."

"You seem chipper today, Moody, doesn't he, Vinnie?"

"Full of fucking beans."

"This Weichek guy, Moody."

"What Weichek guy?"

"That ordered your old pal Wheat to get burned."

"Oh, that Weichek."

"Yeah, that one. You go visit him at all, Moody?"

"When would I have the time? I'm a busy man."

"So you didn't ask him why he burned the body?"

"No, never met the man."

"What would you say if I told you we just went out to Dr.

Weichek's joint in Big Tujunga Canyon and asked him the same question?"

"I wouldn't say anything. I'd wait for you to tell me what he said."

Moody felt his heart accelerating. He had wanted Huttig and Labiosa to stay away from the Weichek Institute at least until he learned what Myra had been doing there. The detectives had him cornered with a palpable lie, and they would proceed to grill him like a fish. He smiled at them. Huttig looked at Labiosa, then back at Moody.

"Weichek never met you either."

"Of course not," said Moody, wanting to vomit with relief.

"That Weichek, he's not a regular doctor, did you know that?"

"What is he, a witch doctor? Ha, ha!"

"No, Moody, he's a head doctor, and I figure you should go see him."

Labiosa said, "You're a wreck, Moody."

"Am I? It takes all kinds. Can I go now?"

"Beat it," Huttig told him.

Moody strolled through Elizabethan England until the detectives were out of sight, then ran through Kunming until he reached Research.

At the front desk, panting slightly, he asked for Myra Nolan, and was told she had called in sick that day. Then Moody knew Myra had not gone to the institute merely to make a quick visit; whatever business had taken her there required her presence for at least an afternoon—and longer, maybe? Was it connected with the fact that Weichek had denied meeting him? He would call her this evening and see if she had returned home. He would call every fifteen minutes until she picked up the phone.

Did Weichek have some kind of sinister hold over her? Was he a blackmailer, like Tony White? Surely someone like Myra had nothing to hide. Of course, there was that hypodermic syringe needle he had found under the seat of her car. Myra, a dope fiend? It was unlikely. Myra an assassin by needle—? The notion slipped beneath his defenses and took hold of his frontal lobe like a gripping hand. It couldn't be! It was too absurd! Now he really did feel sick.

Leaving the Research Block, he ambled in the general direction of his office, and again encountered Roy Schutt. Schutt had pages of script clutched in one hand and a lengthy tear in his slacks. He saw Moody and stormed over.

"What the hell do you mean by keeping a goddamn dog in your office! The damn thing almost took a chunk out of my leg! What kind of an idiot are you, Moody!"

"I don't know," Moody said, and walked on, not caring if Schutt continued to rant behind him. Moody had unwittingly sullied the girl he loved, had permitted an evil, unthinkable notion to invade his thoughts. He had betrayed her at some level he was not quite able to comprehend. He was a disgrace, thoroughly unworthy of her love. But he would call every fifteen minutes until she picked up the phone.

13

THE SEARCH WAS ended. No trace of Russell Keys or his parachute had been found, and it was generally considered impossible for the man to have survived alone in the still-wintry Rocky Mountains for so long. The announcement was on page five of the *Los Angeles Times* and broadcast at the end of the radio news. The case of the Vanishing Airman had entered public consciousness, probably for a lengthy stay, but as news the story was played out.

Moody was glad. Now no one would learn of his cousin's criminal behavior, and Empire would probably go ahead and make *China Skies*, ending the story before Russell returned stateside. Moody already was concocting an appropriate final scene in his head.

PILOT

Well, the Chinese are on their own now.

RUSS

No, they're not. Now there's more than just a bunch of Yanks on their side. Now they've got the whole U.S.A.

PILOT

You figure us Tigers are gonna fit into the regular Army Air Corps after what we did here?

RUSS

Maybe they'll have to fit in with us. We could teach 'em a thing or two. This war's not over yet. For the other guys it's just starting, but for us it's gonna be business as usual.

PILOT

Amen to that, brother.

Cut to P-40's taking off into the wild blue yonder.

Margolis would love it. Roy Schutt would grumble that it was hokey, but would stop grumbling when MM told him it was patriotic. Terry Blackwell would shrug off any judgment and direct it as best he could. Baxter Nolan would secretly ask the cameraman to concentrate on his best side in the close-ups, and Sandy Ryder would count up her lines and complain that she hadn't been given enough screen time. Then Mr. and Mrs. America and their offspring would watch the movie and munch popcorn and cheer every time a Jap plane hit the dirt. It would work. No one would notice who wrote the screenplay, and Moody didn't care.

He took the work home with him once again and was able to concentrate until eight o'clock, when he gave in and called Myra, who did not pick up the phone. He called again at eight-fifteen and eight-thirty, and thereafter was unable to work with the same diligence.

At nine o'clock he left his apartment, taking Bess with him. They strolled together for several blocks, then turned back.

Approaching the apartments, Moody saw a cigarette lighter flame briefly in a car parked across the street from his own. He could not be sure the car had been there when he went out with Bess. Curious, and a little afraid, Moody walked on past his entrance and went two blocks farther, then cut back through alleyways to his own front door, which was hidden from the street.

By looking out through the venetian blinds of his side window, Moody could see the car. Its interior was in darkness, but even as he watched, another cigarette was lit. He was being watched. He was not familiar with the vehicle, apart from being able to identify it as a Dodge. Was it the detectives watching him, or an agent of Dr. Weichek's? Could it be Myra, in someone else's car? She was not at home. He scrubbed this thought from his mind. There was only one way to ascertain the driver's identity, and that was by confrontation.

Moody went down to the forecourt and out through the apartment building's entrance. The Dodge's engine started up. Moody began walking briskly toward it, and the Dodge eased away from the curb, then increased speed as Moody began running to catch up. It was too late to follow the escaping Dodge, but Moody got into his own car anyway and drove off.

He was not surprised, some fifteen minutes later, to find himself parked across the street from Myra's apartment in Alhambra. He had become a sneak, a spy, and he knew that within a few minutes his degradation would be complete when he became a Peeping Tom. He still could turn around and drive home if he chose to, but Moody chose not to.

He locked his car and went to the back of the building, where Myra lived. He had half expected it, but it came as a shock nonetheless to see a sliver of light at the edge of her blackout curtains. He told himself she might have come home in the considerable time since he had last telephoned, but the voice of unreason insisted she had been there all along, ignoring his calls. Maybe the driver of the Dodge had only just departed after having dropped her off.

Every notion that crossed his mind, like a surreptitious hand reaching for receptive thighs in a darkened theater, was shaken off, only to return. He was becoming unhinged, he knew, but he could not stop himself from approaching the open window. He reached through, parted the curtains slightly, and waited for his nightmares to begin.

The room was empty. He saw the old-fashioned sofa Myra had told him belonged to her mother, and on which Myra and Moody had tussled (with the lights out) before retiring to the bedroom. He could see the six-foot yucca plant Myra called Pedro in its sizable terra-cotta pot, and he could see, by standing close to the glass and craning his neck, the entrance to the kitchen. He could hear Kate Smith on the radio singing "He Wears a Pair of Silver Wings." He could not see Myra.

Something moved in the kitchen, then was gone. Moody felt his entire body become tense. He knew it had not been a woman he saw, even though he had only caught a glimpse. A man passed across the kitchen, heading for the sink, beyond Moody's view. The squat shape of Weichek was easily identifiable. He came back, passing briefly in and out of sight, carrying a glass, presumably of water. Was Myra in the kitchen with him? Were they plotting?

Moody hurried around to Myra's front door and knocked. He had to knock twice more before she opened it. Her expression was not reassuring; he could not be sure if it was surprise or guilt he saw written there, or a combination of the two.

"Keith . . . ," she said, her tone reflecting the indecision on her face. "I wasn't expecting you."

"No, I was just driving by and thought I should drop in."

"If you'd given me some warning, Keith . . ."

"Is it an inconvenient time?"

Moody thought he was managing his voice very well, conveying a casualness he did not feel. She was standing in the doorway like a sentinel, denying access.

"Actually, I've got the curse, not to be too delicate about it, and it's bad this time, really. Would I be too much of a rat if I asked you to come back in a day or two, sweetheart? I just feel like hell."

"Of course. It doesn't matter." He was walking backward, smiling broadly. "I'll call ahead next time. Can I get you anything from the drugstore . . . umm . . . painkillers, I mean?"

"No, thanks, I've got plenty."

She blew him a kiss and retreated behind the door, which had at no time been fully opened—a visual clue, Moody decided, to her state of mind; Myra had wanted to conceal her guest, be he lover or conspirator or black-hearted Svengali.

Moody was laid open to the bone. It was betrayal of some kind or other, of that he was sure. She was the one woman he had ever given serious consideration to marrying, although he had never spoken of it to her, and the notion had barely skimmed across his consciousness. He had intended proposing marriage, he convinced himself, and not too far in the future either, maybe after the movie was completed and he felt more secure, and now here she was, denying him entry to her apartment where another man was lurking, a man Moody believed to be a murderer, or trafficker with same. The only one he could trust now was Bess, whom he had left behind with nothing more indicative of his affection than a cheap dog biscuit.

He drove home again, a broken man, and was greeted by Bess like a long-lost explorer. He could do no more work on the script that night; it was approximately three-quarters done now, in any case. He could be self-indulgent for once. He could get blind drunk.

He fetched a half bottle of whiskey from the kitchen cupboard and drank while listening to the radio. He fell asleep after midnight on the sofa, to the strains of Xavier Cugat's "Sleepy Lagoon." Bess lay alongside him, her jaw nestled in his armpit.

BLACKWELL WAS THE first to visit him in his office the following morning. Moody was working his way through a fourth cup of coffee when the director knocked and entered. "Keith, just in case you were wondering, *China Skies* is still on track, with shooting scheduled to begin next month."

"Oh, good—"

"What's wrong? You look like death."

"Nothing . . . hangover, that's all."

"How's the script coming along? Margolis is happy with what he's got so far."

"How about Roy?"

Blackwell waggled his hand and pulled a face. "Roy wants to put Tolstoy on the screen. You let me handle Roy. How much more to write?"

"Not much, another three or four days' work maybe."

"Think of it as war work, Keith. Every scene you write is a smack in the eye for Tojo."

"Terry, you don't really believe that."

"No, but Margolis does. It's a direct quote, so bear it in mind as you pound the keys, my friend. That's a nice-looking dog you've got there."

"Thank you."

Blackwell departed. Moody's second guest arrived less than thirty minutes later. Roy Schutt peered around the door to determine if a dog was present. When he saw Bess, he said, "Moody, come outside."

Moody joined him, and Schutt repeated what Blackwell had already told him and added, "You know, it might not be a bad idea to change the name of the hero, kind of disassociate your cousin from the role, what with the likelihood that he's dead, if you don't mind my saying so, Keith. I've consulted with MM about this, and he agrees. The story was never really an accurate biography in any case, was it?"

"No, Roy, all it ever was is a Hollywood war movie, nothing to do with reality."

"There's no need to take that tone. You're being well paid."

"You misunderstand me. I don't mind changing the name

at all, and we have to bear in mind the possibility that another blackmailer might pop out of the woodwork at any moment and smear Russell's name all over again."

"I don't want to discuss that! MM has made it clear that—*topic* is to be kept under the tightest wraps. You haven't spoken with anyone about it, have you?"

"To the contrary—no one wants to speak to *me* about it."

"Good, and you'd better do the same if you know what's good for you."

"Oh, I know what's good for me all right."

"You know, Keith, you look like hell."

"Thank you."

His third guest was Myra, who arrived just before noon.

"Keith," she said, "you've got a dog."

"Her name's Bess."

"That's so unlike you."

"Am I so predictable?"

"Jeepers, lover, don't get all cross with me."

Myra sat on the sofa and put a cigarette in her mouth. "Sorry about last night."

"It's okay. It doesn't matter, really."

"I just wasn't myself. Not perky old Myra at all."

"I could tell. You aren't perky old Myra today either, and I'm not perky old Keith, and neither of us will ever be perky again, I expect."

"Keith, are you feeling all right?"

"Would you care to tell me I look like hell? I *feel* like hell, in fact I sometimes think I'm actually *in* hell, so that explains the way I look."

"The way you look is explained by overwork. I've heard the script is almost finished, is that true?"

"Pretty much. They want to change the hero's name now that Russell's officially a goner. Naturally I went along with it. Bend over, they said, so I did. They're paying me top dollar to bend over, so that's what I did. Would you bend over for the right price, Myra?"

"Keith—what's the matter with you?"

"With me, nothing. With the world, plenty. I feel I can betray my own project about my own cousin if I want. Betrayal isn't really so bad, not when you get down and roll around in it for a while. Soon it starts to smell like money."

"What are you talking about?"

"I know about Weichek."

"Weichek?"

"Oh, please, don't waste your time and mine by acting innocent."

"Dr. Weichek?"

"No, his brother, Rabbi Weichek."

Myra dragged hard on her cigarette. "How did you find out?"

"Smokey Hayes is . . . I mean, Mortimer Pence is in one of the rubber rooms at the institute. I paid him a visit and saw you there."

"And Weichek talked to you?"

"We had a very stimulating conversation that went around and around like a record, then he had me thrown out."

"Oh."

"Oh, is right. What do you have to say for yourself?"

"He didn't explain?"

"I'm waiting to hear that from you."

"Can you wait a little longer? It's not . . . It's something I don't care to discuss right now, if that's okay with you, Keith."

"Why should I complain? You choose your own friends and associates."

"You sound awfully sore."

"I'm not sore. I can't afford to be."

"Would you like me to go?"

"I think that might be a very good idea."

His face was already turned back to his typewriter when she closed the door behind her. He lifted his hands to resume typing, but no words would come.

And there was a fourth visitor by midafternoon. Bess began growling even before Yapp's head was inside the door. "You gonna make like Frank Buck and get hold of that wild animal you got there, Moody?"

"Come in, Yapp. She only bites when I tell her to."

"That's all I need, is to be dog-bit. I just came from a funeral home, Moody."

"Were you dead?"

"You . . . you don't talk to me like that about this! My own sister, you don't take that tone, I don't care what Margolis thinks."

"Bess, sit! Come in, Quentin."

Yapp sidled into the office but stayed by the door and kept a wary eye on Bess.

"Your sister?" Moody prompted.

"Yeah, dead. Jesus Christ, Moody, you think I don't know they gave you one of the dogs to shove under my nose and let me know to keep my mouth shut, huh?"

"You think I had some part in this?"

"Who was the delivery boy for fifty grand, huh? I told Margolis, okay, I know a guy can look out for Moody when he makes the drop, a personal friend so you can trust him to do what needs to be done, and he did that, Eddie did, only now there's a double cross. You tell 'em from me, Moody— No—don't tell 'em a goddamn thing! I was never here! You never saw me, and I didn't say any of this shit!"

Abruptly, Yapp was gone. Moody looked at Bess. He had been accused of being a party to murder. It was a uniquely awful moment. "Is the whole world going insane," he asked his dog, "or just me?"

THE DAY'S INTERRUPTIONS had slowed his work schedule, so Moody did what he had been doing for days now, and took the work home with him. He was busy with the scene where the hero tells Lin-Ming their unconsummated romance can go no farther because of his girl back home when the telephone rang.

Moody picked up the receiver with some trepidation; would it be Yapp, with more accusations of complicity in a double murder, or Dr. Weichek advising him to avoid the company of Myra in the future?

"Moody?" asked a voice at the other end of the line.

"Yes."

A long silence followed.

"Hey, cuz."

"Is this a prank call? I don't find it amusing."

He slammed the phone down.

Thirty seconds later it rang again, and Moody snatched it up. "Listen, don't do this again. I'm hanging up now and taking the phone off the hook, so if you want to annoy me you're going to be plain out of luck, whoever you are."

"Don't do that, cuz."

It did sound like Russell.

"Russ—?"

"It's me, Keith, the real McCoy."

"But . . . where are you calling from?"

"Drugstore about a quarter mile away."

"Russ, you're alive—"

"Yeah, but I know someone who's dead."

"Who?"

"My good buddy Whitey, that's who."

"Whitey? Russ, I don't understand—"

"Me neither, cuz. You want to explain it to me?"

"You mean Clarence Anthony White?"

"That's him."

"Russ, he was a blackmailer. He tried to—"

"Hey! Shut up and listen. We have to talk about some things, you and me."

"Yes, yes, of course. Why don't you come here."

"I was gonna do just that, but then I saw this big old Dodge hanging around in front of your place, cuz, and the feller inside, he's watching you or else someone else that lives in your apartment block."

"No, it's me he's watching."

"A cop?"

"Maybe, I don't know. You can sneak in along the back alley and they won't see you from the street."

"Here's a better plan. You sneak out the same way. You know Linden's drugstore?"

"Yes."

"Be here soon, and be alone, cuz, because I'm not in the mood to meet with strangers, you got that?"

"Russ, how did you get back here? What happened with the plane?"

The telephone clicked.

Doubting that Russell would classify Bess as a stranger, Moody took her along. They exited along the alley behind his apartment and were able to reach Linden's ten minutes later. Peering inside, Moody saw no one who resembled his cousin.

He stood with his dog beneath the darkened neon tubing of Linden's sign and waited. Soon a tall figure with a familiar shambling walk beckoned from the far side of the street, then began moving away. Moody and Bess followed, gradually catching up with Russell as he entered a small public park. He sat on a bench in the shadows and waited for them to join him. His hair, formerly blond, now was black.

"I never figured you for a dog-owning man, cuz."

"I got this one by accident."

"Where's the money?"

"What money?"

"Don't be stupid. The fifty grand, where is it?"

"How do you know about that?"

"Do I have to draw a picture? I set it up with Whitey, the whole deal."

"But why—?"

"Fifty thousand reasons. Your lousy studio and their lousy thousand bucks for my story. I only took it on account of you, so's you'd get the job of writing the movie."

"I had no idea. I thought you were casual about the whole thing."

"There's ways and ways to make big money, Keith. Working's only one of them."

"So you arranged with Tony White to blackmail the studio."

"Sure, then we figured the best way for me to take my share was disappear, so that's what I did, and according to the papers, I'm a dead man."

"Where did you bail out?"

"Not over the Rockies like everyone thinks. Too cold and too high. I hit the silk after I took off from Salt Lake City, took that bird up as high as she'd go, then set the autopilot and bailed out. Got cold as a witch's tit falling down, but it was only a minute or two, then I yanked on the old rip cord and floated to earth like an autumn leaf. The 'chute and my flying suit are buried out in the middle of nowhere."

"You planned everything, I take it."

"I had civvies on under my suit, and I brung along some sandwiches and a bottle of hair dye. Before the sun came up you could call me Boston Blackie. I hitched a ride into Provo with some old Utah farmer and rode a Greyhound back to Los Angeles, and what happens when I get here? I find out Whitey's dead, locked in a goddamn toilet. So who killed him?"

"A man called Eddie Mauser. Mauser's dead now too."

"How?"

"The police think he had an argument with his wife and they shot each other."

"And the money?"

"I don't know."

"Who else was in on this?"

"Just the Mausers."

"But who put 'em onto Whitey?"

Moody was disinclined to involve Yapp, even though the head of B-feature production had been the liaison between the Mausers and Empire Productions.

"That I couldn't say."

"Couldn't or wouldn't?"

"Russ, did you kill a dwarf Chinese prostitute in Kunming?"

"Did Whitey say she was a dwarf? That wasn't in the script."

"But did you kill her!"

"Settle down, cuz. I killed fifteen Japs, that's all. The dwarf was a little gal me and Whitey knew. Yeah, she was a whore, but we kind of felt sorry for her. I think Whitey was half in love with her. We got the jade cock from the whorehouse where she worked. Nice angle, huh? The documents with the Chinese scribble on them, they came from the same place. For all I know it's a goddamn love letter, or a laundry bill or something, just a souvenir we brung back home with us. It did the trick, though, didn't it?"

"It got your friend killed, and the Mausers too."

"Yeah, well, there's always risk when the big bucks are up for grabs. Whoever did the Mausers has got the cash. So who might that be?"

"Your guess is as good as mine."

"That's a mighty nice thing to say, but I don't agree. I think your guess is gonna be a whole lot more accurate."

"Forget about the money. It's gone, and it was never yours to begin with. It's blackmail money."

"Oh, too dirty to touch. I can handle dirt, Keith. What I can't handle is my friend getting killed and no cash profit to show for it. I don't like that, so you better help me find out where that money's at, or I'll raise a little hell getting it on my own."

"Don't expect me to cooperate. A friend of mine died, too, because of all this."

"What friend?"

"An investigator I hired to find out about Eddie Mauser."

"Tell you what, cuz. We both suffered a loss, so here's the deal—you and me split the money. You get Whitey's share, since he's not around anymore to collect. That's twenty grand and no taxes."

"You didn't have a fifty-fifty split with him?"

"The biggest risk was all mine. You don't bail out of a plane at forty thousand feet at night without taking a big chance you won't walk away from it. You want more than twenty?"

"I don't want anything. If I were you I'd lose myself before someone recognizes you. That dye job won't protect you forever."

"Oh, I'll lose myself all right, don't you worry. Mexico, that's where me and Whitey were headed once we got the money. Warm sun and hot señoritas. Fifty grand, that's like half a million bucks down there. We were gonna open a bar. You want to go into the barkeep business with me, Keith?"

"I'm a writer."

"Got a question for you. When Whitey told you I killed someone, did you believe him?"

Moody stroked Bess's head. "Not at first, no."

"But later on you did."

"Yes."

"How much later? Two minutes?"

"I'm going back home now, Russ. I advise you to go away somewhere before it's too late. You're of military age, people will be looking at you and wondering why you aren't in uniform, and someday someone's going to recognize you."

"Me and Whitey already had our war. I want my money."

"Find it on your own, then. I have other problems."

Moody stood and began walking away. Russell called after him, "Just don't go standing in my way, cuz!"

14

PREOCCUPIED WITH EVERYTHING he had learned, Moody forgot about the Dodge and its occupant until he was approaching his apartment and saw the car parked across the street. He stopped and considered backtracking to make his way home via the alley, then decided to confront his shadow.

He came to the passenger's window and looked inside. The Dodge appeared at first to be empty, then Moody noticed the body slumped across the front seat. Quentin Yapp's face was upturned. There was a lot of blood along his neck and collar that had flowed from the small hole in his left temple. A cigarette stub was still burning between his lips. The driver's-side window was open to allow the smoke out, and Moody assumed that was where the bullet had come from.

He looked up and down the street. No one was in sight. There were no sirens approaching. The killer apparently had used a silencer. Was he also in the neighborhood to kill Moody? Returning to the apartment was likely to prove fatal.

Moody considered his options. Soon someone would find Yapp, and the police, especially if the case came to the attention of Huttig and Labiosa, would want to know why Moody's former boss, the brother and brother-in-law of a recently murdered couple, was himself murdered across the street from Moody's apartment—Moody, the owner of one of the Mausers' dogs by way of another dead man whom Moody himself had claimed was murdered. No explanation he could possibly offer would not sound suspiciously feeble. He would have to remove Yapp from the vicinity.

It was the work of only a few seconds to install himself behind the wheel and Bess in the backseat. Moody was about to turn the ignition key when a gun barrel was placed against his temple.

"Out for a nighttime joyride, cuz?"

"Russ, did you do this?"

"Do what?"

"This that's next to me on the seat, for God's sake."

Russell lowered his army-issue .45 and looked past Moody. "Who's that?"

"The one who's been watching me. His name's Yapp. You shot him before you went to call me from the drugstore, didn't you?"

"For the record—no. When I saw him watching I kept away."

"Then how is it that you're here again, if you didn't know it was safe?"

"Cuz, I followed you because I wanted to see if you stopped by any phone booths along the way to call the cops maybe. I don't think you'll be doing that now, will you?"

"I never had any intention of calling anyone."

"Where were you planning on taking your date, Keith?"

"I don't know. Somewhere a long way away from here."

"And how did you plan on getting back?"

"I hadn't figured it out that far."

"Long-range planning, that requires a military mind. Where's your car?"

"Across the street."

"Gimme the keys. I'll follow you and bring you back here. Deal?"

Moody hesitated only for as long as it took to calculate his chances of success without Russell's assistance. "Deal."

He handed over the keys.

The one logical place he could think of to dump the Dodge and its owner was at the Mausers' dog-breeding property. The simpleton, Herman, might be there still, tending to the dogs until a court decided what should become of the place, so driving up to the front door would not have been sensible.

Moody drove on past the exit taken when Huttig and Labiosa had brought him out to see the bodies, and took the next one. There were not many houses around, and he stopped along a lonely stretch of road. Russell pulled up beside him while Moody wiped his fingerprints from the ignition keys and steering wheel and let Bess out of the backseat. They both joined Russell and were driven away.

"Okay, who's this Yapp guy, and how come you don't care that he's dead?"

"Who says I don't care?"

"It's all over your face."

Moody explained Yapp's role in the blackmail that had gone awry. Russell listened closely, then was silent for some time.

"You figure he's the one took the money?"

"What, and killed his own sister to cover his tracks? That's ridiculous."

"I didn't ask you if he killed his sister. Someone else did that, but maybe that someone didn't get the money, because it wasn't there anymore, because Yapp took it someplace else. Could be the same guy also killed Yapp."

"Why? How could Yapp give out information about the money's whereabouts if he's dead?"

"Maybe he squawked before he died, or the other guy already found the stuff and bumped off Yapp just to tidy things up. Why was Yapp watching you, anyway?"

"Because he thought I'm part of the double cross that got the Mausers killed."

"You? He thought you were working a double cross? What an idiot. You couldn't walk out of a candy store when we were kids without giving back the extra change if they gave it to you wrong."

"That's what he thought, anyway."

"And it got him killed, the stupid idiot. So the one that killed these dog breeders is most likely the one that killed Yapp, right?"

"Possibly. I can't think straight anymore."

"So that'd be someone from the studio. They're the only other ones who know about this whole thing, right?"

"I suppose so."

Russell punched the horn at a driver attempting to cut him off.

"What's their names?"

"Names?"

"The ones who know, and don't tell me you don't know."

"What are you going to do, kill them?"

"Why would I do that?"

"Then you intend beating the truth out of them, at least."

"I might. They'd deserve it, right?"

"If they were the ones responsible—but they aren't."

"Says who?"

"Says me. I know them, and they're not the types to go around killing people."

"But they might hire someone else to do it for them, no? They already did it once, getting this Eddie to rub out Whitey, and maybe they did it again, getting rid of the Mausers, and now Yapp. It all fits."

"It's simply unbelievable."

"Just because they wear suits and ties and drive fancy cars?

Don't kid yourself, cuz. Rich guys, they think they can do anything, and sometimes they can. The facts are, there's someone out there killing everyone connected with this thing. I'd say you're next on the list."

"But I haven't *done* anything! I don't *know* anything!"

"But you might, so they'll be after you. You need a buddy."

"With a gun."

"Right." Russell pulled up at a stop sign. "Now, what's their names?"

"The only ones I know of are Margolis and Schutt. There may be more."

"Swell."

"All they wanted was their money back. They almost certainly have it now. Let them keep it, and they'll leave me alone."

"You think like a girl, cuz. They want you gone because you know their names."

"I'm also writing an important script for them."

"Which is what, half done?"

"More than that, almost completed, in fact."

"After which they don't need you."

Moody had already considered this. Russell let out the clutch, and the car began rolling.

"So if you smack these guys first, you get to live until you're eighty, and maybe we get the money too."

"I don't *want* the money!"

"Well, I goddamn do!"

"Just don't expect me to go along with it."

"Keith, this isn't a movie, and you're not writing it all down before it happens. This is happening *to you*. See the difference? You need to pull your head out of your ass and see what gives. That way you might stay alive, see. Huh? You see?"

"Yes, I see."

"You can't stay at your place anymore. This guy that did Yapp, he might come back for you. I got a place you can share."

"First I need to get some things."

"You'll do it? You're gonna move in with me?"

"If I must."

"Hey, we'll do all right."

MOODY ENTERED HIS apartment from the alley and packed a suitcase, then lifted his typewriter and carried everything back to the car. The Underwood was placed on the backseat with Bess.

"What'd you bring that for?"

"I have a script to complete."

"You what? These guys you're doing it for, they're the ones want you dead pretty soon, or didn't that sink in yet?"

"You may be wrong. I want a completed script to present to them if you are."

"Cuz, you kill me."

Russell's hotel was downtown, on a street filled with blowing trash and stumbling winos. The Belvedere was a ruin, three crumbling stories of dead end.

"Lock the car up," Russell warned Moody.

The desk clerk looked up as they entered, then down again at his racing form.

They carried Moody's suitcase and typewriter up to the second floor. The stairwell and corridors, without pictures, paint, or carpeting, smelled of disinfectant, and behind that odor was another, of ancient urine and vomit and sweat and human despair. Russell unlocked a battered door.

"This is it, home sweet home, like Judy Garland says."

"Actually, she said there's no place like home."

"I guess you'd know. Ever meet her?"

"She's under contract to Goldwyn."

Russell set the suitcase down. Moody stood and absorbed the essence of the room that now was his home. The single light source was of low wattage and without a shade. The bed was a sagging double. The sink in the corner would, on closer examination, prove to have piss stains down the front of the bowl. The wooden floor was warped and gouged and worn down by a million pairs of shoes. Moody sensed the traffic of hopeless souls that had passed through there, and for a moment he was too appalled to do anything but stare at the open window, as if seeking escape from the terrible room. Bess whined.

"Okay," said Russell, "so it ain't the Ritz. Who's gonna come looking for you here, a Hollywood writer like you?"

"No one," Moody admitted. "No one would come looking for anyone here."

"That's right, and the bed's clean, no bugs. It could be worse."

"Indeed it could."

"So now we make plans, right?"

"Right."

By ten o'clock one conclusion had been reached that both parties could agree upon: The only man who might possibly have killed the Mausers and Yapp, and Horace Wheat as well, was Dr. Weichek. Moody was less accepting of this notion than Russell, but could think of no other individual who might logically have cut so precise a swath through the finite membership of those involved in the blackmailing of Empire.

Margolis and Schutt were in all probability behind the killings, but Moody had suspected the doctor from the moment he learned at the morgue that Horace had a needle puncture in his arm. And he did not like the doctor for having had him thrown out of the Weichek Institute, or for the unknown influence he appeared to have over Myra.

Moody was beginning to suspect that Myra led a double life, and had concealed from him the knowledge of an ongoing dope habit, or maybe the current weaning of herself from whatever foul substance she had been injecting. The needle tip he had found in her car was pricking him still. It occurred to Moody that all of Myra's blouses had long sleeves, and he had never seen her naked arms in anything but romantically low lamplight or early-morning sun kept at bay by window shades. If he had looked closely at those arms, would he have seen the telltale marks of her degradation?

"I'm hungry," Russell said. "Let's eat."

He took Moody to an all-night diner washed by cruel light that fell from enameled bowls suspended above the tables like interrogation lamps. The place was clean but joyless, the food plentiful and cheap. They had chowder and yesterday's cherry pie.

Russell selected a toothpick from a small jar on the table and began cleaning his molars, grimacing and leering at his cousin.

"So, this doctor, how do we get to him?"

"I don't know. Reaching him at the Institute is hopeless because of his goons all over the place."

"Then we get him at home."

"I don't know where he lives."

"Don't be so pathetic. This is modern times we live in, the big city, you know, so if you need to find out where someone lives, you do the smart thing and look him up in the goddamn phone book." Russell jerked a thumb at the rear wall. "There's a phone back there. Go check the books."

Moody did it, and remembered those times years before when Russell had ordered him around, sent him on useless errands, and generally done his best to make Moody feel like a flunky. Nothing had changed. Moody found the revival of the master-servant relationship interesting from a psychological point of view, but personally unacceptable. He would do something about that.

The phone books were attached to the wall by chains. Moody checked the inner Los Angeles directory first, then those listing the outer suburbs, then returned to the table.

"Plenty of Weicheks, but no Wendell Weicheks. He probably has an unlisted number."

"Swell. Now we have to hang around on the road to the Institute and nab him when he drives to work."

"We don't know what kind of car he has."

"Okay, come up with a better idea."

Moody hesitated. Could what he was about to do be considered betrayal? Then again, hadn't Myra's secretiveness been just that?

"There's someone I know—" he said, and returned to the phones.

MYRA RECEIVED HIM in her nightgown and robe. Moody knew it was because of the lateness of his call, not some attempt to seduce him. There were dark circles under her eyes. She lit a cigarette as they sat in the living room.

"All right, Keith, what couldn't be discussed over the phone?"

"Weichek."

"What about him?"

"I need his address."

"Why?"

"He had me thrown out of the Institute because I made a scene over what they did to Mortimer. You know he's had electroshock therapy."

"No, I didn't know."

"He looked half dead, and I made a—a fuss about it. The thing is, I want to talk to Dr. Weichek and apologize, so I can get permission to go back there and see Mortimer. It isn't something I could do over the phone. I have to speak with Weichek face-to-face."

"Keith, I don't think you're telling me the truth."

"Does what I want sound so implausible?"

"No, but your eyes aren't looking at me. You always used to look at me when we talked. At first I thought it must be because you think I'm a gorgeous babe or something, then I realized you're just one of those guileless souls who look people in the face when they talk. It's part of what made me fall in love with you, if you want to know, that special eye-to-eye way you have about you. It's not there tonight, Keith."

"Well, I just don't know how to reply. I need to talk with Weichek."

"It's past eleven. You couldn't talk with him tonight."

"Tomorrow, then."

"Just go to the Institute."

"Why are you protecting him? All I want is the man's address, and you're afraid to give it to me. Why is that, Myra?"

Moody did his best to look her directly in the eyes as he said this.

"I'm not protecting anyone. You're acting very strange tonight."

"Show me your arms!"

"What?"

"Show me your arms! You said you fell in love with me, so if you still feel that way, just show me your arms right now! No hesitation, Myra, or I'll suspect the worst!"

A change came over her face; her puzzled expression was replaced by one of resignation, accompanied by a kind of hardness. She slipped off her robe. The nightgown beneath was sleeveless. Myra came across the room and presented her naked arms to Moody.

"See, lover? No needle marks. I've got it right, haven't I? You think I'm a dope fiend because that's Weichek's specialty."

"I don't know what his specialty is. I only know he's got Mortimer locked away and keeps pushing electricity through his skull."

"Maybe that's what Mortimer needs. You're not a doctor,

Keith. You know, I've heard that dopers run out of nice fresh veins in their arms, so they shoot the stuff in other places that can't be noticed. Private places for private vices."

She slipped off her nightgown and stood naked before him, turning slowly so he could see every part of her.

"Any needle marks, Keith? Even one?"

"No—"

"Maybe you're a dope fiend, Keith, and you want Weichek to give you the cure. Am I right? Are you a ravening junkie, Keith?"

"Don't be absurd—"

She sat on his lap and pushed her breasts against his face.

"Prove it," she said. "Strip. Right now. No hesitation, or I'll think the worst."

"Myra, this isn't the time—"

"So you *are* a dope fiend. Oh, Keith, the shame of it, and they say dope addicts are awful lovers too, their cocks don't get hard when their girlfriends want it that way, so how about it, Keith, are we going to see further proof that you shoot bad stuff into your body that makes you limp, hmmm?"

Her hands had already run down his shirtfront and now were tugging at his belt buckle. Moody knew he was losing the advantage of righteous anger and suspicion and still had not gained Weichek's address, the whole purpose of his visit. Her hands were inside his pants now, and Moody's efforts to dislodge Myra from his lap, never very forceful to begin with, were becoming weaker.

"Keith, I think I've found proof that you don't have a dope habit. It's a growing body of evidence, Keith. I think we're going to have to take this into court on a wheelbarrow, Keith. It's looking good, but I still need to see the rest of your skin to be sure—"

Moody toppled them both from the chair onto the floor, and Myra demanded hard evidence in an increasingly hoarse voice, until Moody presented her with it.

Afterward, sharing a cigarette, she asked him for the real reason he required Weichek's address. Moody repeated his story, but without looking at her.

"Keith, you're keeping something secret from me."

"And you're doing the same to me. Your skin is flawless. What's your reason for going out to the Institute?"

Myra took the cigarette back from him. "If I tell you, will you tell me what's eating you, I mean *really* tell me? You look like you've got loan sharks on your trail."

"I can't involve you. It's too dangerous."

"Oooh, too dangerous for me, but not too dangerous for intrepid secret agent Keith Moody, cloak-and-dagger specialist, who fights the good fight against the enemies of the nation. Excuse me while I yawn, darling."

"All right, I'll tell you. You go first, though."

Myra stubbed out the cigarette. "It's Bax," she said.

"Bax?"

"Brother Bax has a little problem with sharp objects. He keeps sticking them into his arm and various other places on his manly anatomy."

"Bax is a dope addict?"

"Not the only one in this town, lover, and not even the only one at Empire."

"God, you don't mean Mortimer—"

"That guy couldn't inject emotion into his lines. No, think again. It's a she."

"Ummm . . . Give me a clue."

"I don't like her."

"Sandy Ryder?"

"The bitch got Bax hooked after his auto accident last year. Take some of this, she said, it'll take the pain away, and he did, like a fool, and now he's hooked on morphine. Dr. Weichek's trying to get him off it. He's trying to do the same for Sandy, but she's not cooperating."

"Does Margolis know this?"

"Are you kidding? Margolis thinks Bax's problem is booze. Weichek handles alcoholics too, and people who like to screw cows for all I know. He's fascinated by everything that people shouldn't do but do anyway. Really, he's a sweet little man who just happens to work with nuts and addicts."

"My oh my—Bax and Sandy."

"You've got to keep it under your hat. Their careers are at stake, and so's your movie. They get canned from the set, and there goes *China Skies*. Promise me you'll keep it a secret. If Margolis ever finds out, Bax is finished. Sandy I don't care about. Margolis doesn't even know she's Weichek's patient. Promise?"

"I promise."

"Now it's your turn."

"I . . . well, knowing what I now know about Weichek, I hesitate to tell you."

"Keith, I'll squeeze your balls if you try to back out of our deal. I mean it."

They smoked two cigarettes each while he explained.

Myra put her robe back on and went into the kitchen to make coffee.

"It's not something you made up?" she asked.

Moody followed her, buttoning his pants. "If I came up with a scenario like this, I'd be fired for making things too complex for the average moviegoer."

"And the only one still alive that you thought might be doing the killing is Weichek? Keith, he's got a mother who's bedridden, a wife who died years ago, and a little boy who's retarded. Does that sound like some kind of crazy killer to you?"

"No."

"Good. The crazy one's your cousin. How does he think he's going to get away with this? His picture's on every newspaper and magazine and newsreel in the country, or was."

"He's got away with it so far. I suppose people just don't expect to see the famous missing Flying Tiger sitting next to them on a bus, or drinking coffee in a diner. He wants his fifty thousand dollars."

"Then he'll have to get it off Roy Schutt or Marvin Margolis. Everyone else who was in on this is dead."

"I can't see either of them as triggermen, can you?"

"No, which puts you back at square one. Why don't you go to the police and ask those two detectives if they can't help?"

"God, no, they'd arrest Russell. I'm not turning over my cousin, even if he's a blackmailer. At least he hasn't killed anyone."

"And if you still have any doubts about Dr. Weichek, look at the way he told the detectives he never met you. Would he have done that if he wanted to make trouble?"

"I guess not. Myra, I'm sorry I thought those ridiculous thoughts about you. I haven't been myself since all this craziness began."

"I think I've already made my forgiveness known. What do we do now?"

"I'll explain to Russell that Dr. Weichek isn't the one we're after, or rather Russell is after. He doesn't know anything about the blackmail or the murders or the money. He's just a doctor who got told by Margolis to cremate Horace Wheat, presumably to take the responsibility off my shoulders so I'd get back to working on the script. Russell isn't going to like that."

"Pooh to Russell. Can't you persuade him to go away?"

"Not until he has his fifty grand."

Myra put her arms around Moody's neck. The coffeepot began to bubble.

"Keith, I've got Bax to worry about, and you've got Russell. Neither one of them is probably worth it, but we're taking care of them anyway, because they're family. The one thing I need to know is, do you and I need to worry about each other? I don't mean worry about assassins and so forth—nobody's after you, because you don't have the money—I mean worry about whether I love you and you love me. Have I made myself clear, or should I start again?"

"It's clear. No, we don't need to worry about that."

She kissed him. "Are you going to stay here tonight?"

"I think I should let Russ know what I found out."

"Get rid of him as fast as you can, sweetheart. He's bad news."

"I know."

BESS LEAPED AT him when he came through the door. It was past 2:00 A.M. by then, and Moody was surprised to find Russell still awake. He was seated directly below the room's only lightbulb, reading the latest pages of *China Skies*. He waved the pages in greeting.

"This is a comedy, right?"

"No, an action drama."

"So how come I keep laughing when I read it?"

"Russ, I have some things to tell you."

"The Tigers were never like this, and neither was I, and who's Lin-Ming and Kathy? I don't know any broads called that."

"Weichek has nothing whatever to do with the money or the murders."

"Say that again."

Moody explained everything to the best of his admittedly incomplete understanding. Russell listened, then became angry.

"If it isn't the doc, then who the hell is it! You say these other guys, Schutt and Margolis, couldn't be doing the killing because they're not the type, but who the hell knows what kinda type anyone else is! So Weichek's got a crippled mama and a retarded kid, okay, I'm real sorry for him, but that don't mean he couldn't be part of this whole thing! Jesus, Keith, did you ever think I could be doing what I'm doing?"

"No."

"There you are! Nobody knows nothing about anyone, not deep down."

"Russ, your argument makes sense, but I don't accept it. Whoever it was that took the money is a long way away by now. There's no reason to believe he, or they, would want to kill again. They have the cash, and the police don't have a clue."

"They got *my* money! I want it back!"

"Fine. Get it back, but don't ask me to help, because I'm not interested. I have a job to do, and I'm nearly done. These pages you find so hilarious are my bread and butter, and I work honestly to earn my pay. I can sleep at night because I haven't committed any crime, and it so happens I'm going to get married soon, so things are all right with me, Russ, even if they aren't with you."

"Married? To who, the one you just went to see?"

"That's right. I just made my mind up to ask her."

"You expect congratulations or something?"

"I expect nothing from you. I'll do one thing, Russ, I'll help you get down to Mexico before your disguise quits working. I don't know what you'll do down there, because you won't have any cash apart from what I can spare, but you can find work, I'm sure, and start over again. They must need pilots in Mexico, and you're a good one. Think about it."

Russell laughed. Moody recognized the bitter, mocking edge to it; he had heard it many times when they were young.

"Keith, you always were a fool. You think if you work hard you'll do okay, and if you marry your girl she won't cheat on you, but there aren't any guarantees for that kinda happiness, not in this world, my friend. The only way to be sure you get what you want is money, and I mean plenty of it, in your hand right this minute. That's what I call a guarantee, and I want mine. I earned it by jumping out of a plane and losing a good buddy. That fifty thousand is mine. I don't care who's got it and how far away he is, I want it back."

Moody began picking up the pages Russell had let fall to the floor.

"Tomorrow I'm going back to my place. Myra's right about there being nobody after me. You do what you want, Russ, but don't expect any help from me, apart from getting across the border. And now I'm going to bed."

"Yeah, you do that, cuz."

Russell smoked while Moody got into his pajamas. The bed, when he eased himself into it with much twanging of springs, was hard and lumpy. Moody pummeled a pillow into submission and thrust it under his head, then prepared himself to sleep. Bess jumped onto the bed and lay at his feet. The last thing he saw before closing his eyes was a stream of smoke jetting from the tight lips of his cousin and swirling upward around the bare lightbulb like mist.

THE SOUNDS OF traffic awakened him. Russell was standing by the open window. Moody saw sunlight and smelled exhaust fumes. Bess was by the door, whining to be let out. He sat up and reached for his glasses. Able to see detail now, he was surprised to find a smile on the face of the Tiger.

"It was the kid," Russell said. "I stayed awake all night, figuring it out. It's the kid. He's got the dough stashed away someplace, waiting for the heat to die down."

"What kid? What are you talking about?"

"The kid that worked for the Mausers. You met him when the cops took you out there. The kid that feeds the dogs and sweeps out the dog shit. He's got it."

Moody got out of bed and began dressing. "Russ, you're clutching at straws. Herman wasn't bright enough to be a part of this. He wasn't even there when the Mausers were killed, Labiosa and Huttig told me that."

"So what? Cops aren't the smartest guys themselves. It was Herman. He killed the Mausers and made it look like they shot each other, then he took the money and hid it."

"He was with his grandmother. They checked up on his alibi."

"Which was his grandma. You think a grandma wouldn't back up any story her grandkid wanted her to, or else watch him get hauled away by the cops? It all adds up. Those cops, they never saw the real kid. He was putting on an act, and it worked. Not for me. I see the real kid. He's a killer and a thief, believe me."

"I have to take Bess for a walk."

"Hurry back, cuz. I'm hot to get out there and talk with Herman."

Moody tied his shoes. "Going to smack him around a little?"

"If I have to. If he's a feeb like you say, he'll squawk pretty fast."

"I wouldn't do that today, Russ."

"Why not?"

"Because last night we left Quentin Yapp just about a half mile from the Mausers'. He'll be found pretty soon, and when he is, the whole area will be thick with police. There's no doubt they'll connect Yapp's murder with what happened to Eddie and Muriel. I'd stay away if I were you."

"Okay, tonight, then."

"Let's just see how things work out."

Moody stood and placed the leash on Bess.

Russell said, "You don't buy my theory, do you."

"Not for one second. Herman is just a not very bright boy."

"So was Billy the Kid, they say."

"I'm taking Bess out, and when we come back I'm putting my things in the car and going home again."

"Okay by me, only you better be back here to pick me up tonight, around ten. You don't show, I'm gonna be mad, cuz."

"Come on, Bess."

"You think about it," called Russell as man and dog left the room.

15

MOODY SHOWERED AT his apartment and fed breakfast to himself and Bess, then drove to the studio. He had smoked an entire pack of Chesterfields, while working his way toward the final pages of the script, when Terry Blackwell came by.

"Say, did you hear about your old boss?" Terry asked.

"Who, Yapp?"

"He's dead."

"No!"

"Found in his car out in El Monte, near where his sister and her husband got killed. The plot thickens."

"I'm . . . flabbergasted."

"Margolis wants to see you."

"Now?"

"Whatever Margolis wants, it's always now."

Moody hurried over to Margolis's office and was ushered through the bronze doors that had closed in his face on the day Mortimer was taken away. Margolis was waiting.

"Keith, we have a killer in our midst."

"Killer, Mr. Margolis?"

"Quentin Yapp has been murdered."

"I was just told. It's terrible."

"Quentin's sister and brother-in-law also were murdered, Keith. There's a pattern here, wouldn't you say?"

Moody wondered if Margolis would go so far as to admit he had told Yapp to hire Eddie Mauser to take care of Tony White. The plan had gone badly awry, and Margolis was not known for public acknowledgment of his failures.

"Are you involved, Keith? Speak now and I can help you."

"I . . . pardon me?"

"The money, Keith, that was supposed to have been returned to this very room, has not found its way back to me. Do you have any explanation I might find believable?"

"I certainly don't have it, and I don't know who does. I'd say Eddie Mauser and his wife intended keeping it, possibly with the connivance of Quentin Yapp, but they had a falling-out. Obviously there's another player in the scheme—the one who shot Yapp—but who that individual might be, Mr. Margolis, I have no idea, and I resent your implication, sir, that it might be myself."

"Did I say Yapp was shot, Keith? He might have been strangled."

"I made the assumption that since the other two were shot, he was shot also. I won't fall into a cheap trap like that, Mr. Margolis."

"Good. I'd hate to see one of my star employees come apart at the mere suggestion of complicity in this dirty business. So, Keith, who's left that has a hand in the deal?"

"I don't know." Moody cleared his throat. "Mr. Margolis?"

"What?"

"It crossed my mind that you and Roy Schutt might have hired someone to take care of Eddie Mauser the same way you hired Mauser to take care of the blackmailer."

Margolis looked at Moody with a basilisk stare.

"Indeed, Keith, and how strongly do you believe this ridiculous and may I say personally insulting theory?"

"Not very strongly. I felt I had to ask, that's all."

"I'll overlook it. At a time like this, when studio money is missing, men are apt to say and do foolish things. Roy Schutt, for your information, is extremely upset about the entire matter, and has taken the day off with my permission. Roy is close to a nervous breakdown because of the strain. Here we are, Keith, doing our best to put together a picture of major importance, a morale booster for the nation, our patriotic duty, no less, and something like this had to come up. It isn't easy, is it, Keith?"

"No, sir, it isn't."

"Finished the script?"

"Almost. Another day or two, Mr. Margolis."

"Good, good. Nothing seems to keep you from your typewriter. Sheer professionalism. I like that. Your star is rising at Empire, Keith, I want you to know."

"Thank you, sir. Sir?"

"Keith?"

"About Mortimer Pence. He's being given electroshock therapy by Dr. Weichek."

"You appear to be very well informed on matters that have nothing to do with you."

"It's just that Smokey . . . Mortimer and I were friends, kind of, and I have to say, Mr. Margolis, that shooting electricity through someone's brain is the kind of thing Dr. Frankenstein might do."

"Your point being?"

"I'd like to have Mortimer released from the Weichek Institute and placed in my custody. That can only happen if you say so, Mr. Margolis."

"Why should I take Pence from expert custodians and place him with you, a man with no psychiatric knowledge whatsoever?"

"To make me happy, sir."

"Happy? Where does happiness fit into this plan, might I ask?"

"Sir, you arranged to have Horace Wheat cremated, isn't that correct?"

"I might have."

"And the reason given to me for your action, sir, was so that I wouldn't need to worry about it myself, because it was all taken care of, thanks to your kind sympathy and generosity. Well, sir, I guess I'm asking for another shot of the same stuff. I can't stand the thought of Mortimer being in that place, having his brain fried."

"I suppose you want him in the picture. You asked me once before."

"No, sir, just out of Weichek's hands."

Margolis continued to stare. Moody stared right back.

"Very well, Keith. Pence is a sick and possibly dangerous man, but upon your head be it. I'll arrange for his release personally."

"Thank you, sir."

"On the day you hand over the last scenes of *China Skies*."

"It's a deal, sir."

"You know, I don't want to offend Dr. Weichek. He's been a good friend to Empire Productions over the years, an invaluable aid in assisting troubled actors to . . . to find themselves again. Actors are not like you and me, Keith, not disciplined. They're children, most of them, and not just the younger ones. An actor is a classroom show-off who has never fully grown up, never lost the need for attention and applause. You may be shocked to hear me say such things, but I feel I can trust you with hard truth in a way that, a week ago, for example, I couldn't have."

"A week ago, sir, you said successful actors, movie stars, were above the salt."

"I did say that, didn't I. Well, Keith, it just goes to show that there are two sides to every question. Do you agree with that?"

"Sometimes, Mr. Margolis, I think there might be three or four."

"And you might even be right. Go back to work, Keith. Don't forget—as soon as the last pages are in my hand, Mortimer Pence is yours."

"Yes, sir."

"And Keith?"

"Sir?"

"If you happen to learn who has Empire's hard-earned money, I do hope you inform me. You know, the fellow who's behind all this is going to have a fight on his hands if he thinks he can simply walk away with what doesn't belong to him."

"I'll keep my mind open, Mr. Margolis."

"Be careful, Keith. An open mind can be like an open mine shaft. You might fall in and die."

"I'll be careful, sir."

"Do that."

Labiosa and Huttig were in his office when Moody returned. Huttig was teaching Bess to stand on her hind legs by making her reach for the iced donut in his hand.

"Mr. Moody, come in, come in."

"Thanks, I will. Please don't give sugar to my dog."

"She never got a bite. So, Moody, you hear about Yapp?"

"Yes."

"When we took you out to Mauser's dog farm you didn't tell us your ex-boss was Muriel Mauser's brother."

"Didn't I? That's probably because I didn't know."

"But you know now, right?" asked Labiosa.

"I do."

"When did you find out, Moody?"

"About ten seconds ago when you told me."

"Expect us to buy that?"

"I expect you to tell me that Yapp's death isn't a coincidence."

"Damn right it isn't," said Huttig. "He was found dead in his car just a little ways from the dog place. How would you explain that?"

"I can't, unless it's revenge."

"Revenge?"

"Someone might have thought Yapp killed Eddie Mauser and killed him for it."

"Think Yapp'd kill his sister too?"

"I didn't say that, I said Eddie. Eddie shot Muriel because she was having an affair with Tony White, and Yapp shot Eddie. I suggest you start looking for a close friend or relative of Eddie's, someone who'd have a motive for a revenge killing."

"Moody, how come they got you writing flyboy pictures and Westerns? They should have you writing the mysteries, you know, Nick Charles and Sam Spade."

"He could cook up a pretty good plot," agreed Labiosa.

"Thanks. Talk to Margolis about it."

"He's the big boss here, right?"

"None bigger. Umm, I think I know who's going to be the next one killed."

"Yeah? Who?"

"Herman."

"Dopey Herman? The kid?"

"I'll bet he knows something. Maybe he was a witness to Yapp's murder. It might have taken place at the house, then the killer took Yapp's body away in the car and dumped it. The kid saw it all, I bet, only he's too scared to talk. If I were you I'd take him into protective custody for a few days. If you're nice to him he might even finger the killer for you. But take him in anyway, is my suggestion."

Labiosa and Huttig exchanged weary looks.

"Everybody's got a theory," said Huttig.

"Everybody wants to be a detective," said Labiosa.

"Vinnie and me, we listen to people with theories and we smile, don't we, Vinnie."

"We smile big."

"And after we quit listening and the person with the theory goes away, we quit smiling, don't we, Vinnie."

"Real fast."

"Because the theory that we smiled about getting, being polite, you know, it's not worth a whole lot. What would you say the average theory we get from John and Jane Citizen is worth, Vinnie?"

"I'd say a good one's worth two cents."

"And we thank you, Moody, for your two cents' worth. Notice how I'm smiling, Moody, and being polite? Vinnie's smiling too, because the department wants us to get along with the public."

Moody took his hat from the stand by the door and put it on his head.

"Gentlemen, I'm going to have a bite to eat in the commissary. Would you care to be my guests?"

"No, thanks, Moody. We'd feel out of place with all those movie stars and producers and writers, wouldn't we, Vinnie?"

"Like two turds on a silver platter," said Labiosa.

"So we'll just run along and do some more police work."

Moody said, "I really think you should take Herman into custody, just to be on the safe side. It wouldn't look good for the police if he's the next one to catch a bullet."

"Might be a three-cent theory," admitted Labiosa.

The detectives walked a short way with Moody, then separated as they neared the visitors' parking lot. "See you around," Huttig told him, "and write a mystery next time."

"I'll certainly try."

"You do that" was Labiosa's parting line.

Moody was looking for an empty seat in the commissary when Myra approached him and suggested they go outside, where the benches afforded more privacy. Once settled away from the other outdoor diners, she said, "Bax is giving Dr. Weichek trouble. Weichek wants me to visit him this evening and talk some sisterly sense into his head."

"I'll come too. I want to see Mortimer again. Margolis told me he'll tell Weichek to let him out when the script's completed."

"He said what? Keith, that's grotesque. Why can't they let Mortimer out today? Why should he be some kind of bargaining chip? It's disgusting."

"I'm not going to argue about that. The point is, in a day or two at most, he'll be released to my custody."

"What are you going to do with him?"

"I don't know. I haven't planned anything beyond getting him away from those damned electrodes."

"All heart and no practicality, that's you."

"Will you marry me anyway?"

"Umm . . . What did you say?"

"I'm asking you to marry me. Mortimer can have his own room."

"Just a minute. You're saying that if we get married, Mortimer's going to live with us? You're not serious."

"Just until we can think of another place for him, a retired actors' home, something like that. We wouldn't have him forever. I love you."

"I love you too. We could always find a place for him *before* getting married."

"But that'd mean waiting."

"Can't you wait another few weeks, darling heart?"

"No. Well, maybe, if that's what you want."

"What I want is for us to be together, alone. And what about the honeymoon? I'm not taking Mortimer with us. The dog, yes, but not Mortimer."

"All right. So—does this mean you said yes?"

"I guess it does. You didn't even get down on bended knee, Keith. I think I've sold myself too easily, somehow. Oh, well. Are you a Hindu or anything unusual?"

"I'm an atheist. How about you?"

"Agnostic, probably. That's a cowardly atheist. I want to keep a little bit of belief in God, just in case I wind up outside the pearly gates one day."

"Better make it a registry office wedding, then."

"But only after Mortimer's found a home."

"What is he, some kind of bargaining chip? That's disgusting."

"Outmaneuvered again. Gosh, you're smart. Think our kids will be?"

"Einsteins, every one."

"Congratulations, Keith. You're going to marry a wonderful girl."

"Thank you."

THEY DROVE TO the Institute in Myra's car, arriving just before sundown, and were escorted to Dr. Weichek's office by one of the white-shirted orderlies. Weichek stood up as they entered.

"Miss Nolan, Mr. Moody, welcome and thank you for coming so very promptly."

"Is Bax being a fool again, Doctor?"

"He's being immature, to say the least. Bax does not respond well to figures of authority, of which I am one, regrettably. I think in this case some advice and a reprimand or two from within the family might be advantageous."

"I've been telling him to quit ever since I found out. He just ignores me."

"That may be, but you have arrived with reinforcements. Mr. Moody, I believe you're writing the next film Bax is scheduled to make, isn't that so?"

"It is, yes."

"And he'll be playing your own cousin, I'm told. How interesting. With a little persuasion from you, I'm hoping Bax will see that nothing less than his career is at stake. For someone of Bax's ego, the loss of his status as a Hollywood star would be substantial, a frightening thing to contemplate. Scare tactics, you see. And we also have with us Miss Ryder, who just this afternoon pledged to me her sincere wish to be rid of her vice once and for all."

"I find that hard to believe, Doctor. She's never once encouraged him to stop."

"Miss Ryder assures me she's ready to begin, and will use her influence over Bax to positive effect. Bax has told me he loves her very much, so her pledge to join him in treatment is significant. We have three individuals representing three excellent reasons for him to turn a new leaf and begin a cleaner life. This is something of a fresh approach for me, using friends and family members to work their wiles on a patient. It's unconventional, but then I've never felt myself constrained to obey the accepted wisdom of my peers."

"I just want it to work," said Myra.

Moody thought he detected a note of despair in her voice.

"I guarantee nothing, of course. We are all adventurers on a sea of discovery."

"I want Bax back on shore, permanently."

"That is the desired outcome, Miss Nolan, for both of us."

"Dr. Weichek?"

"Yes, Mr. Moody?"

"I owe you an apology for my behavior on my last visit here."

"Think nothing of that, Mr. Moody. I do understand that you were not prepared to see your friend Mr. Pence in his condition at that time. It must have been terribly upsetting for you."

"Yes, but that isn't what I mean. It's that . . . other thing. If you'll recall, I made some fairly outrageous accusations."

"Ah, yes, I do recall the nature of the conversation. Let us consign it to the past, shall we?"

"I'd be most grateful if you would, Doctor."

"Consider it done. And now, Bax and Miss Ryder are waiting." He pressed a button on his desk intercom. "Please have Miss Ryder escorted from the waiting room to 106. My visitors and I will meet her there."

"Yes, Doctor," said a voice from the box.

Dr. Weichek led Myra and Moody through the corridors toward room 106.

Moody said, "Doctor, has Marvin Margolis been in touch with you recently?"

"Mr. Margolis? Yes, just this afternoon. I must say you have a charitable disposition, Mr. Moody. Mr. Pence may not be the kind of houseguest who endears himself to the host."

"Has he had more of the electroshock therapy?"

"Not since you were here last. It was never my intention that he should have prolonged treatment. There has been considerable improvement, but my own preference would be to keep him here for further observation. Of course, if Mr. Margolis and yourself are determined to take him from us—"

"I just think he'd be better off with a friend, not doctors and nurses. I don't mean any disrespect by that, Doctor."

"None taken, I assure you. Ah, here we are."

Sandy Ryder, accompanied by an orderly, was approaching from the corridor's far end. She wore a demure skirt and carried a matching purse. She was smiling brightly. Moody thought she looked exactly like one of her own Nice Girl characters, to the extent that he asked himself which scene she was shooting here, maybe one where Russell Keys arrives back in America with his leg in a cast, and his girl Kathy comes to the hospital to be with him. No such scene had been written, nor would it, but Sandy Ryder was Kathy, so far as Moody was concerned, and Baxter Nolan was Russ. It was a uniquely Hollywood perspective, he assumed.

"Hello, Doctor," Sandy called while still some distance away.

"Good evening to you, Miss Ryder. We are to be joined in our efforts by Miss Nolan and Mr. Moody."

"Swell! The more the merrier, I always say. Hi, Myra. Hello, Keith."

"Hello yourself," said Myra, ungraciously, in Moody's opinion.

"Hello, Sandy," he said, mustering a smile that he hoped would cover Myra's indiscretion.

"I suggest we go straight in," said Weichek, producing his key.

"Why does Bax need to be locked in?" Myra asked.

"For the security of the staff and the reasonable protection of the patient, Miss Nolan. Bax is under no obligation to stay here, since this is not an asylum, nor a prison. The minute he leaves, however, I'm duty-bound to inform Mr. Margolis, who pays the bill in such cases. Bax might want to throw in the towel and simply walk away, and if he does so, he walks away from a budding career of incalculable importance to himself and Mr. Margolis. I see a locked door as nothing more than the restraining hand of a friend, urging caution."

"You're saying it's for his own good," said Myra.

"In my own long-winded fashion, I'm saying exactly that."

Weichek inserted the key and turned the lock, then opened the door to allow his three guests to enter Baxter Nolan's room.

It was quite unlike the room in which Moody had seen Mortimer Pence. This room was at least four times larger, with shapely vases containing flowers so heavily scented their presence filled the air with perfume. Reproductions of popular masterpieces were hung on the walls, and an oak cabinet radio was broadcasting the music of Guy Lombardo. The metal-framed hospital bed in the corner was brightened with a cover of New Mexican design. Even the white-painted bars outside the windows seemed part of the decor.

Bax was seated in a Swedish armchair, smoking a cigarette, wearing a silk dressing gown over his silk pajamas. He rose with studied grace and threw his hands wide; an actor's greeting, was Moody's assessment of the move.

"Doctor, so many of my good friends, all at once! Is it my birthday?"

"Not your birthday, Bax, no. More like your day of reckoning. Your friends are here bearing sad tidings."

Bax's eyebrows arched. "Sad? I hope not, by golly."

"They're here to tell you, Bax, that they miss you, and wish most heartily that you would rejoin them outside."

"No sadness there, Doc."

"Sadness lies in the fact that you seem unwilling to leave here, Bax, under the conditions that will ensure you don't return, as you have done in the past. I refer to your unwillingness to give up, once and for all, your foolish and dangerous morphine habit."

"But I'm all cured, Doc. You always fix me right up."

"And when you leave, and the inclination overtakes you, you fix yourself right up all over again, do you not, Bax?"

"A little backsliding, that's all."

"I'll leave your friends with you. Listen to them carefully, Bax."

"I'll do it for you, Doc."

"Do it for yourself, please."

Moody watched Weichek leave, and heard the key turn in the lock. He rather admired the doctor for his strong words.

Bax was embracing Sandy with his left arm, holding his right arm out to receive Myra, but Myra was unwilling to be held by her brother while he still held Sandy, so it was not until Sandy stepped away from Bax that Myra permitted him to touch her.

"Myra," he said, in the same coaxing, gushing tone he had already used on Sandy's name. Now Bax was ready to acknowledge Moody. "And Keith too—how are you, Keith?"

"Fine, thanks, Bax."

"Three visitors. Weichek hasn't allowed that before. Did I do something good? Is this a reward?"

Myra said, "You haven't done anything good since you saved my dog from getting run over when I was seven."

"Harsh words, Sis. Haven't I been a good boy?" he asked Sandy.

"I don't know, Bax, have you?"

"I certainly have. Cooped up in here, what else could I be?"

"Bax, I'm not going to ice the cake. I'm here because I'm sick and tired of being embarrassed to have you for my brother. Keith's here because your idiocy threatens his position at Empire, and Sandy's here to let you know she's going cold turkey herself, right, Sandy?"

"I think I'd prefer to make my own argument in my own way, thank you, Myra."

"Good, you do that. You got him on the stuff, now get him off."

"Ladies, ladies—" Bax soothed, twisting his handsome features in mock agony. "Let's not have a rumpus when we should all be feeling happy to be with one another."

"Speak for yourself," Myra told him, turning away to face the window.

"Never mind her," said Sandy, "what about us?"

"Us, my sugar plum? Well, we're just fine, aren't we?"

"Are we, Bax? Is everything fine for us?"

"Everyone seems to be telling us it is, or will be. You're really going to do what the doc said?"

Moody felt like an eavesdropper. He went to join Myra by the window as she angrily lit a cigarette for herself. Sensing that his presence nearby was no comfort to her and was probably an irritant, Moody moved on to study one of Rembrandt's earliest self-portraits, while trying not to overhear the conversation going on behind him.

Sandy's voice was becoming agitated, so much so that Moody began listening again. "I found out, and there's nothing you can do about that," she said, her tone combining triumph and outrage.

"Sweetheart—you're going to believe what some poison tongue has said about me? I thought you trusted me more than that."

"I did, Bax, I did trust you, and then I hired a detective to make sure I could trust you and not be worrying about it all the time, and guess what, loverboy, you can't be trusted, not even a little bit, not for five minutes."

"Wait one minute, please—a detective?"

"With a camera. Want to share the results with me? I brought them along. How old is she, about sixteen? How many more have there been? Is this the kind of thing you really like, young as yesterday and willing to do anything you want because you're Bax Nolan, movie star?"

"Sandy, listen—"

"No, you listen. After the last one you said it would never happen again, and now I find you broke your solemn word to me, Bax. You have no idea, no idea at all what this has done to me, deep inside, not that you care, not you, you only care about yourself and your little playthings and your stuff, which I'm sick of, Bax, sick and ashamed I ever did that to myself, and so should you be, but you're not. . . . It was going to be the thing that got the monkey off both our backs, the love we were supposed to have, and now I know I'll never shake it alone, not after a betrayal like this . . . so it's over, finished with. My life—gone up in smoke because of you. . . . So good-bye, Bax, darling, and save a seat in hell for me."

"Sandy—"

The first three shots were almost instantaneous, followed by three more, widely spaced. Moody spun around in time to see Bax sinking to the carpet, clutching at his chest, where blood was seeping from behind the silk pattern of his dressing gown.

The gun fell from Sandy's hand. She stood quite still, watching her lover die with a look of great sadness on her face, the first genuine emotion Moody could remember seeing there.

Myra rushed to hold Bax in her arms, a steady moan coming from her throat. Moody watched Bax's face become white as his chest became redder, and then Bax was dead, Moody could tell just by looking. Bax's body sagged in Myra's arms, and his eyes, still open, stared at the carpet on which he lay.

Moody stooped to pick up the gun in case Sandy should try to make good on her promise to finish her own life by reloading. He had barely straightened up when the door flew open to allow Dr. Weichek and two orderlies inside. Moody, holding the gun, became their immediate target, and he was tackled by both men and thrown to the floor.

"It wasn't me—" he began, but the breath had been knocked from him and his words came out as a tortured gasping that conveyed nothing. From his position on the floor, both orderlies sitting on him, he saw Dr. Weichek kneel by Bax and feel for a pulse. Moody could have told him not to bother.

IT WAS INEVITABLE, given the ability of Moody's mind to concoct scenarios based on chance and coincidence, that the police, when summoned by Dr. Weichek, should be led by Labiosa and Huttig. The detectives exchanged a disbelieving look before approaching him.

"Moody, what the hell goes on with you?"

"I didn't do anything. I was here, that's all."

Labiosa said, "We got told it's a mental patient. That right?"

"No, that's not right. He was being treated for addiction to morphine."

"Who was?" asked Huttig.

"Baxter Nolan."

"Nolan? That was gonna play your cousin in the movie?"

"Yes. His girlfriend shot him because he'd been seeing someone else."

"Holy shit. So what were you doing here, Moody? You weren't here that other time, were you, when we asked you and you said you never met with this Weichek guy that runs the place and he said the same thing? Was that a true story from the both of you, Moody, huh?"

"Baxter Nolan's sister is my fiancée. We were visiting, that's all."

Huttig said, "Vinnie, call Ripley and tell him I'm a believer.

No, cancel the call. I don't believe a word Mr. Hollywood Movie Writer here tells us."

"Me neither. He's either a killer that don't look like a killer, or else he's got some kinda mental beam that shoots outta him and makes other people do what he wants, which is kill people. I saw a thing like that in *Flash Gordon*, I think."

Moody was being interviewed in the entry hall. Myra was with Dr. Weichek, and Sandy was in the custody of two uniformed policemen. Labiosa and Huttig studied Moody like a specimen under glass.

"Moody," Huttig said, "just for the record, are you telling us that all these murders that are happening everywhere you go are nothing to do with you, it's just coincidence that puts you where the killings are at every day or two? That right, Moody?"

"That's correct."

"See," said Labiosa, "we don't buy it, this coincidence shit. You're not telling us the whole truth, Moody, not by a long shot. You wanna tell us the truth about all this?"

"I've already done so. If you don't believe me, I don't blame you, but there's nothing more I can say. This is not a satisfactory time in my life, let me assure you."

"That's your fiancée over there?" Huttig asked.

"Yes, Myra Nolan."

"You got taste, Moody. She's a dish."

"Thank you. I'll be sure and tell her."

"She figure to keep on living after she gets married to you, Moody?"

"I'm not a Bluebeard, if that's what you're thinking."

"Bluebeard was a pirate. Nobody's calling you a pirate, Moody, just a magnet for murder, which is a different thing."

Moody said, "The pirate was Blackbeard. Bluebeard was a wife-murderer. I just thought I'd explain that to you for the sake of accuracy on your police report. Do you need to ask me any more questions?"

"Yeah," said Huttig, "but you'd only keep snowing us, so go see your girl."

"I'll do that."

"Only, Moody? Don't think for a minute we aren't gonna be watching you like a goddamn hawk."

"You're very welcome. Did you take Herman into protective custody, as I suggested?"

"No, we didn't. Did we do wrong, Moody? Is Herman gonna be your next victim by accident because you're someplace near the poor bastard? That what you're telling us, Moody?"

"I'm simply offering you good advice, but of course you don't have to listen to me if you don't want to. You fellows are the experts in police work, so you go right ahead and let Herman get killed, he's just a simpleton after all."

"Hey, we don't like that bad insinuation."

"I don't care, frankly."

Moody turned away from the detectives and went to Myra.

She insisted that he take her home and stay there with her. Moody was reluctant to do this, since Russell was expecting him by ten for a trip out to the Mausers' breeding kennels.

It was after nine-thirty when he and Myra were allowed to leave the Weichek Institute. Moody knew Huttig and Labiosa were following him, even though he could not tell which of the shadowy cars in the rearview mirror belonged to them. He had not wanted them to know where Myra lived, but now they would know anyway.

Bess had been left at Myra's while they went to the Institute, and she launched herself at them both when Moody came inside with Myra.

He calmed the dog down, then poured them both a drink. He was hoping to get enough liquor inside Myra to bring about drowsiness, so he could sneak away. His own car was parked nearby, but not so close that the police, if they were watching, could see it. He only had to slip out the back door, and he could get away. Even if they watched his own apartment as well as Myra's, they didn't know of Russell's dive downtown. It was past ten now, and Myra was only on her first drink.

"Keith, I don't know what to do . . ."

"Get drunk," he suggested. "I'm going to."

"Is that all you can say?"

"Yes, that's all I can say. I'm sorry about Bax, really I am, but I don't know what else I can tell you that isn't totally meaningless. He was killed by a stupid, selfish woman who'll probably go to the gas chamber for it, but beyond any satisfaction you might get from that, I don't know what you can do but be miserable for a while, and the time-honored recipe for coping with misery is booze."

Myra tossed down her drink and extended her glass. Moody refilled it, and she drank that too. She sat on the sofa and looked at him. "This afternoon I find out I'm going to get married to a wonderful guy. This evening I see my brother murdered in front of me. I'm not going to be an agnostic anymore, Keith, I'm going to be like you and call myself a bald-faced atheist right out loud for anyone who wants to know."

"That's a big step in the direction of reality, but booze will be better for you in the short term."

"Do you have a secret agenda for me tonight, Keith? You seem to be plying me with strong drink and taking none yourself."

"I want you to relax, that's all."

"How can I relax when I keep seeing Bax's head fall sideways and his eyes stop moving? . . . Oh, God . . ." She covered her face with her hands.

Moody sat beside her, glancing at his watch as he placed an arm across her shoulders: 10:27. Of course, he could simply ignore Russell's instruction and face the consequences tomorrow. That at least would give Labiosa and Huttig enough time to take Herman away from the kennels, assuming they had any intention of doing so. Moody stroked Myra's hair as she sobbed, and wondered if he would ever be free of the tightening noose that had been placed around his neck by his cousin.

"Myra?"

"Yes?"

"I have to go and meet Russell. I'm already late."

"Meet him for what? Tonight?"

"I don't know what. We made the arrangement this morning, before all this . . . other business blew up. I really think I should go and see him. He's a very unstable person I don't know what he might do if I don't show up."

"All right, but come back here after you've met him."

"I promise. I'll leave Bess here with you."

"Hurry back."

"I will."

WALKING INTO RUSSELL'S room at the Belvedere, Moody was prepared for confrontation. Instead, he found his cousin in an affable mood, crouched over a cheap radio that had not been in the room yesterday. Russell waved nonchalantly, his head still cocked toward the radio. The strains of Glen Miller's "I've Got a Gal in Kalamazoo" filled the room with a richness Moody found almost unbearable, considering the bare walls and pitted floor and the desperate man contained by them.

"Cuz, you just missed the news. Heard about your actor pal? Shot six times by his girlfriend, they say."

"I was there when it happened."

"You're shittin' me."

"About three yards away when she plugged him."

Russell insisted on hearing the details. "Okay, so you had an excuse to be late," he said. "I was getting kinda mad at you, Keith. All I've got for entertainment is this radio I got down the street at the pawnshop. Guess what happened. The guy in there says to me I look like that pilot that disappeared, so I said yeah, lots of people have been telling me that just recent, and he says I'm a dead ringer all right, so I told him I'm his twin brother and the guy laughed and laughed. He must not have heard a good radio show in a couple years, the idiot. You ready to roll?"

"Roll?"

"Out to where Herman lives. We talked about this."

"That'd be a wasted trip, Russ. Those same detectives were at the Institute tonight after Bax was killed, and they told me they're taking Herman into protective custody. They say too many people associated with the Mausers are dying, and Herman's probably next, and they may be right."

"Perfect. We go out there and poke around for the money while Herman's in jail and can't interfere. Just what the doctor ordered."

"Russ, if there was a double cross and Herman took the money, do you really think he'd be dumb enough to keep it right there at the scene of the crime?"

"Not right in the house. Maybe it's in one of the dog pens."

"I doubt it."

"You got anything better to do? Your girl, she won't be in the mood for hanky-panky, I bet."

"I'll thank you not to talk about her like that."

"Gee whiz, you sound just like some angry boyfriend in the movies. I think you've been writing that stuff too long, cuz. In real life people don't talk like that. Got your car out front? Let's go."

Russell was silent on the drive to El Monte. Moody drove into the front yard of the darkened house and parked. There were no other vehicles in view.

"Herman, he's got a truck or something?"

"I don't know what he drives, but he goes to see his grandmother on Sundays."

"Well, he's not here tonight. Your cop pals took him away all right."

They left the car and approached the house. Russell tried the door. It opened.

"Hey, Herman's a careless guy."

"Why aren't the dogs barking? I can't hear a single one."

"Maybe the SPCA came and took 'em away. That's another good reason for Herman not to be here anymore. This gets easier and easier."

"It's too easy. You don't think you can simply walk in and pick up the cash, do you?"

"Let's find out."

Russell stepped inside, and Keith followed. Russell turned on the lights.

"I don't think that's a good idea," Moody said.

"It's gone midnight, the neighbors are asleep. I'm not looking for something in the dark. Just try to relax, why don't you?"

"There's just no point in being here."

"Says you, and I don't put a lot of faith in what you say."

Russell opened a few drawers in the kitchen, then said, "Okay, if it's anywhere, it'll be in the attic."

"Why?"

"Because down here is too easy. Herman's not so dumb he wouldn't put it somewhere at least a little bit hard to get at, and that'll be the attic, unless he buried it under a pile of dog shit. Come on."

The trapdoor to the attic was found in the hallway leading to the living room. Russell set a coffee table beneath it, placed a chair on the table, and was able to reach up and push the door in.

"Time to be Tarzan," he said, and boosted himself up into the attic. Moody, below, saw the attic light come on. He could hear Russell's feet stamping around above him.

"Hey, are you coming up here to help?"

"No, I'm not. If you want to hunt for something that isn't there, go right ahead, but I'm taking it easy. I'm relaxing, Russ, just like you said I should."

"You're a goddamn lazy son of a bitch, is what you are! Jesus, Keith, don't you want some of this? If I find it and you're not up here with me, I'm keeping the whole shebang, you got that?"

"Fine! A nothing percent share of nothing is the same as a something percent share of nothing, so go ahead and disturb the spiders!"

"You always were useless! When we were kids you never wanted to get your hands dirty! A real pussy, that's you!"

Moody heard heavy objects being moved around above him while Russell continued shouting. "You don't deserve anything! You've got yourself stuck in a rut with your job and your girl, and you don't have the guts to get yourself out! You don't know a goddamn thing about real life, only what you can make up and put in some bullshit movie! You live in a box, Keith, a tiny little box, and you think it's a thousand miles wide! You're so blind you like it, you pussy!"

Moody told himself not to listen. Russell was a deceiver and blackmailer; his opinion didn't count for anything in the world Moody embraced. He was a loudmouth and a bully, beneath contempt, and yet Moody would continue assisting him, not to find the money, which Moody now saw as beyond their reach, but to avoid the forces of the law. If caught, Russell would be charged with being AWOL, and if his complicity in the blackmail attempt ever came to light he would be put in the stockade forever. Moody did not want that on his conscience, and so he stood and listened to the thumping and bumping and invective from above.

He was not aware of another presence until he felt a gun barrel poking into the small of his back. "Don't turn around, and don't make a sound," a voice told him. "Let's let your friend find what he's looking for, shall we?"

Moody knew the voice. "Roy?"

"I said, don't make a sound. Just keep your mouth shut until he finds it."

"He isn't going to find it, because it isn't here. They wouldn't have left it here."

"Who wouldn't?"

"Whoever killed the Mausers and Yapp."

"And what are their names, Keith? You tell me, and I might be able to cut you a sweet deal. Come clean with me, and you're set for life at Empire. We've got some big productions scheduled for development in the next few months. You can have your pick of them, Keith, if you'll just do the sensible thing and cooperate."

"I don't know who did any of it, and that's the truth."

"Who's your friend in the attic? I'm curious to meet him, Keith. Is he your triggerman?"

"He's my cousin, actually."

"Another cousin? You're a prolific family."

"Russell Keys, that's who's up there, Roy. Did Margolis send you here to get the money? I would have thought fifty thousand was small beer for a studio the size of Empire."

"It's the principle of the thing, Keith. Nobody gets the better of Marvin Margolis if MM can possibly help it. I'm helping him help it, you see. Now, who's up there?"

"Russ!" Moody called, and the gun was jammed harder against his spine.

"What!" came the reply, and Moody heard Roy Schutt gasp.

"It's really *him*?"

"Russ, did you find anything yet?"

"You woulda heard me holler if I did, don't you think! Get your ass up here and gimme a hand!"

"No, thanks, Russ!"

"Well, fuck you, cuz!"

"There," said Moody to Schutt. "Believe me now?"

"It's not possible—"

"He's up there, large as life, looking for the same thing you and Margolis are. I think it's silly for us all to be in contention for the money, don't you, Roy? We should unite to find out what happened. Personally, I'm not interested in taking a cut. You'll have to buy off Russ, though. He's greedy."

"Get him down here."

"Are we going to negotiate like practical men, or are you going to threaten us with your gun?"

"I'm not a violent man, Keith. Let's talk."

"Russ!"

"Shuddup! I'm busy! You want to talk, come up here!"

"We have a visitor!"

"What!"

"Someone's down here with me, Russ! He has a gun, but he wants to talk!"

The sound of Russell's footsteps approached the trapdoor above them, but did not come all the way; Russell was keeping out of sight.

"Who is it, Keith?"

"Roy Schutt, a producer at Empire. He's producing your movie, Russ."

"Yeah? What's he doing here?"

"Looking for the money. The studio wants it back. Come down and we'll talk."

"I don't talk to guys that carry guns, Schutt."

"Then I'll put it away, shall I? Keith, observe." Schutt placed the pistol in his pants pocket.

"He's not holding a gun on me anymore, Russ."

"That's not good enough. Tell him to take out the bullets."

Schutt said, "We're wasting time. Here." He took the gun from his pants and handed it to Moody.

"He's given me the gun now, Russ. You can come down."

Russell's head appeared in the trapdoor. "Show me the gun."

Moody held it up. "Right here. Roy's in the mood for talking, not shooting."

Russell let himself down onto the chair, then the coffee table and the floor. He smacked his hands together to rid them of attic dust as he came toward Moody and Schutt. "How long have you been here, Schutt?"

"I was here before you, looking around by flashlight, when I heard your car. You know, the attic was going to be the next place I looked. What's the likelihood of finding anything up there, Mr. Keys?"

"Nothing. There's too much dust everywhere. Nobody's been up there in years."

"I'm fascinated to be talking with a dead man. Is someone going to offer me an explanation for this amazing encounter? Keith?"

"Some other time," said Russell. "You don't know where it is either, huh?"

"No. Keith has suggested we join forces against whoever it is that's killing everyone and taken the money."

Russell said, "Sounds to me like you don't have much to offer, Schutt, just a smaller share of the prize. We're not interested."

"I'm sure that Empire will offer you compensation for your efforts. Just how is it that you're here, Mr. Keys, and not frozen stiff in the Rocky Mountains?"

"I took my carpet along, that's how."

"Carpet?"

"A flying carpet. Better than a parachute."

Schutt laughed briefly. "Seriously now, gentlemen, hasn't there been enough chasing around the mulberry bush? A team effort, that's the way to proceed."

"Where's your car, Schutt?"

"Parked around back of the dog runs. Why?"

"Why don't you go out there and get in it and drive away, and don't ever cross my path again, okay? Me and Keith, we're in this together, and that means no partners, so get moving."

"You're making a mistake—"

"Not me, pal. You made the mistake coming here. We're not interested."

"Russ, listen to Roy—"

"Shuddup, Keith. I know what I'm doing, and you don't. Schutt, you've got till I count to ten."

"Can I have my gun back?"

"No, you can't. Beat it."

"MM isn't going to like this, Keith."

Moody raised his arms in a gesture of helplessness, and Schutt made a dive for the pistol in his right hand. Taken by surprise, Keith allowed it to be clawed from him. Schutt was arranging it in his hand, trying to fit his fingers around the butt and trigger, when Russell shot him twice at point-blank range with his .45.

Schutt staggered backward, dropping his gun. An expression of surprise grew on his face as he looked down at his chest and saw blooming redness around the bullet holes in his silk waistcoat. He continued moving backward until he collapsed in the kitchen.

"Stupid prick," said Russell.

"You didn't need to shoot him—"

"What, and let him shoot you, or me maybe? And what'd you let him have the goddamn gun for, you pussy! If you hadda pushed him away he'd be alive right now! Don't go putting the blame on me!"

Moody hurried to Schutt's side. "He might still be okay if we call an ambulance."

"Forget it. Two forty-fives in the chest, he's dead."

It was clear Russell was right. Schutt lay like a man profoundly asleep, his mouth agape, the second man in less than six hours Moody had seen killed before his eyes. Huttig's phrase—a magnet for murder—passed across his thoughts like a distant echo.

"Let's get out of here."

"Russ, you insisted on coming."

"Yeah, so? You were right, there's nothing here. We can go now."

"And leave him here like this?"

"What else? You can't report it, not with the cops breathing all over you like they are. He made a wrong move and paid the price. You didn't make him grab for the gun."

Moody stood up. There was nothing he could do, no wrong he could turn into a right without implicating himself and Russell. The only way out of the situation was the hard road that bypassed morality completely and headed straight for survival.

There was thunder overhead, a rare enough sound in southern California to make Moody look up.

Russell said with a lopsided grin, "That's God talking, cuz. He don't like us."

"I don't blame him," said Moody, and Russell laughed.

The drive back to the Belvedere was slow. Rain began falling, and Moody was obliged to reduce speed as his windshield wipers failed to cope with the downpour.

He dropped Russell off without a word, then drove slowly to Myra's, where he parked in the same spot he had vacated two hours earlier. The walk around the corner to Myra's back entrance left him drenched by the time he opened the door.

Moody stripped off his clothing while Bess nuzzled at his legs, then slid into bed alongside Myra, who did not wake up. He fell asleep himself, eventually, and dreamed of dead men watched over by thundering gods

THE SUMMONS TO Marvin Margolis's office came in the afternoon, and Moody was not surprised, on passing through the bronze doors, to see Detectives Huttig and Labiosa there, seated politely on expensive chairs, hats in their laps. Moody had never seen either man without his hat before, and noted with interest that the top of Labiosa's head was completely bald.

"Keith, these gentlemen want a word with you."

"Again?" said Moody. "I already spoke with them at the Institute."

"That was about Baxter Nolan, Keith. This time they want to talk with you about Roy Schutt."

"Why, did someone murder him too?"

"Yes, someone did."

Moody hoped his pretense of shock was convincing. "No . . . ," he said.

Huttig stood up, unfamiliar and uncomfortable with an interrogation conducted while sitting. "Moody, where were you last night?"

"Sound asleep."

"I said where, not doing what."

"I left the Weichek Institute with Myra Nolan and spent the entire night at her apartment. She insisted I stay, after what happened earlier."

"You never went anywhere else?"

"No. What happened to Roy?"

Labiosa said, "They got him at the Mausers' place, shot him dead."

"But what was he doing out there? What did the Mausers have to do with Roy?"

"That's what we'd like to know," Huttig said.

"Gentlemen," said Margolis, "I may be able to help you there. Ever since the demise of Quentin Yapp, Roy had been mulling over the event. Roy and Quentin were close friends, and I believe Roy wanted to visit the scene where Quentin's sister and her husband were murdered. There must be a connection, and Roy wanted to be the one to find it, an overlooked clue, some kind of evidence pointing in a certain direction. Roy was a great reader of mysteries, and unfortunately has now been included in one himself."

"Looking for clues?" asked Labiosa, openly skeptical.

"I believe so, yes," said Margolis, with a face Moody had to admit was perfectly straight. "It may not make a lot of sense to you, but it does to me. I knew the man, knew the way his mind worked. It's such a waste of life, such a terrible tragedy to befall one of the most talented and irreplaceable producers Empire Productions has ever had the privilege to employ. He'll be sorely missed by all."

Huttig listened without comment, then turned to Moody again. "You're saying Miss Nolan will back up your story about spending the night with her?"

"Go ahead and ask her."

Over breakfast Moody had told Myra everything he and Russell had done, and asked her to lie for him if an alibi became necessary. Myra had agreed with little fuss, and had expressed no shock during his account of Roy Schutt's death. Moody had assumed this was because of her lingering sorrow over Bax's murder.

"We'll do that," said Huttig.

"A fiancée," said Labiosa, "that's the next best thing to a wife. A wife, she's not gonna dump her husband in the frying pan, is she, Moody? Even if he deserves it."

"I don't think I need to listen to that kind of comment. All along you two have tried to implicate me in something I find as baffling as you do. I've had enough. I'm going to get a lawyer and make you contact me through him. I have no further comment."

"Okay, Mr. Moody, you go ahead and get a lawyer. You never know, you might need one sooner than you think."

"Gentlemen," said Margolis, "I don't like to hear my employees threatened. Mr. Moody will be provided, free of charge, with the finest legal minds that Empire Productions can muster.

If you wish to accuse this man, who I happen to know is one of the very best young fellows around town, then kindly do so in a straightforward manner, none of this sneering innuendo. Now, get out of my office and off the premises."

The detectives replaced their hats. "Thanks for your time, Mr. Margolis."

"A pleasure," Margolis told them, unsmilingly.

Huttig and Labiosa let themselves out.

When they were alone, Moody turned to Margolis. "Thank you, sir."

"Keith, where's that money?"

"I don't know, I really don't. Is that what Roy was doing last night, looking for it?"

"Weren't you?"

"Sir, I was nowhere near the scene. I regret that Roy has met with untimely death, and frankly, it makes me wonder if maybe I'm next, or you, Mr. Margolis. Who else is left that knows what this is all about, or at least part of what it's all about?"

"No one is going to kill me, Keith. Concerning your own chances, I'm less sure."

"Thank you for the offer of lawyers anyway, sir."

"Empire Productions has far better uses for its legal staff than looking after the likes of you, do I make myself clear? Have you seen the afternoon edition of the *Times*?"

He slid a newspaper across his desk. Moody saw the headline:

HOLLYWOOD MURDER PLOT THICKENS
EMPIRE DENIES RUMORS

"That's the kind of thing I hate to see, Keith, the great name of our studio dragged onto the front pages, besmirched and dirtied and sullied for all the world to see. Empire is my life, Keith. When something like this happens, it makes me very angry. This entire sordid business began with your cousin, the alleged hero, who it turns out isn't a hero at all but a frequenter of brothels and a killer besides. If he wasn't lying dead somewhere in Colorado, I'd suspect he was behind all this killing. It began with him and this ridiculous idea of yours to write a screenplay based on his life, a life of lies, we now know. And what has it brought us but sorrow, Keith? Vast amounts of unhappiness, more blood than a Scottish play, and a picture that has, as of today, become unmakable."

"Unmakable?"

"You heard me correctly. As of this very minute, *China Skies* is no more. The subject of the story is dead, possibly a suicide—has that occurred to you, Keith, that your cousin might have so regretted his foul deeds that he flung himself from his plane at high altitude and chose not to release his parachute? The star who was to have portrayed him is dead, murdered by his costar, who incidentally has had her contract with Empire terminated, effective immediately. The producer-to-be has been murdered while attempting to retrieve from certain criminal types a large sum of studio funds. Quentin Yapp has also been taken from his rightful place among the living, in a murder directly related to the aforementioned events. How, I ask you in the name of God, is this production to go forward?"

"Sir, you could find another producer and another actor and actress and . . . I only have a few more pages to write, a couple of small scenes . . ."

"Is that your answer?" thundered Margolis. "To simply replace those tragic lives with lesser lights? You surprise me, Keith. You shock me with your insensitivity. Are you too blind to see that the *hand of fate*—which I recall you telling me you don't believe in, Keith—the hand of fate, as I say, has turned its mighty palm against us? Can you truly not see that this entire production was blighted from the beginning by forces it could never hope to overcome? I listened to your persuasive voice,

Keith, when you first brought the concept to me, and fool that I was, I accepted your promise that *China Skies* would be a worthwhile picture, something for all of us here at Empire to be proud of, but I should never have succumbed to that voice, Keith, never, never, never, and now it's too late for all those departed souls who made their sacrifice on the altar of your ambition. They have departed this life and gone on to a better place, but you—*you* must linger here in perpetual contemplation of the horror you have wrought, all unintended perhaps, but you did it, Moody, you made this terrible thing happen, started that dreadful snowball rolling downhill, and now look at the death and destruction accomplished by its rushing, crushing terribleness! No, there can be no place for such a man here at Empire."

"Mr. Margolis—"

Margolis held up his hand, possibly in imitation of the hand of fate.

"Your contract has been terminated, instantly and irrevocably."

"But, Mr. Margolis, I haven't done anything wrong—"

Margolis shook his head sadly. "Still you deny your wrongdoing, your principal role in this tragic happenstance. I feel sorry for you, Moody, because you clearly have no conscience and no soul that might be called remotely human. You are without honor, and your services here are no longer required. Vacate your office and empty your desk with all due speed, and may almighty God have mercy on your missing and stunted soul, Keith Moody, because I find that I cannot! Now, go!"

Moody began walking backward despite his wish not to.

"Mr. Margolis? What about Mortimer Pence? You said I could take him out of Dr. Weichek's care when I finished the screenplay. . . . Can I still do that?"

"That verbal contract is also terminated. With *China Skies* canceled, there is no need for any further pages, which, might

I add while we've embarked upon the subject, were never very good, Moody, never a script with the necessary stamp of Empire greatness upon it. Why are you still before me? Go!"

"That isn't fair to Mortimer. He needs someone like me to look after him. . . . He's not a well man, Mr. Margolis—"

The imperial hand was lowered. "Mortimer Pence is another of your casualties, Moody, and I do see some merit in you having to take care of him for the rest of his and your days on earth. Yes, I see the hand of fate at work again as I consider the future lying before you both in times ahead. You will indeed take Mortimer Pence off the hands of the good doctor and take him away with you to a place far distant from here, and live together in disharmony, I don't doubt."

"When can I take him?"

"He's yours, Moody, to have and to hold, the minute you place fifty thousand dollars on my desk."

"But I don't have any idea what happened to the money."

"No matter! Go and find it! If you fail, Mortimer Pence stays where he is. I believe Dr. Weichek is planning extensive electroshock therapy to restore the poor devil to his rightful mind."

"I'll find it," said Moody, recovering slightly.

"See that you do. And quickly, mind."

Moody left, closing the bronze doors behind him.

17

BY AFTERNOON'S END Moody had emptied the desk in his office of all personal items and transferred them to his car. He was tempted to go across to Research to tell Myra what had happened, then remembered that she had taken the day off; Moody had left Bess with her for company. He did have one visitor before leaving his office for the last time. Terry Blackwell came by to express his regret.

"It's hit everyone hard," he said, "just one disaster after another. God, but there was no need for Margolis to take it out on you, Keith. The man's a son of a bitch."

"I'm sorry you won't have *China Skies* to direct, Terry."

"Oh, hell, there's always another picture on the horizon. I'll be okay. I'm the one who came out of this better than anyone else—I'm still alive, and I've still got my job! I guess that wasn't very funny, was it."

"No offense taken." Moody put out his hand. "All the best to you, Terry, and I expect to see your name up on the screen many times."

"Thanks, Keith, and listen, this isn't the only studio in town. Try for a job at Metro or Paramount. Use my name if you think it'll help."

"Maybe I'll do that. For the moment I need to look after Myra."

"Yeah, sweet kid. Losing Bax must've been tough. You know there's already talk about a movie based on the murder. All the younger actresses are hot for the part of Sandy Ryder, can you believe it?"

"I can believe anything about this business, anything at all."

HE ARRIVED AT Myra's by six, after dropping off his belongings from the studio at his own apartment. Walking in, he was greeted by Bess, Myra, and Russell.

"Russ . . . What are you doing here?"

"Passing the time with your girl, cuz. She's a peach."

"How did you know where to find her?"

"There you go again, like with finding the doc. The phone book, cuz. Myra, she's in it, not like Weichek. So here I am, getting introduced, which would've happened sooner or later after Myra gets to be part of the family. When are you two getting hitched, anyway?"

"We haven't decided. Myra, are you all right?"

"I'm better than all right. I took your advice and got drunk. Russell and I are getting drunk together, aren't we, Russell?"

"Yeah, we are, only you had a head start. Fact is, Keith, we're running out of booze. You want to take a stroll with me and get some more?"

"Not particularly. I think we should all have clear heads."

Russell said to Myra, "Did you know that Keith wanted to be an Eagle Scout, but they wouldn't let him in the troop because he was too much of a Goody Two-shoes?"

"Really? Is that true, Keith?"

"No. Margolis fired me today. That's true."

"He what?"

"Out the door. He blamed me for everything!"

"Well, my God, darling, you'd better pour yourself a drink while there's still drink to be had, and tell us absolutely everything."

When he had finished his telling, Moody wanted to be as drunk as the other two.

"The fifty grand for a nutcase?" said Russell. "What is that, some kind of a joke?"

"No joke. Margolis is willing to sell Mortimer like a damn slave, a crippled slave who isn't useful anymore. It's a rotten, rotten deal."

"Kiss good-bye to your friend then, cuz, because we don't have the fifty, and if we did, I wouldn't let you spend a dime of it on some crazy actor."

"Where is it?" Moody said. "Where the hell is that fifty thousand?"

"I still say Herman. Who else is it gonna be? All this killing, it had to be done by someone that's been involved from the beginning, and Herman's the only one left."

"He's right," said Myra, looking at her empty glass. "Now that Russell's gone and bumped off old Roy."

"Hey, that was self-defense. If I hadn't done that, your boyfriend here'd be the dead one, not Schutt. No, sir, don't pin a murder rap on me that I didn't earn."

"I apologize from the bottom of my capacious heart."

"Okay, then. Keith, you want to take another run at Herman? What else are we gonna do, sit here and get old or what?"

"Herman," said Keith, mulling over the name, trying to associate the skinny boy he remembered with the carnage that had taken place so far. It did not jibe, but Russell was right—who else did they have?

Moody called the Los Angeles Police Department, and after being passed from desk to desk eventually was able to speak with Lieutenant Huttig.

"Yeah, Huttig. Who's this?"

"Good evening to you, Lieutenant. This is Keith Moody calling."

"Moody. Whatta you want, Moody? You want to confess?"

"No, actually I haven't done anything wrong, believe it or not."

"Tell that to Ripley."

"Lieutenant, I'm going to make you a happy man this fine evening."

"You drunk, Moody? You sound drunk."

"Not a bit, Lieutenant. I was fired today from the best job I ever had."

"What, that Margolis guy fired you?"

"He did indeed. He said I had brought notoriety and an unkind press down upon his beloved Empire, and he fired me. I didn't do anything, Lieutenant."

"So you're blaming me for that, or what are you telling me, Moody?"

"I'm telling you the cold hard facts of the matter. I was fired for no reason other than the fact that you and your partner walked into Margolis's office and made me look bad, and he fired me for it. Which I did not deserve, Lieutenant."

"That's tough, Moody."

"You see, Lieutenant, Mr. Margolis thinks you and Sergeant Labiosa think I killed a lot of people, which I think you'll admit is a pile of parrot droppings, but Marvin Margolis is not always a rational man, and so he fired me on your say-so. That's what it amounts to."

"Like I said—tough."

"Thank you for those kind words. Now then, Lieutenant, have you done as I advised and put young Herman in protective custody from the real and actual killer, or have you decided I'm an idiot whose opinion can be excluded from consideration? Which is it?"

"We took him in for more questioning, then we let him go again. The kid is eighty cents on the dollar, but no crazy killer."

"Herman—what's his last name again?"

"Smith. Think you can remember that name, Moody? He's

a Smith. That's a very big tribe, the Smiths. Herman Smith is one dumb bunny, and we don't have any reason to hold him, even if you think we have, Moody, so he's out."

"And in the safe custody of his grandmother Helen, I hope, Lieutenant."

"Who told you Helen? It's Matilda. Matilda Smith. Helendale is where she lives. Moody, I don't rate you too high. For the record, I don't think you killed anyone—you just aren't the type—but you sure as hell know more than what you're telling us, so if you got fired, so what. Expect me to cry about it? So long, Moody, and don't forget to write. Ha!"

Moody hung up the phone. "Our assignment for tomorrow, friends, is an interview with Matilda Smith, of Helendale, California."

"Where the hell's that?"

"I'll get the map," said Myra.

THE TACTIC TO be employed was the opposite of that utilized so poorly by the police. There would be no confrontation with Herman, no questions and accusations. The truth, if it resided within him, would be extracted by other means, and the grandmother, Herman's alibi for the murders of Muriel and Eddie Mauser, would be seduced also, rather than sandbagged.

Moody, Russell, and Myra stayed up late, perfecting their plan, then set out early in the morning for the drive north to Helendale, using both Myra's and Moody's cars.

The town was small, sunbaked, quiet. Myra entered the tiny post office, asked where she might be able to locate Matilda Smith, and returned to Moody with the address.

Her home was on the very edge of town, on the dirt road leading farther north, and both cars were driven there. The house was small and weather-beaten, its clapboards long since stripped of paint by desert winds. Several bedraggled trees overhung the roof in an effort to provide shade. There was no blade of grass in the yard where an ancient pickup truck stood.

Once the location was firmly in Russell's mind, he took Moody's car and drove off, heading for the nearest airfield, thirty miles away in Barstow.

Moody and Myra drove back into Helendale and located the only public phone. Myra consulted the dusty phone book in the booth, then inserted a nickel and dialed Matilda Smith's number. Her phone was picked up at the third ring.

"Hello?"

"Hello, Mrs. Smith?"

"Yes."

"Mrs. Smith, my name is Patricia Soames, and I work for *LIFE* magazine. Are you a subscriber to *LIFE*, Mrs. Smith?"

"No. I don't want it."

"Mrs. Smith, this is not a subscription call, this is something quite different."

"How?"

"Mrs. Smith, *LIFE* magazine would like to do a photo profile and feature article about you."

"Me? Why?"

"The feature will be about some of the smallest desert towns in the west, and Helendale was selected, and out of all the citizens of Helendale, your name was chosen to be prominent in the article. Would it be all right with you, Mrs. Smith, if a photographer and myself paid you a visit in the near future?"

"I guess that'll be fine. *LIFE* magazine, you say?"

"Yes, ma'am. Mrs. Smith, do you have other family members living with you?"

"My grandson, he came home just recent, that's all."

"And is he with you today?"

"He's around the place somewhere."

"Mrs. Smith, we were thinking that it might be a nice angle

for the story to have your son take a ride in an airplane. Has he ever been in an airplane?"

"Airplane?"

"Yes, ma'am. We think it would make a nice picture to show a young boy taking his first ride in an airplane. Do you think he'd like to do that?"

"Well, I guess. He's nineteen, only he's more like eleven, if you see what I mean. I guess he'd like to fly in a plane all right, if I tell him he can."

"Mrs. Smith, would it be too much trouble for you if my photographer and myself visited with you this morning?"

"This morning?"

"We happen to be in Helendale right now."

"Well, I won't have a chance to clean the place up if you come this morning."

"Oh no, Mrs. Smith, you mustn't clean the house. *LIFE* magazine insists on absolute authenticity in its features. We want to take pictures of yourself and your grandson and home just the way they are. Is that all right with you, Mrs. Smith?"

"I suppose."

"And the plane will arrive shortly, Mrs. Smith."

"It will? How can you know that?"

"We here at *LIFE* magazine have our little ways and means of getting things done in a timely fashion, Mrs. Smith. We'll be there soon, and I thank you for your cooperation. Good-bye, Mrs. Smith."

" 'Bye."

Myra replaced the phone and winked at Moody.

"You're smooth," he said.

"You need to do something about the way you look."

"You've already agreed to marry me, so I can't be that bad."

"So Herman doesn't recognize you, idiot."

"He only saw me for a minute in the Mausers' kitchen."

"We don't want anything to go wrong, now do we?"

When Myra drove into the dusty front yard of Matilda Smith's home, Moody had his hair parted in the middle and had removed his heavy glasses. He was not wearing the clothes he had worn on the night Huttig and Labiosa had presented him to Herman, and he was confident his appearance had been sufficiently altered to avoid suspicion. He carried a camera with no film in it.

Myra knocked on the fly-screen door, and Matilda Smith opened it to allow them inside. Matilda was at least eighty and walked with the help of two canes. Herman sat in the parlor, his long hair freshly slicked back, a look of eager anticipation on his face. His shirt had been buttoned up to the throat.

"You folks sit down, and I'll get lemonade. It's a hot day, like every day out here."

"I'll get it, Gram!"

Herman was up and sprinting to the kitchen before she could answer. Matilda eased herself into a sagging chair. "My grandson, Herman. He's a good boy, comes to see me regular like he should. Well, I should say he lives here now. Looks after me."

"That's just wonderful, Mrs. Smith," Myra said, smiling.

Herman returned with a tray and pitcher and four glasses.

"Herman, get the glasses that go together, not a hodgepodge like this."

"Okay, Gram."

"He does his best," said Matilda.

Herman replaced the glasses, carrying in the matching set by thrusting his fingers inside. Matilda seemed not to notice. Moody accepted the lemonade that was slopped into his glass from the pitcher and drank with enthusiasm.

"This is excellent lemonade, Herman. Very refreshing."

"I know," said Herman. "Where's the plane at?"

"It's on its way. It should be here pretty soon now. Are you looking forward to an airplane ride, Herman?"

"Yeah! I seen you before."

"Oh, I doubt that, Herman. You may have seen my picture in magazines, though. I'm a very well-known photographer, if I do say it myself."

"You're famous?" Matilda asked.

"Among my fellow professionals, perhaps. Most people have never heard of me."

"What's your name?"

"Mortimer Pence."

"No, I never heard of you."

"That's quite all right."

"Why aren't you taking pictures yet?"

"Oh, I'll get around to that. We just thought, Miss Soames and I, that we'd sit and chat with you awhile, then when the plane gets here I'll go out and take some pictures of Herman with the pilot, and some pictures of the house from the outside, while Miss Soames does the interview."

"I wanna get my picture in the plane!" Herman declared.

"And so you shall, Herman."

"We were never in a magazine before," said Matilda.

"In the newspaper!" said Herman.

"Oh, that. Never mind that." Matilda was not pleased.

"Newspaper, Mrs. Smith?" Myra prompted.

"Not me, just Herman by himself. There was a murder—the folks that he worked for were shot down like dogs. They raised dogs and they got shot down like dogs. The police, they came and talked to Herman, that's all. As if he'd be the one that did it. I pretty soon put a stop to their questions about where was he and so forth. Here with me, that's where, and they left him alone after that. Herman got his name in the paper, though. He cut it out and kept it. Makes me read it to him. He don't have a job now on account of what happened."

"That's a terrible tragedy, Mrs. Smith."

"It surely is. Too much murder in the world, and now there's a war on top of it."

"These are terrible times."

"May I ask if you have any children, Mrs. Smith?" Myra asked.

"Got to, to have grandkids."

"I mean, do your children live around here also?"

"Had a son. He left. Can't say as I blame him. Now it's just me and Herman."

"Herman, were the police mean to you?" asked Moody.

"They axed me if I seen who done it."

"Yes?"

"I never did. I was here. The dogs was barkin' when I come back."

"I see."

"I like dogs. Dogs like me."

"That would come in handy, working for a dog breeder."

"Poodles. They made poodles. That's a kind of a dog."

"And you enjoyed working with the poodles, did you, Herman?"

"I got to kill the ones that turned out wrong."

"Turned out wrong?"

"Some of 'em, they'd be mean or dumb, so Eddie, he put 'em down. He showed me how."

"They don't want to hear about such things, Herman, so shush."

"That's quite all right, Mrs. Smith. In our line of work we often come across unusual stories with a dark side, don't we, Miss Soames?"

"Yes, we do."

"So how do you dispose of a mean dog, Herman? Do you shoot it?"

"Nope, not shoot it."

"Poison? That'd be the way I'd do it."

"Naw, not poison," said Herman, delighted that Moody couldn't guess the answer.

"Well, then, I give up. How do you do it, Herman?"

"Air," said Herman, giggling.

"Air?"

"In a needle. A pointy needle, like with doctors."

"I see. And what do you do with the needle, Herman?"

"Stick it in the mean dog and put air in him, in his blood, and it kills him, kills his heart just like that."

"That's enough," insisted Matilda. "You've made Mr. Pence go all white around the gills, telling him things like that."

"No, no, Mrs. Smith, I'm fine. Tell me, Herman, would the same thing happen if a needle full of air got stuck in a person instead of a dog?"

"Yeah, Eddie said so. Said the same thing happens to people as dogs."

Moody stood. "Mrs. Smith, I'm going to go outside now and start taking pictures. Miss Soames will keep on talking to you while Herman and I wait for the plane."

"You have some more of that lemonade before you go out there, Mr. Pence."

"I will, thank you."

Herman dogged Moody's steps around the yard as he pretended to snap pictures of the house and surrounding landscape. Moody was recovered now from the shock he felt as the means of Horace Wheat's death had been casually revealed. He couldn't believe it had been Herman who injected air into Horace; it must have been Eddie Mauser. Horace must have asked one question too many about Quentin Yapp, and Herman had made this known to Eddie, probably without realizing he was condemning a man to death.

"Herman, did Eddie ever kill anyone with the needle?"

"Kill someone?"

"Yes, with the needle full of air."

"Why would he do that?"

"I was just asking."

"There's the plane! Is that the one?"

A yellow biplane was circling overhead, its engine buzzing. It dropped lower and began lining up for a landing on the straight desert road in front of the house.

"That's the one, Herman."

Russell had seen Myra's car parked in the yard. If it had not been there, this would have signified that Herman was not on the premises, and Russell would have turned back to Barstow for another attempt on another day. He had paid twice the usual fee for hiring the plane because of his demand that he be the one to pilot it.

The plane set its wheels down, kicking up a plume of dust in its wake as it slowed to a halt twenty yards away. Russell waved. Moody pointed his camera and clicked.

"Take a picture of me!" demanded Herman.

"Hop into the plane, and I'll take a couple."

Herman ran to touch the wings and wires. Russell handed down a leather jacket and flying helmet. "Here, Herman, you'll need these."

Herman hurried into his flyer's clothes and told Moody to take the picture. Moody pretended to do so, feeling a little sad at the sight of Herman's battered jeans and sneakers. "Climb aboard, Herman."

The front cockpit was vacant, and Herman scrambled into it, grinning and pulling down his goggles. "Hey, Herman," Russell called, "don't forget to buckle the safety belt."

"Okay!"

Herman waved to his grandmother and Myra, who had come out into the yard.

"Keith, work the prop for me," said Russell.

"His name's Mortimer!" said Herman.

"Okay, Mortimer, just yank it down hard when I yell 'Contact.' "

"I've seen it in the movies," Moody said.

"Fine, so do it."

Moody grasped the propeller.

"Contact!"

Moody spun it down hard. The motor coughed and caught and roared back to life. Moody stepped smartly away from the spinning propeller as Russell turned the plane around using the tail rudder and began hurtling down the road. Within two hundred yards the plane was airborne, rising above a fresh cloud of dust that Moody could feel settling on his teeth. Turning, he saw Myra and Matilda return to the house.

Moody stayed outside to monitor what happened next. Russell gained altitude, then executed a punishing round of loops and rolls and Immelmann turns, followed by swooping dives and mad corkscrewing maneuvers Moody could not name.

The plane was turned upside down and flown that way for at least a minute, then Russell took it straight up into the sky before letting it slip sideways to begin a terrifying dive that seemed too steep and too fast to result in anything but a headlong crash into the ground. At the last possible moment Russell hauled the stick back and the plane assumed a level flight path again.

He flew in a circle twice around the house, then headed for Moody, waggling the plane's wings in a prearranged signal. Moody held both arms over his head in acknowledgment, then hurried back to the house.

Before entering the front door, he went around to the side yard and took a small pair of wire cutters from his pocket. Moody cut a twelve-inch section from the telephone wire where it entered the side of the house, and put this in his pocket along with the cutters, then strolled around to the front yard again. He took an ice pick from his other pocket and plunged it into the left rear tire of Herman's truck, then did the same for the side-mounted spare. Then he went inside.

Myra was sitting with Matilda, making notes on a writing pad.

"My," said Matilda, looking at the ceiling, "that thing certainly does kick up a racket."

"Yes it does, Mrs. Smith," Moody agreed, "but the pilot will be bringing Herman down pretty soon. Miss Soames, are you all done with the interview?"

"Yes, I am, Mr. Pence."

"I think it's nice when young folk call each other Mr. and Miss," said Matilda. "It's nice and formal and old-fashioned, like the way things used to be."

"Mr. Pence and I both agree. Mr. Pence, you haven't taken any pictures of Mrs. Smith yet."

"Forgive me."

Moody clicked his camera several times in the direction of smiling Matilda, then replaced it in its case. "Our job here is done, Mrs. Smith, and I extend my warmest thanks to you."

"My pleasure, Mr. Pence, and you too, Miss Soames."

"Good-bye, now."

"When's Herman coming back? I can hear him up there still."

"Momentarily, Mrs. Smith. I'm afraid we can't wait to greet him. We have another assignment we simply must cover. Are you ready, Miss Soames?"

"Ready, Mr. Pence."

They went to Myra's car and got in. With a final wave to Matilda, standing by the door, they drove off, and as the car turned onto the road back to Helendale, the yellow biplane began its second landing approach. Turning to look over his shoulder, Moody watched it settle onto the road and saw Herman climb slowly from the front cockpit. His legs looked very unsteady as he stripped off the jacket and helmet and handed them to the pilot, who kept the propeller turning.

Herman started walking toward the house. The plane turned, began racing down the road as it had before, and lifted itself into the sky. The house and its occupants were lost to

Moody's sight in the dust kicked up by the car, but he could picture Matilda's expression as she saw the vomit streaks on the shirtfront of her grandson and the look of defeat on his face.

Russell played games with them as Myra drove to Barstow, diving toward them and veering aside at the last moment, and performing stunt maneuvers in front of them, dangerously close to the road.

"That cousin of yours can certainly fly."

"I hope he doesn't crack up between here and the airfield."

"The real show-offs are the ones who know they can handle it."

"Did you have a pleasant chat with Matilda concerning her fascinating family tree and the history of Helendale?"

"Yes I did, the family tree part, anyway."

"Russell waggled his wings at me, so he must have got what he wanted out of poor Herman."

"Matilda's son, the one who moved away?"

"What about him?"

"He became a doctor."

"Doctor of divinity? Doctor of chiropractic? Dentistry? Not a philosopher, surely."

"A medical doctor, at first."

"And then?"

"He branched into psychiatry."

"Really. I never would have guessed, coming from that background."

"Times weren't always so bad for Matilda. He sends money, her doctor son, to help her out with Herman, especially now that Herman's lost his job."

"That's nice. Why are you telling me this?"

"He changed his name to something more suitable for a psychiatrist. Matilda isn't happy about that. She says Smith is a fine name, and there's nothing wrong with it. Any Smith who's ashamed to be a Smith isn't being a good and true Smith."

"Quite right. What did he change it to?"

"Weichek."

"Excuse me? Weichek?"

"He runs a big hospital in Los Angeles, she said. That has to be our Dr. Weichek."

"My God—"

"Did you use the cutters and the ice pick?"

"Like a secret agent."

"Good, because when Matilda finally gets word to her boy about what happened to Herman, she's going to be hopping mad at a fellow by the name of Mortimer Pence. Once he hears that, Weichek's going to smell the proverbial rodent."

"Damn! I should've called myself something else. Me and my whimsy—"

"Too late now, darling."

Russell was waiting for them at the airfield, already behind the wheel of Moody's car. He gave them a thumbs-up as they came alongside. Moody joined Russell, then both cars turned toward Los Angeles.

"WHERE IS IT?" Moody asked.

"Where his daddy told him to put it."

"And that is?"

"At the dog farm, buried at the south end of the longest run, inside the wire."

"Russ, slow down. You don't want to have to explain to a traffic cop why you're speeding when you're supposed to be dead."

"That Herman, he wasn't ready for planes. I just kept asking him over and over, 'Where's the money, Herman! Where's the money, Herman!' Boy, did he scream when I pulled the upside-down numbers on him. He puked twice before he gave up and told me. You don't look happy, cuz. I bet you think we did an awful thing, hoodwinking a little old lady and giving a retarded kid the screaming fits. Hey, nobody died, and we get what's rightfully ours. That's something I can live with."

"Herman's daddy is Dr. Weichek."

"What? Don't dick me around, Keith."

"I'm not. We also found out Eddie Mauser had a way of putting reject dogs to sleep by injecting air into their veins. That's how he took care of Horace Wheat."

"You don't say. Nobody has to cry about that guy, then. I would've killed him myself for rubbing out Whitey if I had the chance."

Both cars stopped for gas in Victorville, and it was decided that Myra would go directly home while Moody and Russell dug up the fifty thousand. They drove nose to tail as far as El Monte, then Myra went on alone as the second car turned off the highway and headed along the road to the Mausers' property.

The yard, when they reached it, was not unoccupied. A dark sedan was parked there. Russell hit the brakes hard and was about to put the car into reverse when Moody told him not to. "We've been seen. I think they're plainclothes detectives. Christ, I hope it isn't Huttig and Labiosa."

Two men in gabardine coats were approaching the car. Russell switched off the engine and Moody got out to meet the men halfway across the yard. While still several yards away from them, he saw the press cards in their hats and lapels.

"Are you fellows cops?" asked the first newspaperman.

"Us? No. I guess you fellows are taking stock of the murder scene."

"Best story since Keys took a swan dive over the mountains."

His partner said, "Three murders in one house, and another stiff found in a car just down the road. It doesn't get any juicier than that. So you and your friend aren't cops, huh?"

"No, not cops. Just sightseeing."

"Sightseeing, pal? At a murder scene?"

"Morbid curiosity," Moody told him. "I've always been this way. So that's the house where it all happened. It looks so ordinary. What are those pens over there for, do you know?"

"Dog pens. This used to be a poodle ranch. Don't you read the papers, friend?"

"I remember now."

"Just sightseeing, huh?"

"That's right. Well, we've seen it, so I guess we'll move along and get out of your way if you're investigating and reporting and whatnot."

"Your friend didn't even get out of the car yet. Doesn't he have a morbid curiosity like yours?"

"No, he hates the sight of blood. Even talking about it makes him sick."

"Don't take him inside, then. It hasn't been cleaned up yet. You know, your friend looks like the missing airman." He turned to the second newspaperman. "Doesn't he look like Keys to you?"

"Some. Hair's darker."

"Let's take a closer took at that bird."

Moody took from his pocket the pass he used to enter the Empire parking lot each day. The logo of Empire Productions was clearly marked on it. He held it up before him for their inspection.

"Gentlemen, my name is Arnold Banks, special assistant to Marvin Margolis, head of Empire Productions. As newshounds you'll know that two of the deaths here were of Empire staff. I'm here to take in the atmosphere and report back to Mr. Margolis on what I find. The two men, Yapp and Schutt, were personal friends of mine, and it was my hope to hold silent communion with them, so to speak, at the location of their demise."

"I get it. So who's the guy that looks like Keys?"

"That, gentlemen, is a rising star at Empire, an actor by the name of Turner, whose resemblance to the dead flyer is startling, as you've already noticed. We intend dyeing his hair blond and putting him into the Russell Keys story currently under development."

"To replace that poor bastard Bax Nolan," said the first newspaperman.

"Precisely. You fellows have got the scoop on this, but I'm asking you not to bother Mr. Turner. He's a rather precocious actor, given to tantrums, frankly, if he's pestered."

"Okay, Banks, we'll keep out of the guy's range, but fair's fair. What's his first name? We won't mention that you told us."

The second newspaperman said, "If you don't tell us, we're liable to call him plain old Mr. Turner, which doesn't sound right for a movie actor, does it."

"Page," said Moody.

"Come again?"

"His name is Page Turner."

"You're kidding me. Page Turner?"

"We see the problem at Empire," Moody said. "He'll probably have a new name before week's end. That's why you fellows need to sit on the replacement-for-Bax angle for the moment. Tell you what, just give me your cards and I'll inform your paper the minute the contract's been signed with Turner. Is that a fair deal?"

"Sounds good," said the first newspaperman, and his partner nodded.

Moody accompanied them to their car and waved as they drove off.

Russell stepped out of Moody's coupe. "Nice piece of fast talking, cuz. You're getting the hang of stepping out of the rut."

"The rut is something I occupied in a former life."

They walked to the dog runs, the farthest of which was considerably longer than the other two. Russell rubbed his hands together. "I can smell that money already."

"We'll need to look for freshly turned earth."

At the south end of the longest run, a few feet inside the wire, in exactly the spot where they anticipated seeing freshly turned earth, there was a four-foot hole occupied by a very dirty shovel.

"Fresh enough for you, Russ?"

"I can't smell the money anymore—"

"I think you'd need long-range smelling ability."

"The little bastard lied, even if he was puking to beat the band—"

"Probably not. The money was obviously here, or there

wouldn't be a hole. It would have been buried a week ago. That was the last Herman knew about it. If my son was a little simpleminded, I wouldn't rely on him to keep a secret for more than a week."

"So Weichek's got it."

"I can't think who else was privy to the deal and is still alive."

"Son of a bitch!"

"The irony is, he now holds both the aces—the man I want to see released, and the money that I have to give Margolis in order to secure that release. I could tell Margolis that Weichek double-crossed him and kept the cash, then Margolis will tell him to give up Mortimer and the fifty thousand, and that'll be that."

"That'd be a deal I don't like, cuz. That's my money Weichek's got, not Margolis's."

"I told you before, all it means to me is the price of getting Mortimer out of Weichek's place."

They began walking back to the car.

"Listen," Russell said, "we're not thinking this through. You want Mortimer, right?"

"Right."

"And I want the fifty grand, right?"

"Right."

"And both those things are with Weichek, right?"

"Right again."

"So we just walk in and grab 'em both."

"Like robbing a bank."

"Only it'll be easier, because there's no guards carrying guns in Weichek's joint."

"Taking Mortimer without permission would be called kidnapping."

"Not if he wants to leave. That's called rescuing."

"I don't know if he *does* want to leave. The one time I saw him, all he could do was give a god-awful scream."

"You're sure you want this guy for a houseguest? He might live a long time and scream every five minutes of it. Did you think about that?"

"I have to get him out, that's all I know."

"That's how I feel about the money. It's personal."

"Russ, taking Mortimer is one thing, assuming he wants to leave, but taking the money is theft. If you get caught, your identity will make the case a page-one issue all over again. They'll never let you out of Leavenworth. It simply isn't worth the risk."

"Any man that says fifty gees isn't worth a little risk has got peanuts for balls."

"Thank you. I'm trying to look after you."

"Funny, that's what I thought I was doing for you."

THEY MET WITH Myra at her apartment, just as she was returning from taking Bess for a walk, and all three sat down over a meal of sandwiches to make plans. Various impractical schemes were proposed and then shot down for failing to meet the three objectives of the perfect plan, as enumerated by Russell.

"One, get Mortimer out. Two, get the fifty large out, and three, get the hell out without the cops or anyone else following along behind."

"Suggestions?" said Moody.

"Call the police," said Myra, "and tell them a man who wants to leave the Institute is being prevented from doing so. This isn't Nazi Germany. You can't just hold someone against their will."

"How does that get us the fifty?" asked Russell.

"It doesn't. That requires a separate plan."

"Screw it."

"How charming."

"The plan includes the green, or it isn't serious. You two don't seem to understand that. I seriously want that fifty."

"All right," Moody agreed, "we think again. Does anyone want that last cheese and ham?"

AT SUNDOWN RUSSELL dispatched Moody to a liquor store for bottled inspiration, and when Moody returned, Myra had a new plan for him to assess.

"We keep thinking in terms of Mortimer and the cash being in the same place, but they almost certainly aren't. Mortimer's at the Institute, but why would the money be there? What's a far more likely place? Weichek's home, which I happen to know by way of Bax . . ." She paused, then recovered herself. "Bax gave me the address, in case of emergencies. Weichek lives in Lynwood. I've got it written down somewhere."

Russell leaned forward eagerly. "So you're saying we go to Weichek's place and lean on the guy till he opens the wall safe or wherever he's got it stashed?"

"Only after we already have Mortimer extracted from the Institute," insisted Moody.

"Jesus Christ, Keith! You keep messing with every plan because it doesn't get you the goddamn mental case you happen to want in your life for reasons I don't get. Why don't you just accept that the guy is nuts and the best place for him is right where he's at!"

"Because . . . just *because*! Indulge me, Russ. I've been indulging you and your obsession with this money that isn't even rightfully yours."

"That's your opinion. Mine's different."

"Stop squabbling, the both of you," chided Myra.

The phone rang. Myra picked it up.

"Hello?"

"Miss Nolan?"

"Speaking."

"It's Dr. Weichek here, Miss Nolan. I'm trying to locate Mr. Moody. Might he be there with you?"

"One moment." Myra placed her hand over the receiver. "It's *him*," she said, her voice barely more than a whisper.

"Him?" said Russell. "Him who?"

"Weichek! He's looking for Keith."

Moody took the phone from Myra's unresisting fingers.

"Tell him he better cooperate or he's dead meat," advised Russell.

"Hello, Dr. Weichek. Keith Moody here. What can I do for you, sir?"

"Mr. Moody, I'll ask you to kindly stay away from my mother and son."

"Mother and son, Doctor? I don't think I understand."

"Moody, I'm not a fool, and neither are you and Miss Nolan. That *was* her accompanying you this morning, was it not? And the pilot you appear to have dragooned into your little enterprise, could that be the intrepid Mr. Keys?"

"How may I help you, Doctor?"

"Moody, I have certain things you want. You may have those things, you and Miss Nolan and Mr. Keys, if you give me in return something that I want. Does that sound reasonable?"

"That depends entirely on what it is you want, Dr. Weichek."

"Do you have a pencil and paper handy?"

"Yes, I do," said Moody, reaching across the coffee table to pick these things up.

"I'm about to give you the private address of Marvin Margolis. I suggest we meet there in one hour from now. None of what has happened so far need stand in the way of a mutually amicable settlement of our grievances. This is not a motion picture. No one need shoot anyone else just to give the appearance of wrongs righted. Do you take my meaning?"

"I do, but I wonder how this philosophy of reconciliation takes into account the fact that you shot Quentin Yapp while he was sitting in his car, not doing you any harm."

"Please, Moody, don't attempt to play the guilt card. You despised Yapp yourself. Shall we meet at the Margolis residence and talk our way out of this impasse, or resort to infantile gunplay? The choice is yours."

"Is Margolis expecting us?"

"All arrangements have been made."

"Including the crocodile pit?"

"Let us keep the conversation on an adult plane, Moody."

"We'll meet."

"Excellent. Pencil poised and ready?"

"Ready."

THE MARGOLIS RESIDENCE was nothing less than a mansion. The roofline, high and angular against the stars, suggested gargoyles and spigots for molten lead. The massive wrought-iron gates stood open to receive Moody's car. He drove slowly along the curved gravel driveway and parked in front of an ambulance, the very one, Moody thought, that had taken Mortimer away from the Empire studios. Could Mortimer be inside?

Russell seemed to have the same thought. "Here's your chance, Keith. Your pal must be in there. You want my gun so you can take him away from the driver and scram?"

"I'd prefer to hear what Weichek wants. A trade is simpler than a holdup."

"Nuts!" said Russell. "You think we're gonna beat the Japs with an attitude like that?"

"Weichek isn't a Jap."

"Weichek," Myra reminded them, "isn't even a Weichek."

As they walked past the ambulance to approach the entrance, the driver nodded at them. "Just one guy," said Russell, "and you passed up the chance."

"Running away with Mortimer now wouldn't get you your money, would it?"

Russell snorted.

"That driver," said Moody, "I think he's the same one that took Mortimer away from the studio. I saw him at the Institute once, too."

Each of Margolis's front doors, even more imposing than the doors to his office, had a lion's head at its center.

"Into the lion's den," said Myra, pressing a button beside the left door. Somewhere within, sonorous chimes announced their presence.

Margolis himself opened the door. "Good evening, Keith, Miss Nolan. Is this the flyer we've all been misinformed about?"

"That's me," said Russell. "How you doing?"

"The staff have been given the evening off," Margolis said, closing the door behind them, "and my family are up at Tahoe for several days."

Moody tried to picture Margolis as a family man but gave up after just a few seconds. Margolis escorted them through a sumptuous hall flanked by suits of medieval armor and into a huge reception room.

Weichek stood by the fireplace, a brandy snifter in his hand. Seated at the far end of a long conference table was Mortimer Pence, scrubbed and sane by all appearances.

"A drink for anyone?" Margolis asked. Moody and Myra declined.

"Whiskey," said Russell, and Margolis poured him one. This sight was so incongruous it became an instant part of Moody's lifelong memories. The drink was handed over in silence. The participants looked at each other.

Weichek said, "I suppose it's my job to get things moving, since I'm the one who invited everyone to join me in Mr. Margolis's beautiful home. To begin with, it's clear we all bear someone else in the room a grudge of one kind or another. I suggest we approach the possibility of reaching a mutually advantageous solution with clear eyes and cool emotions. May we agree on that point before proceeding?"

"Agreed," said Margolis.

Weichek took a sip of brandy. "Well, then, my very first item for consideration is the police. I propose that we leave them out of the conversation completely. Their part in any of this is quite unnecessary. Agreed?"

"Agreed," said Margolis.

"Mr. Moody, I should like to change your low opinion of me by explaining why I shot Quentin Yapp. I did so because Mr. Yapp threatened not only myself but my son. Yapp was particularly incensed at Herman, because Herman, although not a bright boy, is not without charm to a woman denied marital happiness. Yapp's sister, Muriel Mauser, was such a woman, and Eddie Mauser found out about their trystings. He attempted to shoot Herman and shot his wife instead. Bad aim—or was she his secondary target in any case? We shall never know. Muriel fortunately had a gun on her person and managed to shoot Eddie before expiring. Yapp, who was present during this tragic finale, blamed Herman for everything. I think you'll agree that isn't fair. He shot at Herman and missed, and Herman, who sometimes uses his head, took the money and ran. Mr. Yapp seems to have lost his mind, or at least a part of it, shortly thereafter, and began making threats against my boy and myself."

"So you felt you had a right to shoot him," said Moody.

"Yes. I shot him outside your apartment, if you'll recall. I'd say the man was set on doing you harm as well, Moody. A madman is as dangerous as a mad dog, in my opinion, and one doesn't hesitate to shoot a mad dog."

"Sounds reasonable," said Russell.

"Thank you, Mr. Keys. It's a shame your rather clever attempt at blackmail didn't go off according to plan, but there you have the human condition in a nutshell. We must make the best of whatever situation we find ourselves in."

"Why isn't Mortimer saying anything?" Moody asked. "Is he all right?"

"Mr. Pence is in need of a long vacation, aren't you, Mr. Pence?"

"I sure am," said Mortimer, with a wan smile that reminded Moody of the old Smokey Hayes. "I could use me a month in the sun, you bet."

"We'll get it for you," Moody promised.

"Where's the fifty thousand dollars Empire laid out to keep a lid on all this?" Margolis asked.

"In the ambulance outside, beneath the driver's seat. The driver has instructions to hand it over to Mr. Pence and no one else."

"Why Mortimer?" demanded Moody.

"Because I am writing this script, Mr. Moody, and not you."

"Please go on, Doctor," said Margolis.

"Mr. Pence will be placed in the care of Mr. Moody, and that will settle Mr. Moody's account, correct?"

"Correct," said Moody.

"Mr. Margolis, you insist on having back your fifty thousand dollars, but really, sir, isn't that a piffling sum for Empire Productions to be concerned with? Surely your actual need is for a tight lid to be kept on this episode, as you yourself have said."

"Possibly," Margolis admitted.

"Then may I suggest you present the money to Mr. Keys to ensure his continued silence in a distant land. Would that satisfy you, Mr. Keys?"

"That's all I want."

Margolis and Russell began a polite argument over possession of the money.

Moody went to sit beside Mortimer, who barely turned his head to look at him.

"Mortimer, are you sure you're all right? Do you remember me, Mortimer?"

"Sure as hell do. You're the doorman at the Ritz."

"No, I'm Keith Moody. I wrote all your screenplays when you were Smokey Hayes, remember?"

"Yep." Mortimer nodded. "Ritz Carlton. You're Pierre. I always tipped you big, Pierre, and don't say I didn't. Always a big tipper. I'm worth a million."

"Are you? How come, Mortimer?"

"I'm John D. Rockefeller," Mortimer confided in a whisper. "I'm in disguise."

"Oh," said Moody, disappointment washing over him.

"This ain't my house," said Mortimer. "Mine's a whole hell of a lot bigger. I got fifteen mansions bigger'n this here. You come on by sometime, and I'll show 'em to ya."

"I'll certainly do that, Mr. Rockefeller."

"Good. So long, Pierre."

Mortimer turned away. Moody returned to Myra's side, downcast.

"Is he all right?" Myra asked.

"No."

"Mr. Keys," Margolis was saying, "in return for my fifty thousand, I want from you an ironclad promise that you'll never, ever reveal what you did. This entire incident never happened. You're to give me your word you'll remain missing until your dying day. Agreed?"

"Fine by me. That was the plan in any case."

"Very good," said Weichek. "Mr. Margolis, are you happy?"

"Far from it. I want to know what you want, Doctor. You're giving up the money without a fight, and I want to know why. Moody and Keys are satisfied, but what's in this deal to make you happy?"

"I was saving that until last. You and I have yet to receive our fair share of the pie, Mr. Margolis. There must be compensation for us too."

"Get to the point."

"What I require from you is the services of Empire Productions. I'd like you to make a movie for me."

Margolis said, "Go on."

"Yes, a movie of a superior type, about a man who will, before the century's end, be acknowledged as the leading light, intellectually speaking, of the age. I refer, of course, to Sigmund Freud. I suggest we hire Paul Muni to play the role. He does such a good European accent and looks quite striking with a beard. Have you seen him playing Émile Zola? A remarkable performance."

"Freud," said Margolis, his voice impassive.

"A worthwhile subject, I think you'll agree."

"Would you like Moody to write it?"

"Certainly. I have every confidence in his ability."

"What if I say no to the whole deal?"

"Then, sir, you shall not have the very prettily embalmed body of Baxter Nolan to lay to rest the day after tomorrow at Forest Lawn Cemetery."

"What? Bax is lying in the Chapel of Repose at Resthaven Funeral Home."

"Not so. Bax is outside in my ambulance. I picked him up on my way over. I should point out that my driver, Rick, is armed with a pistol. Any attempt to remove either the money or Bax's handsome coffin will be met with a bullet. I say this specifically to Mr. Keys, who has a pistol of his own tucked into his pants waist."

Myra said, "Dr. Weichek, you really are—scum."

"Please, Miss Nolan, your brother is safe. Mr. Margolis doesn't dare risk further scandal by mislaying the remains of his lately departed star. I have correctly assessed the situation, have I not, Mr. Margolis?"

"You might," said Margolis.

"May I assume, then, that all present here are in agreement with the proposals made? Is there any serious dissent? Please be candid."

"Freud," said Margolis. "Moody, can you write a picture about Freud?"

"I'm sure I can, Mr. Margolis."

"Kind of a dry subject."

"Not necessarily, sir. Freud more or less discovered why we like sex."

"He did? I thought we liked it because it feels good."

"Yes, but he . . . ummm . . . Doctor?"

"Freud," said Weichek, "defined the psychological underpinnings of the sex act."

"Sex act," said Margolis. "All right, I'll buy it, but Moody, I want emphasis placed on this psychological sex. Freud used a couch, I believe."

"Yes, sir."

"There you are, Dr. Weichek, you've got your wish—a movie about Freud."

"Thank you, Mr. Margolis. I'm sure it will bring renown to yourself and Empire Productions when the Academy Awards are handed out."

Weichek turned to Mortimer. "Mr. Pence, your services are required. Do you remember the lines I gave you to learn?"

"Uh-huh."

"Repeat them for me, please."

" 'It's all set in there. Hand over the package.' "

"Very good, Mr. Pence. I can see why you were once a famous actor. Go outside now, and tell Rick. Up you get, Mr. Pence. Your audience awaits you."

"Stop that," said Moody. "There's no need to humiliate him."

"Mr. Pence is beyond humiliation. Mr. Pence has had his ego removed by electricity. Nothing offends Mr. Pence now."

Mortimer rose clumsily from his chair and walked from the room.

"You monster!" said Myra.

"Not at all, Miss Nolan. You judge me too harshly. Nobody has been hurt this evening, and all of us have been given something of value. Hollywood is far from heaven, and no one is watching."

The front door opened, then closed with an echoing boom.

"Mr. Margolis," said Moody, "if the Freud picture wins an Academy Award, would you consider making *The Samaritan*, you remember, the picture we discussed in your office not long ago?"

"Certainly, Keith. Success brings its own reward in this town."

Moody knew he had been given nothing. Margolis was allowing words to flow from his mouth without any thought for their worth. Weichek wanted a movie made to placate him; Margolis said it would be done. Moody begged another chance for *The Samaritan*; charity was dispensed. The words promising so much came tumbling from Margolis instantly, without hesitation, without pause for thought, to secure the goodwill of his supplicants. The words meant everything to those who heard and believed them. They meant nothing to the man who spoke them.

There would be no movie about Freud. *The Samaritan* would be stillborn in Moody's imagination. And Marvin Margolis would never pay the price for his empty words. He would continue, year after fiscal year, at the helm of Empire Productions, making no deal with his enemies or underlings that he did not have to make, despite his promises. He was untouchable. His lies would blow away on the wind and be forgotten, and his terrible movies would live on, mile after celluloid mile of them, fantastic and ridiculous and overwrought ribbons, enough to encircle the earth and strangle it. The man was a kind of god, a tin god painted gold, being eaten away from within by the creeping rust of his lies; not even a false god, just a walking cadaver mouthing foul air. And he did not know himself for what he was.

"Why are you smiling at me, Keith? Have I given you what you need, is that it?"

"Yes, I believe you have."

"What is mine to give," said Margolis, "I give gladly. Where's that fool Mortimer?"

Mortimer had not returned.

"Mr. Moody, would you be so kind as to fetch your friend back inside with the money."

"Certainly, Doctor."

"I'll join you, cuz."

"Trust," said Weichek, smiling. "It's so fulfilling to see evidence of trust among us. Don't be concerned for your fifty thousand, Mr. Keys—Rick is a crack shot."

Russell beat Moody to the front door and dragged it open. The ambulance was not there. No one had heard a gunshot; the body of Mortimer was nowhere to be seen.

"Hey . . . ," said Russell, running out into the driveway. "Hey! Where'd they go! Where's the goddamn ambulance!"

"Hightailing it, I guess," said Moody. "You might try headin' 'em off by the old canyon trail, as Smokey would say."

"Get in the car! Follow the sons of bitches! Keith—they took my *money*!"

"Sure looks that way, cuz. Dang varmints."

The others came outside, Margolis last of all.

Weichek said, "Where's Rick?"

Myra began to laugh, then stopped. "Oh, God—they've got Bax."

Weichek stood looking down the driveway, stunned.

Margolis said, "I want an explanation. Keith, anyone . . . an explanation for this outrage! Where is Bax? I must have Bax for the day after tomorrow. . . . Arrangements have been made. . . . I insist on an explanation. . . ."

Myra said to Moody, "Will he be all right?"

"Did you really want him buried in Forest Lawn with a lot of other movie stars?"

"Bax would have wanted it."

"And Sandy Ryder will no doubt be buried in a prison yard. Such is life."

"Keith, please, this is serious."

"Excuse me, I don't agree. I'm leaving here now. Should I go to my place or your place?"

"Your dog is at my place."

"Where my dog goes, my heart follows."

They began walking to the car. Russell took several steps in their direction, then turned back to Margolis. "Call the cops! Have them picked up! Do something!"

Margolis turned and went inside his empty home, closing the doors behind him.

Weichek looked at the stars for guidance. There were many above Los Angeles that night.

Moody and Myra heard, in the far distance, a howling siren.

"You know," said Moody, "if they keep that thing cranked up full blast, they'll be across town in thirty minutes and reaching Tijuana in the wee small hours."

"How do you know?"

"Smokey always said that *banditos* run for the border—it's their nature."

Russell was following them. "Keith? Hey, don't let them do this—"

"It's done," Moody said. "They just did it. Good-bye, Russ."

"Hold on, cuz—"

" 'Bye, Russ," Myra smiled. "Happy landings."

"No, wait—"

They got in the car and drove away.

Weichek strolled across the driveway to Russell. "Mr. Keys, I came by ambulance, all unprepared for emergencies. Might I share a cab with you?"

EPILOGUE

FACED WITH CONTROVERSY the studio could not have endured, Marvin Margolis ordered an empty coffin to be buried in Forest Lawn Cemetery. The coffin was lead-lined, the heaviest available from Resthaven Funeral Home, and the pallbearers suspected nothing as it was carried to the gravesite by some of the studio's notable stars. Several young women, aspiring Empire starlets, threw themselves onto the coffin before it was lowered, crying and wailing for their departed dreamboat. Margolis was hoping the press would depict these scenes as being even more hysterical than the antics that had accompanied Rudolph Valentino's funeral, but the press reports were muted, even snide. Moody and Myra did not attend.

Russell Keys was drunk when he launched himself into a barroom brawl one week later, siding with a group of airmen who had insulted a group of sailors in Long Beach. The bottle that hit him in the neck had already been shattered against the bar, and Russell's lifeblood gushed onto the floor among the stamping boots and broken chairs, so much of it lost in the few minutes the fight lasted that the medical team, when it arrived, could do nothing for him. The bar owner tried to charge the navy for the cost of cleaning up so much blood. An address was found in the pocket of the dead man by a morgue attendant, and this was passed along to the police, who contacted Moody by phone, requesting that he identify a John Doe. Moody presented himself, informing the police that the man was a childhood friend. Moody took charge of the body, accompanied it on an eastbound train, and had the coffin buried in Russell, Kansas. He could not place the dead man's true name on the tombstone without causing a furor, so he asked the stonemason to chisel RUSSELL CUZ instead, and that is the name the vanished flyer lies under today.

Late in 1942 Moody received a letter from Mortimer, postmarked Vera Cruz. It read:

> Dear Moody—
> Now I can say I really am an actor. Fooled you all pretty good I reckon. Did everything but drool. Fact is, Rick was my stunt double a few years back on *High Lonesome* and *Sunset Trail*, which you wrote both of. He got out of stunt work after he hurt his back pretty bad and did driving instead. When he saw it was me that got rounded up and hog-tied in Weichek's calaboose he just naturally wanted to help another cowboy out. We have got us a real nice setup down here, Smokey's Corral we call it, and the locals and tourists too come in for a snort. Someday you should come down and talk over old times. And in case somebody wants to know, we gave that coffin a good spot in the local graveyard with an angel looking down on Bax all sad and forgiving.
>
> Your good pal, Smokey

When she married Moody, Myra was fired from the research department at Empire for alleged incompetence. In 1943 Moody published *Below the Salt*, a novel concerning an actor who undergoes a nervous breakdown and electroshock therapy. It was made into a movie the following year, but the studio (not Empire) assigned one of its own writers to the screenplay. Moody was disappointed with the result but was able to bank a considerable sum.

Sandy Ryder was sentenced to execution in the gas chamber at San Quentin, but many appeals by her lawyers resulted in a stay of execution until 1951, when she was at last put to death. The film based on her life, *Till Tomorrow Comes*, won an Academy Award nomination for the actress portraying Sandy.

Hollywood remains far from heaven.